Any Way
The Wind Blows

[illegible] Helen,
Hope you
enjoy the
read –
Best Wishes, –
Connie

Any Way The Wind Blows

Connie Wallace

Any Way The Wind Blows
by Connie Wallace

ISBN: 0-9668039-0-6

Printed in the United States of America

Acknowledgments

Special thanks to my family and friends,
to my editor, Stephanie Marohn and cover artist Ann Wechlo
for your talent, encouragement and support

1

Leaning her forearms against the cool metal of the tricycle's handlebars, Krake laced her fingers together and squinted to bring the distant figure closer. Every afternoon at ten after five, at the top of a long, sloping hill running down to the paper mill where he worked, she waited to walk Hank home. They only lived a few blocks away, in an old two-story house converted into three apartments. There was no automobile because the year was 1943, money was scarce and everything was rationed. She was lucky to have rubber tires on her tricycle. Her new doll carriage had wooden ones.

His figure grew larger. Now she could make out his gray felt hat, the front of the brim turned down, shadowing his face. Her excitement rose and she shouted, "Daddy! Hi! Here I am!" He raised his arm in answer.

She had gotten her report card that morning and couldn't wait to show him straight A's and knew he would be proud. At last he was by her side, enveloping her in a hug. She buried her face in the dark wool of his tailored suit and eagerly inhaled the familiar smell of Camel cigarettes. His kisses were always wet. If anyone had to teach you to pucker, he had taught her. They always puckered up their mouths so much it hurt, paused a split second and kissed. Nobody ever smooched her like that, only Daddy. Daddy almost made up for everything.

Krake, Krake, skinny as a rake.
A pin-up girl she wouldn't make.
Krake, Krake, skinny as a rake,
She'd better gain weight, for goodness sake!
One potato, two potato, three potato, four,
Five potato, six potato, seven potato, more.

"Do you like this dress?" Anne asked, running her fingers over the yellow plaid skirt.

Krake had been enviously looking at the frock with the eyelet trim. No one else in the first grade class had anything like it. She nodded, wishing it were hers.

"My mother made this, she makes almost all my clothes. I have closets and closets full. Why don't you come over to my house and see? I just got a bed with a canopied top, white lace all around. It's so pretty," Anne smiled sweetly.

On the way upstairs to her room, Anne ran ahead to fling open a white louvered door and reveal a closet full of dresses, skirts, sweaters, blouses, coats and shoes. The room was a little girl's fantasy; pale yellow, flowered wallpaper, four-poster white canopied bed, organdy-skirted dressing table, window seat with velvet pillows, stuffed animals piled on the bed and a shelf filled with miniature dolls. Krake ooohed and aaahed, overcome by the splendor. She felt a little sick inside. What would Anne think of her bedroom? It was nothing compared to this.

The rest of Anne's house fell short of Krake's in size and overall decor which was of some comfort, but she was still left with the feeling that she didn't quite measure up. Hair not shiny enough, bicycle not new enough, not enough clothes, or as fancy a bedroom or well … just not enough. The deadly comparisons had started. How could she know that years later she would become a beauty queen and the havoc it would wreak.

Krake felt no animosity towards Anne, only her own inadequacy. Anne was so pretty, with her coal-black hair, big brown eyes, and beautiful clothes. How Krake coveted those clothes and that canopied bed.

Krake wore two dresses a week. One frock for the first three days of school. The second one after bath night on Wednesday. Very practical and very demoralizing. She never complained to her mother, it wouldn't have done any good. Once Lorraine laid down patterns they were rarely altered. But Krake vowed some day I will have a closet full of lovely things.

On a blustery winter morning, when Krake was in the second grade, her baby brother was born. The snowfall outdid itself that year. In anticipation, a week after Hank Jr.'s birth, she and Daddy crunched their way through drifts of snow to St. Jude's hospital. He left her in the waiting room while he visited Lorraine and the baby. Medical rules wouldn't allow children in patient's rooms and dictated that mother and child remain under hospital care for two weeks.

As she turned the pages of a *Brenda Starr* comic book, she wondered, with excitement what Hank Jr. looked like and whether he would become her dearest friend. How would her life change? She was thrilled to have a brother. When Daddy returned, they went outside and stood below the window he pointed out to her. She shivered, suddenly her mother's face appeared. They waved and blew kisses. Self-consciously Krake straightened her unkempt braids. Daddy didn't know how to braid hair. She felt lonely without Lorraine, missed wearing carefully ironed school clothes and eating hot oatmeal in the morning.

A week later, Lorraine and Hank Jr.came home. What a disappointment! Where was the Gerber baby she had expected? Instead there was a bright red, pinched-up, wrinkled, tiny body in the bassinet bellowing his head off. What a shock! Maybe the hospital had made a mistake. Voicing her concern to Daddy, he assured her that most newborns looked like this but she wasn't entirely convinced.

In a couple of weeks, Hank Jr.'s appearance improved. Krake delighted in secretly watching Lorraine's ample breasts (one chocolate, one vanilla) being stuck in that rosy mouth and Hankie suckling noisily. Wheeling him in the baby carriage was scary and fun and made her feel important. As Hank Jr. grew, however, so did his demands and Krake's responsibilities. More duties were placed upon her and her parents seemed to forget that she was a child too.

When Hank Jr. was two years old and Krake nine, Hank and Lorraine attended a church meeting one evening, leaving Krake in charge. She got involved in a game of hide-and-go-seek with some friends in the backyard. Suddenly, braids swinging, she ran for "in-free," then remembered she was also babysitting Hankie. Her anxious eyes quickly scanned the yard. Where was he? Fear made it hard to swallow. She quickly mobilized her playmates and they scoured the neighborhood, calling frantically, sweaty hands cupped around open mouths, Hankie...Hankie. No answer. No chubby little body appeared.

Torn by fear and guilt, she greeted her parents with the news when they returned from the meeting. Hank called the police and the sergeant in charge informed him that they had just received a call about a lost child bawling in a driveway several blocks away. Apparently Hankie had crossed two busy streets all by himself. Exhausted and confused, he lay down in a driveway and cried. The occupants of the house heard his sobs and rescued him. He was soon brought home safe and sound. She thanked God for his safety but had a hard time falling asleep. Visions of his wanderings kept appearing as soon as she closed her eyes.

Krake was overwhelmed by guilt and Lorraine's accusations of "trying to get rid of your brother" rang in her ears. No one seemed to recognize that she was nine years old, got caught up playing with her friends and simply forgot about her babysitting duties. Lorraine, and Hank Jr. when he grew older, never let her forget her mistake, bringing up the story whenever people seemed too fond of Krake. They were in the make-Krake-feel-guilty business, which became a cornerstone of deep anger in her.

Hankie became a thorn in Krake's side. One day, her friend Joanne called and told her that her cat had just had seven kittens. Did Krake want one? Krake had been longing for a kitty.

"I'm not going to take care of it," Lorraine said firmly, when she went into the kitchen to ask.

"I will, I will," Krake vowed as a hopeless feeling invaded the pit of her stomach.

"I don't believe you. You are so irresponsible," Lorraine reminded her.

"Oh please, Mom. I promise, I promise. Please, please." Krake knew she was just as responsible as anyone else.

"We'll ask Dad when he comes home," Lorraine said, patting a meatloaf into a pan.

In the discussion later that evening with her father, Lorraine pronounced, "Now Hank, I'm not going to take care of that animal. I don't want my house all cat hair, the furniture scratched and those awful smelling litter boxes around. You must talk to her."

Krake's face fell. She'd been pleading for a cat for so long and still didn't have one.

"Let's discuss this by ourselves later, dear. Krake help Mom set the table. We'll talk about kittens tomorrow."

"But, Daddy..."

"Not another word now," he warned, winking secretly, his back to Lorraine.

The next morning, over hot oatmeal and Ovaltine he told her quietly, "If you're very conscientious about caring for this kitten, we'll go down to the Duncan's on Saturday and pick one out."

"Oh, Daddy, thanks, thanks so much." The oatmeal

stuck in her throat. "I love you," she coughed, amid giving her father hugs and kisses. "Thanks, Mom," was an after thought.

"I don't want my curtains ruined by that cat," Lorraine said.

"Don't worry Mom, that'll never happen," Krake assured her confidently, hoping they wouldn't be.

Inevitably the curtains were full of tiny catches, but by that time Boots (four white boots on a black, furry body) had captured their hearts.

Hank Jr. was Boots' sworn enemy. He loved to carry her around by the tail and once cut off all her whiskers on one side. He harassed her so much he merely had to walk into a room and she arched her back and hissed.

As Hank Jr. developed, so did his various ailments. By age four, he was wearing thick glasses. Asthma attacks soon followed, leaving him breathless and very whiny. After several months of testing, it was discovered he was severely allergic to dust and cat and dog dander.

Krake wanted to like Hank Jr. but almost from the beginning it seemed as though he deliberately tried to undermine and torment her. His main vehicle for this was Boots and now he had wreaked the ultimate havoc. Krake's heart was broken. Boots had to go. At first, she couldn't bear thinking of life without her beloved cat. Boots was her confidant, she told her everything. When she was upset by something, the cat would snuggle up to her, licking her face with her rough tongue. Companion, soul mate, her closest friend. It was unthinkable for Boots to be given away. Boots and Daddy were her family.

For awhile they tried to avoid it. Both of her parents were fond of the cat as well. In the end, there was no choice. Hankie's allergies were getting worse. Fortunately they found a home for Boots with some people from New York City visiting her father's secretary. Tearfully, Krake bid her goodbye. She cried herself to sleep for several nights trying to conjure up the black cat-smell she missed.

Hankie's whining and crying had always disgusted her, but after this she began to hate him, especially as his uncontrollable jealousy for anything she had became unbearable. He tyrannized Lorraine and the atmosphere in the house was stifling to Krake.

She found a perfect escape at the movies. The magic and mystery of the darkened movie house drew her like a magnet. For a few hours she was transported to another world. A world of beautiful women and handsome men where the villains were always dressed in black and the hero never lost. A picture of real life was rarely painted, happily ever after was expected. Baby brother, mosquito bites, the measles and skinned knees didn't exist. Krake identified so intensely with the characters, that it was a shock to walk out of the theater blinking at the light of day, and see the mundane streets and herself reflected in the glass over the advertising posters. She was disappointed to see gazing back at her a skinny, auburn haired ten-year old instead of a blond, leggy Betty Grable or sultry, sexy Rita Hayworth.

As soon as she got in the house, she would race to her room, don her mother's silky scarves and jewelry, put on the old pair of black, open-toed high heels Lorraine had given her and wobble precariously down the stairs singing a song from the just-viewed movie.

In eighth grade, childhood dress-up left behind, Krake and her new best friend Liz gorged on popcorn and Jujubees during Saturday matinees or met at Krake's house with the rest of the gang to drink Coke and play canasta.

Liz and Krake exchanged friendship rings, spent every Friday and Saturday night together and shared their innermost thoughts.

Krake shared all but one. That concerned a particular

afternoon after school, when Liz was away visiting her grandmother and Arthur, a boy from their class, walked her home. The house was empty. Krake invited him in to watch TV and they settled back laughing at Pinky Lee's corny jokes. Without warning, Art put his arm around her shoulders. At first, too frightened to move, she gradually relaxed and leaned her head on his shoulder. His hand felt hot and she was afraid to breathe. Although boys were appealing she had had little to do with them before this. Kate Smith was ending her show with the usual "God Bless America," when Art's hand crept down and lightly moved across Krake's breast. She sat up as his mouth pecked her lips. Jerking away, she told him he had better leave. That night, in the safety of her bed she furtively touched her breast and recalled how good his caress felt and decided she was terribly wicked. She was ashamed to tell anyone about her wantonness, even Liz.

Liz, was one of five girls. Nancy, the oldest and a senior in high school, was Elizabeth Taylor beautiful. Sophia, a junior, was equally impressive in her own sensual way. Liz and Krake watched them dress for countless dates, and afterwards went down to Liz's small living room to do leg exercises for their skinny calves, dreaming dreams of Elizabeth Taylor loveliness for themselves.

Liz and Krake, with Anne and another friend Marilyn made up an inseparable foursome that summer. Each had a boyfriend she was crazy about and they constantly plotted ways to engineer dates with them and hopefully some physical contact.

By the end of the summer all of them except Krake had been kissed by their boyfriends. On the last hayride of the summer, she vowed to "make Rick kiss me!"

Ten couples piled into the back of a partially open-sided flatbed truck filled with fragrant hay on a Friday evening in late August. Dusk descended, the air cooled and the truck moved forward. Couples began to don jackets and snuggle deeper in the hay. Everyone was necking by the time the truck was five miles outside of town. Krake and Rick stared out between the wooden slats that striped their view, occasionally exchanging a few monosyllables.

Couples sank lower and lower in the straw until only elbows, knees and an occasional sneaker was visible. All Krake could think about was the feeling of Rick's lips on hers. She tried not to hear the quiet murmurs and shifting bodies nearby. When the truck reached its destination at a pizza parlor twenty miles from town, everyone straightened themselves out and went inside to eat.

"I'm not hungry," Krake answered abruptly when Rick asked if she wanted to go in. Waiting until everyone was out of the truck, she gathered up her courage, sat on her haunches in front of him and cleared her throat. "KISS ME, KELLY!" she spat the words in his face, scared of his response. The blue eyes opened wide, he inhaled sharply, leaned over and gave her a big kiss. They were still kissing when everyone returned from the pizza break, still kissing when the truck started up again, still kissing when they arrived back in town. The sensuous feel of his lips on hers was better than she'd dreamed. When her hands caressed his crewcut she was amazed by its fragility. Krake was elated to have joined the ranks of the "neckers."

Rick was three years her senior. Tall, muscular, with an oddly handsome face, he wasn't a pretty-boy, but rather, unusual looking. Blue eyes slightly tilted at the corners and a full sensuous mouth intrigued Krake. She was drawn to that which was different. In clothes, lifestyle, food, and boys. This preference was in direct opposition to the basic need of the insecure to be accepted. It was a painful dichotomy at times, but one which she seemed unable to alter.

Rick wasn't scholarly, but Krake wasn't interested in his mind. The combination of strangeness and inaccessibility was what drew her. Rick had been going steady with a sophomore cheerleader when she decided to focus her attentions on him. Even at the early age of thirteen and in that particularly unenlightened year of 1951, she felt the coy, waiting game of women was a waste of time. She set about to vamp him. This consisted of letting him know by way of other boys that she was interested, and staring at him whenever they crossed paths.

At first, this knowledge didn't seem to shake his soul, but gradually he began to return her stares. One summer evening at dusk, he came wheeling up on his battered, black bike while she was playing kick-the-can with some neighbor kids, in the road in front of her house. He skidded to a halt beside her and began to talk. She stopped kicking the rusty tin can and sat on the cement curb watching while he performed all sorts of spectacular trick riding feats on his old bicycle. Her energy rose, she felt nervous but exhilarated and didn't realize until she stood up that her behind was completely numb. And so it began. It lasted a year and a half.

During the winter they often went bowling. Once, after a heated game, they got into an argument and she called him a son-of-a-bitch. He stared at her dumbfounded and then walked away. She knew she had overstepped herself and all the begging and pleading and cries of "I'm sorry, I didn't mean it," were in vain. She walked home alone through the drifting snow, feeling panic and confusion. She couldn't believe she'd said it—girls didn't swear like that. But she couldn't take it back, it was out there, bald, ugly and shocking. She was frightened by the depth of anger she had felt when she said it. What would happen? Would she be shunned by everyone?

Daddy swore when he was angry, particularly if he had been drinking. After the silver cocktail shaker of his lethal version of martinis had been emptied, the likelihood of a verbal battle between her parents was almost assured.

"Son-of-a-bitch," was one of his favorite epithets. This had been going on for as long as she could remember. When she was four, she had found pieces of her mother's peach satin nightgown on the stair. Until then, she only knew Hank shouted angry words at Lorraine but after that discovery she began to fear he might hurt her mother. On the other hand, Krake felt some kind of relief when Hank lost control after a few drinks. Lorraine seemed to nag him incessantly and it enraged Krake when Hank didn't stand up to her. An intense anger was building towards her mother.

After a few days of phone calls and Krake running after him apologizing, Rick forgave her. Imperceptibly the balance of power shifted. She felt helpless and frustrated by her loss of position. He even had the audacity to break up with her. They soon made up but Krake knew she had lost something.

That was after her thirteenth summer, when life had seemed magical and perfect, despite the situation at home. Anyway, her father adored her and Lorraine wasn't too bad. She would remember that summer in later years as the last interlude of self-love. From then on, doubts about herself grew until they almost annihilated her. Success, when it came would prove to be a burden rather than propelling her forward.

When she entered high school at the end of that summer she was no longer a big wheel and felt the heavy weight of proving herself. The competition was magnified. Good grades were harder to come by. Classes were larger and more diversified, people new and different. She felt alone and apart, lost in the crowd. The halls were dark and long and unfamiliar. No one knew or cared that she had been president of Student Council, acted in school plays or was singled out for various achievements during the past eight years.

Slowly, she began to adjust, but the feeling of being alone and not quite good enough persisted. Unaware that she was experiencing common growing pains, she kept her discomforts to herself and pretended to be happy.

As soon as she got home after school, she would peel down to her lacy underwear and fling herself across Hankie's narrow bed where she could look directly out the front window at the two maple trees below. Her vision was filled with a leafy green. Music would filter up from the house next door sending her floating off on melancholy fantasies of dancing down the Champs Elysee with Mel Ferrer.

What was wrong with her? Why did she feel like a nerve ending waving in the breeze? She envied everyone who seemed to fit in. Liz, for instance, was a cheerleader going steady with a football player. Football players didn't seem to notice her. She stared at them in their huge shoulder pads and they didn't return her gaze. What's wrong with me? Rick was still around but he was due to graduate and then what? Their necking had advanced to the petting stage, early petting, that is. His hand had yet to slip under her sweater which left her frustrated.

Lorraine had never mentioned sex or menstruation to her. When Krake got her period shortly after her twelfth birthday, she was terrified and, sure she was dying, couldn't shake the feeling of dread even when her mother explained the blood on the toilet paper.

"The curse," happened the afternoon of her first piano recital. Lorraine outfitted her with a sanitary belt and napkin. Attired in a new pale-pink linen dress, Krake self-consciously crossed the stage to seat herself at the piano, not realizing she was walking as though she had a giant dildo dangling between her legs. Her mother told her, amid giggles, how funny she had looked. Angry and humiliated, Krake accused Lorraine of mistreating her by not telling her anything about periods. Lorraine self-righteously replied, "My mother never told me."

Krake swore she would inform her daughter the minute she could comprehend the spoken word. The humiliation and embarrassment of the recital was forever etched in her brain. Automatically assuming that old ways of doing things couldn't be improved upon was against Krake's very fiber. To try, do, experiment, discover, that is what life was about. To sail on the wind and be free. On the other hand, the need to fit in, be approved of, loved, admired and envied was acute.

Things continued uneventfully with Rick, hayrides, movies, bowling, until October of her sophomore year when she broke up with him. For some unknown reason the thrill was gone. She woke up one day and knew it was over. Her virginity was still intact. Near the end of the relationship, they had lain naked in each other's arms on Rick's bed. His parents were away. The kisses were hot and heavy and she was scared something might happen that she didn't want, like going all the way. But aside from some peculiar musky smells filling the room and Rick's hard cock pressed into her flat stomach, she remained impenetrable. Thank heaven for that! Lorraine always said boys never marry girls who had sex with just anyone. Shortly afterwards, she decided to call it quits.

Word spread rapidly that Krake and Rick were no longer an item and John, the star forward of the Alexandria Mills High basketball team, asked her out. Movies and basketball were the two activities they shared.

John asked Krake to the Junior Prom and she readily accepted. Unfortunately, she went into the hospital with a ruptured appendix and missed the big event. Her parents adored him, a local hero and bound for an Ivy League school on an athletic scholarship. Her mother's criteria for an acceptable escort was, superior intelligence or, in John's case, parents who had graduated from a good school and had plenty of money. The fact that he might be a bit boring was irrelevant.

"You know, John," Krake said walking beside him to English class, her first day back at school, "dreams don't always come true."

"What do you mean?" he asked.

"I missed the prom, and never got to wear my pretty dress or dance with you or anything."

"Yeah, I had a white orchid corsage picked out too. Well, my mom picked it out."

Stopping, she looked up at him, "Did you go?" Suddenly it dawned on her. "You took that cheerleader you used to date, Carrie from Phillips Street High, didn't you?"

"Gosh, Krake, it was my prom. My mom rented the tux. I had to go."

"Are you still seeing her?"

"You've been in the hospital. You're still my girl."

"No I'm not. Give me my books, I can carry them just fine." She hurried on to English class feeling relief, he had been awfully boring.

The scar the exploratory surgery left was hideous; red, dimpled, hard to the touch and running from just under her navel to the top of her pubic hair. She grieved over her fate of a lifetime of one-piece bathing suits.

After seeing Audrey Hepburn in Roman Holiday, she had cut her hair in a pixie style. Having reached her full height of 5'6" at age thirteen, she was taller than most of her classmates and at a hundred and ten pounds, striking, verging on beautiful. People turned to watch when Krake walked by.

Her father enjoyed this and liked to go out with her to observe the glances.

Krake wanted to believe she was pretty but didn't. She saw the reflection in the mirror but couldn't see what other people saw. Mostly she felt inadequate; too thin, too bony, too dumb and too poor. These feelings were accompanied by guilt over the minor sensations she caused merely by her looks. The pressure of being the center of attention was embarrassing. It seemed she was supposed to perform like a trained seal and she didn't know what to do. The attention was also gratifying and, in truth, while pretending the glances didn't exist, she looked forward to them.

The summer passed quickly and no one except her seemed to notice that she was without an eligible male for most of it. Her goal in life wasn't developing a career. She planned to go to college, but only for the purpose of finding a husband.

In her junior year, she dated several boys, none of whom interested her. She missed the passion she used to have with Rick. She tried dating him again a few times, but it became clear that once it was gone there was no getting it back. His lips felt slobbery not sensuous.

Over Thanksgiving vacation, she got a call from Stilts, an Alexandria High basketball player and track star who had gone off to college last year. "I'm only home for the weekend. I wondered if you'd like to go to the movies tonight?"

She almost dropped the phone, could hardly believe her ears. She thought she might faint. She had had a secret crush on him for two years. She hadn't thought he was even aware she was alive. Tragically, she had a date! She couldn't break it, Pierre was too good a friend. Reluctantly, she said she was sorry but she was busy that night. He said it really was too short notice and he would be home again in a couple of weeks and try then.

Replacing the receiver she went upstairs to run a bath. Soaking in a scalding, hot tub she thought, Damn! Damn! Damn! Pierre is such a bore. I actually turned down Stilts Stanyon. He'll never call again. I can't wait two weeks. I wish I was dead! She agonized and was curt with Pierre all evening.

He did call. They went to the movies, walked back to his house, played records and danced. Stilts, was sort of famous. He had run the sixth fastest collegiate mile of the year the previous spring. Krake was impressed by him but not intimidated. Dancing on her toes, she barely reached his shoulder and caught a whiff of his manly perspiration. Talking and laughing, they drank two Cokes apiece before deciding to call it a night. Naturally, he walked her home. In the cool night air she stood on the first step leading to her front porch while they chatted awhile longer. Finally he bent down and kissed her. Not slobbery. He promised to call soon.

She counted the days until he did. They began to date on weekends, usually going to the movies, then taking a stroll through the cemetery where they sat on tombstones and necked undisturbed. Johnny Mathis recorded a hit that spring called "The Twelfth of Never." It was "their song," the lyrics promised that their love would last forever. Stilts gave her the "45" and she played it endlessly. This was what she had been born for.

While Krake was enjoying the thrills of puppy love, her father was having difficulty earning an adequate living. Lorraine had been forced to return to work teaching junior high a few years previous and found the teaching experience traumatic. Her class consisted of eighth graders whose interest in English and history was minute. She spent her time maintaining order.

There were horrific fights almost nightly between Hank and Lorraine. Krake would run to her room to try and drown out the noise, but to no avail. She loved Daddy so. Her mother constantly badgered him to make more money. Hank was smart but not aggressive and his feelings of inadequacy undermined any ability to sell himself. Krake learned about this characteristic when Lorraine explained one night why Hank got so drunk at every company party. Her mother said that although Hank was intelligent and capable, he had an inferiority complex.

"What's that?" Krake asked.

"When you don't feel as good as others," Lorraine answered.

"Can he get over it?"

"I don't know, maybe not. When he drinks, he doesn't feel so inferior."

The men Hank worked for at the paper mill were more interested in braggadoccio than brains. He had been looking for another job for several years but was having a hard time of it because he was in his late forties.

Krake walked into the house one day for lunch to find him reading a letter aloud to Lorraine. It was from a publishing house in New York City he had interviewed with recently. They offered him a job and would move him and his family to Belton, Texas where they were opening a paper mill.

Hot panic and grief rose up in Krake along with happiness for her father. She burst into tears. She had lived in Alexandria Mills since kindergarten, gone through school with the same kids, and now with her senior year approaching she had to move. Liz, I can't leave Liz. What will I do without Liz?

That night at dinner the family sat around the kitchen table discussing the relocation. Krake had a hard time relating to it, too enormous. The conclusion was inevitable. They would put the house up for sale immediately. Her father decided to drive to Texas in July and find a house. The rest of the family would fly down in August. School started then, due to the intense summer heat which forced the earlier closing of schools in May.

Krake's relationship with Stilts had been waning of late. She just didn't feel passion for him anymore so she decided to end it. He didn't understand and she didn't comprehend her change of heart either. Using the excuse that she was moving, she tried to hide that her feelings for him were gone. The way her feelings changed so suddenly puzzled her. One day she was madly in love, the next ho-hum. Perhaps it was the image or the challenge she fell for and when reality arrived, she checked out.

All too soon school ended. She sadly bid farewell to her classmates, hardly believing she might never see them again. In the middle of July, Hank left for Texas, alone. He said he was looking forward to the long drive through totally new territory. His sense of adventure was riding in the front seat beside him.

Three nights before her departure, Krake walked down to Schaeffer's Pond. How many times had she been there? In summer to swim, in winter to skate. All the good times, the safe, secure times. She didn't want to let them go. What was Texas going to be like? She couldn't imagine, but she was sure it wouldn't be anything like here. A summer rain drenched her on the way back mixing with the tears blurring her vision. The soft purr of distant thunder kept her company as she walked home through the darkening twilight.

She spent her last evening in Alexandria Mills with Liz, talking until the wee hours. They agreed to write and never, never loose touch.

Krake slept fitfully, awakening early, staring at Liz through half-closed eyes as if to capture the magical friendship they had shared for years. She tried to will her friend inside her. If I memorize her face, maybe I can take her with me. The sheets were soft, there was a big cobweb hanging overhead. She began to look for the spider who spun it and fell asleep.

The next morning Liz's father drove them to the train station in Syracuse. Halfway there, a hitch-hiker held out his thumb to them. As they got closer, Krake recognized that crooked smile. So did Mr. Havel, who stopped. Stilts got in the front seat.

"Hi. I'm on my way to a track meet in Syracuse." Looking at Krake in the back seat, he asked, "How are you?" His eyes searched her face.

She felt so guilty about hurting him she wished he would

disappear. "We're on our way to Texas," she said, looking away. "We're taking the train from Syracuse to New York City. We'll spend the night and fly to Houston tomorrow morning."

"You must be excited." Uncomfortably his eyes darted from the back to the front seat.

"Yeah, in a way." If only he would evaporate and let her talk with Liz. It was their final morning. He didn't get out until near the University, in the heart of Syracuse. Leaning over the seat, he grasped her hand, looked in her eyes for a long moment. "Bye, Krake. Good luck!"

"Goodbye, Stilts. I wish you the best," she said, lowering her eyes until he was outside of the car. Her hand was burning.

"Do you believe that?" she whispered to Liz as Mr. Havel wove his way through heavy traffic.

"It's obvious, he's still crazy about you."

"Gosh, I wish he weren't."

"There'll be a lot of new ones where you're going. Cowboys!" Liz elbowed Krake's side.

"You said it! Ride 'em cowboy!" They laughed.

They made their way through the crowded station to the train where Liz and Krake hugged and bade each other a tearful farewell. Head down, wiping her eyes, Krake climbed aboard, found Lorraine and Hank Jr., and waved a final goodbye to Liz and her father as the train moved forward.

What lay ahead? Fatigue and excitement ran neck and neck. She opened the latest issue of "Seventeen" magazine and began to read. Her mind raced. Would she become the wife of a rich oilman and wear a ruby in her navel? How about a wealthy cattle baron? Learn to ride and shoot? And of course, live happily ever after. No matter what! Are there still wild Indians lurking about, she wondered, with Jeff Chandler playing Cochise? She laughed to herself, not realizing the initial step of a journey spanning a continent had begun. It would end in a nightmare she could not envision.

2

Colored Waiting Room, White Waiting Room, neatly lettered over the two doorways, greeted them in the Houston airport. Krake never knew such signs existed. Then she saw two stainless steel water fountains in the corridor, marked as to whose mouth could drink there. Was the water in each different? She was mystified. This was 1954, the Civil War had made Negroes equal (or was it just free) almost a hundred years ago, hadn't they heard? It was her first taste of racism. Then she got angry. She had a powerful urge to sit in the wrong room, but was nervous enough as it was. Who dared to put up such warnings? The obvious injustice rankled.

As they stepped off the plane in Belton, a bitter, chemical smell met them along with intense heat and oppressively high humidity. She saw her father's silvery hair and ran into his open arms.

Ugh! He exuded the same chemical odor. Later she learned it was from the refineries. His white shirt clung to his back, wet with sweat. A trickle ran down her own leg, much to her horror. She stepped back, swallowing initial disappointment, but smiling bravely to assure him all was well. It was not.

They got in the car after retrieving the luggage and headed into town. FLAT! FLAT! Miles and miles of nothing.

Oil refineries that looked like life-size erector sets marred the landscape, flashing lights and emitting fumes no human should breathe.

As the car neared the residential area of Belton, the hideous spectacle of the refineries past, the landscape was more acceptable. There were plenty of trees with Spanish moss romantically festooning their branches. The well-tended lawns in front of the houses were deep green, a richer shade than the green of the northeast.

They pulled into the parking lot of a small restaurant her father had been frequenting during his stay this past month.

Inside, Krake's senses were bombarded with nasal, twangy, voices, smells of frying everything, western music on the jukebox and the chlorinated taste of cloudy water delivered by the waitress.

The menu seemed to be written in a foreign language. Chicken fried steak, which turned out to be a dry, thin piece of overdone beef fried in a chicken batter covered with milky, white gravy. Grits. Okra.

Even the hamburger Krake ordered was alien, the burger topped with lettuce, tomatoes, pickles and onions, slathered with mayonnaise and mustard and not a sign of ketchup anywhere.

Exhausted by the trauma of the exodus across country and the unfamiliarity of everything, they soon vacated the restaurant. Hank drove the three blocks to the Lone Star Lodge and all fell gratefully into the beds in the air-conditioned rooms. The house Hank had purchased wasn't ready for occupancy so the motel was their home for the first few days.

Krake woke the next morning to the hum of the air-conditioner. The room was cool, Hank Jr. still asleep. This is kind of exciting, she thought as she stretched awake, and it was lovely to be with her father again. She had been lonely without his love and support.

After breakfast, "No thanks, no grits," she adjourned to the motel swimming pool to work on her tan. A tan had been of utmost importance for the last three years. It symbolized wealth, glamour and success and was an essential part of acceptability.

That first morning in Belton she lounged in a chair by the motel pool as the stifling, hot air of a Texas morning settled over her. Sweat poured off her body in rivers. She took frequent dips in the bath-water warm pool.

Just before noon, a good-looking man in his mid-twenties came out of one of the rooms and took a lounge chair on the other side of the pool. When Krake got up to go into the water, the stranger cast admiring glances at her nubile form filling out the plaid strapless swimsuit..

He spoke with a thick drawl, "Hi, Y'all! How's the pool?"

"Wet," she replied her eyes twinkling flirtatiously.

Laughing, he came over and sat in the chair next to hers as she toweled off. Soon he was subtly flexing his smooth muscles and telling her of his exploits on the wrestling team at Southern Methodist University and asked if she would like to take a day trip over to Louisiana to see the alligators down on the bayous.

"Well, I'll have to ask my parents," she demurred, but quickly added, "I'm sure it'll be OK." The adventure of it appealed to her.

The next morning she and Louis set off in a big, yellow Buick. Louis, "Call me Lou," was a traveling salesman for an auto parts manufacturer in Dallas.

The thirty-mile stretch between Belton and the Louisiana border was flat and yawnable. The twenty miles to Lake Charles was more of the same until they left the main highway and bumped down a dirt road to a small, wooden shack next to a dilapidated dock falling into the murky waters of a swamp.

They got out and walked up the broken steps into the building. It was a restaurant, bar and general store. Pungent, spicy smells assailed their nostrils as they entered.

"What's that cooking?"

"Crawfish jambalaya," the brown-skinned, wizened face behind the counter answered. "You otts' try it." He then spoke to a young woman in a language Krake didn't recognize. The woman beckoned to them to follow her to a few tables covered in soiled yellow oilcloth. She pulled out a chair for Krake. Once seated, they looked through a fly-specked window down into the swamp. There was a wooden ledge outside the window with a bowl containing pieces of broken bread. Before long a fat, gray squirrel jumped up and began to eat.

Lou ordered a bourbon and Coke for each of them, along with a serving of jambalaya. The overhead fan whirred as they ate and drank and watched the squirrel. Unused to drinking, Krake felt the effects of the alcohol immediately. A warmth crept up her spine along with exhilaration. Occasionally, the dark, shiny head of an alligator would surface in the dank water below. It was all so thrilling and different from Schaffer's Pond. Lou ordered another bourbon and Coke followed by some chicory coffee. The perfumed spicy taste was so unusual and strong, Krake had a hard time finishing it. Their conversation during the meal was centered around Lou's job and his college exploits, which were boring, interspersed with compliments on Krake's beauty, which made her nervous. The second drink eased this feeling and lent a becoming flush to her cheeks.

Finally, Lou said they should be getting back. Krake secretly wanted another bourbon and Coke, but was too shy to ask. She swayed a bit as she negotiated the steps. The bourbon was having an effect.

Instead of heading back to the highway, Lou took a dirt road running along the edge of the bayou. Out of sight of the restaurant, he stopped the car and lit a cigarette. Krake smoked one too. In the area of smoking she felt fairly adept, having started the year before. He began kissing her, gently at first, then with more pressure. Presently his hand slipped under her skirt and found its way between her legs. She protested, but the combination of bourbon and lust removed her objections. His fingers pulled aside her lace panties. He rubbed and pushed his fingers inside her which hurt a little, and then he unzipped his pants, pushed her head down and thrust his penis into her mouth. It was the first time a male organ had been in her mouth. She didn't know what to do. He whispered, "Suck it, baby!"

She did obediently. He began to moan, soon the flesh in her mouth jerked and out came a creamy, hot liquid. Trying to hide her repulsion, she let it run down her face and wiped her chin on his pants.

What had happened? She was so naive about sex and at sixteen still a virgin. No one talked about it and she could only assume he had had an orgasm. Embarrassed and guilty, she wanted to run away but couldn't.

Lou zipped his pants, lit a cigarette and headed the Buick back towards the highway. Krake straightened her clothes and using her reflection in the rear view mirror applied lipstick to her still sticky lips. They rode in silence back to Belton. She avoided looking at him and was relieved when he said he was leaving early in the morning for New Orleans. She never saw him again.

She told her parents about the jambalaya and chicory coffee, but not the swampy orgasm. Lying in bed that night, she realized she had not had the courage to ask him to stop. Her fear of rejection and of his probable displeasure had kept her silent. She had enjoyed the feelings of lust he had inspired though. Did that make her a whore? Maybe. But the penis had been so big inside her mouth she had nearly gagged and when his semen erupted, it disgusted her. Is this what she had to look forward to?

Two days later, she and her family moved into their new home. It was not air-conditioned. A single-story ranch style bungalow, it had an attic fan and lots of flying roaches the size of small tanks. The house seemed small compared to the one in Alexandria Mills, much less privacy, with every room opening onto another. But a gardenia bush sent a heady smell wafting through Krake's room. She had only seen these exotic blossoms inside white cardboard boxes with clear plastic coverings.

Tall, skinny pines stood in the backyard along with a beautiful passion flower vine twining around a wire fence. New houses were being built a few blocks away and the local inhabitants (i.e., snakes) disturbed by the construction constantly slithered across yards, causing mayhem. Lorraine saw a copperhead beside the back door one afternoon and for over forty years never used that entrance again. Drainage ditches ran down between houses and were a haven for 'gators and water moccasins. Spanish moss hung silver-green and feathery from all the trees.

That year in Jefferson County there were 40,000 mosquitoes per person. The dull grinding of crop-duster engines could be heard morning and night as they sprayed the swampland, killing the larvae. Krake, very susceptible to mosquito bites, was in constant agony and covered with welts.

The heat was unbearable. Krake arrived at school at 7:45 a.m., when it was still cool. By ten she was soaked with sweat, her shoes actually squishing as she walked to class.

The kids at Belton High dressed differently than in Alexandria Mills. Even though it was ninety degrees, the girls wore full skirts with two or three petticoats underneath. Their socks were thin, not like the bobby socks of the East Their loafers were suede, while Krake's were smooth leather. She was the only girl with a pixie haircut, Bermuda shorts and a Bermuda skirt.

The boys wore jeans and boots and cowboy shirts which she thought belonged only in a Republic Pictures movie. Not an oxford button-down shirt, a pair of suntans or dirty white bucks to be seen.

The boys went crazy for Krake. On the weekends, carloads and pickup trucks full came over to her house. They crowded into the tiny, closed-in back porch, hung over chairs, sat on the floor and consumed innumerable Cokes.

"I'm going to buy stock in the company," Hank said.

Lorraine clucked and fluttered and gave them all chips and charm. Krake felt flattered, but awkward with all the attention, like a prize hog at the fair.

The girls, rich or not so rich, accepted Krake immediately. Krake was drawn to the sophisticated in-group, so unlike the Junior-Miss bunch she had been a part of in Alexandria Mills. She had never met people like this. They smoked, drank, had cars, closets full of clothes, and plenty of money. Texas oil and rice farming money.

One of the girls, Lynn Farrow, invited Krake to spend the night. The Farrow house was only a few blocks from hers. What a difference a few blocks made. Lynn's two-story brick mansion with four white columns and a circular drive belonged to the moneyed upper-class residents of the exclusive West End. The three-car garage housed Mr. Farrow's navy-blue Lincoln, Mrs.Farrow's white Cadillac and Lynn's red Oldsmobile convertible.

Lynn's room was out of a movie. One entire wall of the large bedroom was devoted to closet space. Inside were boxes of shoes neatly labeled "red flats," "black heels," "gold sandals," "lizard pumps," etc. Boxes were a necessity to keep away mildew. There was a separate dressing room and an adjoining bath. Krake, who had never been in a house with more than one bathroom, had never seen anything like this.

She recalled her first visit to Anne's house back in Alexandria Mills. The stakes certainly had gotten higher.

Lynn was open and friendly. Her hospitality and warmth soon put Krake at ease and helped push aside her feelings of insecurity. They played croquet in the backyard, and the next morning the maid served them breakfast out on the terrace. Trying to maintain a conversation was difficult, her head was spinning from all the luxury she suddenly craved. Somehow she felt she didn't really belong in this setting and fearful of seeming too impressed, she was unusually quiet.

Lynn's boyfriend was from Port Heron, a small town on the Gulf of Mexico, thirty miles from Belton. He fixed Krake up with Charles Lacey, the son of Port Heron's Ford dealer. On their first date, Charlie picked Krake up in a 1955 black Thunderbird! This was Ford's new sports car causing a sensation everywhere.

They drove down to Galveston, Krake leaning back in what was to her an odd little car with the wind whipping her hair, dreaming of becoming Mrs. Charles Lacey...Charlie would take over the car dealership from his father, they would belong to the country club, have three darling children and live happily ever after. What more could life possibly offer?

Krake and Charlie dated for a couple of months. Everything seemed to be fine until one night after watching *Love Me Or Leave Me*, with Doris Day and James Cagney, Charlie dropped a bomb. They were parked at the Treadaway mansion, a haunted house partially destroyed by fire, hidden in a tangle of trees and Spanish moss. Lynn and Don were necking in the back seat when Charlie whispered in her ear that he wanted to date other people. She didn't want to make a scene and disturb Lynn and Don, so she said nothing. She was crushed. He dropped her off at the end of the evening and said he would call. He never did.

Krake was home alone the next night baby-sitting Hankie. She played the sound track of *Love Me Or Leave Me* over and over and proceeded to get rip-roaring drunk to the poignant strains of "Ten Cents A Dance" and "Mean To Me." She was in such pain. How could Charlie have done this to her? Why? What had she done? What was wrong with her? She drank all of her father's pinch bottle of Haig and Haig, smoked a pack of Pall Malls and cried.

Her parents told her the next day that when they got home, they found her sitting in her father's green naugahyde over-stuffed armchair, smoking an imaginary cigarette, going through all the motions of putting the cigarette to her lips, inhaling and blowing out air. This was her second blackout.

She had experienced her first drunk a few months earlier, not long after the start of school. Waiting for Lorraine to pick her up one afternoon, she overheard two of her classmates talking.

"What do ya' want to do tonight, go 'gator giggin' or 'nigger knockin'?" one asked the other.

Krake couldn't believe her ears. Later she learned it was commonplace for boys to go out to the bayous near town at night to catch alligators prowling the banks of the Neches River, or venture down to "nigger town" and attack anyone who happened to be on the street, as long as they were black.

She was still digesting this remark when Sophie, squinting through her rhinestone sunglasses, sauntered by and invited Krake to a purple passion party that evening. Sophie, rail thin, very tan, and always faultlessly dressed was the epitome of worldliness, cigarette holder and all.

That evening they all met at Sophie's apartment, located across from the high school. Each morning, before classes began, seven or eight girls gathered at Soph's to smoke and gossip about boys. This lent a decidedly decadent note to the start of the day. The whole concept of apartment living conjured up images of people like Robert Taylor, Lauren Bacall and Barbara Stanwyck leading lives of unmitigated glamour.

As soon as everyone arrived, they took off in various trucks and cars to meet at an abandoned oil rig. In the back of one of the pickups was a large container of grain alcohol and Hawaiian punch, known fondly as "purple passion." It went down so easy, sweet, with just a little burning sensation at the back of the throat after swallowing.

They drank fast and soon were back in the vehicles, screaming and laughing, headed for the high school football field. Krake vaguely remembered getting out of Sophie's car and rolling around on the ground, giggling. The wet feel of the dew-laden grass soaking her underpants only added to the hilarity. She blacked out after that and awoke in her bedroom at home, with a tremendous hangover.

Sophie told her the next day that she had passed out. They brought her home and revived her enough so she could make it inside to her bed. Krake remembered none of this which helped in her denial.

Her first drunk! Her first blackout! At seventeen. She liked the first part of it anyway. After that initial cup of purple passion, she began to relax and didn't feel so alien. It didn't matter then that she couldn't drive and didn't have a car or shoes in boxes or live in a mansion. Well, it didn't matter as much. Her feelings of inadequacy and inferiority disappeared. Happiness and laughter welled up inside and bubbled over.

Her father was an introvert, her mother an extrovert, which was probably why they were together. She was a mixture. Her intelligence and creativity were hard to hide, but fear of rejection and failure kept her silent. Her thoughts were that if she made no comments or expressed no opinions, then she wouldn't appear stupid. Just smile and look pretty and everyone will like you. The epitaph under her photo in the yearbook read, "Still water runs deep." If they only knew how she really felt about the racism and not having a lot of money and blue jeans and grits she might not be so popular.

It was her desire to please, along with too much to drink, that led to her losing her virginity. It was Thanksgiving and her father served his lethal martinis before dinner. She got the extraordinary rush from the alcohol that she had grown to love and she wanted more. Some friends came by and took her to a wealthy boy's home for a swimming party in his indoor pool. There were both high school and college kids there. After a few bourbon and Cokes, some of the girls stripped (she didn't) and cavorted naked in the water. A couple of hours and plenty of bourbon and Cokes later, Krake agreed to let the host drive her home in his new, black Jaguar.

Ryan, a ne'er do well, probably an alcoholic, was in his early twenties and very sexy with black, Elvis hair. He guided the car down by the Neches river to a secluded spot. After a few amorous kisses, he slid her down on the seat and quickly penetrated her untouched body. She vaguely remembered a sharp pain, something wet oozing down her thigh and not much else.

On the drive home she realized she was no longer a virgin. It was only nine o'clock when Ryan left her at the door. She knew she would never see him again and didn't want to. She felt so dirty and wanted no reminder of her transgression. Her parents were watching TV, a late rebroadcast of the Macy's Thanksgiving Day Parade. Almost running by them she wondered, can they tell? She was shocked that it had happened almost without her knowing. Her alcohol muddled mind went into denial and after a long shower, she gratefully fell into bed.

A few days later her crotch began to itch. Upon examination in the confines of the locked bathroom, she was horrified to discover small, crab-like creatures sucking on the flesh of the labia majora. Now in the same category as a prostitute, or close, she concluded that this was her just desserts.

She didn't know about crabs and was ashamed to ask anyone so every evening after dinner she spent hours in the bathroom picking them off until they were gone. Lorraine's voice would probe, "What are you doing in there?" The shame and embarrassment of the whole episode lowered her self-esteem another notch.

On the surface, however, Krake was part of the gang and found two good friends, Kay and Marilee. And despite being a part of the sophisticated, we-don't give-a-damn, black-sheath-with-matching-cigarette-holder crowd, Krake's enthusiasm for stage acting led her to try out for the senior play, *Our Miss Brooks*. Having watched movies from an early age, she harbored a fantasy of being an actress. Being more than ever exposed on stage was outweighed by the lure of escaping reality and venturing into a different place and personality, a freedom she seldom found at home. Too many people to please and be responsible for there. She was cast as Maureen, the sexiest girl in Miss Brook's high school. She didn't feel sexy. Sex in the fifties was Marilyn Monroe and Jane Russell. Krake was too thin to fit that standard.

Maureen was a minor character, appearing only in the second act. In the assembly performance for the school, however, her entrance was greeted by catcalls, applause and rebel yells. Whistles followed her every move in her revealing, low-cut costume. Embarrassed and confused by this reception, she was grateful to make her exit. Her self-consciousness increased around boys.

Our Miss Brooks played two weekends for the public and Krake's presence didn't go entirely unnoticed. The review in the local paper read, "Krake Forrester, as the provocative Maureen, stole all of her scenes." Because of her acting ability? Krake knew better.

Neither Marilee nor Krake had dates for the Senior Prom. Because they dated college students none of the high school boys would ask them and no college guy would attend a high school prom. After graduation ceremonies the two of them went to the local drive-in, the Hogs Shed. They smoked and drank olive Cokes. This was an ending Krake hadn't counted on. Nothing had turned out the way she dreamed it would. One of her favorite fantasies had been that she would be Prom Queen. And she always thought that she and Liz or Anne would attend the same college, maybe a girl's school like Skidmore which was now too far away. She missed Liz and her friends in Alexandria Mills. You could bet none of her old gang had missed their Senior Prom. She wanted to participate in all the rituals; pick out a prom dress, put on her corsage, dance in the aromatic gymnasium with a boy who adored her. She didn't know why she had missed it. What had gone wrong? She pretended she didn't care, but truthfully, she was sad and lonely. She and Marilee were quiet as they drank their exotic Cokes. It wasn't because she didn't trust Marilee that Krake remained silent. She couldn't admit her feelings even to herself.

For a graduation present, Kay's mother had invited a friend over to read their palms. Kay went first. The palm reader took her slender hand and after looking at it closely, announced that Kay would be married within the year. They all gasped. College hadn't even begun. She would have to work fast.

To Marilee, the palm reader said, "You will find your true love in two years, marry and have a lot of children; boys, I think." How unlikely for footloose, fancy-free Marilee.

Krake held out her hand, not breathing. "Long lifeline. Now the love line. You will find love and happiness late in life."

"How many children?" Krake asked.

"I don't see any children."

No children. Love late in life. Krake was disturbed. What about living happily ever after? What else was there? She had no thoughts of a career. College was only a romantic stepping-stone to marriage. She didn't expect to graduate. But everybody knew what fakes fortune-tellers were.

3

Krake spun her wheels for two years at that haven of southern Baptist doctrine, Baylor University in Waco. Her first semester, she was put on permanent social probation for drinking. Undaunted, she continued to drink on weekend dates with airmen from a nearby base. The game plan became one of breaking the rules and not getting caught. Innumerable restrictions made this a full time job. She hardly went to class.

The summer between Krake's first and second year, her mother went back to New York for three weeks. While she was away, Krake was chief cook and bottle washer. Between cooking for her father and brother as well as herself, washing clothes, keeping the house immaculate and attending summer school, she had never worked so hard in her life. Krake gained a new understanding of the significant role her mother played in the family. She had had no inkling of how much effort it took to run a household smoothly. She was impressed by what Lorraine had been managing all these years and on the fringes of her awareness was the knowledge that homemakers got no credit, no validation. She asked herself if she really wanted to be one. But her answer to the question--what else was there?--she still came up blank.

Krake was miserable at Baylor. Except for her roommates, she didn't establish rapport with anyone. The southern Baptist student population seemed petty and judgmental. She felt her morals were nobody's business but her own. She knew she was wasting her time and Daddy's money, so towards the end of her sophomore year, she dropped out.

In the fall, Krake entered Belton College as a drama major.

You had to major in something, didn't you? On the first day of classes, as she entered the stuffiness of the Quonset hut where Drama 201 was held she saw him. He was talking animatedly with a couple of people; seated on a high stool, long legs angled out, arms gesturing, his head thrown back in laughter. Brown eyes acknowledged her as she took a seat in the last row. While arranging her books and purse, she covertly watched his every move. The attraction was instantaneous! Whenever their eyes met, she felt a thrill. Oh, I must meet him, I have to date him, she thought, and suddenly self-conscious, pulled her skirt down to cover her knees.

Soon the classroom was full of chattering students. The tall, lanky object of her affection glanced at his watch, stood up and walked over to the podium in front of the classroom.

"Hello, I'm Alan Burgess. Welcome to Drama 201."

She didn't hear any more for awhile, her disappointment acute. The professor! Professor Burgess, the Drama teacher! Oh, no, I'm sure he's married, has lots of kids and I'll never be able to date him. But, he'd looked at her in such a different way.

When she tuned back in, he was calling roll. Each student stood up, gave a brief resume of themselves and walked up to hand Professor Burgess their enrollment card. She was so nervous, she nearly stammered over her name during her introduction. Her legs felt weak as she slowly made her way towards the warm, brown eyes staring at her intently. Her gaze met his and didn't waver. Fortunately he had the podium in front of him or she might have let go of all reason and walked right into his arms. She handed him her card and made the long way back to her seat. Is he watching me? Please God don't let me trip.

She left the class experiencing a mixture of joy and sadness. In 1957, a student and professor dating was unheard of, yet she was sure she had just met the man of her dreams; tall, funny, smart and possessing an exciting energy. Resigning herself to the unpleasant facts of reality, she began her studies.

That semester the Drama Department was doing the Broadway musical *Brigadoon*, Alan Burgess directing. Drama 201 required working "crew" for the play. Krake still didn't know if Burgess was married. She was afraid to ask anyone for fear of revealing her feelings.

She started dating Tom, a student in her English class who boldly asked her out the first day. He was good-looking in a Rock Hudson sort of way, so she accepted and found she enjoyed his company and his kisses. As the semester progressed, she realized she was feeling a sense of belonging. The students were open and friendly and not as judgmental as those at Baylor.

During rehearsals for *Brigadoon*, Krake watched Professor Burgess direct and fell more and more in love. The huge auditorium was almost empty on those nights and she would sit marveling at his talent. He had taken her fellow students, kids who sat in class looking so ordinary, and transformed them into Scottish highlanders doing a sword dance, or maidens waltzing to "Go Home with Bonnie Jean." Magic and he was the magician. Even the twanginess of the Texan accents was hardly discernible. She sat there in those uncomfortable wooden seats and wished with all her heart that he was hers. She tried to will him to her. Staring at the back of his head or his profile, depending upon her angle, she sent forceful thought waves-you will ask me out, I am the woman you belong with, you will ask me out. Never more than polite, he seemed to hardly notice her. He was totally absorbed in the play.

The next play on the roster was *Rumpelstiltskin.* Krake read and won the part of Marianne, the miller's daughter. When she was informed she had to wear a long, blond wig, she questioned Burgess, "Why do heroines in fairy tales always have to be blond? Couldn't they have auburn hair like mine?"

"Princesses are always blond," he replied, the subject closed.

She hated the wig, thought it looked foolish. It was homemade and resembled a yellow mop.

She was late for the first rehearsal. A fellow cast member picked her up. One of the numerous trains that crisscrossed Belton had chosen to unhook cars as they were driving to campus. This was a lengthy procedure which took twenty minutes. Panicked at being late, she rushed on stage where Professor Burgess was already blocking the first scene.

"I'm sorry to be late," she said breathlessly, "but we got held up by a train."

Burgess looked at her, raising an eyebrow, "Did it take much?"

She stared at him uncomprehendingly for a moment, realized he was joking and laughed in relief.

"You'll have to leave in time to allow for that in the future," he sternly directed. "Tardiness is not tolerated."

She meekly went into the wings and waited for her entrance cue. When it came, she set foot downstage left and walked a few steps when Burgess' booming voice stopped her.

"Vocalize on *Greensleeves*!"

"What?"

"Do you know the tune?"

Of course she knew the tune! "Yes."

"Well, go back and come out again humming a few bars of *Greensleeves*."

Krake had a lovely voice, sang a solo in church when only three and participated in the choir for years. But her insecurity took over and *Greensleeves* came out as a croak. Burgess gave her an incredulous look. She continued with the dialogue, but was consumed with shame.

During the course of rehearsals, she slowly began to relax around Burgess. He did her makeup for dress rehearsal. Sitting in the dressing room with him leaning over her carefully applying blue shadow to her lids was almost more than she could stand. With only a slight movement she could reach up and kiss him. He seemed detached and unaware that her heart was about to pound its way out of her chest.

"I will do this only once," he advised. "Next time you're on your own."

She had never used eye shadow, liner or eyebrow pencil. Her beautifying ritual consisted of moisturizer, mascara and lipstick. "I can't," she told him.

"There is no such word in the theater," he replied and strode off, leaving her in a state of panic.

Luckily her friend Alice assisted her the next day for the opening matinee performance. As she was waiting for her entrance cue, Burgess who was checking the lighting stopped and wished her "Good Show!" Nervously she nodded, praying her croaking of *Greensleeves* wouldn't drive the audience right out of the auditorium. The first act went well and everyone was excited by the smoothness of the performance.

In the middle of the second act, she went up on her lines. Totally blank! The man playing her father mumbled some gibberish and they continued. No one seemed to notice, except Burgess. When she exited, he stopped her and asked what had happened.

"I forgot my lines. Was it awful?"

"It wasn't good."

She was mortified. The rest of the cast told her they didn't notice, but it was his opinion that mattered.

That evening, Tom, the good kisser from English class, picked her up for the cast party. They arrived early in spite of the fact that Tom stopped to get some bourbon to mix with the Cokes and 7-Up. Inside long wooden tables encircled a dance floor. Soon everyone from the Theater Arts Department was seated around them. Burgess was sitting across the table and a couple of chairs to the left of Krake and Tom.

Liquor flowed, people danced and Tom went back to the store for more booze. Krake took a deep breath, looked at Burgess across the table and blurted out, "Isn't this our dance?" She waited for his answer. He gazed at her a long moment then smiled, stood up and led her onto the dance floor. She turned to face him. He took her in his arms. For three or four turns he held her at arm's length, then drew her close. She was afraid she might faint, or worse, stumble. Neither happened. She thought, I must remember what song is playing so it can be our song. Johnny Ray's mournful voice was singing *Cry*. How disappointing! Not too romantic, but very prophetic.

The song ended and the next one started. They kept dancing until Tom returned with the liquor. It was so difficult for Krake to walk back to him, away from Burgess.

Off and on for the rest of the evening she would look over at him and say, "Isn't this the dance I promised you?" They would dance, her head fitting just beneath his chin. Unable to see over his shoulder, it became a fantasy of being alone together. Fearful that even a breath of air might disturb the magic of the moment, she let her breath out in tiny puffs, trying not to shatter utopia. She drank more and more to give her courage.

Between dances, Jean and Betty, established members of the Drama Department who lived in the same apartment complex as Burgess and were good friends with him, invited Krake to a late party after the cast party. Krake told them she didn't want her date to come along.

Conspiratorially, they whispered, "Just get in the car with us. Ditch him!" She was drunk enough and obsessed enough to do it.

Telling Tom she was going to the ladies' room, she grabbed her coat and purse and ducked outside. The next thing she knew she was crammed in the front seat of Jean's car along with Betty. Four men, including Burgess were in the back. As they were leaving the parking lot, Tom came running alongside the car, opened Krake's door and pulled her out. Fortunately they weren't traveling too fast. Krake hit the macadam and Tom dragged her on her knees for a short distance. She shouted after the retreating car, "Call me!"

The vehicle sped away into the darkness.

She looked down at her knees, painfully scraped and bleeding. Tom helped her up and silently they walked over to his brown Hornet.

They said nothing on the short drive home either. She knew she had treated him badly, but his possessiveness and control was unwelcome. Krake got out of the car, quickly let herself in the house and headed for her bedroom. She was packing an overnight case when the phone rang in the hall. It was Jean saying they'd be right over and yes, plan to spend the night. Lorraine was awake and whispered an OK to Krake's request to stay over at Jean's.

The party turned out to be at Burgess' apartment. A little anxious, Krake entered for the first time. Burgess came directly towards her, as if he had been waiting for her to arrive. Glancing at her injured knees, he guided her to a chair. Kneeling, he gently washed the raw flesh with some peroxide and covered the damage with gauze. She was stunned, enormously pleased and slightly drunk. Everyone was and the soiree soon broke up.

Disappointed that no future date had been made she climbed the stairs to Jean and Betty's apartment where she slept on a lumpy worn-out sofa. She woke early and was lying there when she heard a knock on the door. Motionless, she let Jean answer it. Burgess had come to borrow some sugar. She hoped he would stride over to the couch, awaken her with a kiss and carry her off on his white charger (or in his green Plymouth coupe). He thanked Jean for the sugar and left.

Jean, Betty and Krake sat around a breakfast table littered with empty Coke bottles and overflowing ashtrays. She marveled at how effortlessly she fit into this campus life. From the first, Jean and Betty and most of her fellow drama students seemed like her family, They were similar to her friends in Alexandria Mills, honest, direct, familiar and comfortable and most of all, trustworthy. Jealousy didn't seem to be an issue.

Over scrambled eggs and raisin toast the three discussed *Rumpelstiltskin* and *Brigadoon* and drama in general. Krake asked Jean for a ride home. Jean said Mr. Burgess had offered to give Krake a lift if she needed one. At their urging she called him. He was very friendly. "Come on down, Earl is here, cleaning the apartment. I can leave as soon as he's finished."

Earl, another Theater Arts major, was clearing away the party clutter when Burgess let her in. Burgess wanted to know if she had heard the score of the new Broadway musical, *West Side Story*. It had just opened on Broadway and Burgess knew Larry Kert, who was playing Tony, when they were both at Columbia in New York City. He spoke highly of Kert's talent and that of his co-star, Carol Lawrence, and expressed the opinion that this was the best Broadway musical in years. He played the album for her.

In spite of her acute nervous state at being nearly alone with him in his apartment, she thought the music wonderful. Usually she had to hear musical scores several times before she really liked them. Not this one. The hi-fi was turned up so conversation was impossible. While he and Earl cleaned, she listened. It was a bit overwhelming. Her mind listened to the compelling music for awhile then drifted off into various daydreams of being married to Burgess, alternating with panicked thoughts of how to comment on the music or any other subject that might be brought up. She glanced around at the typical 50's Swedish modern decor and found no trace of Burgess except for the rather elaborate hi-if system.

The silence was deafening after the finale. She didn't know what to say, how to express her feelings at the genius of the music and lyrics she had just heard. He seemed to understand her lack of response.

Earl left. Panic! Burgess sat down on the studio couch next to her after making them a cup of Lapsang souchong. While brewing the smoky tea, he talked of his love for the musical theater. Shyly, she made feeble attempts at conversation. Her background in this field was lacking except for seeing the *King and I* on Broadway a few years earlier and memorizing the lyrics of the popular tunes of the genre.

The tea finished, he suggested they leave and ushered her out. His shoulder brushed against hers as he opened the car door. The accidental touch burned on her skin as they drove home through the still, warm air of the December day. The trees were bare of leaves, the sky pale. He dropped her at her door and drove off without asking for a date. She was crushed.

By Wednesday of the following week she was desperate. She accompanied Jean, who was now playing Cupid for real, to the local grade school where the drama department was presenting *The Clown Who Ran Away*. When Burgess saw her seated on the stairs of the auditorium in a clown costume, he asked her what she was doing there.

"Betty has a cold and asked me to take her place," she said, shyly wrinkling her bulbous red nose.

This consisted of passing out candy to the audience after the show, so Krake had little problem replacing her. Afterwards she went back to Jean's and bravely stopped by to see Burgess. She babbled about the fun the grade-school children had at the play. She occupied her hands by doing his sink of dirty dishes. He tried to stop her, but she insisted. Finished, she stood drying her hands. She had let the pixie-cut grow out and now the steam from the dishes caused her long hair to curl around her beautiful face. He stood in the opposite corner of the cramped studio apartment.

Everything seemed to go dark, a phenomenon which occurred whenever she felt terrified. "Are you ever going to ask me out?" she managed to say.

Silence. Clearing of the throat. "You are strange."

"I know it. Well?"

"Yes."

"When?"

"I guess, , ah, Saturday night?"

"OK."

He wondered aloud, "Let's see, do I have anything planned for for Saturday night?"

"If you do, give me a call," she said. Just then her father, who she had called to pick her up, honked the horn. She left hurriedly before Burgess could change his mind.

4

Friday afternoon, Krake stopped by Kay's house. She and her new husband, Chip, were in Belton visiting her parents for the weekend. True to the fortune teller's prediction, Kay had eloped with Chip before Christmas vacation of her freshman year of college. They lived in Houston now and had repeatedly invited her to visit them. Kay wasn't interested in finishing school and was working as a secretary for a large oil company.

Lying across Kay's familiar beige, chenille bedspread, Krake told her a little about Burgess. Her feelings were too precious to share at length. After painting their toenails a crimson Fire and Ice, they spent most of their time gossiping about former classmates at Belton High. Specifically Sophie's surprise marriage to a roughneck from Buna. She met him at a roadhouse one night and ran away to get married the next morning. He must have quite a rig under his jeans. Sophisticated Sophie was now living in a tiny house out near the refineries and was pregnant with her second child.

Their conversation ended when Hank stopped by to pick her up on his way home from work. She promised Kay she would come back after supper to watch TV.

When Hank and Krake got home, Lorraine greeted her daughter with, "Someone called, a man, he sounded older."

Krake's heart dropped. "What'd you tell him?"

Lorraine was struggling to unmold a Jell-O salad and didn't answer.

"Mom, what'd you say to him?"

"I told him you'd be home around six and to try then. He didn't want to leave a message. Krake, can you help me with this? I never can get these darn things out."

Undoubtedly it was Burgess calling to cancel their date, she concluded by the time the salad was unmolded. Shortly before six the phone rang. Krake answered it, braced for the probable rejection. "Hello."

"Hi, this is Professor Burgess, how are you?"

"Fine," she answered, holding her breath.

"Jean, Betty, Larry, Dave, Ann and Eddie and some other students are going to a midnight show tonight at the Jefferson. Would you like to go?"

She couldn't believe it. Real casual, "Sure."

"Good. I'll pick you up at 10:30, the movie starts at 11:30."

"See you then," she said. "Bye."

"Bye."

She put down the phone and twirled and pranced out to the kitchen. Her cheeks were flushed with anticipation and pleasure.

"Mom, guess what? That was the 'older man,' Professor Burgess, you know, the drama teacher. He asked me to go to a midnight show at the Jefferson."

"That's nice, dear. Sit down, we're ready to eat."

Her stomach churning with excitement Krake ate, went back to Kay's and watched TV. She couldn't concentrate on anything, in fact had a hard time carrying on a conversation. Hank picked her up again about nine and as soon as she got in the house, she headed for the bathroom and the preparing-for-a-date routine. After bathing in lilac bubble bath, shaving her legs to a silky smoothness without too many nicks, she chose her favorite blue cashmere sweater buttoned up the back and matching skirt, gave up on her hair ever falling into a perfect pageboy, and applied Fire and Ice lipstick. The hour and a half she had allowed herself was barely enough. Just as she was blotting her lips the doorbell rang. It was HIM! Introductions over, Krake and Burgess departed, stopping for a beer (she had an olive Coke) at the Hog Shed. "What shall I call you, Professor Burgess, Alan, what?" she asked.

"Just call me Burg."

At the theater, a line wound around the corner for the midnight show. Spotting Jean, Betty and the others, they joined them and were soon seated in the art deco magnificence of the Jefferson. *The Cabinet of Dr. Caligary*, a classic horror flick was the feature. He didn't hold her palms-up, resting in her lap hand, but in the middle of a supposedly scary part strong fingers gripped her knee. Frozen, she didn't utter a sound. Should she have screamed or jumped or what? While she was agonizing over her inability to react, the awful movie ended and it was time for the stage show. This featured a magician who called forth the head of James Dean, killed in a car crash two years before. This obviously artificial talking head was the beginning, highlight and climax of the show.

Exiting into the night, the group headed for the coffee shop next to the theater. The James Dean spectacle was the subject of much jest and many rude remarks. She had only taken a few sips of coffee when Burg announced they were leaving.

On the way to her house, they discussed James Dean and *Rebel Without A Cause*. Before she knew it, they were sitting in the driveway. She felt shy and scared. It was 2:15 a.m., the house was dark, her parents and Hankie in bed long ago.

Burg offered her a Lucky Strike and they smoked together. They spoke again of the foolish magic show. Presently Burg leaned over and kissed her lightly on the mouth. All she could do was sit there like a dummy and think, I can't believe it. Professor Burgess is actually kissing me! His lips pressed harder on hers, her arms went around his shoulders, they were really kissing, tongues and all.

Time was forgotten. Cigarettes tossed out the window. Love was beginning. It crept in through the half-open window on Krake's side of the car. It enveloped them slowly until it covered every pore. They saw it and touched it and held it and were it. How, she thought, did this happen? Krake knew she'd never felt this way before. It was the epitome of every fantasy and dream. They kissed and talked. They kissed and smoked. They kissed and laughed. They kissed and kissed until Burg looked at his watch, exclaiming, "My God, it's five o'clock! I'd better get you inside. Your father won't think very highly of me, keeping you out this late on a first date."

"He's asleep," she assured him. Burg walked her to the front door. Just before kissing her good night he said, "I can't believe this is happening."

Standing on the step looking him squarely in the eyes, she, with the wisdom of the ages, replied, "Well, it is."

In her room, she undressed and got into bed as the faint rays of the first light of dawn began to streak the horizon. She couldn't sleep, too excited. Who could she tell? No one at this hour. She went over and over every second of the evening.

At eleven o'clock, she could feign sleep no longer and got up in time for lunch. She daydreamed and dawdled over her egg-salad sandwich until Lorraine inquired if she were ill.

"No," she said, "... well, kind of."

"Were you out late?"

"The movie ended about one-thirty and we went out for coffee with everyone. Then we sat in the driveway and talked for a long time." Her eyes quickly averted when her mother's hazel ones stared at her. "Why do I feel guilty?" she wondered. She always felt guilty. Lorraine never uttered the word "sex" but made clear the negative results of having it. She had told Krake several times, "Men never marry those kinds of women. That's why there are prostitutes, Krake. Men just have to have it and since they can't get it from nice girls like you, they have to go to prostitutes."

Sexuality mystified Krake. The sweet, sensual longings she felt while necking, could they be bad? Why? At times when she got drunk, she let boys fondle her. She didn't care, it felt good. They never pressed her to go all the way after she said no. The shameful feelings that Ryan engendered in taking her virginity had never left. Besides one dose of the crabs was enough.

In the late afternoon, the phone rang. It was HIM!

"How are you?" she inquired, hoping to avoid some kind of rejection.

"Fine and you?"

"Fine. Listen, I know we made a date for tonight originally but since we went out last night I won't hold you to it." A pause. "Don't you want to?" he asked.

"Well, yes, but I didn't want you to think you had to."

"Oh," he paused, puzzled. "Larry and Linda are coming over to my place, we'll listen to records. I'll pick you up at eight-thirty."

"OK, see you then," Krake said. "Bye."

"Bye."

She hung up, embarrassed, mortified, she didn't know what to do. Her insecurity was running wild. She calmed down and decided to wear cashmere again, soft for necking.

The evening was pleasant. They listened to *West Side Story* and *South Pacific*. Burg and Krake ended up standing in the narrow hallway near the tiny bathroom necking, in full view of Linda and Larry. There was no place else to go. His lips were warm and familiar. No, she hadn't dreamt it. They really had necked in her driveway until five that morning. The kisses were so special she never wanted them to stop. She wished he could swallow her up like a snake swallowing a dinnertime rodent whole.

The evening ended early. Neither one of them had had much sleep, if any, the night before. On the drive home he told her he was going to San Francisco to spend the Christmas holidays which began the following Wednesday. Confiding that he hoped to sell his plans for a theater to San Francisco State and arrange for a teaching fellowship to complete his doctorate, he kissed her good night and left, saying he would see her soon.

She began scheming immediately. He would be staying with a favorite aunt in Houston both before flying to California and for another two days when he returned. Aha! That was it.

Wednesday, she stopped by his office after class. He looked happy to see her, wished her a Merry Christmas and a Happy New Year and said he would see her when he got back.

"I'm going to be visiting some friends in Houston after New Year's. When will you be coming back to Belton?"

"On the 5th, classes start the 6th."

"Great, could I hitch a ride with you? I'll be coming back the same day."

"Well … sure."

"Thanks."

"I'll call you when I get in to Houston on the 3rd. We could go out to dinner and the theater the next night, if you like."

Krake's heart beat wildly. "OK, sure," she replied.

They exchanged phone numbers and parted. She was thrilled. Now, if only Kay and Chip were going to be home then. A quick call to Kay settled the situation. She had done it! Her first major manipulation of circumstance for her benefit. She was scared and hopeful at the same time. The thought of spending a whole evening alone with him was terrifying. But they might get to know each other better. But then he might not like her. Shit, she had to risk it.

The thought of going to dinner with Burg kept her sane during the holidays. She even honored Lorraine's request to stop saying "shit". She finally boarded the Greyhound bound for Houston. She hated buses. This one stopped at every podunk town between Belton and Houston. Today she didn't mind. She was going to see him tomorrow.

Houston was huge even then. Sprawled out like an oil spill on the prairie. Kay and Chip picked her up at the station and drove endless miles to a suburb where they had recently purchased a house. It proved to be a typical tract box but she enjoyed witnessing the first of her high school friends indulging in all the trappings of the married bliss she coveted.

That evening as planned, Burg called and arranged to pick her up the next afternoon at five for dinner and the theater.

At four o'clock, she bathed, shaved her legs, splashed lotion all over her body and dressed meticulously. This was the era of garter belts and stockings. Being thin with prominent hipbones, her garter belt rested uncomfortably on these protrusions, leaving red grooves in her skin. Painful, but what price glamour?

She had gone shopping the week before for the dress. A raw-silk sheath with a white, long-sleeved blouse-like top, a navy blue skirt and a pleated vibrant green cummerbund. Matching green satin high-heeled mules, called spring-o-lators, and an ivory satin clutch bag completed the outfit. She looked terrific and felt very grown up.

Promptly at five, the doorbell rang. Grabbing her purse, she opened the door, nervously pushed right past him and headed out to the car. He opened the door as she stood waiting and slid in. As he was walking around to get in on the driver's side, she glanced in the rear-view mirror at her still perfect reflection, licked her lips and turned slightly towards him as he got in behind the wheel. To her surprise he leaned over and kissed her hard on the lips. She had expected a more formal greeting, no kissing until the end of the evening. A blush suffused her body. "I missed you," he murmured and started the car. She turned hot and cold, hoped her lipstick wasn't smeared and tried to make small talk (never her forte) until they arrived at his aunt's house. He told her on the drive that his Aunt Louise was the only one of his relatives he felt close to. He had lived with her while attending the University of Houston and always stayed there when he was in town. The house, a large, two-story cream colored brick, sat back from the street.

Tall and white-haired, Aunt Louise was friendly and served hors d'ouevres and wine before leaving them alone in the vast living room. Burg pointed out antiques and some baby pictures of himself on the marble mantelpiece. He began to tell her a little about his family. Aunt Louise had raised him because his parents divorced when he was nine. His brown eyes shifted restlessly when he talked about his mother. His Howdy Doody grin of a mouth turned downwards and his tone became serious as he explained that both his parents had married others soon after they parted.

"My mother never really liked me," he continued. "She doesn't know or understand anything about the theater or my world." His mother had been a manicurist in a beauty salon when she married his father. "We rarely see each other, which is good, because I don't have anything to say to her. She and her husband run a Bronco Burger in Tyler. I guess they're happy. Whenever I see her, all she asks is how much money I make and could I send her some."

"What about your Dad?" Krake asked. For a prince, his background was surprisingly ordinary.

"He's semi-retired now. Lives in a beach house down near Galveston with his second wife. He works on fishing boat engines when he needs cash, but mostly goes fishing and drinks beer." His voice drifted off remembering the limited relationship with his immediate family. "Aunt Louise is the closest thing to a mother I've known," he sighed. "She's always been there for me."

Krake felt his sad loneliness and resisted an impulse to give him a hug. He returned the photos to the mantle, then took her in his arms, giving her a long, intense kiss.

She felt so shy, self-conscious and vulnerable. The fear that it all would suddenly vanish kept her slightly aloof and distant. Also the fear of tripping. Negotiating in high heels had always been a challenge, but according to her dress code they were a must for dressy occasions. The glamour of the 50s.

After thanking Aunt Louise, they got back in the car and headed for the Old College Inn, a well-known restaurant near the theater district. The building was brick with brick floors. Krake prayed that the stiletto heels wouldn't catch in a crevice as she followed the maitre'd to a table for two in the back dining room.

Safely seated in a ladderback chair, she began to relax slightly. Burg removed a brown paper bag from his inside coat pocket. A half pint of bourbon. This was Texas in 1958, Harris County was semi-dry. That meant a restaurant could only serve wine, no hard liquor. People brought their own and then were sold a set-up, a mixer and ice for the booze. She declined his offer of a drink, knowing the effect it had on her. She wanted all her wits about her for this, their first evening alone.

Burg carried the conversation and dinner was fun. He told her all about San Francisco and Chinatown. Descriptions of the charm of the city entranced her. Her mind began to plan ahead to the time they would visit there together. They would be newlyweds and have a glorious honeymoon at the St.Francis or the Mark Hopkins.

Burg told her that he had sold his plans for a theater to San Francisco State and the teaching fellowship was secure whenever he chose to use it.

We have to be married first, flashed through her mind. She hoped it wasn't visible on her forehead. Perhaps her eyes were flashing "marriage" on and off. She quickly looked down at the pale pink shrimp in the cocktail dish which had just been placed before her. Securing one on a tiny silver fork she popped it in her mouth, then raised her eyes and met his staring at her from across the table. A slight smile played at the corners of his generous mouth and his slim fingers enclosed her wrist as she was spearing another shrimp.

"I missed you," he said. The brown eyes held hers for a moment.

With a noisy gulp she swallowed the shrimp whole. During the meal (she tasted nothing, could have been eating cardboard food cut-outs), his warmth melted her reserve. By the time the chocolate mousse came she could not only taste it, but was telling him of her awful recitation during kindergarten graduation ceremonies when, due to a recent bout with chickenpox, she scratched all over her body throughout the speech and was totally perplexed by the laughter of the audience.

Smiling, he glanced at his watch and announced they had better go. She once again negotiated the treacherous bricks and while he paid the check, repaired her lipstick in the ladies' room.

They drove the few blocks to Theater,Inc., the premier musical theater company in Houston. *Kiss Me Kate* was the current offering. The performance was captivating and afterwards they went backstage to meet the infamous, temperamental Leslie Johns, Theater Inc.'s founder and managing director, a flamboyant figure well known for her outrageous behavior. Burg had worked crew backstage here for a year while attending the university.

Introductions were informal. Leslie shook Krake's hand heartily with her heavily ringed fingers, talked briefly to Burg, then departed for a press party at the Shamrock Hilton.

Burg showed her around the dimly lit backstage area, explaining the reason for different gels on the various lights and the intricacies of the lighting and sound effects systems and relating some of his experiences working there. He was indeed in his element. The glow from his eyes indicated his utter devotion to every aspect of this world.

Eventually they returned to Kay's house. Kay and Chip were in bed. They listened to records in the living room. Burg sat on the uncomfortable couch, pulled her down on his lap and ran his slender fingers through her hair. She entwined her arms around him as the satin spring-o-lators tumbled to the floor. When he removed his jacket, she could feel the hard muscles of his chest through his shirt. A slight odor of starch and sweat added to the sensuousness of the contact.

She loosened the bow tie he usually wore. The tie was hard to get used to. Nearly everyone else wore conventional ties and her need for conventionality was constantly with her. He said he wore them because they added width to his thinness. Couldn't argue with that.

His kisses were so passionate she felt she could have spent forever exploring his mouth. After a half hour of making discoveries, he said he should be going. Reluctantly, she walked him to the door. He left after a lingering kiss and the promise to see her the following afternoon.

The next day Kay invited Burg to join them for dinner. When he arrived, Chip took him out to the garage to look at the 1930 Model A coupe he was restoring.

Krake and Kay retreated to the kitchen to make the ever popular dish for the young married set, hamburger stroganoff. While Krake was slicing tomatoes for the salad, Burg came up behind her and kissed the nape of her neck. No one had ever done that before. His lips were moist and warm and the gesture so tender she could hardly breathe. She wanted to turn around and embrace him, but not in front of Kay.

On the drive back to Belton after dinner, they talked about the next semester and stopped for one last cup of coffee. They didn't want the evening to end, but school started in the morning so they unwillingly parted.

"Good night, sweet prince," she whispered to herself as she quietly closed the front door.

5

January was cold and rainy. Burg dripped too with the flu. Krake stopped at his apartment where he was grading final exams. Although she was permitted to sit on his lap while he recorded students marks, she was denied the pleasure of kissing on the mouth.

"You'll catch whatever I have, it's not worth it." He sneezed.

"It's worth that and a lot more," she said.

The fact that he genuinely cared for her was a constant wonder. He was her idol, her fantasy, her dream prince. She loved *Grimm's Fairy Tales*, and every Saturday morning as a child had listened to *Let's Pretend* on the radio. Handsome princes, evil Queens, blond Princesses and definitely Happily Ever After.

This man, her drama professor, winner of a grant to study theater at Stratford-Upon-Avon for a year (only twelve of which were given throughout the entire United States when he received his), intelligent, talented, handsome with huge, brown eyes that melted her heart, the thought that he might be crazy for her was mind-boggling. Her uncertainty was a paradox because she had the daring to attempt almost anything, but lacked belief in herself. She had been bold enough, after a few drinks, to ask him to dance, but sober, she was plagued by self doubt. He hadn't told her he loved her. Although his attentions indicated that he did, she wanted to hear the words.

Krake's home life was one source of her ongoing uncertainty about herself and her abilities. Her mother seemed to undermine her, but it was subtle, indirect and hard to decipher. For instance, when Krake wanted a new dress for an upcoming dance, Lorraine agreed to take her shopping. Krake would select a dress and Lorraine suggested buying matching shoes. This task accomplished they returned home. Flirtatious and happy, Krake modeled the new outfit for Daddy. Everything seemed fine until the following evening at dinner when Hankie started his routine. "Why does Krake get everything and I get nothing? She's so spoiled and greedy, nobody can have anything but her. She's mean and selfish. I can't have a new baseball mitt and she has twenty-two pairs of shoes and got another pair yesterday. I want a bee-bee gun!" Lorraine backed him up and another argument began. The support of her mother was there one day and gone the next. Krake often wondered if Lorraine planted the seeds of discontent and rivalry. Why would an adolescent boy care how many shoes or dresses she had?

Hank Jr. was a difficult child. Had he been born fifteen years later he would have been diagnosed as hyperactive. The whole family had a hard time coping with the manifestations of this condition. Thrusting his hand into a floor fan in a restaurant or drinking out of the finger bowls was annoying but much of the time he was uncontrollable. Since neither one of her parents were well versed in administering discipline, Hankie had the run of the house or wherever he was. His unpleasant habit of voicing loud discontent over almost everything made situations miserable.

After Hank Jr. arrived, Christmases, which had been special times, were a disaster. He pouted, "I don't like this. I want a Flexible Flyer sled, not a Snow Skimmer. Waah, this broke! All I did was try to bend it in two. Krake got more than I did. Look, she has two sweaters, shoes, a bathrobe and three necklaces. I just got a sled, a coloring book, dungarees and a toy gun. Waah!"

Hank Jr.'s jealousy was a constant thorn in Krake's side. Her mother was jealous too. The rivalry that sprang up between them was initially for her father's attention. Lorraine, vastly insecure herself, envied Krake's good looks. Compared to her daughter, she was plain. A great admirer of physical beauty, Lorraine placed anyone possessing it far above her, revering and resenting them simultaneously. Krake headed the list. The fact that Hank Sr. adored his daughter and she him added to the atmosphere of suspicion and envy.

It gradually became clear to Krake that Lorraine was using Hankie as her Charlie McCarthy. Placing the ideas in his mind, she backed him up when he opened the field for battle. The unfairness of it, the treachery, inflamed Krake.

After years of this, she spent less and less time at home. The rift between her and Lorraine and Hankie grew wider. She thought all she suffered as a result of this game was anger, but underlying the whole dynamic was distrust. Distrust of others and mainly of herself. This permeated her being so totally it almost destroyed her. When people let her down, she felt it was her fault and hated herself. As a teenager she had nary a clue as to the truth. She only knew she didn't have her mother's love. No matter how good the grades, how popular or how pretty she was, it was never enough. Different from her mother in many ways, she enjoyed the unconventional, the dramatic, the sensual and the exotic. Daddy enjoyed this aspect of her, but it frightened Lorraine. It was hard to be herself around her mother, yet she needed and wanted Lorraine's support.

Instead of support, Krake's "true love" became the latest target. Burg was a different type than Lorraine was used to. His long, lanky body and expressive gestures caused her to remark, "Are you sure that man isn't effeminate?" This was years before the term "gay." "A black umbrella, I've never seen a man carry an umbrella."

"Mother, he lived in England for a year. That's where he got it. Even the dogs carry one over there," Krake responded angrily.

"Oh," her mother said with a sly smile, satisfied to have gotten a rise out of her.

Undermining, judgmental, and negative, Lorraine's power was formidable and left a lasting impression of self-doubt in Krake.

In February, Burg cast Krake as the lead in *Picnic*. The previous summer, the movie, starring Kim Novak and William Holden, had been a huge hit. Rehearsals were fun. The rapport Krake felt with her fellow drama students was to be unequaled the rest of her life. Inseparable, they went to school all day, taking a break at Jean and Betty's to watch *Days Of Our Lives* and eat lunch. They rehearsed into the evening and adjourned afterwards to Edward's, a local hang-out a few blocks from campus. Krake always had Champale and never enough. One drink more, just one drink more, played endlessly in her mind. But this relationship was important and Burg seemed so far above her in intellect and creativity and age that she had to be in complete command of her faculties, so her drinking habits were curtailed. Burg rarely drank more than two or three drinks in an evening and neither did she.

On weekends Krake was with Burg, alone or double-dating. The fact that they saw each other every night at rehearsals contributed to their growing closer. Krake always had the job of bringing him his coffee at breaks. He wasn't cool, he drank it with cream and lots of sugar. The "beats" always had it black.

On stage she was inhibited around him. When Larry tried to choreograph the dance sequence between Hal and Madge at the picnic, he had to literally stand behind Krake, grab her hips and move them from side to side to loosen her up. Later, at Edward's, they had a good laugh over that. "Krake," Larry joked, "you need to rock your pendulum around the clock. Dig?" She was fearful of making a mistake in front of Burg, but her natural abilities as an actress pulled her through.

The opening night performance went well and the reviews were kind. She was so nervous she had no idea what kind of a performance she gave. Rather than concentrate on the audience, she thought about making Burg proud. Playing Madge wasn't easy. The ingenue roles never were. Unfortunately these pretty, naive women's parts were written without too much depth or meat to sink your teeth into. She found it more fun to play the wicked witch than the princess. But princess material she was, despite not being blonde.

When not rehearsing, she and Burg attended local theatrical productions and met the actors. She began to learn about professional theater. The actors talked of working long hours with little or no pay, but they seemed to have a real love for what they were doing and the whole thing seemed glamorous.

Krake and Burg had confined any caressing to above the waist. He never made any further advances, but if he had, she wouldn't have resisted. She knew her mother thought the only reason she was so popular was because she slept with all her dates, but she hadn't. With Burg, she didn't feel that restraint. This was love.

Right after the closing of *Picnic*, Krake cut her hair. Short curls capped her head.

"Sophia Loren, that's who you look like," said Larry as he was dropping her off at Burg's for a short visit. Burg had another cold and was staying inside for the weekend. Krake persuaded Larry to take her over to the apartment to show off her new hairdo. Apprehensive, she let herself in. He was lying on the studio couch, smoking. Casually, he looked at her. "Turn around."

She turned self-consciously, praying, "Please God, let him like it."

"Mmmmm..."

Her confidence waned.

"I like it."

"You do? Really?"

"Mmmmm.... yes, I do. You would probably look good with your head shaved."

Relief, relaxing, "How are you feeling?"

"Better, now."

Giggle. "Larry's picking me up at nine. I had to give him dinner to get him to bring me to see you."

"I thought you said you'd be here by seven."

"Sorry, dinner was late and so was Larry." She sat on the edge of the narrow couch, leaning down to kiss him.

He turned his head. "No, you'll catch this."

"I don't care."

"Listen, kiddo, this is no fun."

"It could be." Wickedly, she tickled him. He caught her hand in his. She stared into his eyes. Silence.

"Krake...I love you."

"You what?" Did I really hear that?

"I love you."

Oh, my God, he loves me. "I love you," she finally said.

He drew her down on his chest, her head resting under his chin. They remained like that for awhile savoring the moment. Her thoughts were filled with the overwhelming fact that he actually said that he loved her. The dream was coming true. See, people do live Happily Ever After. Finally she stirred, lifted her head. "Want some tea?"

"Yeah, love some."

"As much as you love me?"

"Hmmmm....let's see."

"Never mind, you creep!" Laughing, she walked to the stove and put the kettle on.

Larry's knock ended their rendezvous. Burg was coughing and sneezing as they left. Luckies overflowed the ashtray.

The final play of the spring semester was *Death of a Salesman*, given for Religious Emphasis Week which took place late in April. Cast in the small part of a hooker in the second act, Krake worked mostly backstage on props and costumes. Alice was playing "the woman." She had fallen madly in love that spring with a local disk-jockey named Lyle who Burg cast as the neurotically emotional son, Biff. It was frustrating to watch Alice and Lyle in the student union, unable to keep their hands off each other. Krake and Burg couldn't indulge themselves like that, could only smile and give each other special looks whenever they met on campus. According to college rules, they weren't supposed to date.

The selection of *Death of a Salesman* was radical for this small Texas campus, especially as a topic for discussion during Religious Emphasis Week. Burg welcomed all the controversy, in fact, thrived on it.

The production was staged in theater-in-the-round style, a new experience for most of the cast. In this medium the actors have to create the space between themselves and the audience because the audience is within the actor's line of vision at all times. The lighting helped, but it took some getting used to.

The play opened to brilliant reviews and genuine enthusiasm among the religious leaders participating in the after-performance discussions which dealt with the problems of deceit, adultery and suicide. Immediately after the play closed, however, Burg was censured by the head of the Drama Department, ordered not to present such a modern, controversial play again. Krake supposed deceit, adultery and suicide were considered more appropriate if couched in the iambic pentameter of the Bard.

Burg usually called Krake once a week to make a date for the coming weekend. A week and a half passed after *Salesman* closed and no call. She called him. "What's going on? Why haven't I heard from you?" For some unknown reason she never used a salutation when calling him.

"I was just getting ready to call you. Can you go out for a beer in an hour?"

"Sure."

"0K, I'll see you soon."

She hung up. Fear gripped her. What could it be? Had he changed his mind about her?

An hour later they were headed across town. Not to the Hogs Shed, too visible she soon learned. Burg related what had taken place the previous Monday when he was called into the head of the Drama Department's office and told he could not be seen leaving or entering the campus with her. When they drove by the college grounds, he asked her to lie down on the front seat. She complied, relishing the idea that she was forbidden. They went to the Longhorn, a seedy drive-in on the other side of town where all the good ol' boys hung out.

Burg ordered two beers. He looked at her and said, "I'd ask you to marry me right now but since you have a year and a half of school left, I think you should be able to be with your friends. If we were married, you couldn't be. You'd have to sit in the faculty lounge in the student union, for instance. I feel you'd miss a lot. What do you think?"

Reeling with shock and happiness that he had asked or rather told her he would marry her, she paused a long moment then replied, "I suppose you're right. I didn't realize I couldn't be with my friends."

He assured her that as soon as she graduated they would marry and move to San Francisco. There he could complete the two years left on his doctorate while teaching drama at San Francisco State.

She invited him to come for dinner on Sunday evening and he drove her home.

Krake prepared Eggs Bernaise that evening. The dish, ham slices, eggs, potatoes and a cheese-wine sauce melted together, was a hit. As they were eating in the dining room, off of Lorraine's pink Haviland china plates, Burg expressed admiration of the meal to Lorraine.

"Oh, no, I didn't make this, Krake did," her mother protested.

"You did?" he said wonderingly. Krake nodded.

"It's delicious."

She flushed at his approval.

Dinner over, Krake and Burg retired to the jalousied back porch. There, as was their custom, they necked and petted. Sitting on a glider which tended to move back and forth only added to the excitement of hands on flesh, mouth on mouth, bra unhooked, tongue encircling nipples, until Burg suggested they go across town to his apartment.

A warm, late-spring rain had begun to fall as they dashed up the concrete stairwell to his apartment. In each other's arms, Krake pressed against him. Blouse and jeans were swiftly in a heap on the floor. She managed to strip off Burg's shirt, but was suddenly overcome with shyness and unwilling to unzip his pants. He did and stepped out of them. The shorts followed and their naked bodies dissolved into one. Krake soon felt the long, hard sheath between her legs. It must be enormous, she thought, it extends all the way underneath me. He picked her up and carried her to the sofa-bed. Lying on top of him, she nervously took a sip of beer that was sitting on a table by the bed. Burg laughed.

She murmured, fearful of his finding no maidenhead. "I've done this once before. It was three years ago. I was drunk."

He stopped her with a kiss. "It doesn't matter."

Oh, I hope not, she prayed, I hope you don't think I'm a whore, then was swept away in passion.

Later they lay quietly, side by side in the narrow bed. As she rested in his arms, the lonely sound of a train whistle interrupted the soothing patter of rain on the roof. If only we could stay like this forever. I'm so content, so peaceful. They had finally done it. She didn't think she had had an orgasm, but never mind, there was plenty of time for that. The fact that this physical barrier had been conquered was enough. The special intimacy this fleshy coupling engenders took over. After all the months of anxiety, insecurity and wondering, she could relax.

The next week hurried by. Thursday noon he stood behind her in the cafeteria line and whispered, "I love you." She floated to a table, sat down and found him sitting several people over to her left. The smiles exchanged left no doubt as to their feelings.

Friday night they went to the drive-in and watched a double feature. Later when people asked her, she couldn't remember what was playing. She had a vague recollection of some French refugees riding on the back of a wooden cart in war-torn Germany, shot in black and white.

Finishing off an entire six-pack at the movies, they were quite relaxed by the time they reached Burg's apartment. The lovemaking was memorable. She had her first vaginal orgasm. They were so enamored they didn't want to part, but had plans the next day to see the play, *Inherit The Wind*, in Houston.

Burg got a drink of water for himself, then brought the half-full glass over to her. She buttoned her shirt one button and looked up as he put the glass down on the bedside table.

"Do you think you can be happy with me?" he asked as he knelt down between her legs, head resting on her stomach, arms encircling her hips.

"I'm so happy I don't even know how to tell you. I can't wait until we can be together for good."

"We may not be able to wait a year and a half," he whispered as he gave her right breast a kiss, then brought her face down to his. "we'll have the kind of family I always dreamed of."

The next day, Krake fussed and fumed. They were driving to Houston with Larry and Linda. Aunt Louise was preparing an early dinner for the four of them. Should she wear her Bermuda shorts and change at Aunt Louise's? No, the hassle of bringing a garter belt, stockings and all the paraphernalia seemed too much trouble. She decided to be all ready for the theater and dressed with care. In the spring of 1958, the hemlines had risen to just below the knee. She was wearing a yellow and white gingham chemise with a rope of white beads and low white heels. Her lipstick and nail polish were Revlon's newest, Persian Melon.

Promptly at a quarter to four, the black and chartreuse '57 Chevy coupe pulled into the driveway. Larry, Linda and Burg got out. When they saw her they protested, "Go change! Get into shorts! You'll get all wrinkled riding over there. You can get gorgeous at Aunt Louise's. We're all bringing our good clothes."

"OK, OK," she said and went back into her bedroom with Burg following. He grabbed her and began kissing her. Disengaging herself, she started to undress. Standing in her slip, he kissed her again and ran his hands over her body. Her nipples hardened and desire rose. Thank heavens her parents had gone shopping. Reluctantly she led him into Hankie's adjoining room, seated him on the bed, telling him to stay there or she'd never be able to get ready.

She changed quickly and packed a small bag of essentials. They piled into the Chevy, Krake and Burg in the back seat, Linda and Larry in the front. That was the last thing she remembered, settling down into the black vinyl upholstery with Burg's arm around her, laughing.

6

News of the tragedy spread quickly. Alice was in the bathtub getting ready for a date with Lyle when the phone rang. It was Krake's mother. What was she doing calling her? "Krake's in Houston with Burg," Alice began.

"No," the voice on the phone interrupted, "there's been a bad automobile accident. We don't know yet how it happened. Krake's in critical condition at St. Elizabeth's Hospital. Her father and I are here at the hospital if you and Lyle want to come down."

"What about Burg and Larry and Linda? Weren't they with them? Are they hurt? Where did it happen? When?" The questions tumbled out as Alice tried to learn everything at once.

"Larry and Linda are injured, but will be all right. Alice, dear, I hate to tell you this... Mr. Burgess was killed. The doctor just told us."

"It's not true!" Alice pulled the towel tightly around her, water puddling the hardwood floor. She leaned against the wall for support.

"Have you seen Krake? Have you talked to her?"

"She's still unconscious, they won't let us see her."

Lorraine's voice cracked.

"Lyle and I'll be there as soon as we can, Mrs. Forrester. Don't worry, Krake will be fine." Alice hung up the phone.

They came in anguish, in horror, in disbelief. Burg, their shining star, their leader, mentor, confidant and friend was dead. Few of them knew anyone who had died and they were emotionally shattered. People were supposed to meet the grim reaper when they were old, had gray hair and wrinkles and had led long, full lives, not when they were young and incredibly vital.

Larry suffered a broken collarbone when his shoulder hit the steering wheel. Linda had a cut on her forehead, from being thrown against the dashboard. Apparently, just as Larry turned the Chevy onto the highway two cars veered into their lane when a Cadillac ahead of them made an unexpected right turn. Larry saw this and pulled onto the shoulder but the oncoming autos struck the back of the car. Burg was sitting at the point of impact and his body took the brunt of the crash. His neck snapped and he died immediately. Krake was shielded from the direct force by him. She sustained a broken pelvis which pierced her bladder, blood clots formed in her chest and brain and her skull was fractured. She was semi-comatose for ten days.

Two days after the accident, Lorraine attended Burg's funeral in Houston. She squeezed into Jean's red Chevy along with Betty, Larry, Linda, Alice and Lyle. Lorraine had an ability to relate to her daughter's friends on a close, personal level. Krake, however, mystified her. She didn't know how to reach her much less understand her behavior. Raised in a society whose class distinctions weren't too far removed from its Anglo-Saxon forebears, elements of money, position, and expressing the utmost discretion in personal matters were her main criteria for living. Her standards for Krake were exacting, but towards Krake's friends she was generous and easy-going.

The funeral was moving in the genuineness of the emotion displayed. The church overflowed with mourners; friends, relatives and students. This charismatic teacher touched many with his love for life and people. In discussing it later with Krake, Lorraine mentioned she saw Burg's mother taking photos after the service. Lorraine felt this was strange and not in good taste. So did Krake, particularly when his mother sent her copies. She tore them up. Keeping mementos of this death was too painful. No reminders were necessary.

Hank visited Krake's hospital room that Monday night. Lorraine wasn't due back from Houston until late. Much to his relief, she was conscious. As soon as he walked over to the bed, her eyes opened. "Daddy, where am I? What happened?" Her voice was so soft he could hardly hear it.

"You were in an accident, honey. Two cars hit Larry's as you were leaving Belton on Highway 90." Hank's hand found hers.

"Am I OK?"

"Yes ... well, you soon will be."

"Where's Mom?" her eyes darted to the empty doorway.

No answer.

"Where's Burg? Why isn't he here?"

Hank lifted her hand and brought it close to his chest, "Krake, I have some sad news. Burg was killed when the two cars hit you."

She threw his hand away. "No! No! No! It's not true!" She began to sob hysterically. Helpless, Hank rang for the duty nurse who administered a sedative. Krake lay comatose for another week.

The following Tuesday, the doctors ordered an angiogram of her brain. They were fearful that the clots hadn't dissolved and were trying to determine why she was still unconscious.

After Krake was wheeled down the corridor to the x-ray lab, Lorraine remained in her room staring at the empty bed, praying. This beautiful girl just beginning adult life must not die. Before Krake was born, she had prayed the baby would be beautiful. Now she asked that she live.

An hour later the attendants wheeled Krake's still form back to the room and transferred her into bed. Lorraine moved closer and saw the eyelids fluttering, then the blue eyes of her daughter looking at her. Krake stared blankly for a moment, then tears formed at the corners of her eyes and spilled out, running down her pale cheeks.

The second after regaining consciousness, she remembered that Burg was dead. The pain tore through her with such intensity she could hardly breathe. Her life was over. She wished she hadn't survived. In the days that followed she ate what was put before her and slept and tried to be cheerful for her friends and family, but she felt the opposite. She wanted to talk about the accident and about him with everyone. Were they aware she had spent every waking moment thinking, planning and dreaming about him? Now a huge unfillable void existed. Harsh reality had been limited to substituting thin ankle socks for thick ones. Her heart was brimming with love and there was no one to give it to. She longed to feel his arms around her, his lips on hers, hear his voice, smell his skin, hear his laughter, see his joy, feel his love. The aching loneliness was unbearable. "Please, please talk to me about him. Please," she silently asked. Everyone avoided the subject, wanting to spare her pain, and she was unable to ask for what she needed.

The second week of her hospital stay the Episcopal minister on campus, a young, good-looking, friendly man came to see her. He had been in close association with Burg, having conducted the panel discussions following the *Salesman* performances. He wrote a moving obituary of Burg for the college newspaper.

After the preliminary, polite questions concerning her health, he sat down at her bedside and began to talk. About everlasting life, death, sorrow and ended by saying, "Krake, a person with your looks and personality, without character in this world, would be deadly. This will give you character."

She didn't understand, but she never forgot those words. Amid the heart-rending shafts of painful grief, it was a light. She didn't realize the depth of the statement, only that something she needed would come out of this.

A week later she went home in an ambulance. She couldn't walk yet, had been in traction during the entire hospital stay. She now graduated to a wheelchair. In two weeks they told her, she could begin to walk with the aid of crutches. Some of the neighbors peeked out from behind curtained windows as the big, white hospital ambulance rolled in the driveway. A few came outside and waved as she was transported inside the house in a wheelchair.

As Hank Jr. carefully wheeled her into the bedroom, she caught sight of the Christmas card Burg had given her, a caricature of him done by a student. She had it framed and it sat on her desk. The floodgates opened, she burst into tears. Hankie, frightened he had hurt her in some way, fled. She remembered the last time she was in this room with Burg pursuing her amorously as she changed into shorts to go to Houston. What if she had already been in shorts when they arrived? They would have been on the highway sooner and the accident wouldn't have happened. She sobbed and sobbed. It was becoming more real.

Yes, he is dead. I am never, ever, going to see him again. I can hold my breath or give all my money to the poor, or shave my head or paint myself blue, I will never see him again.

In the unfamiliar, clinical atmosphere of the hospital room where she was constantly waited on, reality was suspended. Now she was in her own room, a part of the real world where she would be expected to function again. How could she? The weight of grief lay so heavy on her shoulders she was pinned.

Days passed. Reading had always been her refuge. The accident prevented this form of escape. The fractured skull and brain concussion had a lasting effect. A nerve controlling a muscle in her right eye was paralyzed so she saw double from eye-level down. (Eventually she was fitted with glasses which she wore to correct the double vision.) She couldn't read unless she held a book over her head. All she could do was listen to the radio and the record player. Often she felt like screaming. She couldn't walk, she couldn't read, she was a prisoner of her grief. Time seemed to stop. Only the pain continued, relentlessly, unrelieved.

School had ended while she was in the hospital. Before everyone scattered for the summer, she decided to give a party. It was a month since . . . Still confined to the wheelchair, she coerced Jean into being hostess, to pass around potato chips and dips and keep everyone supplied with drinks and to play music. The first party without him. Hank and Lorraine went to the movies, Hank Jr. stayed overnight with a pal down the street. Jean put Bill Hailey and the Comets on the record player as soon as she arrived. In a little while, people began to gather, and soon the music was louder, competing with high-pitched conversation and laughter. Just what she needed.

Jean, looking down at her, asked, "What do you want to drink?"

"I don't know, anything."

"I'm drinking Southern Comfort and Coke, that OK?"

"Sure, sounds good."

Jean handed her a glass brimming with the sugary drink. She took a long gulp. Sweet, yes, but also warm, and for the first time in a month she began to relax. She actually laughed at Larry's imitation of Dr. Tanner, the head of the Drama Department, reprimanding everyone.

She proceeded to get quite drunk. The new joke around campus after that was, "If you haven't seen a drunk in a wheelchair, you haven't seen a drunk!" She had forgotten how alcohol made her feel. For a few hours she had a buffer against the pain.

The party was the last time this group of special friends were all together. The wonderful, magical year was over. Alice went back to her home town, Larry to summer stock in Massachusetts, and Jean and Betty graduated.

Every morning of that endless summer, Krake woke up, felt the pain and like an automaton began the day. Donning her bathing suit, she got the required tan in her wheelchair. When she began to use crutches, she and Jean went to a neighborhood movie house to see *Vertigo*. In the lobby, she caught sight of her reflection in the wall of mirrors and gasped. It looked like she was using four crutches and had no legs. All the hours she and Liz had spent doing those calf lifts were wasted. Her legs were bone thin from disuse. Covering her dismay, she joked about her skinny legs.

By August, she could navigate pretty well and took her final exams. She made her usual A's and B's, but being on campus was difficult. She would think she saw his tall, lanky figure going into the theater or crossing the patio outside the union. Her heart would stop, then she'd realize it wasn't him and the pain returned.

That fall, Burg's replacement, Dr. Jeder arrived on campus. His directorial debut was Shakespeare's *Julius Caesar*. Krake went to the tryouts. Everything was different. New teacher, new students and she wasn't cast. Instead she became assistant director, a glorified term for gofer. But sitting in the auditorium beside Jeder, noting his blocking and anything else of import, she felt safe, and realized that she had always felt exposed on stage.

Philip Brownley, a new member of the Drama Department, became a close friend. A year behind her in school and captivated by the theater, his warm personality drew Krake. A credible actor, he was cast immediately in productions. Discovering they lived a few blocks apart, Philip became her ride to and from school and play rehearsals.

A new clique formed, composed of those left from last year and some new members of the department. Fresh rituals developed. Philip and Krake together with Ann and Eddie became inseparable. On Friday or Saturday night, they would meet at the Brownley's spacious ranch house and listen to Broadway musicals while getting rip-roaring drunk. Krake usually didn't remember exactly how she got home or half of the previous evening. The pain of Burg's death was so much a part of her now, she found her only relief in drinking.

Krake needed the distraction of a social life but no one from the opposite sex appealed to her. Philip was perfect. Slightly in awe of her, he never approached her in any way except as a good friend. Once, while parked in her driveway after a party, they kissed. Nothing, for either of them. Friendship was their destiny. They shared a special rapport and love for the theater. Attending social functions with him was enjoyable. He was an excellent dancer, a drinker and provided a safe place for her to dwell. She couldn't fill the void left by Burg, the companionship provided by Philip met some of her needs.

That spring, for Religious Emphasis Week, Dr. Jeder chose *The River Line*, an obscure English play about the French underground in World War II. Krake didn't read for any of the parts. She had decided she was never going to act again. Jeder hadn't cast her in *Julius Caesar* and the vulnerability of acting was too much for her to handle anyway.

She was in the property room at the theater one afternoon, looking for items needed in the new play when Dr. Jeder walked in. "Why didn't you read for a part in *The River Line*?" he asked.

"I didn't want to."

"Why not?"

"I don't know. I think I'm better off working backstage."

"I'd like you to read for the part of Marie."

"Really?"

"Yes, you're the only one I have who can do it." The last words were flung over his shoulder as he left.

Nervously, she read for the part and got it, the lead and only female in a cast of seven. She had to learn a French accent. Researching the character, she consulted with the government professor from France who had actually hidden English and American fliers in his house outside Marseilles during world War II.

Her character was the head of an underground cell in Paris, transporting Allied fliers who had been shot down out of occupied France, under the very noses of the Germans. In the second act, Marie is confronted with evidence that one of the men she is hiding in her attic is a traitor. Even though the accused American is her lover she can't take the chance of discovery. She orders him killed. The British flier who performs the deed in front of her is the man she later marries.

When Krake walked out on stage the first afternoon of rehearsals, she felt like she had come home. All the fears and inhibitions experienced last year were gone. She was free! The only thing missing was Burg.

The accent was a challenge. Philip, playing her husband, said he thought she would never get it. Finally mastering it, the play and particularly her performance were a resounding hit.

The turquoise chiffon dress she borrowed from Alice to wear in the first act became Alice's wedding dress a month later. An unexpected pregnancy was the cause and Krake as maid of honor could hardly stop crying throughout the ceremony. She was genuinely happy for Alice and Lyle, but wanted to be standing next to Burg saying the vows.

Philip bought a few bottles of champagne to the ceremony and they toasted the couple as they drove off in Lyle's latest acquisition, a 1930 Model A coupe. Etched forever in Krake's memory was the silhouette of two heads close together as seen through the small, oval back window of the old car as they headed into the sunset.

Alpha Psi Omega, the honorary dramatic fraternity, held its annual awards banquet in May. Krake went to the ceremonies with Philip, Ann, Eddie, Alice and Lyle. Periodically during the evening, each of them would steal out to Philip's car for a quick swallow from the pint bottle of bourbon Lyle brought. None of them were quite sober by the time the awards ceremony began. Fortunately they were seated at a table in the front of the reception hall near the speaker's podium so Krake didn't have far to walk to accept the awards she won that night. Not only was she named Best Actress for her portrayal of Marie, but also won Best All Around Drama Student. If only Burg could see her now. If only ....

In the fall, she was cast as Kate in *Taming Of The Shrew*.

"Type-casting," her mother said.

In truth, Krake was an angry shrew at home. Not towards Daddy, but in response to the diabolical schemes Lorraine created to make her wrong. That's how Krake perceived it, anyway. Krake's formidable anger lay just below the surface, partially inherited from both parents, partly the result of Burg's untimely death coupled with her lifelong complaint that people's, mainly her mother's, conception of her was erroneous. She was always amazed and hurt when she heard people comment that she was stuck-up or a rich bitch or "she thinks she's so great." Lorraine could push this volatile button using no hands. With her low boiling point, Krake found an acceptable release in playing a shrew. Screaming, yelling, spitting and kicking was so much fun she didn't want rehearsals to end.

On opening night, at the end of the first act, her exit was accompanied by loud applause and as she and Petrucio entered at the top of a long staircase in the final scene, the audience stood clapping and shouting bravo. She and her costar were a great match. They played off each other and had enormous fun.

The last performance of Krake's college career came on a rainy night in January. She and Ann, who was portraying an eighty-year-old curmudgeon to her servant girl in *Devil's Disciple*, were on-stage waiting for the curtain to rise. Ann was rocking in her chair, Krake huddled by the fire. They looked at each other with tears in their eyes. This was their last performance together. They had to follow their own paths. Giving each other a mental hug as the curtain rose, they whispered, "Good show!"

7

Cavorting about nightly as Kate, by day she completed her degree requirements student teaching an eighth-grade class at the junior high.

It was a rude awakening the first time she took charge of the class. As Lorraine had complained years before, the most difficult part was keeping order. Why weren't they quiet? It was hard enough to teach without the constant whispering and inattention.

One plus was that the play she had the students write for assembly progressed nicely. They came up with a story line of four bank robbers who, after making a heist, flee to their hideout and are tracked down by a clever cop. During the time they are holed up, the robbers and their molls carouse a bit, smoking and drinking.

Krake never gave the story line a second thought. After the presentation in assembly she was called into the principle's office and reprimanded for allowing such an improper scene. She laughed inwardly at how ill-suited she was for teaching. It was clear that she couldn't spend her life teaching speech and drama, as much as her mother hoped she would. It might be easier to get herself to a nunnery.

What was she going to do? Scheduled to graduate in January, she never dreamed she wouldn't be married by now.

No wedding bells were chiming and there were no prospects in sight. A career? She hadn't envisioned one. What do I want to do? Become an actress? Could she? Dare she?

One day in the student union, she asked Dr. Jeder if he thought she had enough talent to consider an acting career. Pushing an unruly lock of black hair away from his furrowed brow, he replied that talent had little to do with success in the field, but yes, she did. How should she go about it? Do summer stock, regional theater? Find any place where good professional theater was being performed and try to become a part of it, was his advice.

There was a famous regional stage company in Houston called the Alley Theater. A small theater-in-the-round, its well-known director was a woman named Nina Vance renowned for her innovative style and treatment of the classics as well as her presentation of contemporary playwrights. Why not go there and talk with them? she thought.

She wrote a letter asking for an interview at the Alley during Christmas vacation. Not wanting to incur any unnecessary wrath, she decided to wait until learning the outcome of this venture before informing her parents of her plans. The Alley wrote back and said they would see her the Monday after Christmas.

So on an overcast December afternoon, she found herself standing in front of the one-story building which housed the Alley. Mrs. Vance was in New York City so the interview was conducted by two members of the company. One of them vaguely reminded her of Burg. She still recreated the dead man any way she could. Warm and friendly, they put her at ease and she talked freely of her love for the stage and her desire to act. They explained the apprenticeship program and at the end of a half hour, assuring her they would be in touch, she left feeling hopeful.

In less than two weeks, a letter arrived. She ran into the bathroom, tore it open and the words, "You are the recipient of a place in the Alley Theater's scholarship apprentice program," leapt out at her. The scholarship meant that she wouldn't have to pay to work for nothing. Looking in the mirror, she hugged herself and danced a jig.

She went to the kitchen where Lorraine was chopping tomatoes for a luncheon salad.

"Mom, where's Dad?"

"I think he's out in the garage fixing the lawn mower."

Opening the screen door, Krake called, "Daddy, can you come in here for a second? I have something to tell you and Mom."

Hank put the wrench down, wiped his hands on a greasy cloth and came inside. "What's up, Princess?"

"Daddy, Mom, you'll never guess what's happened."

"What?" they chorused.

"I know you want me to teach school, but I hated student-teaching ... I'm going to be an actress. Wait, wait ..."

Lorraine's face was contorting as her voice began a protest.

"While I was in Houston after Christmas I had an interview at the Alley Theater. They've accepted me as an apprentice on a scholarship!"

"Will you be making any money?" Lorraine demanded.

"Not at first. But it's a start. I'll be working backstage, in the box office, as well as acting. A lot of famous actors started as apprentices."

"Who?"

"Errr ... ummmmm ... Helen Hayes, I think, lots of famous ones."

"How will you support yourself? We've sent you through college. Now it's your turn. I can't do any more." Hank sat down at the kitchen table.

"I know, Daddy, I've thought of that. Could I use the $5,000 insurance settlement from the accident?"

"It's your nest egg. Are you sure you want to spend it like this?" Hank lit a Camel.

"Yes."

Lorraine looked at her angrily. "Krake, people in the theater have no morals. They are promiscuous and lead dreadful lives."

Sarcastically, Krake flung a retort, "Tell me, Mother, how was it when you were in the theater?"

Eyebrows raised, "What do you mean?"

"You seem to know so much about it I assume you must have been an actress yourself."

"I know because I read Dorothy Kilgallen." This was said with great conviction.

"Oh, Mother, I can't talk to you." Krake retreated to her bedroom and slammed the door. Her spirits dampened, she phoned Philip who came to her rescue. Ann and Eddie were thrilled by the news. They bought some booze and celebrated at Philip's.

Everyone at school was excited. The local paper did an article and Dr. Jeder said she was off to a good start. Lorraine continued to grumble, but her father supported her decision. She knew he was apprehensive about her choice of careers, but allowed her to decide for herself. Still, she wanted her mother's approval.

The weekend after finals she began her new life. Through Nan, the set designer at Belton, she located a place to live. Three friends of Nan's sharing an apartment on Houston's west side needed one more to help with the rent and were happy to have her join them. Nan drove her to Houston one bleak January morning. Krake was so excited she wasn't even scared. A big city! Professional theater! Anything could happen!

The three-story cement apartment building was an unattractive dirty yellow, located in an older section of the city thirty minutes from the theater. Two of her three roommates were home when she and Nan arrived. May, an attractive, blond part-time-typist-waiting-to-be-discovered model, and

Olivia, a chemistry major at the University of Houston, welcomed her and helped carry the bags up to her room on the second floor. Small and furnished, it had a large closet which was Krake's main requirement for her voluminous wardrobe.

An hour later, Nan dropped her off at the theater. Krake stood on the sidewalk and surveyed the small one-story white building before her. Taking a deep breath she walked up the old brick pathway and through the double glass doors leading into the lobby.

Inside, she knocked on a door marked OFFICE. A short, fat, balding man peered at her through bifocals. A stubby unlit cigar stuck in his mouth, he mumbled, "What d'ya want?"

Nervously batting her eyelashes, Krake said, "Hi, I'm the new apprentice, Krake Forrester. I was supposed to start tomorrow, but I thought I'd stop by and maybe meet Mrs. Vance and take a look around."

"I'll see if she's here. You wait." The man shuffled off. Soon he returned and pointing to a door at the end of the lobby, said, "Mrs. Vance will see you. Go on in."

Krake walked down the darkened lobby and softly tapped on the closed door.

"Come in," a woman's throaty voice invited. A tall redhead stood behind a rather large desk, extending her hand. "I'm Nina Vance. Welcome to the Alley. Sit down." She indicated an upholstered chair near the desk. Krake sat and answered questions about her background and experience in the theater. When she mentioned where she was staying and that she was planning to take the bus to and from the theater, Mrs. Vance protested, "No! This city is not a place for a young girl to ride the bus at night. Find Will Stoner, he lives out that way. Tell him I told you to ask to ride with him. I think he's in the dressing room. By the way, the man who looks like a bullfrog smoking a cigar is Elmer, the business manager. He's a good friend to have. Be sure you always say hello to him."

When Krake left Nina's office, she made her way along the narrow, dark passage that ran from the lobby to the back-stage area.

Will was in the dressing room talking with some other actors. He was tall and dark with wavy hair and a strong face that lit up when Krake shyly introduced herself and asked him for a ride.

"Sure. I'm leaving in thirty minutes. And I'll pick you up on my way back at about seven-thirty. I have to be here by half-hour."

She must have looked puzzled by the unfamiliar term.

"You know, eight p.m., thirty minutes before curtain. The stage manager always calls half-hour, fifteen minutes, five minutes and places."

Will was starring as the defense attorney in the current production of *The Caine Mutiny Court Martial*, which Krake was to see that evening. Will's exuberance and open friendliness made her feel comfortable on the ride to and from the theater that day. He casually mentioned that he had been one of the men who interviewed her for the apprenticeship program in December. She pretended she remembered him but she didn't.

Watching the performance of *Mutiny* that night from a seat way in the back, she was thrilled to be a part of such a fine acting company and more than a little intimidated by the high level of skill displayed.

Her first job was to help gather props for the next production. Eugenie Leontovich, the Russian actress who won a Tony award on Broadway in 1956 for her portrayal of the dowager empress in *Anastasia*, was directing and starring in William Saroyan's *The Cave Dwellers*. In this strange, whimsical fantasy play, Krake was chosen to portray the Leontovich character, the Old Queen, as a young actress playing Cleopatra. The part required that she lie on a couch and kill herself with a prop asp, while saying, "Antony, Antony."

Her costume was the one that Eugenie had worn when she played Cleopatra in Paris in the 30s. Because Krake was a half-foot taller than the diminutive Russian, the gold lamé dress had to be redesigned into a skimpy two-piece garment. With heavy Egyptian makeup, she unknowingly caused a mild sensation backstage every time she walked by the male members of the crew.

Will Stoner, in a huge, furry costume, played a bear.

She and Will had become fast friends on their daily trips to and from the theater. One morning when he picked her up a striking brunette sat next to him in the front seat. There was a collapsible wheelchair in the back seat. "This is my wife, Tonya." Krake and Tonya exchanged smiles. Will told her later that they had dated before he shipped out for Korea. While he was overseas Tonya contracted polio which left her paralyzed from the waist down. When he returned and found her a cripple, he married her. "It was not so much love as pity," said Will. They had been married for five years. Krake heard whispers around the theater that Tonya was a real bitch. She didn't know, their few encounters were brief and polite.

Will enjoyed educating Krake as to the traditions and superstitions of the theater. He also helped her with her lines, taught her how to apply stage makeup and hovered around like a mother hen. Krake worked on props from ten until two, when afternoon rehearsals began. The woman whom she assisted in gathering props was a tough, wiry redhead named Megan. Krake, very much in awe of her, felt soft and weak by comparison. Megan's capabilities in building sets, setting lights, driving fearlessly through city traffic while drinking an ever-present can of beer, was awe-inspiring. They worked well together. Krake would make endless phone calls trying to locate an item. When she found it, she and Megan would drive across town in Megan's beat-up MG, retrieve it and give the donors free tickets and program credit.

At night Krake worked crew. A theater-in-the-round, the Alley required the crew to change sets in the dark during scene breaks. The four posts holding up the roof located at each stage entrance were spotted with pieces of iridescent tape. A crew member dressed in black was assigned to activate their luminescence with a flashlight before each act. Every piece of movable furniture and props were also spotted. That way the blackout wasn't so black.

Krake's standard crewing outfit consisted of a black sweater, black Bermuda skirt and black tights. When she appeared as Cleopatra in the last act of *Cave Dwellers* she shed her blacks and donned gold lamé.

She and Will, hugely hairy in his bear-suit, would stand side by side not speaking, at entrance C waiting for her cue. In total darkness she ascended a makeshift stairway to a couch, arranged herself provocatively, grabbed the asp and holding it to her breast as the lights came, moaned "Antony, Antony" and died. Quite a departure from the lead roles she played in college.

The day before *Cave Dwellers* opened, Will told her she mustn't tell anyone if she got a surprise the next day. He emphasized not telling anyone. She assured him she wouldn't.

The following afternoon a telegram came for her. Her first opening-night telegram! Thrilled, she read, "To a young actress on her first opening night of many in the professional theater. Break a leg!" It was unsigned. She showed everyone her mysterious missile—who could have sent it? Finally, Hillary, the set designer said, "I bet Will Stoner sent it."

She found him in the dressing room brushing the bear suit.

"Did you send this?" she asked.

"Krake," he sighed, "I asked you not to tell anyone. I hear you've shown the telegram to the whole company."

This was the surprise he had cautioned her about. She hadn't connected one with the other. They were good friends.

Why should it be a secret if he sent her a message of good will in the age-old tradition of the theater? She soon learned why.

It was an opening night ritual at the Alley to have a champagne celebration after the first night's curtain descended. Thirty minutes into the celebration Will maneuvered Krake into a small hallway leading to the box office by saying he had a newspaper photo of the cast he wanted to show her. As soon as they were out of sight of the others, he leaned towards her and said, "I think I'm falling in love with you."

Shocked, she whispered, "But you're married."

Frowning, he muttered, "Yeah, but it's awful. I think we're going to get a divorce. She left this morning to stay with her sister for a week."

"Oh, ummm, are you going to Tod's party?"

"No, I'm going home."

Krake had a date with Tod which Will knew about.

"I'll pick you up in the morning at ten for rehearsal. Have a good time and be careful," he warned.

"I will." Krake started towards the lobby to find Tod, stopped and faced Will again. "I think I may be falling in love with you too, Will." She quickly lost herself in the throngs of people laughing and toasting with champagne. Whenever anyone said, "I love you," out of gratitude she felt obliged to respond in kind no matter what she really felt. She had dismissed Will as a potential suitor because he was married. Now he had changed all that.

She liked Tonya, but didn't like the way she treated Will. Will had confided one afternoon over hot chocolate that Tonya hadn't attended a performance of his in over two years and didn't support his acting career at all. This revelation was appalling to Krake's romantic views of marriage and her sense of caring.

The crowd held her in its protective arms until she located Tod standing by the open bottles of champagne. He gave her a hug and poured them each a glass of the bubbly.

"I've got the prettiest date in the West tonight," he said, pulling her close, but letting her go as Mrs. Vance approached.

"Here's a handsome member of my junior staff, dear Tod, and our pretty little apprentice getting to know each other." Nina's voice was pitched high to be audible over the crowd. Looking directly at Krake, she asked, "How are you getting along Krake?"

"I'm having a wonderful time, Mrs. Vance," Krake shouted. "I'm learning so much."

"I imagine you are. Hopefully, in the next play you'll be on-stage longer, although your small scene was remarkable, I must say." Nina laughed as she turned away to speak to Leontovich.

Tod finished his glass of wine. "You ready to have a party?" he asked as he tried to take her glass. "I'm not through," said Krake and downed the half-full glass in one gulp. "Now we can go," she smiled. In the car driving to his apartment Tod said, "I think Will Stoner has a crush on you."

"No," she protested, "he's married." Had he overheard?

"I hear his wife's a bitch. Beautiful, but a bitch!"

Krake said nothing but felt the flush of conquest.

The party was typical, with dancing and more drinking. Krake passed out on Tod's bed. She didn't stir until morning when the gray light of dawn crept in through dirty window panes.

Shit! She licked her dry lips, I never went home last night. What happened? Did Tod and I have sex?

Krake's movements awakened Tod who, when asked, hastily assured her nothing happened. "You passed out, girl," he laughed. "I couldn't have moved you if I tried."

"What will everyone think?" she cried.

"Nobody cares," he comforted her.

Little did she suspect that the Legend of Krake Forrester had begun. She felt ashamed when Tod drove her home. Still wearing the slept-in green velvet dress from the night before, her head ached, her eyes burned and she felt nauseous. She couldn't remember much of the party. Philip and the rest of the gang weren't here to assure her she was innocent of any wrong doing, except drinking too much.

When Tod dropped her off, she barely had time to change into work clothes before Will's car pulled up in front. She avoided telling him she had only gotten home thirty minutes before. They talked little until late that afternoon when he waylaid her in the dressing room.

At one end of the long room lined with mirrors was a small dressing area reserved for the female star of the current production. He motioned her in and closed the door. Like a father he began, "You stayed all night at Tod's. This is just what I warned you about. People love to gossip. I heard the story several times during the day."

"Nothing happened. I fell asleep and he couldn't wake me. I swear nothing happened,"

"How can you be sure?"

"I was there, wasn't I? Please believe me, nothing happened!"

Will mumbled through clenched teeth, "I'll try," and left.

She sat in the hard, straight-backed chair staring in the mirror. She felt sick. Apparently everyone thought she had slept with Tod Evans and she hadn't. Still, members of the company were treating her the same as always. Maybe this kind of behavior didn't matter to them.

On the way home that afternoon, Will drove to the zoo. They got out and walked in the chilly February air, stopping by the monkey cages to watch the hairy creatures eat insects off each other. When they made faces at them, the monkeys made faces back. Laughing, they got back in Will's old Nash Rambler and shared a cigarette. He reached for her and they kissed. Krake's first thought was, his lips are too big and mushy. He's slobbering all over me. She didn't want to be there or kiss him, but she was and she did. The kissing continued for awhile, then looking at his watch he realized the time and drove her to her apartment. She ran in, grabbed a bite to eat and was bathed and perfumed by the time he returned. They made it to the theater by half-hour and parted to assume their duties for the evening's performance.

After the final curtain, Krake and Will drove to Hermann Park and necked by the lake. The second night's performance had been down due to hangovers and fatigue. The kissing helped the depressed feeling disappear and she liked the kisses better. Before any petting could begin, she pleaded tiredness so he drove her home.

She sank into her bed with relief and exhaustion. So much happening. Too much, perhaps.

They became an item at the theater. Never one for subterfuge, Krake's interest in Will was obvious. Will did little to mask his feelings either. The relationship blossomed. Will contributed to Krake's education, specifically in the areas of food and sex. For the first time since Burg died, she felt some relief from the gnawing pain and loneliness. She was needed and desirable, warm and happy. She had fallen in love again. They were more open with each other than she and Burg had been. Alcohol played a part in this. With Burg, she was too anxious, afraid of making a mistake and therefore unable to risk letting go. Now she drank and booze released her inhibitions.

Necking with Will progressed to oral sex. The first time he went down on her, Krake couldn't believe anything felt that good. His wet, rough tongue finding her smooth, hard spot amidst the folds that lay between her legs excited her like nothing before. He was an amorous, passionate man who taught her what good sex was. The alcohol freed her to explore her own sexuality while clouding the experience and her memory of it, lessening any guilty feelings.

When they weren't devouring each other, they went to exotic restaurants. Middle eastern food--tangy hummus on pita bread, dolmas and kibbe—intrigued her. Will was taking over where her father, who had introduced her to many culinary delicacies, had left off.

On their way to the theater on Saturday mornings, they would stop at a Jewish delicatessen where she sampled her first bagel, lox and cream cheese. Not as fishy smelling as my pussy, she concluded. Preceding the evening show, they tried Japanese and Chinese food.

On Sundays the Alley had two performances, a matinee and an evening show. Usually hung-over, the company would go to a nearby Chinese restaurant between shows. The Great Wall served an all-you-can-eat buffet which Krake looked forward to. Piling her plate high with egg rolls, sweet and sour pork, cashew chicken, beef and snow peas, she would return for seconds and sometimes, depending on the severity of the hangover, thirds. "You oughta see that little girl eat!" people commented. Cooking and eating were two of her favorite diversions.

When Krake's parents came to see *The Cave Dwellers*, she introduced them to Will. They seemed to like one another. Krake didn't reveal the extent of their relationship or that Will had asked her to marry him. She just said he was a friend, omitting the fact that he was married. His married status bothered her and she was concerned that there might be some difficulty in getting a divorce. Shortly after he had declared his love for Krake, Will asked Tonya for a divorce. She agreed, then asked whether there was anyone else. When he said yes, she guessed who. Will had never spent the night with Krake but he was with her constantly.

Two weeks later, on a Monday when the Alley was dark, Krake and Will drove over to Belton to have dinner with Hank and Lorraine. After dinner, while Krake and Lorraine were doing the dishes, Will took Hank aside and told him when his divorce was final, he wanted to marry Krake. Hank liked Will and was pleased he exhibited such old fashioned grace as to ask for his daughter's hand in marriage. Lorraine was showing Will old photos of Krake in the living room when Hank whispered to Krake his congratulations and said he would tell Lorraine after they left.

Later they went to a party at Philip's and ended up drinking until almost two in the morning. Will literally dragged Krake away so they could drive back to Houston and make the early call of ten a.m. They were both working crew for the new show, *Moon For The Misbegotten*. Lack of sleep and excess booze made the day an effort.

Exactly a week after their visit to Belton, Will picked Krake up for the evening's performance. He looked perturbed. "Tonya's pregnant," he said quietly. Stunned into silence, Krake wondered how this could be.

As though reading her mind, he sighed, "I was thinking of you and made love to her, once, over a month ago. I never dreamed..." They clung to each other, neither realizing the significance of the event.

A week later, just as Krake and Will were getting ready to leave her apartment to have breakfast at the Swedish Pancake House, the phone rang. Lorraine's voice came clearly over the wire, "Krake, I just received a letter from a lawyer in Houston. He say's he's Will Stoner's brother-in-law and if you don't stop seeing Will, your name and ours will be dragged through the divorce courts. You will be named as corespondent. He also threatens to make it impossible for either of you to work in the theater in Houston again. Krake, you must stop seeing Will."

She was surprised, then angry. "Mother, I'm twenty-two years old. Why did he contact you and not me? You and Daddy have no legal say in what I do anymore."

"I don't know, I only know you must stop seeing him!"

"Mom, I love Will and he loves me, we're going to be married as soon as he gets his divorce." She felt ill.

"Krake, they're going to make a public scandal. Our whole family will be disgraced."

"I'm sorry this happened. You and Daddy aren't a part of this. They were wrong to involve you. It's my business, I'll handle it the best way I can. Don't worry," Krake tried to reassure her.

"I will worry."

"Please don't," Krake repeated.

"I can't help it. Let me know what happens," her mother pleaded.

"I will. Bye Mom."

"Goodbye. Try and act responsibly in this."

As soon as she hung up, Krake ran into Will's arms, telling him what her mother had said. "Darling," he whispered, "we'll get through this. I'll call Tonya's brother. I'll take care of this, don't worry." Her thoughts echoed her mother's, "I will worry."

Three days later *Moon* opened. A week into the run, during the last act, Megan rushed up to Krake as she was working props at D door and whispered, "I'll take over. Go up to the light booth and hide. Leslie Johns is here looking for you."

Leslie was Tonya's sister and the director Burg had introduced her to the night they saw *Kiss Me Kate* at Theater, Inc. two years before. She had a reputation for being an eccentric, some said a crazy woman.

In the light booth, the technicians advised her to crouch down in the corner. She did. The show closed and the lighting crew left. She remained huddled in the dark. Finally, after what seemed like hours, Megan appeared. "Come on down, she's gone. Mrs. Vance talked to her and now wants to speak to you in the dressing room."

Fear closed around her heart. "What does she want?"

"I don't know. Just go. I'll wait out front and take you over to George's. Will's already there." George's was the after-performance hangout, a smoke-filled bar a few blocks from the Alley.

Hesitantly Krake made her way to the dressing room. Nina was sitting at the makeup table, gazing in the mirror. Seeing Krake's reflection in the glass, Nina turned and motioned her to sit down. Smiling, she said she had just had a talk with Leslie Johns. Krake was sure Nina was going to say she couldn't have such a slut working in her theater. Mrs. Vance laid a hand on her shoulder and said, "We are a theater, not a church. We are here to interpret life, not to judge it. Any help I can give, whether it be the name of a good lawyer or a shoulder to cry on, I'll be happy to."

Krake was astonished. Nina Vance, one of the foremost directors of regional theater in the country and someone whom she held in the highest regard, was willing to put herself on the line for her. In fact, already had. Not only that, she went on to tell Krake that she had recently gone through a divorce herself and knew how difficult it was. Nina mentioned she had warned Leslie Johns to stay away from the Alley and Krake Forrester. At the end of the conversation, thanking her profusely, Krake left.

Megan was waiting in the topless MG. They sped off in the cold night air to the warmth of George's where Will waited. After drinking a couple of beers, Krake and Will went to Hermann Park to smooch by the lake. What a night!

The idea that Will would be a father wasn't real to Krake. It seemed to be Tonya's baby only. Her fear was that she might lose him. The thought of the difficulty facing Tonya as a single parent wasn't in Krake's consciousness. Will assured her that he was determined to do all he could for Tonya but that she, Krake, was his number one priority. He did talk to Samuel, Tonya's brother, but Samuel was adamant that Will stop seeing Krake. Will flatly refused. Samuel repeated his threats that he would make it impossible for either of them to work in Houston theater again. How he meant to accomplish this was never clear, but there was concern in Will's voice as he relayed this conversation.

The Saturday after Leslie appeared at the Alley, Will decided to spend the night at Krake's apartment. Her roommates were going to be gone and she and Will had never spent an entire night together. After the evening's performance, they stopped only to purchase a bottle of burgundy before heading across town to Krake's apartment. No sooner had they put on music and seated themselves on the couch when there was a sharp knock on the door. Will went to the window and looked out. He turned, exclaiming, "My God! It's Leslie."

"Don't let her in!" hissed Krake, filled with fear.

The knocking continued, accompanied by a shrill caterwauling, "Will Stoner, let me in! I know you're in there! Will! Will!"

Will reluctantly opened the door. He had experienced run-ins with Miss Johns before.

A slight brunette swayed through the doorway. Her eyes scanned the room and came to rest on Will. He led her to a chair opposite the sofa. She sank down into it. Krake and Will sat on the couch, waiting. John's head lolled forward on her chest. Krake, in amazement, wondered if she had fallen asleep. No, raising her head she stared at Will, ignoring Krake. "What are you trying to do to Tonya, kill her?"

Will denied this was his intention. Leslie drank bourbon and branch water, non-stop. Will was constantly refilling her glass. She had brought all the ingredients, including the heavy crystal highball glass. Waterford, no doubt.

"Will you're going to, if you don't stop carrying on with her." Leslie indicated Krake.

"Leslie, I'd like you to meet Krake Forrester."

"Hello," Leslie said, without looking at her.

"Hi," Krake managed, swallowing deeply.

"Leslie, Krake and I love each other very much and want to get married."

"You're already married," Leslie reminded him.

"I know that!" Will snapped.

"And about to become a father. Will, I've known you for years, I never thought you'd do a thing like this. Don't you want the baby?"

"Tonya and I haven't been happy for a long time, you know that, Leslie."

"She's pregnant now and that changes everything."

"How?"

"Tonya told me she wants to stay married and have this child. Please let her."

"But I don't love her," he said.

"It doesn't matter," Leslie told him.

"I love Krake." Will looked at Krake.

"Stay with Tonya until the baby comes, then you can leave." For the first time that evening, Leslie looked her way. "Krake, make him listen. You're going to kill my sister and her baby if you don't."

Krake didn't know what to say. "Will and I want to be together."

"Yes, I understand that," Leslie replied, "and after this baby is born you will be. Please, please give him up for a few months, then you can have him back. I'm afraid Tonya will miscarry if you don't. She's always wanted a child. Now she's going to have one if you and Will don't cause her to lose it."

Krake looked at Will. Will looked at her, paused and said, "Leslie, Krake and I will talk this over. I understand your concern for your sister, but I have a life too."

Leslie appeared somewhat placated and began to talk about her casting troubles with Theater Inc.'s latest production *New Girl In Town*, a recent Broadway success starring Thelma Ritter. She and Will debated the assets of the various members of the acting community, of which Krake knew almost nothing.

When it was nearly dawn, Leslie made her exit. And what an exit! After using the bathroom at the head of the stairs, she lost her balance, tumbling headlong to the landing, where she lay without speaking, eyes closed. Krake knew it was staged. Will and Krake ran to her just as she gasped that she needed a doctor. After examination, Will said she didn't. Reluctantly she got to her feet, made a few final pleas for Tonya and the baby and left.

They watched with relief as Leslie's white Cadillac pulled away. One of her assistants had spent the entire night waiting outside in the car. Krake expressed astonishment that anyone would do that. Will admitted that Leslie always had flunkies who would do whatever she wanted, hoping to be used in a show.

It was five a.m. and sleep was impossible so they went out for breakfast. Over pancakes and coffee, Krake and Will tried to figure out what would be best for all concerned.

8

Everything changed after Leslie's visit. Will agreed to stay with Tonya until the baby was born. He assured Krake he would seek a divorce after the birth. Krake realized Will felt he had little choice but she was still hurt and disappointed by this turn of events. He had expressed almost no feelings about the baby, only a sense of obligation. He too seemed to have trouble realizing it was real.

Will had directed plays for Kerrville summer stock in the scenic rolling hills north of San Antonio for the past two years and wanted Krake to be a member of the company. Mrs. Vance had been consulted and was in agreement. Krake had been dreaming of months of theater and passion; that is, before Tonya's unexpected pregnancy and the ensuing wrath. Now Tonya was going in her place.

Two things happened to soften the blow. Philip decided to be a part of the acting company in Kerrville and agreed to be a go-between for the lovers. The plan was that Krake would write letters to Will addressed to Philip and he would mail the ones from Will to her.

Secondly she was cast in her first supporting role in a major show at the Alley, *Sunrise at Campobello*. Playing Anna Roosevelt she had three good scenes and made friends with some new members of the ensemble.

Will had a bit part as a reporter because he was busy organizing the schedule of plays for the summer. They were together most nights after the performance. On one such evening, necking in the front seat of the Nash parked by the lake, Krake's eyes opened to the glare of headlights shining through the back window. Will, squinting in the rear-view mirror exclaimed, "My God, it's Tonya!"

Zipping his pants, he started the car and they drove out of the park. The beige Oldsmobile, which had been fitted with special hand-driving equipment for Tonya, followed. They raced through downtown Houston, Tony close behind, running red lights and ignoring speed limits. Several times, when they were forced to slow down, the Oldsmobile rammed them.

On a poorly-lit, narrow, curvy street, Tonya's headlights suddenly disappeared. Will slowed down ... no Tonya. He stopped the car and got out. "I'm going back and see if she's all right," he said. He returned before long and told Krake, "Wait here. She went into the ditch on that last curve. She's all right. I think I can get the car out."

Krake waited several minutes and was starting to get out and see for herself what was going on when Tonya's car passed by and Will slid behind the wheel of the Nash. He hardly spoke and dropped Krake at her apartment without so much as a kiss good-bye. Both were shaken by the incident. Krake kept remembering the Oldsmobile hitting them from the rear. "Hell hath no fury," rang in her ears.

The next day, Will told her he had promised Tonya he wouldn't try to see Krake until after the baby was born. Tonya would just keep on endangering them, herself and the child. He had no choice.

They managed to sneak away for dinner and a motel before he left for the summer. Will could excite and please her sexually like no one else. Well, there had been no one else, hardly. They made love continuously until she bid him a tearful farewell at dawn. This continued ability to get it up after coming in every available orifice was amazing.

Depressed and lonely, it was a relief to Krake when twelve summer apprentices arrived the first week in June. She was an old hand by now and helped them all adjust and learn the menial tasks she knew by heart. She explained the backstage area to them, demonstrated how to clean paintbrushes when working in the shop, what approach to use with merchants in obtaining props and how to quietly maybe, (she was famous for dropping trays full of dishes) change sets during a blackout.

Soon after Will left, she moved closer to the theater. A member of the junior staff suggested they room together when she heard Krake was looking for a place. In truth, Krake didn't think too much of Lily Anne's acting abilities. She found her brittle, blond looks and high-pitched voice irritating, but Lily Anne was sweet and likable. She was a graduate of the University of Texas and had also studied dance in New York.

Her apartment was a plush one-bedroom with a pool. They found they had a lot in common. They both loved to cook and eat. On Monday nights when the Alley was dark, they began to entertain and people looked forward to their parties. On one such evening after gorging on Lily's lasagna, a group went to see Alfred Hitchcock's new thriller, *Psycho*. Afterwards Lily and Krake sat up until dawn and neither one of them took a shower the rest of the summer.

Will's letters came regularly and were as amorous as the man himself. He said he missed her terribly and Sir William missed Lady Krake as well, so they started to plan a way to meet when summer stock was over at the end of August.

Larry came to visit and she told him about Will. He seemed happy for her. He was one of the few people in her life now that she could talk to about Burg. They reminisced briefly about the school year that ended so tragically. Larry said he thought Burg would be proud of her and pleased that she had fallen in love again. He was on his way to New York City to conquer Broadway. She wished him well and as they parted, she wondered if she would ever see him again.

In July the company was informed that the Alley had received a Ford Foundation Grant starting that fall. The moneys provided for a resident acting company to be composed of ten people from all over the country. Mrs. Vance traveled to New York and Los Angeles to interview prospects. The Ford Grant was providing for salaries of two hundred dollars a week. An excellent wage for any actor in 1960.

Most of the present company, consisting of local actors, actors from regional theaters and jobbers from other areas who came to do one specific role, would go their separate ways. The theater was to be closed for three weeks in September for renovations. A new technical staff would be hired. Both Krake and Lily Anne, however, would remain in their present positions.

At the close of the summer season, an annual event was staged for the public - Apprentice Night. The young actors adapted various scenes from well-known classics and had a real opening night at the Alley Theater. Krake was cast as Ondine in the Jean Anouilh play of the same name. In the Broadway production, Audrey Hepburn and Mel Ferrer starred and were subsequently married.

Krake selected an iridescent, blue-green clinging dress to wear along with a long fall into which she braided seaweed. Her makeup was exaggerated green eye-shadow highlighted with silvery liner. The end product was sensational, a surrealistic sea creature. Her performance was average, but the moment she was transformed into the Ondine and returned to the sea she felt the energy coming from the audience that told her she had captured their hearts. After the performance, she got exceedingly drunk on Lily Anne's opening night present of, her favorite, green chartreuse.

One afternoon during a quiet period when the new apprentices were busy rehearsing, Krake and one of the members she had become friendly with were discussing upcoming projects. Just as Krake was about to leave for the shop, Geneva looked intensely at her, cleared her throat and said, "We don't usually do this, go preaching or break our anonymity but I couldn't help notice the way you behave at parties and the way you drink. You remind me of myself a few years ago. I think perhaps you should talk to someone. I'm a member of Alcoholics Anonymous. Yes, I'm an alcoholic. Would you attend a meeting with me?"

Krake was stunned. Denial rushed to her lips, but she didn't speak, just looked stricken.

"It's only a thought. I care a lot about you and if I can prevent you from suffering like I did, it would make me feel good." Geneva repeated, "Would you go to a meeting with me?"

"When?" Krake murmured.

"Next Monday night. I'll pick you up."

"OK, I guess," Krake slowly answered. Saying NO to anything while sober was almost an impossibility. The person might not like her if she did.

"Don't be nervous. It's anonymous. No one even says their last names at meetings."

Krake didn't want to go. Don't be nervous! How could she not be nervous? It was unthinkable to give up drinking. What would she do instead? How could she possibly enjoy herself? Krake knew that alcohol affected her differently than others. But she loved the feeling it gave her of being cozy and secure and like nothing could harm her. It was also exciting and fun. She did things drinking she could only dream about sober. She admitted she wasn't a pleasant drunk. At parties, people didn't think her cruel sarcasm very funny. Sometimes rage would overtake her and be spewed out on everyone. She usually didn't remember these instances so she pretended they didn't happen. And then there were the blackouts. Fortunately, she was smart enough to get drunk most often in the company of friends so no bodily harm had come to her. Yet. Was she an alcoholic? The very question sent chills through her. She couldn't, wouldn't give up the only thing that made her feel safe and was a buffer against the slings and arrows of life. And what about the sex? Yeah, what about the sex.

On Monday night, waiting for Geneva to arrive, she wished heartily that she hadn't agreed to go. A sleek gray car rolled up with Geneva in the back seat. As Krake slid in beside her, Geneva introduced the two men in front. Krake immediately forgot their names and gazed around her. What kind of a car was this? Nothing she was familiar with. She saw a double RR on the dash. A Rolls Royce! Her first ride in a Rolls Royce and she was going to an AA meeting? How disappointing. The destination should have been the Houston Opera or somewhere equally glamorous. An AA meeting! Disgusting!

The evening proved forgettable. The small room in a Methodist church was dark and full of smoke. Among the mostly male attendees, she recognized several prominent Houstonians. Damn, I can't tell anyone. Everyone appeared to be older and, aside from the smoke and laughter, which surprised her, she remembered little else.

The next day Geneva took her to a private meeting with four members of the National Council On Alcoholism to evaluate her drinking. She told them about her drinking patterns. No, she wasn't a daily drinker. She only drank at parties, never alone. She forgot about stealing her father's scotch when she was a teenager and replacing what she had drunk with water. That really didn't count because it was out of boredom and she had had only a few drinks alone in her bedroom while reading Mickey Spillane and jacking-off. At the end of the discussion, they told her she was a "potential alcoholic." At twenty-two, she was too young to have the established drinking patterns of long-time alcoholics. They did emphasize that if she continued to drink the way she was, from one drink to oblivion, she would become one.

Whew! Off the hook! She knew she wasn't one. Really! The very idea that she couldn't control her alcohol intake or her behavior after ingesting some was absurd. An alcoholic? That term was meant for Ray Milland in *The Lost Weekend*, not a pretty, talented young woman.

Geneva never mentioned it again. Sometimes at the barbecues Geneva gave, Krake would watch her laughing and talking with people downing booze while she drank 7-Up. There was an inner light shining from Geneva's eyes that Krake envied. Where did it come from? Unless in the throes of a love affair or halfway through a bottle of champagne, Krake never felt radiant.

A week before the theater's closing, Nina had a party for the summer apprentices, including Krake. After hors d'oeuvres and drinks, Mrs. Vance seated everyone around her for critique. Some she encouraged to remain in the theater, others she gently tried to dissuade from pursuing an acting career. When she got to Krake, she said, "And you definitely have a place in this business. Maybe not on the legitimate stage, perhaps TV or movies." Krake was thrilled. Mrs. Vance believed in her.

After the gathering the summer apprentices left for various destinations. Krake was sorry they were going, they had been fun to work with. But she was eager to see Will and the world of repertory theater was demanding and insular. They all needed a respite.

Lily Anne had invited Krake to visit her family in San Antonio. Hal, the assistant lighting director, was on his way to Los Angeles to work as lighting crew at Desilu Studios and offered them a ride. He was stopping to see some cousins in San Antonio and was glad of the company and the additional money for gas. The drive from Houston to San Antonio was uncomfortable for everyone. Hal's old Chevy didn't have air-conditioning, sweat rolled down their bodies and soaked their clothes. Krake was wearing a blue and white mattress-ticking skirt and sleeveless top with sandals and a long braid kept her thick hair off her neck. All she could think of was seeing Will again. They had arranged to meet at the Hacienda Hotel in downtown San Antonio at three that afternoon. Hal would drop them there and Will said he would drive them to Lily's.

She didn't see him anywhere as they pulled up to the old stone hotel. Krake and Lily Anne headed inside and Hal began unloading their luggage. As Krake stepped into the revolving glass door, a man came from the other direction, exiting. Was it? Yes, it was. Will! At the same instant, he saw her. They did a Laurel and Hardy bit of revolving through the door before they were in each other's arms.

"Krake, I hardly recognized you, you're so tan."

"Oh, Will, I'm so glad to see you."

Lily Anne stood discretely aside while they embraced and embraced and embraced. Finally, disengaging, they went outside to retrieve the bags from Hal. That accomplished, Hal and Lily Anne went into the bar for a drink.

Krake and Will went up to his room to get reacquainted. As soon as they closed the door, they devoured each other. "I missed you so much," she repeated. Their lips sealed in starving kisses, his hands came up under her short-cropped top and quickly undid her bra. As it came loose, his hands encircled her full breasts, fingers rubbing the nipples. He undid her skirt which fell to her ankles. She stepped out of it while unzipping his jeans and kicked it aside. His hands ran down her body and slipped under her panties and between her legs. She arched herself into his hand and involuntarily moaned. He picked her up and carried her to the bed. Quickly shedding his clothes, he lay beside her.

"Hi, Sir William, Lady Krake has missed you and so have I." She self-consciously used the silly names he called their sexual organs. Her hands reached for his large erection and she bent down and took him in her mouth. She sucked and pulled, but not too hard, remembering once when she had done that and he erupted in her mouth before she had been satisfied. He lifted her up to him and kissed her long and thoroughly as he parted her legs and his fingers discovered her wetness. Then he thrust himself into her waiting warmth. He moved slowly at first, but soon, unable to wait any longer, he pumped hard and brought them to an electrifying orgasm. Spent, sweating and happy, they remained together on the bedspread. Their joy was interrupted by the sharp ring of the phone on the bedside table. Will reluctantly answered it. Lily Anne's high-pitched voice was audible to Krake curled up close to him.

"Will, I'm sorry to bother you but I think we should be heading for my parents' house. They're expecting us."

"All right, Lil, we'll be down soon." He replaced the receiver and they both burst into laughter. "At least her timing's good."

They dressed each other, kissing and hugging, unable to stop touching. They met Lily Anne and Hal downstairs in the bar. Will, becoming a little paranoid since the Laniers knew him from Kerrville, thought it might appear too suspicious if he drove them. They put the luggage back in Hal's Chevy and drove out into the late afternoon steam bath. As they approached the Lanier house, Krake wasn't surprised to see a large, imposing stone mansion with a turret at one end. Hal deposited the luggage and disappeared before the door opened. Mrs. Lanier motioned them inside to a black and white marble-floored entry hall ending at a polished mahogany staircase circling to the second floor. Opposite, a huge living room opened onto a brick patio. Lavishly furnished, the living area had a fireplace at either end with a huge crystal chandelier swaying slightly in the center over a magnificent Oriental carpet. The furnishings were Louis XV, not to Krake's taste, but beautiful nonetheless.

Mrs. Lanier could have been Mt. Rushmore for all the warmth she exuded. She smiled artificially as Krake stuck out her hand in greeting. When no corresponding hand was extended, Krake quickly withdrew hers. The chilling tonal quality of Mrs. Lanier's voice was also disquieting. Krake decided she would keep out of her way as much as possible. She was only planning to stay five days anyway. No wonder Lily Anne was such a bundle of nerves. If Lorraine objected to Krake's being in the theater, what horrors had Lily Anne faced?

After brief introductions, Lily Anne and Krake made their way up to her second-floor bedroom. The combination bed-sitting room was large and elegant. Heavy silk chiffon curtains let in only a glow of light at this hour. Krake shivered a little, whether from the cold air blasting from the central air-conditioning unit or the coolness of Mrs. Lanier's greeting, she wasn't sure.

The hungry girls showered quickly and went down to the long table in the formal dining room for dinner. Dr. Lanier, a respected neurosurgeon, had returned and Krake felt a genuine warmth in his greeting. He and Lily Anne and Krake had a lively discussion regarding the coming year at the Alley. Dr. Lanier was quite knowledgeable about plays. He had seen a lot of Houston theater during his undergraduate years.

The phone rang just as they were finishing a delicious meal of crab salad and cornbread fritters. It was for Lily Anne. When she returned, she announced (as planned) that it was Will Stoner, who was visiting friends for a few days in San Antonio, calling to see if he could stop by and bring along his technical director at the summer theater. "I told him to come over," said Lily Anne to her parents. "I hope that's all right."

Her parents assured her it was. They had both seen Will's plays at Kerrville and were familiar with his acting career at the Alley. The girls excused themselves from the table and went upstairs to redo lipstick and make themselves generally irresistible. They congratulated each other for having pulled off this deception.

Twenty minutes later, the doorbell chimed, Dr. Lanier opened the door and welcomed the visitors. The girls descended the curving staircase and introductions were made. Lily's mother was much friendlier to Will, batting her eyelashes and giggling. She totally ignored his companion.

Abel, an aspiring actor and Will's technical director, immediately took a liking to Lily Anne. Her mother's rudeness seemed to matter little. They were soon immersed in a shared personal passion, a game of scrabble. When Dr. and Mrs. Lanier left to attend a benefit auction, Will and Krake went for a walk. They didn't get far. The moonless night was pitch black, lit only by the spangling of stars in the vast Texas sky. They soon found a spreading magnolia tree in a far corner of the Lanier's property. In the soft grass they repeated the ancient act of love. They laughed softly thinking how shocked proper Mrs. Lanier would be if she could see them now.

They returned to the house in response to Lily Anne calling. Will was ready to leave, it had been a long day. The lovers parted, promising to meet tomorrow. Krake hugged her happiness to her as she covered herself with the satin coverlet, said goodnight to Lily and fell asleep.

They slept late. At eleven, Sadie, the Lanier's "colored" cook knocked on their door. ".Miss Lily Anne, I fixed your favorite, blueberry pancakes. You girls get up now and come down to breakfast before it's cold."

Seated in the sunny, glassed-in breakfast room, Krake could see why the rich, fruity cakes were revered. Mrs. Lanier expressed her pride in Sadie's abilities and said, "We treat her just like one of us." The highest accolade a white person could bestow on a black.

Stuffed after gorging herself, Krake went upstairs to bathe and dress while Lily Anne stayed in the kitchen to try and wheedle a buckwheat and grits pancake recipe out of Sadie.

Lolling in the hot bath, she gazed around at the splendor of the surroundings. The tub was an oversized pink marble creation. The gold faucets had pink quartz inlaid handles. The sink and tile were pink with tiny gold flecks which sparkled when the light hit them. All the towels and rugs and curtains were a pale seashell pink. It was disappointing that the water didn't run out pink as well. Krake leisurely dried off and slathered pink lotion all over, then returned to the bedroom to dress. Where was her black bra? She looked everywhere and was headed down the stairs in her robe to ask Lily Anne if she had seen it when the icy voice of Mrs. Lanier floated up.

"I don't want that woman in my house. I just spoke with a friend of Tonya Stoner's. It seems Will has been having an affair with that tramp. Your roommate! Tonya's pregnant too. The very idea! I suppose she thought she could carry on with him under my roof. No, I should say not! I want her out of here, now!"

Her voice pierced Krake's heart. She slowly turned and made her way back to the bedroom. Throwing her suitcase on the unmade bed, she began to dump her clothes in it. Her mind was whirling. Where would she go? What would she do? She had very little money and couldn't call her parents for help. What defense could she give for being kicked out of Lily's house because she was a tramp? It would only confirm Lorraine's views of her.

Why was she to blame? Tonya didn't love him. Only when he wanted someone else had he become desirable. Did people really believe anyone could break up a happy marriage? Did they really believe in the myth of the seductive other woman? Why should the man be blameless? Will made the first move. She would never have attempted to date him, hadn't even considered him a contender until he told her he was falling in love with her. He said he didn't love Tonya and wanted a divorce. Was Will Stoner being called a tramp? NO! Krake, the evil one, had taken advantage of this poor, helpless, six-foot, 185-pound man. The hurt and shame welled up inside of her. It was the old double standard, of course. It would be a few more years before Betty Freidan began to raise women's consciousness, so Krake could only wonder helplessly at the imbalance of blame. If she did speak out about it, would anyone listen?

When Lily Anne slowly entered the room, Krake spoke, "I heard what your mother said and I'm packing." Tears filled her eyes as she turned away. There was silence.

Lily said, "I'm sorry, Krake, I don't know what to do. Where will you go?"

"Beats me. I'll have to call Will," Krake replied. She swallowed, breathed deeply and then used the pale pink phone on the table. Will came quickly. He didn't come in, the Laniers were formidable. Krake ran out with her bags, got in the car and they drove away. She looked over at Will and began to cry. When they were out of sight of the house, he pulled over to the curb and took her in his arms.

"Why me?" she sobbed. "Why does everyone blame me?"

"That's the way most people think," he murmured as he gently kissed the top of her head. He let her cry until she was exhausted and feeling a little better. She looked up at him, "What are we going to do?"

"We're going to get a room at the Adobe Inn down by the river. We can stay there tonight and I'll book you on a Texas Airlines flight to Belton tomorrow evening."

A river runs through San Antonio and along its banks, in the heart of the city, are a string of restaurants, shops and lodging. The Adobe Inn was a moderately priced, one-story motel set back from the street. Lush orange trumpet vines and magenta bougainvillea covered the red-tiled roof. A fountain played in the courtyard. It was very romantic looking, she decided. The idea of spending the night with Will was exciting. They dropped her luggage off at the room, intending to take a walk down by the river but the intensity of their love/lust was overwhelming and soon they were in bed. The physical intimacy and Will's tenderness lessened the pain of the morning's events.

Renewed, they set off to enjoy a leisurely brunch at an open-air restaurant nearby. As they sat down, Will said, "Someday, Krake, we'll have breakfast together every morning."

"Yes!" she smiled, but didn't quite believe it.

After their meal, they went to see the Alamo, which had recently been the subject of a John Wayne movie. They left the car in a huge parking lot across from the mission. Only a few tourists were wandering around so they explored the famous site practically alone. Holding hands, walking over the rough stones they tried to imagine what horror the massacre must have been. All the while, talking and laughing, Krake felt a sense of dread. Would they ever be together as a married couple? She was still feeling the hurt of the brutal rejection this morning. She wondered if Will knew how badly she felt, how alone. She tried to memorize the discomfort of the sharp stones under her feet as if she could imprint it in her mind so strongly that none of this would disappear. If only she could stop time right now and be with Will forever. Her powerlessness was defeating.

That night was the first night she had ever spent with a man and he was married. The romantic love they had started with had been torn by fear and hatred. This wasn't part of Happily Ever After. But her doubts were pushed aside by idyllic lovemaking followed by a leisurely stroll through the ruins of Franciscan missions the next day.

Late in the afternoon, on the way back to the motel, Will bought a wide silver bracelet she had admired earlier. Krake loved the way it shone in contrast to her dark skin, it was the first gift he had given her. She vowed never to take it off.

They headed for the airport lost in thought. The silence continued as they bought Krake's ticket. Near the gate they stopped and kissed. She forced herself to turn away and walk to the plane.

9

When she arrived home early, Hank and Lorraine accepted her excuse of returning sooner than expected from Lily's because Mrs. Lanier was ill. They were glad to hear that Philip was joining the theater group, but Lorraine's opening remark to her never varied, "Wouldn't you like to teach school?" Not a word of encouragement or support. In answer to the next inevitable question, she said she hadn't seen Will all summer, which was almost true. Daddy said he liked Will but he didn't want her to get hurt. Krake told him she missed Will terribly and didn't know how the whole thing was going to turn out but only hoped it would be all right.

"Whatever happens we'll be here. You can always come back home."

"Thanks, Daddy. I can't give up now, I've just left." She hugged him, grateful for his love.

During the two weeks she was at home, she only had one brief phone call from Will. His voice was warm and caring though. He told her he would arrange a meeting through Philip as soon as she was back in Houston.

When Krake arrived at her apartment, no one was there. She made a grilled-cheese sandwich and a salad and after watching a little television went to bed. This was the first time she had been alone in the apartment. She felt scared and lonely and stayed awake for hours trying to figure out what lay ahead for her and Will. She was pretty sure she was no longer an approved roommate for Lily Anne and couldn't imagine where she would live.

At seven forty-five a.m., a loud knocking on the door awakened her. A familiar voice called her name harshly, "Krake, Krake Forrester, get up!" Someone had let themselves in and was knocking on the bedroom door. "Get out, you whore!"

My God! It was Mrs. Lanier. Just then she burst into the bedroom, ripped the blankets and sheets off Krake's body and yelled, "Get dressed and get out!"

Krake lay there, stunned. But only for a moment. She leapt up, grabbing a blanket to cover herself, and tried to decide what to do first.

"I'm going to take a bath, then I'll get dressed and leave," she said.

Why she persisted in her regular morning bath she didn't know. Perhaps because the ritual was some sort of security to cling to. She felt stripped of everything, her privacy, her dignity, herself. She ran an inch of lukewarm water into the tub and got in. She sat there frozen in horror as the loud, grating voice came through the door.

"You whore! You slut! How could you do this to another woman and a paraplegic who's pregnant? (Krake had to admit her choices were unbeatable.) You're the worst form of human being on earth. As soon as you're dressed, I want you and all of your things out of here. You are not to associate with Lily Anne in any way, ever again. You prostitutes shouldn't be allowed to be around decent people. Get out! Get out, now!" This was accompanied by fists pounding on the bathroom door.

The glare of morning light reflected off the chrome faucets. The room seemed to be a white shroud encasing her in shame. The horror of Mrs. Lanier's words pierced her. She looked down at the inch of water surrounding her body to see if it was turning red. Red with the blood of shame and self-hatred. She couldn't move, her breathing stopped. She wanted to scream, but couldn't. I must get out of here now!

Krake didn't bother washing. She got out of the already cold water and hastily dried off with a towel. Cautiously she entered the bedroom ... no one in sight. No double-barreled shotgun staring her in the face. She dressed to the constant harangue from the living room. Clothed, she grabbed her purse and ran past the figure in the chair and out of the apartment, out to the freedom of the street, where she flagged down the first car she saw.

"Please give me a ride to the Alley Theater," she cried. "I'm late for rehearsal and my ride can't pick me up. He's down on Westheimer Boulevard with a flat tire."

A middle-aged man with wispy hair sticking out from under the brim of a dilapidated straw cowboy hat barely noticed her. In minutes he deposited her in front of the theater. She was so shaken by the early morning's ghastly wake-up call she could hardly speak. She managed to thank him and ran inside to the box office where she was supposed to work that day. No one was there. She sat down in the brown swivel chair, covered her face and cried. Where are you, Will?

Megan found her a short while later. Krake told her of the predicament. As of that moment she had no place to live. Mrs. Lanier's voice kept ringing in her ears, "Whore, slut!" The tears streamed down, she couldn't stop them. She would dry her eyes, try to talk on the phone and start bawling all over again. Finally Megan said she had better take the phone reservations. Philip came in and Krake told him the whole story, which helped; at least she stopped crying. Word spread through the theater and by noon most everyone had been by or at least looked in to see "the evil one." Each breath she drew was painful. It was hard to meet people's eyes. She knew they believed she was a whore. Was she?

The day dragged on. She began to answer the phones and take reservations for the opening show. *The Library Raid*, the Ford Foundation Grant's first offering, was a new play written by a young playwright from New York. Howard Taubman, the New York Times theater critic was coming down to review it. Word was Peter Lorre might attend the opening night performance. None of this seemingly exciting information meant a thing to Krake.

At three o'clock the phone rang and a soft feminine voice asked for Krake Forrester. "This is Mary Moore," she said. "I'm a dancer who was in the children's show, *Bozo The Clown*, with you."

"Oh yes, I remember you, Mary."

"I hear you need a place to stay and my roommates and I are looking for someone to share the rent. One of the women I live with is leaving shortly. You'd have to sleep on the couch until she left, maybe two weeks or so, but then you'd be sharing a bedroom. Would that be of any help?"

Any help? It was a bloody miracle!

When Krake replaced the receiver, she breathed a sigh of relief. She wouldn't have to sleep on a park bench tonight. Someone actually wanted her to room with them. Philip drove her there after the box office closed for the day.

Not a word was mentioned about Krake's departure from her last apartment. Mary told her she could put her things in the bedroom she would be sharing with Harriet.

She and Philip went to her old place to pick up her belongings. They worked quickly. Krake was extremely nervous and fearful that the "dragon lady" would reappear, to breathe more fire. The burns were third degree as it was. After making several trips, they had their arms full with the last of it, had just rounded the pool and were on their way to the parking lot when Lily Anne and her parents nearly ran into them. The narrow sidewalk seemed even narrower as the five people stopped and stared at each other.

With all the bravado she could muster, Krake spoke, "Hello, Lily Anne." She ignored the dragon and her mate. Lily Anne's eyes darted away as she responded with a barely audible "Hi." Mrs. Lanier's face was cast in stone. "Did you get everything out?"

Krake's tone became imperious, "Yes, but if I've left anything behind, do let me know and I'll send someone to get it!" If only I don't burst into tears, that's all I ask. She glanced at Dr. Lanier who was smiling at her, or was that a lecherous grin? This family is insane, she decided. Philip gave her a firm shove and she swept by them with nary a backward glance. Leaning against the side of the car, she inhaled deeply. She had forgotten to breathe.

Moving into Mary's went faster because both Mary and Harriet helped. Philip gave her a big hug before he left. Falling asleep that night wasn't easy. The sofa was lumpy, but better than the bed of nails at Lily Anne's. She had been back at the theater for two days, it seemed like two years. A constant theme ran through her head: why am I going through this alone? Where is Will? Why doesn't he give me any support? Aren't we in this together? Or are we? She couldn't sort it out and she chose to believe that everything would be all right.

Philip got word to her that Will wanted to meet her on Monday at Philip's apartment. She was full of mixed emotions; happy that she would see him and at the same time apprehensive. She wondered where he was and what kind of job he had, if any. Nina had finished hiring the company for the Ford Grant season and he wasn't among them. What was he doing for money? How would they see each other now that they weren't working together? He would find a way.

On Monday she walked over to Phillip's place. The Nash was parked out front and Will was waiting inside. She knocked on the screen door. When he opened it, she was in his arms before he could step back inside. Kissing her, he pulled her into the room then told her to sit down, he had something serious to say. Her heart sank as she sat opposite him.

"Krake, this is going to be a difficult period of time for us. We can't see each other until after the baby's born. Tonya's doctors say that because of the stress our relationship put on her she could miscarry or have a premature birth. I know it'll be hard, but we really have no choice. Please say you understand."

The pain was monumental. Not to see him for three or four months seemed like an eternity. They would be in the same city. Not to be able to feel his warmth, know his love or be a part of his passion? How could she stand it? She couldn't believe it was happening again. She had found a man she truly loved and he was leaving her. Burg was gone forever. Now Will had to play out a farce and might never return. Abandonment again. Rejected again and powerless to prevent it. She shared none of this with Will, told him she would do it for the baby's sake. What did her feelings matter compared to the life of a baby? What did she matter? Not much, was the message. She, the strong woman, would carry on stoically when in reality she was but a baby herself. A twenty-three-year-old baby. She didn't know how to cope with loss, temporary or permanent, and didn't know where to go for help.

They kissed fiercely and he pressed her to him so tightly she thought he might crush her. Better to die in his arms than to be without him.

"Goodbye, I love you," Will said.

"Goodbye, I love you too," she said, and cried all the way back to the theater. She told Elmer she had a stomach-ache and needed to lie down. He told her to go home, that he could handle all the calls that afternoon. She did. Fortunately her new roommates weren't there, so she went into her soon-to-be-bedroom, curled up on the bed and cried herself to asleep.

She was nothing without a man. Her self-worth depended on one being there, loving her. All the 40s and 50s movies she had grown up on supported this idea. And the times told her the same. Without a man, a woman was not complete and life had no meaning. Certainly her existence wasn't justifiable on its own. Through all the pain, only the concept of Happily Ever After kept her going. Aside from finding the man she could share her life with, she had no goals, direction or plans, but let herself be buffeted about by whatever came her way. The only thing that seemed to fill the void was alcohol. Drunk, she didn't care.

Krake woke up when Mary came in from her Monday night dance class. "Hi, what're you doing here? I thought you had rehearsal tonight."

"I do, but I'm not feeling very well." Krake got up, came in the kitchen and sat down at the round wooden table.

Mary offered her a Coke and joined her. "Krake, we don't know each other very well, but I like you. I've heard about you and Will Stoner and I'd hate to see you hurt."

Krake didn't answer right away. Finally she looked across at Mary, tears welling in her eyes. "Oh, Mary, I've already been hurt. So much that it's hard to talk about. I'm afraid if I try to tell anyone, I'll fall apart. Like saying it will make it real."

Mary reached over and put her hand on Krake's. The touch made her jump, she tried to pull her hand away, but Mary's closed tightly around it. "Krake, it might help if you told me. I won't say anything. You can trust me." Mary's dark brown eyes were warm and Krake needed someone so badly.

"I saw Will today and he told me we couldn't see each other until after the baby is born. I can't handle it. I just don't see how I can go on." She burst into tears, put her head in her hands and sobbed.

Mary came around the table and held her in her arms until she stopped. When she finally quieted down and dried her eyes on a paper towel Mary handed her, Krake apologized, "I'm so sorry."

"Sorry for what? For being sweet and trusting and falling in love. Nonsense! It's Will who should be sorry. He created this mess and now because a little pressure's put on he walks away from you. Back to where his bread is buttered, if you know what I mean. I think he loves you, but he's weak. He doesn't want to give up the easy ride he has with Tonya. Her family money supports them when he's not working, you know. Honey, that s.o.b. doesn't deserve to kiss the hem of your Bermuda shorts. Forget the bastard! I bet every guy on the Ford Grant, who's not queer, that is, would give his you know what for a date with you. Krake, you're beautiful, talented, intelligent, funny. He's not worth it, none of 'em are. You start appreciating yourself. That's the best thing you can do. You are your own worst enemy. Start loving yourself." With these sage words, Mary retired to "dip" her tights and get ready for bed.

Krake sat at the table and finished her Coke, then headed to the bathroom for a long, hot bath. The pain wasn't gone, but it had subsided. Later, lying on the couch, thoughts whirled about in her brain. Tonya has family money, that's how they survive, Will had never mentioned that. Hmmm … her eyes closed and she dreamed of witches in wheelchairs chasing her.

The next day at the theater, things seemed better. Her thoughts were occupied with work and adjusting to the new corps of actors on the Ford Grant who consisted of four women and six men. Only two were left from the original company, Megan and one of the men. Krake made friends immediately with Ellen, a tall, very attractive New Yorker in her mid-twenties. She got her start in show-biz when George Abbott spotted her at a casting call for the road company of *Bells Are Ringing*. Not primarily a musical comedy performer, she soon found her way to the soaps and had recently finished a year on *Days Of Our Lives*. Very homespun and down-to-earth, she was an easy choice for Nina to add to her company.

In contrast, Grace, a sleek brunette with an angular face and a slight British accent was the epitome of sophistication and style. Canadian by birth, Grace lived in London for several years before coming to the states to enroll in the Yale Drama School. People were a little in awe of Grace, but in reality she was as warm and perhaps even more open than Ellen. These two roomed together not far from Krake's new apartment and she found herself dropping in on them frequently.

Lewis, a forty-ish, darkly handsome movie and TV actor from Los Angeles, was the man in the company she related to most. The member she related to least was Tom, another Hollywood actor. Both were homosexuals but the difference was that Lewis liked her and Tom didn't. Krake found throughout her life that many homosexual men and women disliked her. She supposed she represented everything feminine that repelled both sexes.

The Library Raid was in full rehearsal and she was busy gathering props and running in to say her one line as the French maid. In addition, she had been cast as Snow White in the children's play. A dwarf was cast as Doc with the remainder of the dwarfs to be drawn from the students in the Creative Dramatics class taught at the Alley Theater Acting School in an old house across from the theater. When Mrs.Vance heard Krake had a degree in education and a major in drama, she was recruited to teach at the school.

Her only experience was a Creative Dramatics class at Belton College, for which she instructed ten-year-olds for a month. Krake taught the four-to-six year-olds at the Alley School once a week. They loved her and to her surprise she fell in love with them. Children had always intimidated her, plus endlessly baby-sitting Hankie had left a bad taste.

One assignment she gave them was to stand with their backs to her and portray emotions using only their bodies. It was amazing how free they were, in contrast to her self-consciousness. One rainy afternoon, one of the four-year-olds ran up to Krake as she was leaving, threw her arms around her and said, "I wish you were my mother!" Krake was so moved she didn't know what to say. When six of her students were chosen to play the dwarfs, she was enormously pleased.

The Library Raid opened a week before *Snow White and the Seven Dwarfs*. Opening night was a black-tie affair. All the local celebrities, the two Ford Foundation Grant writers, Peter Lorre as well as Howard Taubman were scheduled to attend. The air was electric with excitement.

That afternoon she and the new technical director painted the arms of the seats in the newly refurbished theater. Fortunately, it was quick-drying paint, since they finished only three hours before the curtain went up.

Krake didn't have a thing to wear! Truthfully, she had so many clothes they were a problem to transport and store. But this was a special occasion. When they were finished cleaning the brushes, she asked Paul if he would give her a ride out to Battlesteins, a nearby department store where her father had a charge account.

Paint-spattered, sans makeup, hair in a ponytail, dressed in dirty jeans and an old shirt, she rushed into the elegant foyer of the store. Sales clerks looked at her with disdain. She didn't care. She had thirty minutes before the store closed. She grabbed a black chiffon shirtwaist from a rack, ran into a dressing room and slipped it on. Not great, but it would do. Then out to the jewelry department. On the way she spied black silk high heels spattered with rhinestones, the latest thing and very expensive. One second's hesitation and they were hers. She was the last customer as the lights began to dim and she rushed out the door. Daddy would probably faint when he got the bill, but he was used to it. Krake's clothes, his cross in life.

The play went well and the audience was appreciative. Apparently the quick-drying paint didn't live up to its promise. Patrons complained that their forearms stuck to the seats.

Krake tried to act concerned, but it was all she could do to keep from laughing. Talk about a captive audience!

Drinking champagne in the lobby after the play, Krake met the two Ford Grant writers. Brian Forbes, a slim blond, elegantly handsome man, had written lyrics for many Broadway musicals and his poems appeared regularly in *The New Yorker*. In contrast, Gerry Grovner was a short rotund, cherub-faced imp with an infectious laugh. He had published two novels, a book of poems and a collection of short stories. During this year they were supposed to absorb as much knowledge of the theater as possible and perhaps write a play to be produced at the Alley.

After the theater party broke up, there was another at Marshall Brooks' mansion in River Oaks. Over the years, Mr. Brooks had donated millions to subsidize the fine arts of Houston. The Houston Ballet, the symphony and the Alley Theater were among the most recent beneficiaries.

Krake and Philip went to the Brooks' together and exclaimed in whispers over the magnificently furnished rooms. Not long after they arrived, Tonya and Will Stoner appeared in the doorway. Tonya, dressed in a pale green maternity smock, her dark curls piled on top of her head, was very pregnant and barely able to fit into the wheelchair Will was pushing. It was the first time Krake had seen her since the night in late April when she had "car chased" them through the streets of Houston. The face Krake saw tonight was tense through the laughter over some remark Will had just made to her.

Krake's heart sank. She got in line for drinks at the bar. As she waited a masculine voice whispered in her ear, "I love you." She turned around and met Will's gaze as he stood behind her. He quickly looked away and Krake saw Tonya wheeling herself towards him. Fortunately, Krake's turn to order came and grabbing the glass of wine she retreated to a large leather chair in the living room.

Will's words created a stir of feeling. warm happiness suffused her body along with intense frustration. She took a sip of wine and looked around. Seated on one end of a long divan directly across from her was Peter Lorre. Engaged in conversation with Marshall Brooks, he occasionally glanced her way. Peter Lorre was the prize of the evening and she vowed to make him come to her. Will was with Tonya, well, she'd show them. She sat and sat. Various people stopped by for conversation and to refill her drink. She watched as several socialites asked Mr. Lorre for his autograph. Not me! He was now talking to a young man she didn't know. Eventually the man rose and came across the room towards her. She had about given up. Bored, restless, she needed to use the bathroom. The stranger, an aspiring actor from Dallas, leaned down to her. "Mr. Lorre would like to meet you. He wondered if you would come over and sit beside him for awhile."

"Oh," she replied, feigning indifference. Inwardly, she felt the rush of conquest. He didn't exactly come to me, but he has requested my presence. She nodded her acceptance, excused herself and made a beeline for the bathroom. She relieved herself, quickly redid her lipstick, patted her French roll and smiled to herself as she dried her hands on the B-monogrammed towel. She was enormously pleased.

His features were softer than on screen, although the eyes drooped under their heavy lids in that characteristic way known to movie-goers. His smile was warm. He patted the sofa cushion next to him indicating she should sit. Even sitting down, she was taller. His face and body were bloated with fat. Turning slightly, he spoke in that distinctive, quietly nasal voice, "You're a fascinating looking woman, I couldn't help wondering who you were."

"Krake Forrester, Mr. Lorre." His hand barely held hers as she extended it. "I'm an apprentice at the Alley. I've admired you as an actor for a long time." This was pure flattery, she had never thought of him as an actor, only as a famous person. "Why are you here? This is quite a way from Hollywood."

"I'm interested in regional theater and am visiting all the regional companies that are recipients of the Ford grants."

Several glasses of white wine made her courageous. "Oh, Mr. Lorre," she breathed, "some people have told me I should try Hollywood. What do you think? I really don't like Texas. I'm happy working at the Alley, but I don't want to stay here forever."

Peter Lorre was silent for a moment. He took a sip of his drink and clearing his throat replied, "I have children about your age and I'll tell you what I would tell them. I wouldn't recommend Hollywood to anyone. It's one of the toughest places in the profession. I can't stop you from going there, but that's my answer."

Krake was disappointed. Ever since mincing down the stairs in Lorraine's high-heels when she was four, she had fantasized about being a movie star. Will had said, just recently, that she had the looks and personality for it. She wanted Lorre to tell her he would make her a star. They chatted a while longer about acting and the evening's performance. Krake noticed a faint smudge of paint on his French cuff and smiled. Philip came over, met Lorre and asked if she was ready to go. She nodded yes, bid adieu to her conquest and they left.

She knew she looked great, but for what? Will Stoner told her he loved her, and went home with his wife. Peter Lorre, co-star of Humphrey Bogart, Sydney Greenstreet, Lauren Bacall and Mary Astor, asked to meet her but told her not to go to Hollywood. She only wanted to go to sleep in Will's arms. What did her mother always say? "If wishes were horses, beggars would ride."

10

Krake started drinking heavily, as heavily as her unusually susceptible body could handle. After a few drinks her whole being was alive with the possibilities of life. She could attempt anything and succeed. Become a famous movie star, be loved by everyone including the perfect man, have untold wealth which would enable her to buy her family all they dreamed of and then, maybe, her mother would love her. Lorraine had given Krake the impression that no matter what you did, if you had money, it was OK.

She busied herself at the theater playing Snow White. The children adored her. Little did they know she was usually suffering a monumental hangover and played the beauteous sylph only partly present.

The Ford Grant writers took a liking to her and formed the "Krake Forrester Fan Club Of Greater Harris County." When *Snow White* opened they sent her a telegram wishing her luck and praising her beauty. She was thrilled by this attention from these important men. Her relationship with Brian Forbes was rather distant and formal, his wife was always hovering around. With Gerry Grovner, it was entirely different. Warm and charming, his obvious enchantment with her was a great support. Gerry was a fun-lover and so was Krake. Married, with three small children, he loved his family, but that never interfered with their special relationship. She became his muse. He made her laugh and brought her gifts, mainly books - his and others, like George Bernard Shaw's "Letters to a Young Actress." He often referred to the day when she would rise naked from her bath, like Venus rising from the sea (the old porcelain tub in her apartment didn't seem quite right) and he would pour champagne over her and throw yellow roses onto her perfect body. Sometimes he would ask, "When are we running away to Aruba?" It was understood between them that he was devoted to his wife, and this would never occur. But Gerry's adoration helped her accept Will's absence. She tried to forget him, and the combination of Gerry, Philip and booze were her mainstays.

The next major Alley show, *The Happy Time*, was a comedy about a French-Canadian family. Philip was cast as the adolescent son, Bebe, with Krake as his girlfriend, Sally O'Hare. One day during the early stages of rehearsal Krake used a different voice when saying her lines. Harsh, raspy and throaty, she never knew where it came from. Suddenly her character emerged. Sally's heretofore mildly amusing lines became hilarious. She couldn't open her mouth without causing laughter. The response of the cast and Kevin the director, gave her confidence. She loosened up and took chances. Her choices were applauded and she finally felt like one of them. A professional actress!

Sally was fun to immerse herself in. She wore braces on her teeth (strips of aluminum foil wrapped around rubber bands), her hair in braids, thick glasses perched on her nose. An ugly navy-blue sailor suit with long socks and oxfords was her costume in the first two acts. Her transformation occurred in the third act when she wore her hair streaming down her back, the glasses disappeared and she was attired in a pink and white gingham dress. Bebe was overwhelmed.

Suddenly people noticed her talent. Insecurity made it difficult to promote herself, but she knew she had a gift for acting. Her shyness and self-doubt worked against the talent, but when she felt safe it surfaced. Another contradiction.

When she exited in the first act on opening night performance, the audience burst into applause. She stood backstage, stunned. They were applauding her, clapping, laughing, and shouting "Bravo." Megan, standing near the property table, gave her a big grin. Suddenly self-conscious, Krake retreated to the dressing room. After the show, many in the audience came backstage to congratulate the cast, especially Krake and Philip. They were a hit!

Krake dressed carefully for the opening night party in a sophisticated red suit with her hair in a French twist. Her fantasy was that people would say, "Where is that fabulous actress who played Sally O'Hare?" Someone would point to her and say, "Right over there." They would exclaim, "But you're so beautiful and much older than Sally O'Hare! You're a great actress." Her fantasy failed to materialize. No one paid any attention to her and the reviews only named her in the cast list. She drank herself into a blackout.

One night during the run of *Happy Time*, Nina sat next to Krake backstage where she was waiting for her entrance cue. They exchanged inanities for awhile, then Nina leaned over and spoke softly in her ear, "I have never seen anyone give a better performance on Broadway. What did Kevin do to motivate you? He said you just brought it in."

Krake, suddenly shy said, "I don't know how it happened." This was only partially true. She knew it was able to happen because she felt safe with Kevin. She had watched Nina, brilliant director that she was, tear people apart in rehearsals. For Krake, this treatment paralyzed her with fear blocking her creative juices. Kevin was kind and generous. He talked with his actors privately concerning their performances. Kevin was an actor too, which must have made a difference. Krake's precarious self-esteem couldn't survive a "Ninalation."

During one performance of *Happy Time*, Krake appeared drunk on stage for the first and last time. She and Gerry had been drinking his martinis at her apartment late one afternoon and against all reason she had three. Her limit was none. She arrived at the theater late, three martinis to the wind. Megan, who was stage managing, saw at a glance her state of inebriation. She quickly brought a pot of coffee and helped her dress for the first act. As she was braiding her hair, she said, "I don't want to alarm you, but Will and Tonya Stoner are sitting out front." Krake gasped. Of all nights for him to come. The only time she had drunk anything before a show. And Tonya! She hadn't been to an Alley production in years. Now, here they were sitting front row center. Megan explained that she was telling her because she didn't want Krake to be caught off guard by seeing them when she was on-stage. Thank God for Megan.

Krake's performance that night was terrible. Poor Philip had to carry their scenes completely as she swayed to and fro, slurring the dialogue. As he related afterwards, "I looked up and you almost fell on me. Your breath was awful and your eyes were completely glazed over. As if that wasn't enough, Tyrone chose that particular evening to go up on his lines. He'd lean over and whisper, 'Help me Philip.' What a disaster!"

Krake cringed, remembering also how she literally ran out of the theater after the performance, managing a "hi" as she passed Will and Tonya in the lobby. She went home and cried herself to sleep. Of all people to humiliate herself in front of. How did she manage to screw things up so badly?

Gerry Grovner wrote a children's play, *The Peasant and the Princess*, which went into rehearsal during the run of *Happy Time*. He wrote it for Krake and a male member of the company. Playing Princess Rosebud and a lion in the second act, she again reached into her bag of tricks and pulled out a lion's voice. Gruff and growly, she was the sexiest lion in the woods. She played Princess Rosebud as Ophelia, scattering rose petals and humming. The Alley promoted the play as the premier work of a Ford Grant writer and the opening was a gala evening affair. Ellen and Grace gave her a unique rose-shaped mirror which she used during the performance. Krake kept that mirror for years until the satin back and stem were in shreds. Brian and Gerry wrote a sixteen-stanza poem about her "pre-Raphaelite" beauty. The local papers gave the production a big spread.

One day after rehearsal when she stopped by the cleaners to pick up a dress, the owner asked if she was Krake Forrester. She nodded and he said he had seen her in *The Happy Time* and thought she was very good. Her feet never touched the ground until she went to bed that night.

In spite of all the pluses in her career, Will was gone. The pain wasn't. Each morning she awoke to a knife-like jab in her heart. She knew it was over. Her drunken escapades involved seducing whomever struck her fancy and were now common knowledge in the closely-knit (gossipy) theater community. This type of behavior was something Will would never forgive. Not that there had been that many seductions, mind you, but even one would have been too much for Will. She longed for love. The love she had had with Burg and thought she had found with Will. The desire to move on to another part of the country was strong. But the pain over Will bound her to Houston. So she laughed and drank and had short-lived romances she barely recalled.

One morning after a drunken opening night party for Ibsen's *An Enemy of the People*, she awoke or came to in a strange bed in an unfamiliar room with a man whose back was towards her lying at her side. Who is he? she wondered. Where am I? What happened? She forced her mind to ignore its aching and gradually some of the previous evening's events returned.

Playing the lead in *Enemy* was Tyrone Hughes, an Irish member of the company from New York. Tyrone, 40, hadn't distinguished himself in the supporting roles he had played, but as the lead in *Enemy* he gave a stellar performance. She remembered walking into the opening night party and deciding she was going to sleep with him. How she had managed it she didn't remember, but here she was lying next to him. Staring at the back of his head she noticed black streaks on the pillow which matched the black of his hair. Dyed! She sighed. She didn't want to be here and hated herself for letting it happen. Why did she always lose control when she drank? The fact that chunks of time were obliterated from her memory both disturbed and excited her. She could pretend that all that occurred during those lapses hadn't. The excitement came from the danger of what might have happened. Like conquering the unknown, being there yet not.

The conventional morality she had been raised with never made much sense to her. It was so hypocritical. What difference did it make if you made love to someone because you were lonely? The warmth and comfort of welcoming arms could keep the chill of aloneness at bay for awhile. Was the sanctity of marriage the only way to obtain this? Why was it all right for a man to satisfy these needs and not a woman? Was she a moral leper because she "had to have it" too? None of it made sense.

Hughes stirred and turned towards her, interrupting her thoughts. He opened one bloodshot eye. "Mmm, Krake." He reached over and began kissing her. His stale whiskey breath was repelling and she pulled away. "Ty, I've got to go back to my apartment. I feel awful."

"So do I," he agreed.

Tyrone didn't have a car, didn't drive and so he called a cab. Safely back in her own bed, she felt better. Nothing happened, because I don't remember it.

The apartment she returned to that morning was her own. She had wanted the privacy of her own place. As soon as she completed her apprenticeship in January, she was put on junior staff and given the huge salary of $25 a week. With this enormous amount, she found a furnished one-bedroom apartment located on a tree-lined boulevard within walking distance of the theater. It was the first time she had ever lived alone and she was often scared. Her fear wasn't completely unfounded. Houston had the sixth highest crime rate of cities in the U.S., according to the papers. She avoided reading them finally because of the explicit headlines and graphic detail of every murder and rape. She sometimes got a bottle of wine to help her fall asleep.

Ever since her triumph in *The Happy Time*, Lewis Berry, the friendly homosexual, had been urging her to consider Hollywood. One evening when she was looking exceptionally pretty, he murmured in her ear, "You ought to be in pictures." She laughed, but he said he was serious. She told him she couldn't do that. He told her to see *A Summer Place*, with Sandra Dee and Troy Donahue, that was playing in a downtown movie house. "Then tell me you can't do that." She went and decided maybe she could.

One Sunday morning after a late night party, she found a telephone number scribbled on a note pad on her desk. She didn't know whose number it was or how it got there. Curious, she dialed the digits. On the third ring, Will Stoner's voice came on the line. She recognized it immediately. "Hello, hello." She could hear a baby crying in the background. Word was Tonya had given birth to a girl in January. "Hello, hello," he repeated. Krake slowly replaced the receiver and sat down. How had she gotten the number? She had absolutely no recollection of obtaining it. Tears fell. It was over, over.

Krake wanted out of Houston. California ... why not?

Lewis said if she had some photos made he would send them to his agents, the Bellamy brothers, in Los Angeles. The Alley's photographer obliged and Lewis mailed them off. She anxiously awaited the results. At long last, Lewis said that he had heard from them. Her heart stopped. The Bellamys didn't know if they could be of any help, but if she came out to Hollywood they would see her. Acute disappointment! Her fantasies had been something along the lines of "She's the new Rita Hayworth! What a body! What a face! Send her out at once and we'll make her a star!" Lewis hastened to reassure her, "The fact that they'll see you is encouraging. They'll probably take you out to Warner's. This is good news."

She wasn't too persuaded, but wanted to get out of Texas so badly she grabbed at it. "I don't know anyone in LA. Where will I stay?"

Lewis mentioned the Hollywood Studio Club, a branch of the YWCA, which housed single women in the arts. It provided a protective environment with a housemother and rules and served two meals a day. Most of the five thousand dollars of Krake's insurance money was left so she could live on that for awhile. Everyone at the theater was enthusiastic about her venture. When she called her parents and told them, they were concerned, but since she had her own money they couldn't say too much. She was nervous yet excited.

She spent two weeks with her family before she left. The bickering hadn't changed, it was the only way she and Hankie communicated. They were almost strangers. Texas humidity and her negative family smothered her and only confirmed her decision to leave. Her father's presence no longer made up for anything. He was more passive and absent than before. She said goodbye to Lorraine and Hankie at home and her father took her to the airport. Seven years ago she had arrived at this same airport from upstate New York. Now she was making another major move. This time on her own.

Her father was still on the runway when the plane began to move. Tears ran down his face and hers. She saw his hand waving in the twilight as the plane lifted off. He loved her like no one else. He hated to let her go, but knew he must. She had to live her own life.

11

Krake had a three-hour layover in Houston. Everyone at the Alley said they would come out to the airport to see her off. No one showed up. She supposed it was too much to expect that after doing a show her friends would drive out to help pass the time until her plane departed. But it was disappointing.

On the flight to Los Angeles, the seat beside her was empty, but not for long. A pale, pimply-faced man about her age sat down.

"Hi! I'm Sid Blackstone. You sure are pretty. Do you mind if I sit here?"

"Thank you. I'm Krake Forrester. No, I don't mind." Lie.

"Krake, that's an unusual name."

"Yes, it was my mother's maiden name."

"Do you live in Los Angeles?" He stared at her, grinning.

"No, this is my first trip."

"Oh, are you going to visit a friend?" He settled in and talked and talked. Always polite, she answered his questions, told him of her plans to find work acting. He then revealed that he was Jerry Lewis' cousin, once removed or something like that. She wanted to be left alone, but not facile at repelling unwanted attention, she patiently listened to inane stories of life on the West coast, secretly wishing he would disappear. Without thinking, she told him a friend of her father's was meeting her at the airport and driving her to the Hollywood Studio Club. The minute the words were out of her mouth, she regretted them. Now he was saying he would call and take her out to see the sights.

At last Sid nodded off and she lay back in her seat and dreamed of becoming a movie star. She felt deep in her bones she would. How? She knew no one. Armed only with the introduction to the Bellamy brothers, she was enormously hopeful.

The sun rose as the plane began its descent into LA International. A light brown haze covered the city. The view was mostly small houses stretching on forever. Sid, awake now, assured Krake he would call and they deplaned.

A middle-aged, dark-haired man, graying at the temples stepped forward and stopped her. Elton Henry, was a business acquaintance of Daddy's. When Hank told him that Krake was coming to LA to live, he insisted upon meeting her and seeing she was safely deposited at the Studio Club. This relieved her father's anxieties somewhat, and she was grateful to have someone there.

They retrieved her luggage and, walking the length of several football fields, found his black Lincoln in the nearly full parking lot. It was six a.m. She was limping, having badly stubbed her toe a week before, but nevertheless insisting on wearing heels for her entrance into her glamorous new life. A star would never arrive in a town she was going to conquer, in flats. In endless traffic, the ride from the airport was interminable. It's ugly here, she thought, but quickly pushed that aside to answer Mr. Henry's questions about her acting experience. At last they pulled into a parking lot on Vine Street just down from Hollywood Boulevard. The building was shaped like a brown hat. The Brown Derby! She gritted her teeth and managed to walk inside without limping. Fortunately they were seated immediately so she could slip off the torture chamber of a shoe. Trying to be blasé about this thrilling beginning, she ordered the most exotic item on the menu, eggs and tomatoes.

"Eggs and tomatoes? I've never heard of that. Is it good?" Mr. Henry asked.

"Delicious."

Actually it wasn't bad. They ate and then he drove her the few blocks to Lodi Place and stopped in front of the big stone building called the Hollywood Studio Club. Advising her to call if she needed anything, he left her and her three suitcases in the lobby.

They informed her at the desk that her room wouldn't be ready until noon. It was eight-thirty. Homesickness assailed her as she sat on one of the chintz-covered sofas. She felt like crying or throwing up, she couldn't decide which. She thought about calling home, telling them it was a big mistake and that she was coming back. No, she couldn't do that.

At eleven-thirty, the housemother informed her that her room was ready. Her foot was now so swollen she couldn't get her shoe back on. Hobbling, with one shoe on and carrying the other she ascended in the elevator to the second floor. She walked down a long, poorly-lit corridor with many doors opening on either side to the room at the far end. She knocked softly, opened the door and entered the hospital green space that was her new home. A strikingly beautiful redhead was making up in the mirror over a dresser on the far side.

"Hi, I'm Nancy Kendricks, your roomie. I'm on my way to an interview so you'll be able to move in here in peace."

"Hi, Krake Forrester. Got here this morning from Texas. I guess I'd better go downstairs and get my other suitcase."

"What's wrong with your foot?" Nancy pointed to the shoeless one.

"I stubbed it a week ago and it still hurts. I don't know what's wrong."

"Let's go downstairs and get your bag. If I get back in time, we'll go over to the emergency clinic and get your toe checked."

"Gee, thanks," murmured Krake.

Together they retrieved the luggage and as soon as Nancy left Krake lay on the bed. This room was so cold and ugly. Even after putting some of her cosmetics on the dresser and hanging up a few clothes, it remained anonymous. Contemplating the fact of being in a strange city miles from anyone or anything she knew, she fell asleep. Nancy opening the door awakened her. She rolled over, sat up, brushing hair out of her eyes.

"Sorry, I didn't mean to wake you. I'm not a very quiet person," Nancy apologized.

"Oh, that's all right, I'm a light sleeper. What time is it?"

"Almost five. The clinic's walk-in section closes at four-thirty. I guess we'll have to see about your toe tomorrow." Nancy kicked off her high heels and flopped down on the bed opposite Krake.

"That's OK, it feels better if I don't walk on it. How was your interview?" Krake was eager to learn all she could about "the business."

"Awful! They were looking for a young housewife type to do an Avon commercial. A cattle call! I guess I'm too glamorous." Nancy was changing into jeans and an old shirt.

"What's a cattle call?" Krake asked.

"That's when everyone in town who remotely answers the description of what they're looking for gets sent on the interview. Today there were at least a hundred and fifty women waiting to be seen."

Krake sighed. Did she have even a chance?

The next morning, Krake called the Bellamy brothers from the pay phone in the lobby. Their secretary made an appointment for her the next afternoon. Pleased and excited, she decided to take a walk. She went to the emergency clinic five blocks away. The sky was pale, the glare intense. The air was warm, but a light breeze kept things mild. No humidity. She felt pounds lighter, rested and ready to tackle the unknown.

This feeling was tempered slightly by the news that she had a broken toe. Treatment? Wear flat, open-toed shoes for four to six weeks. It couldn't have been worse. How could she go on interviews wearing flat-heeled shoes? She decided to go right back to the Club and rest her foot all day and tomorrow wear the black, pointed-toed high heels to meet the agents. This seemed symbolic of the way she always felt, trying to look perfect, but knowing something was not quite right.

The following afternoon she took a taxi out on Sunset Boulevard to the agents' office. The secretary ushered her in almost immediately. Behind an enormous desk sat a middle-aged, balding, overweight man with a cigar stuck in his too-full lips. To his right stood a thin, tanned man looking at his watch. She walked in and sat in the chair that was offered directly in front of them. They didn't say anything after "hello," just looked. Then they asked about her acting experience. When she finished the short résumé, Irving, the man behind the desk, spoke, "You're too skinny, not blond, just not a Warner Brother's type. That's where we send the majority of our clients. You're not right for Warner's."

She got hot all over, wanted to run but sat still and said nothing. Bernie, the thin one, quietly suggested she go into the bathroom and take down her hair. She went down the hall and took out the pins holding her beehive in place. Hair fell around her shoulders that she tried to shake into some sort of order. She didn't have a brush, never dreaming she would need it.

"Turn around," they said when she returned.

"That's better," they said.

"Well," said the cigar to the reed, "want to take her out to see Solly?"

"I'll call and see what I can do. Sweetie, give me a call on Friday. I'll try and set something up," Bernie promised.

Out on the sidewalk, she decided she had better not repeat the extravagance of the taxi ride across town so hobbled painfully across the busy boulevard to a bus stop and sat on the wooden bench. What am I going to do? I can't cry right here. She felt herself leave her body for a moment, floating overhead among the skyscrapers until the bus came. She asked herself over and over on the long ride back to the Studio Club, what am I going to do?

With a sinking heart, she related the afternoon's experiences to Nancy who didn't seemed too alarmed.

"They're trying to set up an interview for you with Solly Biano, head casting director at Warner Brothers. Maybe he'll like you."

"I sure hope so. What's he like? Have you met him?"

"Yes, a couple of months ago after the Playboy spread. He's OK and if he likes you, you could be cast in something."

Nancy had been the Miss April centerfold in Playboy Magazine. She said she had done it for the money, $5000, to subsidize her acting career.

"Come with me tonight," Nancy urged. "I'm going to a party at Ricky Blaze's. It's better than moping around here."

Ricky Blaze was a character actor of forgettable talent who had a great affinity for beautiful women. He had met Nancy when they were auditioning for parts in a short-lived series at Desilu Studios. She became a regular at his parties and he liked to be seen with her on his arm. He told Krake he was glad she could join them. They left in his Cadillac, listening to him drop names.

"I've got to call Cary. He said he would try to make it, but his back's been bothering him. I hope he can come. He always loves my parties." Ricky glanced in the rear-view mirror to catch Krake's reaction.

Krake was duly impressed and intimidated. Cary Grant? Really? What would she say if she met him?

High in the hills, overlooking Hollywood, Ricky's house was a two-story Mediterranean style, attractively surrounded by the lush foliage of southern California. Krake looked around for stars, but didn't see any. Sitting at a table where several people were talking, they had rum drinks and ate hors d'oeuvres. A rather pleasant-looking brunette with a round face introduced as Debbie, dominated the conversation.

"Oh, Ty drank a lot. I can just see him sitting at the bar every morning, drink in hand."

Ty? Oh my God! It's Debbie Power, Tyrone Power's widow. She looked so ordinary. Power had died recently in Spain while making a movie, leaving a young widow and baby. Krake was thrilled. The impact of sitting at the same table with Tyrone Power's widow was enough to render her speechless. She was grateful when the party was over and she could stop smiling. Her jaws ached. It seems Cary couldn't make it to Ricky's that evening. Oh well, I nearly met Cary Grant and I've only been in Hollywood a week.

Bernie Bellamy called on Friday to say he had arranged a meeting with Solly Biano for the following Tuesday. He would pick her up and told her to be sure to wear something sexy. Sexy! How could she possibly wear something sexy, her feet in flat-heeled shoes? She agonized over what to wear. Her trunk hadn't arrived from Texas. The sexiest dress she had was an olive-green knit with a deep scoop neck. It was sleeveless and very tight. What shoes? The only possible choice was her one pair of mid-heeled thong sandals. The half-inch heels gave her legs the angle they needed to look good, but the color, white, was all wrong. Why hadn't her trunk come? She hated to spend money on shoes when she had so many pairs already.

Feeling less than glamorous on Tuesday, she rode with Bernie to the Warner Brother's lot in Burbank. The ride took nearly an hour. It was hot as they walked from the parking lot to Biano's office. Bellamy stopped.

"Walk ahead of me," he commanded. Krake walked self-consciously a little way ahead.

"Not bad," he intoned," not bad."

They entered Biano's office and were ushered into his private enclave. A slight, white-haired man behind an enormous desk rose and shook her hand.

After introductions and a verbal résumé, Krake pointed to her shoes. "I broke my toe and these are the only shoes I can wear." She had to stop herself from adding, "I know they don't go with this dress."

It did seem to relax everyone a little. Biano said he would like her to do a scene or reading for him in a week. Bellamy set up an appointment.

"Do you think he likes me?" she asked on the way to the car.

"He wants to see you again, that's something." Bellamy drove her back to the Studio Club where she found a note from Nancy saying she would be in Chicago for a week on a Playboy photo shoot. Moan, no one to talk this over with and help pick a reading for Biano.

Fortunately, she had a copy of one of Gerry's short stories she had done on closed-circuit television in Houston last summer. Set in the south, it was a whimsical account of love. She decided to do that since she knew no one with whom to do a scene. The Studio Club atmosphere was strange. Seemingly a dorm, there was little of the sound of girlish chatter heard down the halls. When she had spoken to several of the women she passed on the way to the dining room or the ironing room, they had looked at her in astonishment. Had she lapsed into Greek? Was she wearing the wrong head, or skirt, or, God forbid, garter belt? Could they sense from her voice that she was licentious and no good? Gradually she learned it was competition, nothing else. Every new face, especially an attractive one, was looked upon as a threat. With hundreds of women vying for every part, the threat was real. The ensemble feeling of theater was absent.

What was she going to wear? The ever-present dilemma. She decided to walk down to Hollywood Boulevard and see if she could find anything halfway decent. She walked briskly, like her mother, always fast, rain or shine. She passed the Hollywood Ranch Market, a 24-hour grocery store. That was a first for Krake. She stopped to buy cigarettes, but the man behind the counter wouldn't sell her any. You had to be twenty-one. She didn't have a driver's license or a birth certificate.

"I'm twenty-three."

"Sorry, no ID, no cigarettes."

She had been buying cigarettes for Daddy since she was ten. She continued on to the famous corner of Hollywood and Vine. On the near left was the Broadway department store. She went in, found the junior department and saw numerous dresses she liked, but they were too expensive. She walked further down the Boulevard. It was like being in a carnival. She could hardly keep her mouth from gaping open. In 1961, this "boulevard of dreams" was seedy, but had remnants of respectability. There were a lot of shops full of souvenirs and cheap mementos. She rushed past Frederick's of Hollywood, glancing quickly through her sunglasses at the scantily-clad mannequins in the window. Oh my God, it's really here. Further on there was a shop with cheap clothes in the windows. She went in and bought a white cotton sheath for $10. She was elated. She had never bought such an inexpensive dress. Would it look all right? On her lithe, tanned body it seemed wonderful. With no one's opinion to rely on except her own, she decided to let go of her shopping training, which consisted of buying labels instead of clothes. Lorraine, like most of her contemporaries, spoke in labels. "My Mr. Mort, my Herbert Levines, my Dalton," and everyone knew what she meant. But Krake had to make her money last, so she abandoned all that.

She was both frightened and excited to be this much on her own and, unaware of the courage she exhibited, wished only that she felt secure and confident. She wandered down a few more blocks to Pickwick Books, the largest bookstore she had ever been in. Overwhelmed by the rows and rows of books, she left and retraced her steps to the Club. When she turned the corner and started down Lodi Place, she saw Sid Blackstone in front of her. God! Why me? She smiled, shoved the cheap dress under her arm (the vestiges of snobbery clinging to her) and extended her hand.

"Krake, I've called and left messages. Didn't you get them?"

Busted! She declared her innocence and he talked her into going to dinner with him that night. It was better than eating the institutional food, or was it? He took her to a hamburger joint not far from the Club. He insisted afterwards that they had to go up to Mulholland Drive to see the lights.

It was dark by the time they reached the ridge that stood between the San Fernando Valley and Hollywood. The view was spectacular. They got out of the car and stood on the edge of the world, where the city lights met the starlight. She gazed in amazement. Sid's arm crept around her shoulders. She moved away. He followed. Why couldn't this be Burg or Will? When they got back in the car, she quickly lit a cigarette. She had bought a pack at the hamburger joint. Being with a man made her legitimate and her age wasn't questioned.

Conversation waned and soon, cigarettes out, he kissed her. Why can't I just say no? I can't hurt his feelings, I'll endure this. She pleaded tiredness. He drove down to the lowlands and promised he would call soon. Never would be too soon. She thanked him for the burger and view and retreated to her green sanctuary.

The following Tuesday she read for Biano wearing the new white dress and matching sandals. He had no response. She didn't know if she had been good or terrible. Bernie said he would let her know if anything came up. Don't call us, we'll call you. Stricken, she tearfully put in a call to Lewis who was in New York City reading for a Broadway play. His voice sounded good, familiar. "Don't worry. If the brothers can't help someone else will. Got pencil and paper?"

"No."

"Remember this name. Ben Knox. He's in the phone book, used to work with the Bellamys. Tell him I told you to call. Don't worry, sweetheart, it'll work out."

She thanked him and hung up. Yeah, easy for you to say, Lewis, easy for you to say.

She called information, got Knox's number and called him. He agreed to see her the next day. Back on the buses, she made her way to his small office, closer in on Sunset. He opened the door himself. His face lit up. She sat down in his office and he proceeded to say he could find her work easily. He thought she was beautiful and "If Lewis recommends you, I know you can act. Do you have any photos, a composite?" She showed him the pictures from the Alley.

"These'll never do. I want you to go to Maximillian on Wilshire across from Bullock's department store. She's photographed all the greats, been in the business for years. Expensive, but worth it." He gave her a phone number and a hug.

"What'll I wear?"

"Don't worry, Maxi'll tell you."

It took a week before Maxi could fit her in. Krake brought her overnight bag to the studio with the changes Maxi had suggested. A tiny woman in her sixties, Maximillian invaded the dressing room where Krake was trying to apply makeup. She had arrived with her hair in a French roll so Maxi could shoot the sophisticated poses first. Maxi insisted upon doing her makeup. She applied eyeliner and false lashes and outlined Krake's lips slightly outside their shape. The total effect was startling. Hollywood glamour. Maxi was overjoyed at Krake's photogenic qualities and they worked together for over two hours. Krake loved the total attention and basked in the glow of flattery and floodlights. She became a movie queen of the

40s for the afternoon. First she was Merle Oberon, then Rita Hayworth and finally Hedy Lamar. At the end of the shoot, she hated to scrub off the wondrous makeup, but knew the harsh light of day wouldn't be as flattering.

A long week went by before the photos were ready. In the meantime, Ben arranged a meeting with his biggest male actor, Tom Herriot, to prepare a scene for various casting directors. Tom, a totally unpretentious man in his late twenties, won her heart immediately. Married, with two children, he had been working in TV for three years, appearing on *Gunsmoke*, the *Untouchables* and in a continuing role on *The Young Doctors*, a daytime soap. They decided on a scene from Tennessee Williams' *Twenty-Seven Wagons Full of Cotton*, which had recently been made into the Carroll Baker movie, *Babydoll*. The first read-through was stilted and awkward. Krake felt they needed a director. Ben tried to help, but he really didn't have the expertise.

Maxi's office called to say the contact sheets were ready. Krake rushed down, picked them up and took them over to Ben's office. This process took the entire morning, two buses to get to Maxi's and three to get to Ben's. Public transportation in this sprawling city was poor.

When Ben saw the contact sheets, his mouth fell open. "You are so photogenic! I don't know which ones we should pick, they're all good."

They were. She looked like every movie star she had ever emulated. In reality, because of the "star" makeup job, the photos didn't look much like her. Ben chose three for 8 x 10s and a composite.

Soon she and Tom were doing *Twenty-Seven Wagons Full of Cotton* all over town. As soon as Ben showed her photos to a casting director, he wanted to meet her. When she was in their offices, they only said, "You don't look much like these photos." How stupid! Didn't they realize you were specially made-up for a photo shoot? But their comments made her feel even more inadequate.

On an interview for a *Dobie Gillis* spot, the casting director said she had the part after hearing her read. She was so excited. As she was leaving, he shouted, "How tall are you?"

"Five foot six," she replied.

"I'm sorry, you'll be too tall wearing high heels to play opposite Dwayne Hickman."

"I'll wear flats." Her happiness took a downward spiral.

"Sorry, this is a very sexy role and the character has to wear heels."

Slowly she walked into the sunlight. She wanted to scream. So close! So close! Then NO! Because I'm too tall.

Ben sent her on an interview for a play, Lewis John Carlino's *The Brick and the Rose*. She didn't want to do stage, but Ben convinced her that it was part of the process. Casting directors were known to frequent these local productions and might decide to use you in something. Sitting on a stool in a drugstore was a myth as far as being discovered was concerned. The criteria for landing a part seemed almost as whimsical.

The tryouts were held in a small theater on Santa Monica Boulevard. Several people were in the audience and two seated on the stage when she arrived. Richard Wells, a handsome, curly-haired actor, looked familiar. She read with him and was given the part of the ingenue. Richard said she was the best and asked where she was from. When she mentioned the Alley, he said he had worked there for two years before coming to Hollywood. Now she remembered seeing pictures of him in the theater's photo album. He had played the lead in *The Fugitive Kind* and was rumored to have been Nina's lover.

As they were leaving the theater, the owner, a former Houstonian, learning that Krake had worked at the Alley, asked if she knew Will Stoner. Her heart took a nosedive. "Yes, but I haven't seen him in awhile," she said.

"We were both in the Armed Forces special services program in Korea. He went back to Houston and I came out here."

That night, plagued with thoughts of Will, Krake didn't fall asleep until dawn. The pain persisted.

12

Many of the small theater groups in the area offered acting classes. It was one way to help finance production costs and serious actors were always working to improve their skills. At Ben's urging, Krake enrolled in a group called the Players. During the first session, she recognized a freckle-faced strawberry blond from the Studio Club rehearsing in a corner of the large hall. After class, Krake introduced herself and Gail offered her a lift back to the club.

Gail's parents had lived in Spain since McCarthy's witch hunt blacklisted her father, Trevor Trent, a screenwriter who attended a few subversive meetings, or so they said. They had moved to Spain when Gail was in grade school. The Trents had sent Gail back to the states to continue her education at Hollywood High. After graduating, she got an agent and began to make the rounds. She had had small parts on a few sitcoms, the latest being *The Real McCoys.* She and Krake decided to rent an apartment together.

The Brick and the Rose rehearsals were slow and plodding.

Richard asked her out. Not to relieve the boredom, she hoped. He took her to the Jade Gardens on the Strip, an expensive, dimly-lit Chinese restaurant with unusually attractive decor. They sat in the bar until their table was ready. "I never drink this much, but tonight I just feel like it," Krake said, downing her fourth Black Russian. She didn't remember eating dinner, but she had a vague memory of necking in the front seat of Richard's borrowed car until the Club's twelve o'clock curfew.

Richard was warm and easy to be with, like the boys she had grown up with. Simple, with basic values like respect and consideration of her feelings. Not a bit like Terry Phelps, the record producer Nancy fixed her up with. They had double dated a few weeks before, going to Malibu for dinner. The meal was good and on the way back to Hollywood, Terry invited her to go swimming at a client's house in Zuma Beach the next day.

He picked her up at eleven and they drove the scenic route out Sunset Boulevard to the Pacific. The night before it had been too dark to see the lovely homes set far back from the street with expanses of geranium beds. In upstate New York, geraniums were considered exotic. Lorraine was always trying to keep one alive. Here they grew like weeds.

On the way, they stopped at a large, Spanish-style house with a circular drive. It belonged to another of Terry's clients. He had to pick up a musical score that needed new lyrics. A Mexican servant let them in. High vaulted ceilings with roughhewn beams met her eyes in the entry way and living room. Krake sat stiffly on a fawn-colored suede sofa while Terry went to find his client who was taking a sauna in his downstairs gym. A huge cabinet housing an elaborate stereo system was emitting unfamiliar musical sounds. Abstract music of drums, flutes and vibes. Looking around at the cavernous living room furnished in rustic Mexican furniture with a Goya spotlighted on one wall, she felt mouse-like and almost squeaked when Terry came back.

They continued out Sunset and she marveled at the beauty; lush, green-leafed canyons with glimpses of houses covered with gold, orange and magenta bougainvillea and trumpet vines. It was the antithesis of flat, steamy Texas. The air felt alive, not oppressive. The blue of the sky increased as they left the smog and neared the Pacific Coast Highway and the deeper blue of the sea rose to join it. I wish I could live out here, she thought.

Terry parked the red Mercedes convertible right on the highway and opened a door in a wall a few feet away. They went through a flowering garden and entered another door that led into a vast, glassed-in room overlooking the ocean. People were talking and laughing, some on lounge chairs, others seated at tables, a few playing cards. Everyone was friendly and after brief introductions, she went into the master bedroom to change into her swimsuit. The airy room had views of the pounding surf and bamboo furniture covered in tropical prints. Her white one-piece felt too revealing, so she hid in a beach towel. She and Terry descended the steps down to the beach and spread a blanket the hostess had provided.

The cold Pacific hurled itself at her feet. Never a strong swimmer, she was apprehensive but ran in anyway. After a dozen steps she was hit by a huge wave and knocked flat. So much for the hair. She got up gasping and continued on. SMACK! This time she got up more slowly. A series of inconsequential lappings at her thighs was relaxing. She turned to say something to Terry when the biggest wave so far picked her up and swept her into its churning fury. She held her breath, wondering if she would drown. She was tumbling around when Terry's hand grasped her shoulder and pulled her on shore. She sat there blinking and coughing, trying to appear unaffected by it all.

"I'll say one thing for you, you've got guts," he said as they returned to the blanket. "Have you ever swum in the ocean before?"

"Not anything like this. I've been in the Atlantic and the gulf in Texas but it doesn't get like this except in a hurricane."

"You have to be careful here. Those waves can suck you under in a second."

Back at the house, they dried off, changed and had a bite to eat. Then Terry announced he had to get back, something about an early appointment in the morning. She asked if she could make a collect call to her father. Terry told her to hurry. She sat down on the tropical prints in the bedroom and called home.

"Hello," Hank answered.

"Hi, Daddy."

"Krake, are you all right?"

"Yes, Daddy. I'm at a beach house on the Pacific ocean. It's the most beautiful place I've ever seen. The flowers, the white sand, this house, everything. I wish you were here. You have to come out as soon as you can. You'd love it."

"It sounds great, Princess. As soon as I get some money together, we'll come for a visit."

"Oh, Daddy, you have to live here. I know you'll want to. It's so much prettier than Texas."

Just then Terry leaned in the door motioning that he was leaving.

"Daddy, my date has to go so I'll say good-bye. I miss you so much."

"I miss you too, honey. Write us," he urged.

"OK, Daddy. I love you. Bye."

In front of the Club, Terry kissed her goodnight, pawing at her breasts. She pushed his hands away. He took her to dinner the next Friday night and afterwards pawed her again. She resisted. "Are you going to go to bed with me?" he asked.

Shocked, she murmured, "No."

"I'll say goodbye," he replied. "I have no time for this. I don't date women I don't sleep with." She got out of the car and he drove away.

Confused and hurt by this treatment, she didn't think he really meant it. He did. He never called again. No one had ever treated her so insensitively, like she was a piece of ass and nothing more. "Tits and ass" was becoming more of a reality. At least Richard courted her. Being an out-of-work actor, the dinners were usually hamburgers and the flowers plucked from hedges, but the caring was there.

Gail and Krake finally found a duplex on Gower Street above Franklin Avenue. A small living room, two bedrooms and a bath plus a kitchen supplied with dishes and silverware seemed adequate. Furnished and a rent of seventy dollars a month convinced them this was it. In one morning they moved the boxes and trunks of clothing from the Studio Club to the apartment.

In the afternoon, Krake was alone when a man from the hardware store delivered the items they had purchased earlier. Without a word, he put a hand of each of Krake's breasts. She backed away, covering herself, and exclaimed, "No!" "You know you were asking for it," he commented and left.

She ran to the door and locked it. She had "asked for it?" What was this world she had flown so willingly to? Men don't date you because you won't have sex? Delivery men feel free to touch your breasts in broad daylight? Did she have WHORE tattooed on her forehead? Were her mother's suspicions correct? What an utterly disgusting creature she must be!

As soon as Gail returned, Krake told her what had happened. Gail reassured her that she had done nothing to provoke the attack. "The delivery boy probably assumed you were an actress," she said. "I mentioned I had an appointment at Twentieth, remember? When people in this town think you are an actress, they feel it gives them license to do what they want." She reminded Krake that they couldn't tell the landlady they were actresses or she wouldn't have rented to them. In order to have a phone installed without a big deposit, Krake had to call Elton Henry who told the phone company she was his secretary, thus eliminating the $75 deposit they would pay because they were unemployed actresses. This stigma attached to acting was a puzzlement. A difficult profession requiring dedication and hard work for little pay, it seemed people would give it some respect, but that wasn't the case.

A month after they moved in, Thanksgiving arrived. Krake cooked a Thanksgiving eve feast for Richard, Gail and her boyfriend, Mark; duck stuffed with apricot dressing and served with fruit sauce, two bottles of Leibfraumilch, and assorted side dishes. The four of them ate the wonderful meal by candlelight. After dinner, Gail and Mark retired to her bedroom while Richard and Krake cleaned up. Krake wanted more wine. There never seemed to be enough. But all the stores were closed except the Hollywood Ranch Market and Richard didn't want to go all that way. Krake had no choice but to fight the craving. They washed the dishes and retired to the bedroom.

Although they had been dating for two months, Krake and Richard had not had sex. They were mostly with other people when they were together, besides both enjoyed courting. Richard was particularly amorous after the duck and wine and Krake thought, why not?

The next morning they got up early and stole out to have breakfast at a tiny restaurant near Hollywood Boulevard that specialized in omelets. Afterwards, they walked to Richard's room on Beechwood Drive. Krake looked around at the unappealing furnished room with a hot plate and was grateful for her apartment. Richard pulled her down on the bed which dominated the space. Krake's body responded to his sensual touch. Her sexual passion seemed akin to her drinking, she always wanted more. While making love, she felt she had power over her partner. Afterwards the power seemed to shift to him, as if she had given something up. With each encounter her vulnerability increased while her desire lessened.

As far as birth control, Krake was a woman of her times. She closed her mind to the possibility of pregnancy. Even condoms were not an option. If a man had a condom it meant the woman was a whore. Everyone just hoped for the best and so far Krake had been lucky.

Right after Thanksgiving, Krake received a call from Lester Hadley, a member of the Ford Grant at the Alley. He was in Hollywood now. A friend of his from the Actors Studio in New York had written a play and was looking for an ingenue lead. Lester had thought of her. The play, *Virtue Wins*, starred Isabel Jewell, a B-movie actress of the thirties and forties who had fallen into obscurity. Krake agreed to read.

Lester picked her up the next day and they drove to an apartment complex on Cahuenga. They descended a flight of stairs to a large, well-furnished basement apartment. A tall, heavy-set man with thinning blond hair shook her hand. "I'm Donald Meyers, the guy who wrote this thing. You must be Krake." A small, delicately formed woman who looked like a child emerged from the kitchen. "Hi, I'm Sarah, Don's wife." A couple from the Actors Studio were there, Brice Parkinson and his wife, Angela Storm. Brice took one look and said she was too sexy to read for the part of the ingenue but would be perfect for Paula Kondra, the secretary. The reading took well over two hours and Krake knew she was terrible although no one said anything. She still held out the hope that they would use her.

How quickly she had changed from the fairy princess and Sally O'Hare to a siren! The term sexy didn't feel comfortable. To her it implied confidence, 42-Z tits (not her 34-Bs) and maturity, none of which she had. Although she had said to herself that she didn't want to do theater for awhile because there was no money in it, these people were talented, had depth and were part of a world she would like to be in.

The next morning Lester called and said she had the part. A week before, *The Brick and the Rose*, had lost its backers and been put on hold. She knew Ben would be pleased to learn she had been cast in something else.

The show was to be presented in the Hollywood Center Theater on Las Palmas in the heart of Hollywood. Richard went with her on the first day of rehearsals and became assistant stage manager and Brice's understudy. Krake would be understudying Angela, cast as the ingenue.

Since she was in only one scene in the second act, she didn't have to come to rehearsals until after Christmas. Needing money, she and Gail tried selling Avon Cosmetics. It was a total disaster.

Krake rang the doorbell and said, "Avon calling," just like on TV, but could do nothing more. Frozen with fear, she sat like a lump while Gail introduced the products, demonstrated their use and gave out samples. They took one order in two weeks. Discouraged, they applied to I. Magnin's on Wilshire Boulevard and got jobs as Christmas help, Krake in cosmetics and Gail in lingerie.

In the orientation session the Saturday before they began, they were told the history of the store and informed they could only wear black, brown or gray clothing. There was to be no smoking or flirting and they must be polite. The pay was $1.25 an hour. They arrived for their first day wearing high heels, flat-heeled shoes not being considered chic. The older, more experienced saleswomen advised them to bring a change of shoes. After standing for eight hours, they knew this was probably the most valuable advice they would get.

As Christmas approached, the store got busier and busier. The second week of the three-week stint, Ben called to tell Krake she had an appointment early the next morning with the casting director of a daytime TV show called *A Day In Court*. She rose at six, dressed for work in a brown wool sheath, hair in a French roll and braved the rigors of the bus system to arrive at the casting director's office just before nine. She was not due at Magnin's until ten.

The main character in the script was a fifteen-year-old who runs away from home to live with an older sister, the part

Krake was reading for. The casting director, Helen Travers, explained that the script dealt with the older sister's suitability to be the legal guardian. In 1961, an unattached female under the age of 25 living alone was looked upon with suspicion. Her character was supposed to be very sexy. Krake still found this strange as applied to her.

When she got home after work, Ben called and said she was cast. Her first TV show! Yahoo! It was scheduled for production the following Tuesday when she was supposed to be at Magnin's from ten to six. She called in sick.

The show was filmed at Desilu Studios. Krake wore her hair down and the revealing olive-green dress. Helen Travers hardly recognized her. The day was a blur. It was her first time on a sound stage and she felt nervous. People were milling around everywhere. The courtroom set was small, but surrounded by several cameras, boom microphones, lights and makeup tables. They shot her scene right after lunch. The director merely told her when to enter, where to stop and how to sit. She never was introduced to the girl playing her sister and there was no rehearsal. Feeling lost without one and confused as to what was expected of her, she muddled through two run-throughs. They shot it in one take and were finished by two-thirty. She had no idea what her performance was like. It was so different from stage work. There, you had some knowledge of what to do, how to approach a character and if your performance was good.

In this medium, hitting your mark seemed to be the most important thing. The good news was that she made as much money in one day as working three weeks at Magnin's.

At the end of three weeks, Gail and Krake's feet were aching and any patience they had left was wearing thin. The store manager spoke about them staying on to learn the marketing end of the retail clothing business. They said they would think about it. It took a split second. No, acting was in their blood.

After Christmas, with daily rehearsals of *Virtue*, Krake spent almost every night at Richard's apartment. They came and went to the theater together and often only stopped by the duplex to get her mail. She felt guilty, had a hard time looking Gail in the eye. She knew she had abandoned her, but the need to be with Richard was stronger. She hated sleeping alone and felt incomplete without a man sharing her life. Just as Daddy had been her main source of support, now Richard was.

The play was absorbing and rehearsals were fascinating. Brice Parkinson was an actor's actor. Schooled in the Method, by its best known promoters, Lee Strasberg and Elia Kazan, Brice was a revelation. This was the first time Krake had observed Method acting and she was amazed at his meticulous attention to detail. Early in rehearsals she found him lying prone backstage before his entrance cue. Alarmed, she leaned down and asked if he was all right. He mumbled a reply. "What?" she couldn't hear him. He roared up, "Leave me alone, can't you see I'm preparing?" Startled by this response and not understanding, she kept her distance for awhile.

One day during a break, she started dancing an Irish jig to some music blaring out of a portable radio. Brice watched from the audience and spoke as she finished twirling. "Have you studied acting?"

"No, I've just done it. I did take a class at the Players a couple of months ago, that's all." In college, the acting portion of drama classes had meant being in plays.

"I thought so. I teach an acting class at my house in the Valley and when this play is over I'd like you to join it. You have a good instrument, but it needs tuning."

She was enormously pleased and puzzled. I have a good instrument. What does that mean? She was afraid to appear stupid by asking.

His wife, Angela, was well schooled in the art of performing. Having been everything from a Copa girl at New

York's famed Copacabana Club to playing Carol Cutrer in an off-Broadway revival of Tennessee Williams' *Orpheus Descending*, Angela taught Krake a lot. She had what Walter Winchell had called, writing in his column about her, the "Geraldine Page fire."

The most colorful member of *Virtue's* cast was Isabel Jewell. Krake didn't remember seeing any of her films although her Playbill biography stated she had been in over 100 movies and TV shows, starring in *Lost Horizon, Tale Of Two Cities* and *Northwest Passage*. She had won the film critics award for her portrayal in *Marked Woman*. Her long stage runs in *Counselor at Law*, with Otto Kruger, and *Of Mice and Men*, with Wallace Ford, were a source of pride. Krake vaguely remembered her role as Belle in *Gone With The Wind.*

One afternoon after rehearsal, when Donald was giving Isabel, Krake and Richard a ride home, Isabel urged Donald to drive further up into the Hollywood Hills. There on an obscure promontory stood an adobe-colored mansion. Black iron gates prevented them from driving up the steep driveway, but from what they could see, the house and grounds covered half the hillside.

"That was my house," Isabel sighed.

"When?" asked Krake.

"From 1942 til 49."

"What happened?"

"Isabel paused, "I got sick and had to stop working for awhile."

Everyone knew what happened. The booze! There was always the danger that Isabel's drinking might surface before *Virtue* opened. As a precautionary measure, Donald had rented a motel room for her and her invalid mother near the theater for the run of the play. It was arranged that the costume designer would stay in an adjoining room; ostensibly to help care for Isabel's mother, but in reality to keep an eye on them both.

Krake's TV debut on *A Day In Court* aired in the middle of January, just before the play opened. Krake didn't have a set so on the broadcast day she went to the department store on the corner of Hollywood and Vine, took the elevator to the third-floor major appliance section, discreetly changed channels until she found the program, and sat down amidst the surrounding activity to watch. She refrained from shouting to passersby, "Hey, that's me!" There was one shot of her walking away from the camera and her butt looked huge! The camera adds ten pounds, they say. Ever since the Bellamy brothers told her that she was too skinny, she had been indulging in huge breakfasts of French toast and jam and at night lots of ice cream. Her clothes did seem a bit tighter, but the rear view of her on screen was appalling. Despite the standard of the times, a big ass had little appeal as far as she was concerned. She went on a diet of popcorn and red wine immediately. The first of a lifetime.

Despite a torrential downpour, *Virtue Wins* opened to a packed house. Listening backstage, Krake heard everyone receive entrance applause. Would she? Her scene wasn't until the second act. When it came, so did the clapping and she was grateful. Although bravos and three curtain calls marked the end of the play, the reviews were mixed. However the main criticism was directed at the play rather than the acting. Attendance dropped off. Some nights, there were more people on stage than in the audience.

The play ran three weeks. During the final week, Angela and Brice called in sick. As their understudies, Krake and Richard had to go on. Krake panicked, with good reason. The character of Norma had many lines and was on stage three-quarters of the play. There was no time for rehearsal. As soon as they reached the theater, they appropriated the stage manager's script and attempted to learn the blocking. Never dreaming she would be called upon to perform, she had not bothered to really memorize Norma's lines. Now she fervently wished she had. Isabel rehearsed with her backstage until places were called.

The entire performance assumed an unreal quality. She missed cues, forgot blocking. The stage manager whispered her lines as did her fellow actors. At last it was over and they took their bows. Isabel stepped forward, raised her hands to quiet the applause of the sparse audience, and taking Krake by the wrist, led her forward.

Her voice rang out, "I want you to know this girl, Krake Forrester, went on tonight without a rehearsal and gave an excellent performance. Don't you agree?"

The audience clapped. Krake was very moved. She embraced Isabel backstage and never forgot the gesture. She had no clue as to the quality of her performance, was only grateful to have gotten through it. Richard's acting job had been adequate too. No one made mention of his achievements that evening. Maybe it was obvious she needed the support.

Two days before *Virtue* closed, Krake succumbed to the persistent nagging feeling and went to pick up her mail. She hadn't been there in weeks. She told Gail that she would be moving at out the end of the month, that she and Richard were moving in together. Gail didn't seem surprised or particularly disturbed by this because she was planning to return to Spain for her annual visit with her parents. Krake picked up her pile of mail, but didn't go through it until she got to Richard's. Near the bottom was a yellow telegram. Assuming it must be from someone wishing her well on the play's opening, she tore it open. The words seared themselves into her brain. "Nina Vance has recommended you for our new series at Revue. Will you contact the studio immediately? Sincerely, Peter Tewksbury."

She screamed! The telegram was dated two weeks ago.

Richard ran in from the bathroom. "What's wrong?"

"I just went over to Gail's to get my mail and found this." She showed it to him. "What'll I do?" She started to cry.

It was six-thirty in the evening. She tried the studio in vain. Everyone had gone home. She couldn't sleep. An opportunity had dropped in her lap and she hadn't known it. Why had guilt stopped her from picking up her mail? Why hadn't Gail called when the telegram arrived? Why? Why? Why? She agonized all night.

Early the next morning, she called Tewksbury's office. His secretary informed her that the series was cast and there was "No reason for Mr. Tewksbury to see you. Sorry." Krake cried and cried. She was irresponsible. Her mother had told her that over and over. It was true. She wanted to yell and tear things in two. Instead she wept and got drunk. The hangover dulled the sharp ache of a missed opportunity.

13

The acting class met on Tuesday afternoons in the pool house behind Brice and Angela's. The group ranged in age and acting experience from a teenage studio contractee, a leopard-clothed vamp who constantly complained that men were hitting on her, to a character actor in his seventies, a veteran of forty-six stage plays. Sitting in canvas chairs arranged in a semi-circle, the fifteen of them began with exercises called sense memories; for instance lifting an imaginary brick after lifting a real one and trying to duplicate the experience.

The process was an entirely new one for Krake. She quickly learned how out of touch she was with her senses, physical and emotional. Her awareness of the infinite ways the body and psyche react to stimuli increased immensely. She learned that certain memories evoke certain emotions. For the first time, she went into herself to find the key elements in creating a character.

Brice assigned a scene from a Dorothy Parker short story entitled "Here We Are," an amusing look at honeymooners starting married life. They learned their lines rapidly and rehearsed constantly. As her classwork kept missing the mark, Krake became depressed, insecure and confused. Hadn't she won awards for her college acting? And Nina had said her portrayal of Sally O'Hare was as good as a Broadway performance. She was at her wit's end one afternoon when they began the scene.

"Well, here we are," Richard said.

"Yes, here we are," she replied and burst into tears.

It was unrehearsed and came out of the hopelessness she experienced about never becoming a good actress, at least by Actors Studio standards. She said her lines through the tears and it was good. Just what he wanted. He came up and hugged her at the end, "I knew you could do it. This is what I've been talking about. Find a real emotion, past or current and use it in the scene you're doing on stage. The more unexpected the better." She caught a glimmer of what Method acting was all about.

Ben called when they returned home after class and asked her to go on an interview for a play being done at the Stage Society. She refused. They had a big fight on the phone. He had sent no casting directors to see *Virtue Wins*. She was tired of working for nothing and wanted to make money. That was the reason she had come to Hollywood instead of going to New York. He told her she needed all the experience and exposure she could get, but she remained firm in her refusal and ended up telling him to send her the photo composites and the film she had bought of the *Day In Court*.

"I'm getting another agent!" she said, slamming down the phone.

Looking for one proved demeaning. Most established agents were reluctant to take unknowns because they would have to pound the pavement to get them jobs. These men sat behind big desks and said she was too pretty or not pretty enough, or too tall, or too thin, or just not right for this office. Some advised her to wear falsies. She left many interviews feeling lower than a snake's belly.

Two days after the blow up, Ben called and said he had been working on an interview for her with *Ozzie and Harriet* and it had come through. They wanted to meet her. She did have a contract with Ben, so she went. The series had been running for years although she had seldom seen it. Since high school, she had been too busy to watch much TV.

Ozzie and Harriet was shot in the old red-brick Charlie Chaplin Studios in Hollywood. She had no sooner taken a seat in the casting director's office when Ozzie Nelson walked in, exuding warmth and charm. She read and he said he was pleased. She left feeling hopeful. Ben called that evening with the news she had been cast. The part was a sexy girlfriend of Ricky's.

The script came the next morning by messenger. She rehearsed her long scenes with Richard over and over. A week later she reported to makeup at seven a.m. Harriet Nelson sat in the chair next to her. Krake said hello and Harriet nodded by way of response. That was the only interaction they had the entire day. Harriet appeared to be a very private person. Since they didn't have any scenes together, there was really no reason to converse.

Ozzie, on the other hand, was very outgoing. He insisted Krake come on the set and watch the show being filmed. He had written the script himself and was directing it. When it came time to shoot her scenes with Ricky, he hadn't appeared. Krake rehearsed with the script girl. Ozzie gave her blocking and despite the blinding lights she managed to hit her marks pretty accurately. The technical aspects were more complicated than stage work and made a performance of any depth harder to achieve.

Ricky finally dashed in, didn't know a single line of dialogue and had to be fed every word from the script girl, off camera. This was distracting and made Krake very insecure. Added to it was the fact that as soon as she stood next to Ricky, Ozzie had asked her to remove her high heels since she was the same height. Any feelings of glamour left with them. It must not have showed because Ozzie kept saying, "Haven't had anyone like you, who can act, in a long time." He invited her to view the dailies the next afternoon. After watching her overly dramatic rendition of a sexy girlfriend, she wished he hadn't. She fled as soon as the lights came on in the screening room. Humiliated at blowing it she didn't tell Richard of her poor acting. She never saw the show, having no TV set.

In spite of the disappointment over the performance, she had gained some ground. In order to work on the sitcom, she had to join the Screen Actors Guild which was ordinarily difficult to get into. A producer or director had to be willing to take a chance on hiring a newcomer. Most casting directors were too afraid to risk it because if the actor was bad they, the casting directors, might be fired. But Ozzie Nelson had to answer to no one. The membership fee for the guild was $200, which for an out-of-work actor was not so easy to come by. Krake dipped into her cost-of-living fund to pay it. This was worthwhile because others jobs would follow more easily, one hoped, and the union offered many benefits.

Her relationship with Richard was going well. They had found a studio apartment in a 1930s stucco red-tile roofed, pseudo-Spanish style building, only a block from his room on Beechwood. They enjoyed each other, the sex was good and she was happy. Granted he had no money, no automobile and wasn't aggressive about going after acting jobs, but he nonetheless provided the stability she needed. His various jobs, selling encyclopedias or vacuum cleaners, paid part of the expenses, and she was dependent on his love. She drank only on Saturday night, after they walked down to a nearby store and bought a Sunday paper and a bottle of cheap red wine to wash down the popcorn, which she always finished.

One day in June, Krake received an official-looking envelope from a trade magazine called *Film Marketing and Far East Movie News* published in Tokyo. Unbeknownst to her, her Gramma, (Lorraine's mother) had written to her nephew, whom Krake had never met, regarding her granddaughter's career. The nephew, Charles Craig, editor and publisher of the magazine, sent a list of names of people in the business he suggested Krake contact. He had already written to some of them about her.

Looking at the list of producers, agents and heads of publicity departments at various studios, Krake suffered an attack of stage fright. When she tried to call one of the names on the list, her deep-seated inferiority complex took the receiver out of her hand and placed it back in the cradle. All sorts of imaginary fears took over. How could she get out to Culver City or the Valley? The public transportation system was so poor it would take her a whole day. Excuse after excuse popped up, but fear was the true culprit.

One day she finally managed to call Agents For Artists, a prestigious firm where one of the men on the list worked. His name was Abner Weinstein and he answered before she had a chance to hang up. When she explained who she was, he asked her to drop by the office that afternoon. That afternoon! Much too soon. She would rather fantasize for awhile, but she agreed. Two buses and an hour later she arrived at his office on the far end of the Strip. It was past the Bellamy's office and as the bus went by, she flipped them the bird.

The Agents For Artists offices occupied the whole top floor of a new high-rise. She sank into a sofa in the waiting room. Soon, a young, medium-height, stocky fellow emerged and walked over to her. "Krake Forrester?"

She nodded.

"I'm Abner. Let's go back to my office."

He escorted her down a long hallway. The room was pleasantly furnished in beige and brown Swedish modern. Abner explained he was a writer's agent, but knew a lot of people on the acting end and would be of any assistance he could, although he mentioned nothing specific. Krake had stuck her mother's amethyst ring on in case he should ask her out. He did. She told him she was sort of engaged to an actor.

"Well, maybe we could have lunch sometime."

She guessed that would be OK.

"Have you ever been to the Hamburger Hamlet?"

"No.".

He seemed shocked that she hadn't and added, "It's only a couple of blocks from here. When I get back, we'll go." Abner was traveling to Japan to negotiate a deal with Kurosawa.

At the end of the interview, Abner walked her to the elevator, the doors of which were just opening. Three men stepped out, one of them very tan.

Abner greeted him, "Hello, Bing. Just coming in from the links?"

"Hello, Abner. Yes, we finished thirty-six holes at Mission Hills. Shot a 79 and an 85, not too good." He looked at Krake and smiled.

"Bing, I'd like you to meet Krake Forrester, from Texas. Krake, this is Bing Crosby."

He was shorter than she had imagined (all of them were) and very good-looking. She said, "Hi," then bid Abner adieu and rode the elevator down to the street. All the way home on the bus she went over the incident. Bing Crosby! I was introduced to Bing Crosby! She wanted to tell everyone, but settled for Richard who wasn't too impressed.

A few weeks later on a Saturday afternoon, Krake, Richard, and Sarah were driving with Donald in his car on Hollywood Boulevard. They stopped to buy a paper to check out the movie schedule. Sarah leaned out the front window to hand the man hawking papers some coins. The headlines screamed, "MARILYN MONROE COMMITS SUICIDE." They were deeply shocked and all began talking at once.

"How could she have done it?"

"No, not Marilyn!"

"Why?"

"How did she do it?"

"She was my favorite comedienne."

"She was so sexy."

"Yeah."

The day was saddened by the unexpected loss. Krake was mystified. How could this MOVIE STAR, who had everything, take her own life? It must have been an accident. Yes, that was it, an accident. Donald said he had taken classes with her at the Actors Studio, that she was quiet and shy, almost a recluse. One night after class, he had walked her home. She hardly talked at all. With Donald, there was no need.

That Thanksgiving, Sarah and Donald invited Richard and Krake to dinner at a screenwriter's house in the Hollywood Hills. Donald and the writer, Joel Levy, had collaborated in New York on a script for *The Naked City*.

Thanksgiving Day dawned overcast and muggy, but after months of glare, this kind of weather was a relief. Krake missed summer rains. Rains you could walk in and not catch a cold. Rains with lightning zigzagging across the sky to the second-later accompaniment of thunder. Endless days of sun and smog got boring. A good rain could clear things up, let the scenery put on a fresh face. Goethe once said something to the effect that people who lived under palm trees have to pay the price. The seductive inertia of heat and sun could be paralyzing.

Over the Thanksgiving meal, copious amounts of alcohol were consumed. The discussion was about how Hollywood compared to New York. Joel was adamant that only hacks wrote for the movies and TV.

"What about Fitzgerald, Faulkner and Nathaniel West?" Donald countered.

"That was a long time ago," Joel said. "Now it's just a way to make a buck, TV writing is just something to fill in between advertisements. There's no artistic principle in Hollywood, no integrity. And the acting is a joke. Anyone can act on film, they just reshoot a scene if it's no good." Joel said.

Krake didn't agree. She tried to interject her thoughts about the lack of direction on the *Day In Court*, but Donald and Joel didn't hear her.

The night wore on, Krake got drunk. She suddenly realized that Sarah and Donald were gone. Danielle, Joel's girlfriend, wanted to play strip poker. She was a wardrobe assistant, soft-spoken and very pretty. At her insistence, they agreed to play. Krake quickly lost socks, shoes, a bracelet, ring and finally her sweater. Soon everyone was stripped to their underwear. Sipping warm brandy, she didn't notice Richard and Danielle leave the room. The next thing she knew she was sitting on the floor in her panties telling Joel that the minute she met a man she wondered what he looked like naked.

"I must be an awful pervert," she said. "Only men have thoughts like that, huh?"

"Hell no" Joel snorted. "I think you're healthy to have those ideas." He moved closer and put a hand on her bare knee. "Would you like to make love?"

Drunk enough to tell the truth, she replied, "Not really."

"That's what Danielle and Richard are doing." He took a swallow of his scotch.

"Where?"

"Upstairs in the bedroom." He pointed towards the ceiling.

"I don't believe it."

"Come up and see." He pulled her to her feet and led the way up the carpeted stairs. He opened the bedroom door and stepped aside. She stood silent watching Richard's bare buttocks pumping up and down between Danielle's legs. Joel gazed over her shoulder. His presence made her turn and quickly descend the stairs to the living room.

Dressed again, Krake spent the remainder of the night on the balcony overlooking the vast expanse of the city. Confusing thoughts of morality versus pleasure kept her awake. What has happened to me? Here I am in Hollywood and I feel so disconnected. As though this has nothing to do with me. I thought I would feel a part of things here. But I'm so ashamed to be a part of this. All I ever wanted was a home with a husband and children. Why can't I get it? What's wrong with me? Doesn't Joel care that Danielle's fucking Richard? Do I care? Over and over the same thoughts, until she jumped when Richard's hand touched her shoulder and he said they were leaving.

Joel took them home in his big rented Mercedes. She gratefully pulled down the Murphy bed and crawled in. Still feeling the effects of the alcohol she realized that the sight of Richard fucking another woman was acting as an aphrodisiac. She reached over and hungrily kissed him. Was this the sense of possession men felt? She had to fuck him and fuck him and fuck him. You are mine, her body said. Am I better than she is? Am I prettier, sexier? Do you still love me? All of these questions she whispered in his ear. The more they screwed, the more she wanted. Finally, Richard, pleading fatigue, fell asleep.

What kind of perverse creature am I? Krake thought. This world I'm in is far different from anything I've ever known. Do all these people find free love and sex satisfactory? Don't they find one person and remain true? What happened to the Prince and Happily Ever After? Doesn't it exist? The strange thing was she wasn't jealous of Danielle. She regarded the whole event as a drunken aberration that had little to do with reality.

Hours later she awoke, relaxed but empty. Neither of them referred to the incident.

In Brice's acting class, Krake had been rehearsing a scene with a tall, thin, Anthony Perkins type named Harold Grimes. His agent arranged for him to do a scene for Monica Howser, the head of new talent at Revue Studios, the television section of Universal Studios. Brice thought she would be an excellent partner for him so they spent afternoons at Krake's rehearsing a scene from *Cat On A Hot Tin Roof*.

In addition to acting, Harold dabbled in interior design. At Christmas he brought her many varicolored gels along with sequins and glitter, frills, bows and ribbons. Krake decided to really decorate the apartment. It was her and Richard's first Christmas living together. Worth a few decorations at least. She covered the window panes in the dining room with the translucent gels and the light became a myriad of hues, reflecting off the silver and purple wallpaper. She went to the Hollywood Ranch Market and bought ten dollars worth of groceries and got a three-foot tree, free. Using the glitter and frills she transformed the plastic fruit she had bought into shiny ornaments. The decorations were so heavy, Richard had to wire up each spindly branch. Krake sprayed snow everywhere, fastened evergreen branches tied with red velvet ribbon in every available space and covered the front door with red foil striped with some wide, green ribbon. The apartment became a giant Christmas present, the illusion of a happy holiday residence.

Christmas day arrived. Their money was so tight they had agreed not to exchange presents. Krake did manage to buy a large chicken which she stuffed and along with sweet potatoes, squash and cranberry sauce they had a delicious meal. She had sent a ten-dollar box of California oranges and dates to her family. Daddy sent a box of various kinds of tea and Alice and Lyle sent a black ceramic teapot. Those were her only gifts.

The day dragged on. There was no one in the apartment except Richard. While growing up, although the opening of gifts was spoiled by Hankie's complaints, she had always had a delicious holiday meal with friends dropping in to exchange gifts. Even at the Alley the acting troupe had met at someone's apartment to exchange gifts and indulge themselves in Christmas cookies and candy and hot toddies. Krake and Richard's few friends were having their own celebrations without them. They had received no invitations. If they had more money, they could have invited Donald and Sarah for dinner, or gone out to a movie. Krake hid her feelings, but it was the loneliest Christmas she had ever spent. This situation needed some changes. The loneliness was painful and for the first time in her life she hated Christmas. Usually optimistic, she had never experienced such a lost feeling during a holiday or felt so alone.

Her mother's unhappiness with her chosen profession was a constant source of grief. It was so tough to get out there and expose yourself, lay yourself on the line. And for what? Rejection, that's what. Cold, brutal rejection. Some producer looks you in the eye after you have given a reading for a part and says, "When are you going to get a nose job?" Then to have the people close to you withholding their support was hard. Although Lorraine was the only one who expressed her disapproval openly, Daddy had seemed to withdraw since she'd come to California. She had no relationship with Hank Jr. Their seven-year age difference had proved to be insurmountable. His jealousy and dislike of her ate away at her self-esteem too.

With every rejection, Krake's insecurity grew. The competition, the lack of real friends and a sense of belonging took their toll on her. She didn't understand this value system. Everything was based on appearance. It seemed that people only wanted to use you, to see how you could be manipulated to benefit them. Fit you into some preconceived mold. Don't be different or unique. Be like Sandra Dee and we'll know what to do with you. Don't ask us to be creative where you are concerned. Don't ask us to help or work with you. Come to us complete, the perfect embodiment of the image of the day. Don't ask us to look beneath the surface or treat you like a valuable human being, like anything but a piece of meat. What else would you expect to find on a cattle call? Sequels are easy, originals are risky. No guarantees there and what we want are guarantees.

Alice and Lyle called on New Year's Eve, met Richard via phone and had a long chat with Krake. It raised her spirits, but also emphasized the lack of meaningful friends in her life.

In early January, Harold and Krake did the scene for Monica Howser. Short and heavyset, she was businesslike and cast Harold in a segment of *The Virginian*, to shoot the following week. It was Harold's moment and his partner was barely noticed.

Krake had been wanting to make some changes for weeks. Right after the audition, she went to a beauty shop on Doheny Drive. She was tired of long hair and had hers cut in a shoulder-length flip which was all the rage. She swished it around and loved the feel of it touching her cheeks. With the new hair, she looked less like the Maximillian photos than ever, so she decided to have different ones taken as soon as she found the right photographer.

She had finally found a new agent as well. Melbourne Brooks had been a powerful force in Hollywood during the thirties and forties. Now in his seventies, he handled mostly bit players and a few old character actors. He loved the Maximillian photos and insisted Krake have them put in the Players Guide, a large index of actors who belonged to SAG, AFTRA or Equity. Personally Krake thought it a waste of twenty-five dollars. She was wrong. In early March, Roger Corman, who directed horror films for American International, called Melbourne. Corman had seen her in the Players Guide and thought he could use her in his next film, an adaptation of the Edgar Allen Poe poem, *The Raven*.

Corman was trying to find someone who resembled the English actress Hazel Court, playing Lenore. He looked Krake over and decided she would do. As he explained, she would only be in one scene, but it was a crucial one. Vincent Price, Peter Lorre and an unknown named Jack Nicholson, playing Lorre's son, believe she is Price's dead wife, but she is only Boris Karloff's servant girl. The explanation was longer than the scene but she was excited. Would Peter Lorre remember her?

Hazel Court was a strawberry blond so Krake would have to wear a wig. She went to Max Factor's on Hollywood Boulevard. She was informed she had a large head and it was hard finding one to fit. They compromised by covering her widow's peak with makeup. Then she went to Western Costume and took the freight elevator to the second floor. She stepped out into a maze of costumes. Racks and racks. Everywhere you looked, costumes. First she tried on a colorful gypsy dress, a red and orange striped skirt with a black velvet bodice covering a flimsy peasant blouse. Looking in the mirror she longed for Glenn Ford to appear behind her. The dress was too bright though. Next she donned a long, fitted black taffeta with a low-neck and a v-tapered waist. Lifting her hair off her neck, she could have been Olivia De Havilland in *The Heiress.* Bit it rustled too much. She settled for a plain, fitted, gray and black cotton gown which showed off her small waist. To think they are paying me to do this!

With only one line she felt a little foolish attending rehearsal, but was grateful to be included. The day her scene was shot her call was for eight a.m. First, the makeup artist went to work. While he was intently creating her face, she heard Vincent Price at a nearby makeup table tell the cosmetician that both his wife and daughter had babies two weeks apart. Krake went to wardrobe and put on the costume. Lastly, the hair stylist fitted the wig. She hardly recognized herself in the mirror.

While looking for the bathroom, she literally ran into Peter Lorre behind one of the "stone" walls of the set. Nervously, she introduced herself and reminded him of their meeting two years ago at the Alley Theater. "You probably don't remember me. You advised me not to come to Hollywood and the first movie I'm in is with you. Funny, huh?"

"Yes, I do remember you, dear. I wish you luck." With that he shuffled off, seeming preoccupied. The sound stage was partially covered with a huge replica of a medieval castle. A curving staircase rose, ending abruptly in midair. She found an old broken couch off to one side where she could watch all the activity. Things progressed slowly. Boris Karloff and his wife sat side by side until it was time for his takes. He seemed so frail. When he ascended the staircase, it made her anxious, afraid he would fall. His wife was attentive and had tea ready for him on the breaks. Everyone, including Corman, treated him gently.

The man playing Lorre's son, Jack Nicholson, eventually came over and sat beside her. He was handsome, with the devil in his eye and Krake liked him immediately. He seemed genuinely interested in helping her with her part. He knew Brice and they talked at length about the Method. He helped her create a life for the servant girl and find her motivation for the scene. After he had completed his scenes and left, she felt lonely.

At a quarter to five, when she was the only one left on the sound stage besides the crew, they shot her scene. Corman, sitting beside the camera, said her cue, "summoning forth the truth." This was Karloff's line, but he had gone home long ago. She walked down a long corridor and entered the hall where the main characters (supposedly) were gathered. In reality, it was empty. She took her mark opposite Karloff's chair and said, "You rang, sir?" Corman read Karloff's and Price's lines. She turned and walked slowly back down the hallway. They rehearsed once and shot it.

"I think we got it, but let's do it once more just to be safe." Corman looked at her. "Wouldn't want you to have to come back and do this all again."

Oh, no. It was over. She had waited eight hours for twenty minutes work. She didn't care, it was so exciting. Just like in the ...!

14

After Abner returned from Japan, Krake went out to lunch with him now and then. She rode the bus to his office so he and Richard wouldn't meet. The contrast with the ride to the restaurant in Abner's new Chrysler made her want more. I ought to have a car like this, instead of the 1954 Jaguar sedan she had purchased after the *Ozzie and Harriet* stint. Not with her earnings, mind you. On a whim, she bought it with part of the insurance money that was left. She couldn't drive, but it fulfilled a dream she had had since seeing Kim Novak drive an olive green one in Vertigo. The car was nine years old and the dual parts were regularly wearing out. First one fuel pump, then the other. The vehicle was enormous and drank gallons of gas, but she felt like a princess leaning her head back on the cracked, faded red-leather seats. She wanted to sit in the back seat and have Richard chauffeur her around but restrained herself.

After lunch with Abner, she felt discontent returning to the small apartment. Poverty was oppressive. So when Abner invited her to go along on a business trip to San Francisco, she easily agreed, making up a story for Richard about visiting an old girlfriend.

Abner was a perfect gentleman, installing her in her own room and seemingly satisfied just to have her company. He wined and dined her and she felt marvelously pampered.

Back in Hollywood, Abner let her off a block from her studio apartment, kissing her lightly on the cheek. She regretfully went into the apartment. Richard was cool and distant. She felt guilty though she hadn't even kissed Abner. But she had lied to Richard. She hadn't known how else to handle the situation. When they got in bed, he warmed up considerably. She began to kiss his back and stroke his cock which sprang to attention. He turned over, pulled her legs apart and thrust inside. He rapidly came to orgasm without satisfying her. The guilt lessened.

Krake had found a young photographer in Brice's class who shot some photos of her outside in Griffith Park. Two days after her return from San Francisco, he dropped them off. They were excellent. Her shorter hair and the naturalness of the poses and setting enhanced her looks. Most importantly, they looked like her. She had done her own makeup and the whole thing worked. She took them to class to show Brice. While he was looking at them, a friend of Brice's who had observed the acting class on several occasions, walked up. Lasalle James was a contract player at Revue and someone Krake admired.

She had first met him at a party at Brice and Angela's . It only took a few drinks and they began flirting with each other. As the evening progressed, Krake became more outrageous. Playing charades she had them all in stitches over her portrayal of *Desire Under The Elms*. Lasalle had married his now ex-wife in Paris, so Krake began to speak French.

The next day Angela called and said Lasalle was crazy about her. "He thinks you're the most beautiful and funniest woman he's met in years. He wants your phone number. I told him you lived with Richard and he said he'd wait."

"Angela, what did I do? What did I say? I remember very little after we played charades."

Angela laughed, "Whatever you did it was the right thing. I bet he calls."

In a week sure enough. He was thinking of joining Brice's acting class and wanted to talk to her about it. They met for lunch at a cafeteria on Hollywood Boulevard. All during the meal, he kept watching and waiting. Waiting for her to be outrageous. On a Diet 7-Up that was impossible. She clammed up, was extremely uncomfortable and couldn't wait for lunch to be over. She felt she was swimming in deep water without a lifejacket. He was cute, but of no help. If only she could remember what she had said that night, but she never recalled anything from a blackout, even when people told her what had transpired. They did discuss Brice's class and he decided to join. The thought of him watching her feeble attempts at creating roles made her nervous, but what could she do? At least it would be an opportunity to get to know each other better

After lunch she said goodbye, aware of his disappointment at not finding "the most beautiful and funniest woman he'd met in years."

Now she felt a wave of insecurity wash over her as Lasalle and Brice looked at the photos. I bet they aren't any good. Maybe she was ugly.

"These are terrific," Lasalle said. "I'd like to show them to Monica Howser." Lasalle left with them after class and called the following week. "Monica Howser wants to meet you. Can you go out to the studio on Friday? I'll meet you, we can have lunch in the commissary and I'll introduce you to her."

Krake didn't offer that she had already met Monica Howser because she felt fearful that Howser might not want to see her again. "I don't drive and Richard will have the car," she replied. "Could I possibly ride out there with you?"

"I just have the scooter, but you can ride on the back. Wear a scarf!"

Hanging on behind was very nice, her arms around his waist. They went through the front gates of Universal without stopping (the guard knew Lasalle) and pulled up at the curb beside a one-story building with double glass doors. Quickly dismounting, Krake straightened her dress, took off her scarf and fluffed her hair. She glanced at the reflection in the door as they entered the commissary. The image wasn't bad.

Krake hardly tasted the tuna salad. Her mind was a jumble of thoughts. Should she mention to Howser that she had done a scene for her with Harold Givner a few months ago? Monica might feel she should have remembered her and be embarrassed.

Should she lie about her age? If so, when was she born? How old was she when she graduated from college and what year was that? All the mind fucking was interrupted by Lasalle, "It's almost time for your interview. Do you want to freshen up?"

She retreated into the restroom where she decided she had worn the wrong outfit. It make her look fat. She was so thin, no one could possibly take this worry seriously. But Krake had no real sense of how she looked. Regardless, it was too late now for anything but fresh lipstick and a prayer that Howser would like her.

On the elevator to Howser's office, Krake was silent, hands clasped in front to hold herself together. They entered the office and sat down. Krake was too shy to ask Lasalle how she looked. It wasn't long before the secretary ushered them in. Monica Howser came from behind her large desk, smiling, and shook Krake's hand. After introductions, Lasalle gave Monica a peck on the cheek and left. Krake took the proffered chair and Howser sat behind the desk facing her.

"Tell me about yourself, your acting experience," Monica began.

Krake filled her in on her stint at the Alley and told about the few parts she had done in Hollywood. At the close of the conversation, Monica asked her to do a scene.

Thinking this might be a good time, Krake replied, "I've met you before, you know." Howser stared at her, saying nothing. Suddenly fearful that she had said something wrong, Krake quickly went on. "When do you want to see the scene?"

"In a month or so, whenever you get it ready."

That night she danced around the apartment singing, "Monica Howser wants me to do a scene, Monica H. wants me to do a scene!" She ended the verse by jumping up and down on the Murphy bed making the floor shake. "Yippee!"

Richard was pleased, but she didn't want him to give her so much as a congratulatory hug. They had been living together for over a year and she knew staying here was safe, but she wanted to move out on her own. For the last few months, she had had a longing to go out dancing, eat at nice (expensive) restaurants, and have fun. Only twenty-five, she felt like forty with him. The whole scene had become depressing. She was in one of the so-called glamour spots of the world and wasn't participating. Her sphere was narrow. She had to make some changes.

Abner helped her find an apartment, a studio with a small kitchen, for $75 a month. Krake decided she could afford it for a little while. Her insurance money was almost gone, but stardom was imminent. Abner offered to loan her money if she was desperate.

All that remained was to tell Richard. Naturally he was upset. He didn't understand what was wrong and she didn't want to hurt him. "I still love you, but I need to be on my own, just for awhile," she lied.

Reluctantly he helped move her things in the old Jaguar.

The new apartment was two blocks from the noisy Sunset Strip. An area inhabited mostly by transients, it was exciting and a trifle scary.

The first night she hardly slept, mostly because of the strange surroundings. She missed Richard's warm body, but the sense of freedom she felt surpassed any longing. Her time with Richard already seemed like a long-ago love affair. She still cared, but the passion was gone.

Two days later, hearing she had left Richard, Lasalle called, wanting to take her to dinner at some friends who lived near the strip.

Amid the urban sprawl of Los Angeles, the Hilliard's was a charming one-story Spanish stucco house. A small blond child raced through the wide oak doorway and flung herself into Lasalle's arms. "Lasalle, Lasalle, come play house with me," she said, amid giggles as he tickled her.

A slim, ascetic looking man with short-cropped brown hair, appeared in the doorway. "You must be Krake. I'm Matt Hilliard. So glad you could come for dinner." He introduced her to his wife Jocelyn and they all went inside.

After a relaxing meal with plenty of good food, Krake not only played with Becky, but agreed to baby-sit the following Wednesday with Becky and her cherubic baby brother, Andrew.

"What a wonderful family," she commented as they left.

After babysitting and spending another evening with them, Krake wanted to spend more time there. It's been so long since I've met any real people, she thought, they're so sincere and loving.

After two more babysitting visits, Jocelyn and Matt asked if she would like to rent the room in the garage used as an office. Compact, it had a single bed, a desk and a dresser. Matt, an actor and director, generated income in these two fields sporadically. Jocelyn's hat-checking job was ending and her only means of a regular income was the dance class she taught once a week. They periodically took in a boarder to help out.

It didn't take long for Krake to decide. "Yes, I'd love to live with you. I can move in at the end of the month." She needed the warmth and activity of the Hilliards. When she was with them she didn't feel so alienated from everything. She longed to be part of a family.

Watching the arms full of clothes marching by, Jocelyn burst out laughing.

"What's so funny?" Krake inquired, pausing on her fourth trip to the garage.

"Lasalle said you had little money and hardly any clothes. He should see this. Matt's going to have to put an addition on the garage."

"Does Lasalle think I'm going to wear my good clothes to crawl around on that dirty floor in acting class?" Krake asked indignantly.

Matt put up long steel rods outside his former office to accommodate the wardrobe and even had a phone installed in her room. She slept better from the start knowing her new-found family was only a few yards away.

Lasalle suggested she ask Matt to direct her scene for Monica Howser. When she approached him, he quickly agreed but stipulated that when she began to earn money, she would pay him. That seemed fair. Matt also selected one of the frequent visitors to the house, Lane Gibbons, a struggling actor and painter, to be her scene partner. He chose a light comedy, *Under the Yum Yum Tree*, as the best vehicle to display her talent.

The hot summer days passed. Becky had a small, round plastic pool that she and Krake lolled in during the afternoons, legs hanging out with the hose running water over both of them as they chatted about this and that while their bodies turned brown. Jocelyn passed by one day when they were indulging themselves and, looking at Krake, said affectionately, "You're a true Sybarite."

"A what?"

"A Sybarite, sybaritic, you know."

"No, I don't."

"They were the people who lived in the ancient Italian city of Sybaris, who were known to be very sensuous and fond of luxury and pleasure."

Krake laughed, "So that's what I am."

Abner stopped by often and on several weekends they went to Agua Caliente racetrack in Tijuana. He was an expert handicapper and always won something. She loved going to the track to watch the people, glamorous in their tans and gold jewelry. The horses were beautiful. Sometimes they went down to the paddock under the grandstand before the race to look at them up close. The sleek, powerful bodies rippling under the satin coats of black and brown, white or dappled gray were a delight to her senses. The colorful silks of the jockeys and the smell of hay and manure completed the sensory experience. Occasionally she would put five dollars on a horse, but usually she had no money to spare.

After the races they would go into Tijuana to have dinner and watch the jai alai games. Seated behind the protective iron grillwork surrounding the court, they observed the players running and hitting the ball. Abner bet on that too. Jai alai bored Krake, she preferred the horses.

During these jaunts, they usually stayed in La Jolla in a motel on the cliffs overlooking the Pacific. Abner always reserved separate rooms, for which she was grateful. She liked him as a friend and ignored the fact that possibly he felt more than friendship for her.

Matt was being hard on her in their rehearsals for her scene. "You have to sound natural," he said. This character is fairly close to you, so just be yourself . . . No that sounded phony, don't act, just be." She was confused and discouraged, but plodded on. Howser would hate it. Why did she think she could act? Any fool could see she couldn't. Won "best actress" in college? Big deal!

Krake had hardly thought of Richard in the three months she had been living without him. He had stopped by her apartment near the strip a couple of times. They had sex and he left. She didn't miss him.

She and Lane, her scene partner, had had a brief fling when they first met. The Hilliards was a haven for a number of working and out-of-work actors, directors, writers and artists. People dropped by at all hours. This kind of atmosphere intrigued Krake. Lorraine made such a fuss when people came to dinner. Krake admired Jocelyn's ease and relaxed attitude about the whole thing. If people happened to be around close to mealtime, they were expected to stay and share whatever was on hand. The constant company was stimulating and Krake's feelings of being alone diminished.

Lane first came over a week or so after she moved in and stayed for dinner. Sitting across from each other at the table, the mutual attraction was strong. They ended up at his trailer a few blocks away. Lane's apparent sensitivity made the lovemaking special. I think I'm in love, he is so sweet, thought Krake.

He came to dinner at the Hilliards again the next night and when the phone rang, Krake answered it. "It's for you Lane, a woman." A flash of anxiety crossed his face as she handed him the receiver. He spoke softly. She could only catch, "Yes, I'll be home soon." He handed the receiver back, she hung up.

After an awkward silence, the conversation resumed. In a short while, Lane excused himself, saying he hated to eat and run, but...

Krake followed him out to his car. "Who was that on the phone? Why do you have to go?"

"I wanted to tell you last night, but I couldn't." Her heart sank. "That was Allison, my girlfriend. She's been out of town for a week and just got back."

"Your girlfriend! Why didn't you tell me? How could you make love to me when you have a girlfriend?"

"I'm sorry, Krake, I didn't mean to hurt you. I've got to go." He jumped in the old Plymouth and beat a hasty retreat.

Krake didn't want to go hack inside. She couldn't face anyone, feeling so hurt and humiliated. A drink, I need a drink! She sat in the Hilliards' Peugot and cried. When Matt came out to look for her, he got in next to her. She sobbed out the story and he held her while she cried.

"Honey," he began, "Lane isn't honorable. He doesn't respect women or understand how they operate. You make love with emotions which include trust. A lot of men only experience lust. Lane saw a beautiful woman, desired her and that's all. He didn't mean to hurt you, but he doesn't have a clue as to what it meant to you. He doesn't realize how he betrayed you."

She finally quieted down, went back to her room in the garage and wept some more before finally falling asleep, wondering why love always seemed to elude her.

A week later, when Matt mentioned he thought Lane would be a good scene partner, she didn't know if she could face him. She managed to and now considered him just that, a scene partner.

As her twenty-sixth birthday approached, Krake wondered if she should tell Jocelyn how old she really was. She had learned to take a couple of years off her age because she still looked eighteen. Now she was saying she was twenty-two and no one seemed to question it. Her real age was disquieting to casting agents whose lack of imagination prevented them from casting a twenty-six-year-old to play a teenager. It rankled that she couldn't be her own age. People didn't like it if you threw them curves and she needed approval, so she kept her secret.

A week after a lovely surprise birthday party the Hilliards gave for her, Krake scheduled the scene for Howser. Nervously, Lane drove his old car out to the Universal lot. Once in Howser's office, Krake introduced Lane and they rearranged the furniture to set the scene. As usual, Krake had no idea how it went, but Howser laughed at the comedy and seemed genuinely pleased as she bid them goodbye.

Lasalle called just as she got home. "She wants to give you a screen test," he exclaimed. "She thought you were very sexy. Said she'll call you tomorrow. I'm proud of you, babe."

Monica called and asked her to come to the office to discuss the details. Krake floated in the next day. Monica hugged her and said that in December, Revue Studios was testing four people for seven-year contracts. Two women from New York City, Krake and Morgan Stillman, a male model from Hollywood. Revue Studios was the only production company building a group of contract players for work in TV series and movies. Monica also said a young director from New York was moving to the coast in a few weeks. Revue had just put him under contract. When he arrived, they would start rehearsing the scene for the test, the other part of which was a personal interview.

Monica looked at her. "F. Scott Fitzgerald seems right for you. What do you think?"

"Sure, I like Fitzgerald." Thin, rich women slunk through her mind.

"I'll see what I can come up with. In the meantime, there's one thing you should be attending to."

"What?"

"Your teeth. They cross slightly in front, I'm afraid they'll cast shadows under lights. I don't want anything like that to prevent you from being put under contract. Would you agree to have them capped?" Monica leaned across her desk.

"If it's essential, I will. I'll borrow the money." All she could think of was the four years of braces she had endured and the money Daddy had spent. She could never tell him.

Monica stood up. "I'm very happy that we're testing you. You are definitely contract material."

"Thanks, I'm happy too."

"Who is your agent? I should talk to him."

"I don't have one." She had left Melborne Brooks months ago.

"We'll take care of that," Monica said firmly.

When Abner took her to dinner that night to celebrate, she asked him if he would loan her the money to have her teeth capped. He readily agreed. She promised to repay him when she became a big star. Krake had been waiting for Abner to apply pressure to sleep with him now that she was no longer living with Richard, but he hadn't. Once, over lunch, he did say that he was in love with her. She had felt panic that if she didn't respond with "I love you, too," he would stop seeing her. But she couldn't lie to him. She quickly explained that she wasn't ready for another relationship. Abner accepted this and never raised the subject again. Krake was relieved. Her friendship with Abner fulfilled her constant need for a responsible man, a Daddy.

15

A few days later, Abner took her to dinner at the house of a friend of his, a publicist. He said there would be several of Harvey's client's she might enjoy meeting. When Krake and Abner arrived, her eyes fell on him immediately. Fairly tall (for Hollywood) at about 5'10", brown hair and eyes, full lips and a sexy way of moving. Damien! It was Damien! An honest to God Teenage Idol! A couple of years ago, she and Lorraine had seen him on the *Ed Sullivan Show*. They both agreed he was a lousy singer, but very good-looking. That seemed to be the consensus of opinion, but it didn't diminish his popularity.

In person he was handsome, strikingly so. Krake was glad she was wearing one of her favorite outfits, a low-necked green and white gingham dress with matching kerchief, which she left on, a la Audrey Hepburn. It framed her tanned face just right. He was alone. His girlfriend was appearing in a play so she couldn't attend the dinner. Gee, too bad.

Although they didn't speak more than a few sentences to each other, Krake was acutely aware of him all evening and thought she felt the same attention from him. Whenever their eyes met, the attraction was evident. Sitting opposite one another during dinner, he asked if she was going to leave the scarf on. She nodded. He said he liked it. The party broke up early and he left to pick up his girlfriend Cheryl at the Friars Club where she was performing. Krake fantasized all the way home.

The following Thursday, Harvey called inviting her to go with a group of friends to see Bob Dylan and Joan Baez in concert at the Hollywood Bowl. Damien would be there. Cheryl was still in the play so he wouldn't have a date. Gee, too bad. They picked her up promptly at 7:30 to have enough time to park and find their seats by the 8:30 curtain. She found herself in the back seat of the car between Damien and another publicist from Harvey's agency. The feeling of his body pressed against hers was exciting. It was only side by side, but you had to start somewhere. Besides it was their first date. Well, anyway they were together.

Once at the bowl, they climbed for what seemed an eternity to their seats almost on the top row. They were so high up it was a wonder no one got a nosebleed. The temperature dropped with the descent of the sun and a wind came up. Krake was freezing. Harvey had brought two thin, wool blankets and they huddled under them. The show began, the tiny figures of Baez and Dylan hardly visible on the stage far below. During one song Dylan sang the lyric, "and Damien singing on the radio." She wanted to shout, "Here I am sitting with him! Yes, me! Right here!" Dylan must have gotten word that Damien was in the audience. Everyone laughed and a few people turned around to look at them. All the time she sat next to him she thought how nice it would be if he held her hand or put his arm around her. He didn't. After two hours of good music and a cold hotdog at intermission, they went to the Friar's Club.

They sat around a tiny table and ordered drinks. A good-looking redhead appeared, cast hostile glances at Krake and sat on Damien's lap. Everyone drank, made small talk and then left Damien to Cheryl.

Two weeks later Harvey called and said David Wolper was doing a TV special on Teen Idols. Damien was featured and Harvey assigned to do the publicity. They needed a pretty girl for a photo layout and he thought of her.

"Are you interested?" he said with a laugh.

"You know I am," she replied, the mistress of understatement.

"They're shooting first thing Tuesday." This was Sunday night. "Can you make it?"

"You better believe it. What shall I wear?"

"Something casual, bring a couple of changes."

She was a nervous wreck. Should she wear her new pant-suit? Damien had just seen her in that. Still, it looked good. What else? The black sweater and the beige corduroy slacks, the green raw silk pants and matching green and violet chenille blouse. What else? What else? She nearly drove herself crazy trying to decide. Finally, she chose three outfits which she put in a small suitcase along with some cosmetics, praying she could apply them flatteringly. She was still in doubt as to her makeup abilities.

Damien was already at the photographer's studio fooling around with a lipstick-red motorcycle. First they posed as young lovers holding hands, then sipping a Coke out of a glass with two straws and eventually on the back of the motorcycle. The photographer didn't like any of the clothes she had brought except the green pant-suit. He had a pair of red slacks and a sweater hanging in the dressing room which fit her perfectly and she wore that for all the motorcycle shots. Shooting the layout was fun. She enjoyed the attention and hugging Damien made it worthwhile. He seemed so nice, didn't preen or act smart or do anything to indicate the presence of an inflated ego. They worked most of the morning and when the final shot was complete he asked if she was hungry.

Food! Who could think of food at a time like this? "Sure, I'm starving!"

"Do you want to go to lunch?"

"That would be nice. Thanks."

She hurried into the dressing room, threw herself a kiss in the mirror and quickly removed the red sweater and slacks, donned the familiar green pant-suit and met him at the studio door. He escorted her outside to his metallic blue Jaguar XKE convertible. She was so full of excitement she could hardly restrain herself from sitting on the hood, but she got in instead. He drove to the Cock 'n Bull, an English Tudor style restaurant at the end of the strip. It was dark inside the mahogany-paneled room. They sat at a small table just inside the bar. Damien ordered drinks. He had a scotch and soda, she, a plain Coke. Too risky for booze. They sat talking inanities and smoking. After a while he asked, "Are you ready?"

Thinking he meant ready to leave, she slowly replied, "I guess so."

He doesn't like me. He's decided not to eat lunch. He stood up and left the room. Was he a complete idiot? He'd left his jacket and cigarettes too. She gathered them up along with her own belongings and loaded down followed in the direction he had gone. As she entered the next room, she saw him standing, plate in hand, in line at a salad bar. She felt like dropping everything and running. He hadn't meant they were leaving, only going to get salad. She forced herself to walk towards him. He looked questioningly at her burdens. Red-faced, she mumbled, "I thought we were leaving."

"Oh no," he laughed, "you have to serve yourself salad here."

God, why me? He must think I am so stupid. He'll never ask me out. I wish I were dead. Miraculously she calmed down and ate the meal which consisted of salad and rare roast beef with Yorkshire pudding. Damien eased her embarrassment by ignoring it.

She felt the warm breeze ruffling her hair on the drive home and knew this was what she wanted. He was what she wanted. Every fantasy of a '40s movies kid was coming true. A blue Jaguar convertible and a handsome teen idol. What else was there? All too soon they were turning down the hill, pulling up in the Hilliards' driveway and saying goodbye.

She went in the house which was deserted, put down her purse and crossed to the window to watch him drive away. She clasped her hands, please, please God, let him call and ask me out. Later in her room she relived the day over and over.

A week went by and no word. She had an appointment near Paramount for an independent film that was being cast. A friend of Brice's was directing and he had recommended her for the female lead. She was riding on a bus down Santa Monica Boulevard to the appointment when a man climbed on board, talking rapidly. All she heard was, "The President's been shot! They don't know if he's dead or alive!" No, it couldn't be true. The beautiful, charismatic leader who had inspired everyone, shot!

She arrived at the director's small office and waited and waited in an anteroom for the interview. The secretary finally emerged and said that the director, Hal Weiss, had canceled all appointments for the day. President Kennedy was dead.

Stunned, she caught the bus home. It let her off a block from her street. A few doors away was a flower shop. She stopped and bought a dozen yellow chrysanthemums. She placed them in a vase on the dining room table as Matt and Jocelyn sat glued to the news on TV. There they remained for the rest of the day. People stopped by to share the devastation of the event. The image of Jacqueline Kennedy, horror on her face and blood staining her pink suit, haunted Krake. She thought of Burg and went out to the garage and wept for him, for Kennedy and for all the senseless tragedies in the world.

The next morning as she was sipping her first cup of coffee in front of the TV, the image of Lee Harvey Oswald filled the screen. He was walking towards the camera surrounded by security guards when a sharp crack sounded and he collapsed into the arms of the men around him. Matt sprang from the couch shouting, "He's been shot, somebody just shot him!" The TV announcer echoed these words and in seconds the camera focused on a short, heavy-set man with a gun who was suddenly covered with policemen, like bees on honey. Jocelyn ran in from the kitchen with Becky close behind. The four of them stood transfixed watching this historical event, stunned into silence by the open display of violence once again. The gunman was identified as Jack Ruby, a Dallas restaurant owner and a big fan of Kennedy's.

Krake had mixed feelings about Oswald's death. She had already convicted him in her mind. She didn't feel too badly about this murder except that she felt taking anyone's life was immoral. Matt expressed frustration over the fact that killing Oswald prevented ever knowing his motivation or if he was just a hired gun. For three days, until the state funeral, no one ventured out. The TV set was on around the clock. They were all in mourning.

Every aspect of the funeral, the riderless horse, the black-veiled widow, the flag-draped coffin atop the caisson, the honor guards, the drums, the children, epitomized the end of an era of compassion, style and grace in the White House. It shook people to the core. Kennedy had appealed to Krake and her friends in the entertainment industry, both to their aesthetic sense and their political views. He had inspired them and given them hope for the future. His death was disillusioning. Truly the loss of a dream.

Gradually things began to regain some sense of normalcy. Two weeks after the tragedy, Krake returned to read for Hal Weiss and got the part. The film was a modern Western, she was cast as the local sheriff's girlfriend who has an affair with a drifter. Hal Weiss also wanted her to represent his independent film company as a Deb Star nominee. The Hollywood Press Club sponsored this annual event and all the major film companies had representatives. Krake was pleased, but apprehensive about the competition. She hated to be placed on display and judged on nothing but her physical appearance. Yet, she had chosen to come to Hollywood, the pinnacle of superficiality. Still, it was more by default that she had come. If she was not destined to be a wife and mother, then why not go for being rich and famous?

The eternal question - what to wear? She possessed no formal gowns and no money to buy one. Jocelyn suggested they go to a rental shop on Vine and see what they could find. A long, slim, white strapless dress with beading on the bodice seemed suitable. Rental fee? Ten dollars a night. Jocelyn offered her long white gloves to go with it and Krake bought a cheap pearl pin and matching earrings. That evening when she fastened the pin in her hair she thought as she surveyed herself, not bad, not bad. But apparently not good enough. As she progressed down the seemingly endless row of judges, shaking hands, she heard Army Archerd whisper to his companion, "I bet she's a good actress." Hey, I don't want to be voted "most likely to succeed." I want, "prettiest."

There were forty women competing for ten Deb Star positions. After they met the judges, they had to walk singly out on the brightly-lit stage of the Press Club, twirl around, curtsy and depart. Backstage, waiting to be called, several of the women were talking and laughing together, but Krake was too insecure and shy in her ten-dollar dress to approach anyone. In typical Hollywood fashion, there was no question of there introducing themselves to her. A beautiful blond at the other end of the room smiled warmly, however, and wished her good luck as she passed by to go on stage when her name was called. "Krake Forrester, representing Weiss Films, Inc." A smattering of applause, the bright lights obliterated everything but the stage. She curtsied and exited, extremely glad it was over. Another hour of waiting and they announced the winners. Krake was not among them. After all, she and the film company she represented were complete unknowns.

The day following her defeat Monica called and told her Michael Lawrence, assigned to direct her screen test was leaving New York City and would be arriving in Los Angeles in a few days. They set a tentative rehearsal date for the following Monday.

On Monday afternoon, Krake found her way to the dance studio serving as a rehearsal hall, located behind some bungalows on the Universal lot. She entered a large mirrored room. Michael Lawrence was sitting on a bench at the far end. He rose, came towards her and introduced himself. He had a copy of the novel as well as a *Great Gatsby* script. They read the scene together. Krake would meet Bradley, her scene partner, at their next rehearsal on Wednesday.

Krake was relieved Michael was directing the test. Her experience with Hollywood directors, limited as it was, led her to expect only concern with her height or position to the camera. The acting part had been left solely to her. This was entirely different from the stage where she and her directors worked closely on the development of the character she was to portray. Michael appeared to care about her acting. Only time would tell.

The Wednesday rehearsal with Bradley Forbes was a disaster. In looks, this male model was the epitome of a matinee idol. Dark wavy hair, an aquiline nose, classically chiseled face, and warm, if rather blank, brown eyes. He was six feet tall which meant she wouldn't have to play the scene on her knees. As they read, however, it became painfully obvious that the dialogue was above his power of comprehension. He sounded like Elmer Fudd playing Romeo. She and Michael exchanged a raised-eyebrow look and plodded on. Hopefully, he would be better once they got on their feet. No, worse! He never looked at her. His gaze was riveted on his reflection in the wall of mirrors.

Two rehearsals later, Monica called a meeting, explaining that after careful consideration, she and Michael decided although she could carry the scene, Bradley couldn't.

Would you be upset if we changed the scene to one from *Reluctant Debutante*? Both Michael and I feel that Brad's lack of experience would pull your performance down as well. What do you think?"

Hating to relinquish a scene that was right for her, but acknowledging their correct assessment of Brad's acting abilities, she agreed. Monica gave her a new script which she memorized that evening. The next day's rehearsal went better. Brad still never looked at her, only at his reflection. It was impossible for her to play off him and have some exchange of emotions. This was a love scene, but he was in love with himself.

Again she was left on her own to create the character. Michael was too busy coaching Bradley through every sentence. She didn't see how this test could happen, but maybe a miracle would occur, like Brad contracting a rare, tropical disease and Anthony Perkins being called in at the last moment to play the scene.

Frustrating rehearsals continued and just before Christmas Monica called saying she had a day job on *Chandler*, a television series about life in a small college in the Midwest. Krake was grateful. She knew Monica was aware of her financial condition and was trying to help. Krake's part of girl-student consisted of a few lines with boy-student after graduation exercises. It was used as a tease introducing the segment. For the eight hours she spent on the set, mostly waiting, she was paid two hundred dollars.

Christmas was fun in contrast to the aching loneliness of the last one. Matt waited until the children were asleep on Christmas Eve, went down to the railroad yards and brought home six trees. "They were giving these away," he explained, carrying them in one by one. Suddenly a forest sprang up between the kitchen and living room. The house was filled with pine scent and they decided not to decorate. The trees looked so pristine standing there, like the "forest primeval."

Krake slept on the daybed next to the trees so she could experience the children's reaction. A light sleeper, the first sound she heard was the sharp intake of Becky's breath followed by a muffled, "Ooooh," then scurrying feet across hardwood floors and shouts of "Mommy, Daddy, come here, come here. Look what Santa's left."

Krake got up, put on her robe and sat on the daybed watching the faces of Becky and Andrew, who was in Jocelyn's arms. Not quite sure about it all, he began to cry. Jocelyn soon quieted him and he and Becky began to open presents. The pure wonder Krake saw restored her feelings about this time-revered holiday. The presents they exchanged made it festive, but most importantly, Krake had a family again. Krake gave thanks for her good fortune.

The night before the screen test Krake slept in the house. Matt said they needed to get up at five so he could drive her out to the studio in time for her six o'clock call. He gave her a mild sleeping pill. She said otherwise she wouldn't sleep a wink. Too soon Matt was shaking her awake, saying it was time. Her suitcase was already packed. She only had to put on jeans and a sweater, brush her teeth and they were off.

The guard at the gate waved them through after checking her name off his list. Matt squeezed her hand saying, "Good luck, 'Goody Two Shoes,' " planted a kiss on her cheek and drove out of sight in the darkness. She hesitated a moment, please God, please God, let this test be good, and entered the building.

Voices floated out of rooms on either side of a long hallway. She stuck her head in one and saw a tall, blond man who she recognized as Hugh, the makeup artist from *Chandler*. He used green makeup on her eyes to compliment the green formal dress she would be wearing. When he was finished he said someone would be there to wash and style her hair.

As soon as he left, she slipped on a black and yellow print challis robe and fuzzy new slippers, a Christmas present from

Matt. They were so big and funny-looking, like two yellow dust mops. Soon a gray-haired woman knocked and entered, motioned for her to sit in a chair in front of a wash basin and swiftly shampooed her hair. With a towel wrapped around her wet head, she was handed a cup of coffee and informed the cream and sugar could be found on a table at the end of the corridor. She shuffled along in her mops and fixed the coffee the way she liked. Lots of cream and sugar with a hint of coffee. She returned to the room slowly sipping the comforting liquid. As she was finishing, a short bleached blond came in, set her hair and put her under a dryer. While she was sitting under the blowing heat, several others entered, took a look and vanished. She recognized no one. Finally a hair stylist arrived, seated her in front of a mirror and arranged her hair in an upsweep. Krake didn't like it. Her face was too bony for the severity of the style. However, her scene took place after a country club dance so the hairdo suited her character. After the stylist left, she sat and waited.

Where was Hugh? He had said he would be back after her hair was styled. Sitting, sitting, waiting, waiting. It seemed like hours, but it was only twenty minutes or so. Out of boredom and nervousness, she began to wander up and down the hall, poking her head into rooms where everyone seemed busy. Someone passed her in the hall and spying the slippers suggested, "Why don't you make yourself useful and clean the floor? It really needs it." She proceeded to skate up and down the hallway in her twin mops. Soon people in the various makeup rooms were standing in doorways, watching and advising.

"Over here, I see lots of dust, right here. This place has never been so clean."

"Can we hire you on a regular basis?"

She felt right at home, like she had always been here. anxiety left and pleasure took its place.

Hugh had to come looking for her to do her makeup. When he finished she looked at herself in the mirror.

"Yes, it's very nice, thank you."

She didn't like it. The eye-shadow was green to go with the dress and wasn't as flattering as the purple he had used for *Chandler*. He left as the wardrobe .mistress took her to her trailer outside the sound stage where they were shooting. The green dress was carefully lowered over her hair. She looked all right, nothing special.

At eight am. sharp, she walked on the set. Amid cameras, cables, furniture and crew scattered about, she spotted Monica talking to Michael. Wading cautiously through the maze of cables, she had almost reached them when Monica looked up. "Don't you look beautiful, just like a debutante."

Her eyes darted past Krake to Bradley who had appeared resplendent in a black tuxedo. He paused a few feet from them to let the total effect sink in.

Michael jolted Brad out of his pose by snapping the scene marker sharply behind him. He began to place the marks they would have to hit in the first segment of the scene. These were the first color tests Revue had shot and the lights were very intense. Krake had been warned, but nothing prepared her for the blinding heat.

They rehearsed the segment being shot first and it was as if Bradley had never seen the script. For each segment the procedure was the same. They rehearsed and shot the portion once, then Michael would take Bradley aside and talk intently, sometimes for ten or fifteen minutes. They would repeat the scene and hopefully Michael would decide to use it. Sometimes they repeated it two or three times. Michael had to coach Bradley on practically every word. Meanwhile Krake waited. She began talking to the cameramen, who were just as bored. One of them offered her some Chiclets. She chewed three of them into a big wad and left it on the side of a camera to return to the set and shoot another scene. When she came off, one of the crew would ask, "You want a shot of gin?" referring to the gum. She would have another

Chiclet. Each time she named the Chiclets differently; bourbon, scotch, vodka, rum, always some kind of booze. There were wads of gum stuck all over the cameras by noon. That part was fun.

The execution of the scene was tortuous. She felt her performance, if you could call it that, was poor. Bradley was impossible to interact with. The constant stopping and starting made any form of concentration unattainable. The makeup people surrounding her, fixing her hair, powdering her face down between takes making her feel special, were some consolation. They finally shot the last take just before noon.

After lunch in the commissary, Monica accompanied Krake back to her trailer and helped select a dress for the interview. Monica left to watch the two New York actresses' scene as the interviews weren't going to be shot until four p.m. Krake lay down on the narrow bed, closed her eyes and the next thing she knew Monica was coming in the door.

"Were you asleep? I knocked, but you didn't answer."

"I can't believe it, one of the most important days of my life and I fall asleep." Krake sat up.

Monica gasped, "Look at your makeup, it's ruined." Smudged green eyes met Krake's gaze as she looked in the mirror. "Put the dress on and we'll go over to makeup. I think Bud Westmore is still here. He'll fix you up."

"Where's Hugh?" Krake inquired.

"He left at noon."

An inward sigh of relief. She entered a makeup room that was filled with the sounds of Italian opera. A dark-haired, handsome man greeted her. "Oh, making you up will be a pleasure."

A short while later she looked at her reflection. Wow! Her hair was down around her shoulders and the makeup was artistry. Singing along with Puccini arias coming out of the overhead speakers, he had created a movie star. She thanked him and he gave her a hug, wishing her good luck.

Monica was waiting and expressed approval at her appearance. Together they walked to a small sound-stage close by. The room was lit only in the center and three cameras stood ready.

Lasalle was there. He had been assigned to ask her questions off camera for this portion of the test. During the ten-minute interview, the camera was trained only on her face to catch responses from all angles.

Taking a deep breath, she entered the pool of light and sat on the canvas chair provided. Lasalle stood to the side of the camera, outlined in the dark. He asked about her previous acting experiences; college, theater, what plays she had done, what working in repertory was like and why she had left. He started walking around, always off camera so she had to turn her head to answer thus giving a view of all facial angles. At one point, standing behind her, he asked, "What do we always shout when we play 'Blockhead' at the Hilliards'?"

Her eyes bugged out. At Christmas Becky had received a game called Blockhead. This consisted of various-shaped, wooden blocks which you stacked as high as possible. The person who put on the block that knocked the stack down was called a "blockhead" and was out. They yelled, instead of "blockhead," "fughead." Because of the children, they cleaned up "fuckhead."

"Lasalle, I can't say that here."

"Sure you can." They started to laugh.

"No, I can't. This is my screen test, Lasalle."

"You can say it."

Laughing, Krake refused and they went on. Krake opened up completely and was her charismatic, charming self. Everyone clapped when they were finished. Krake knew it was good, thank God for Lasalle!

On New Year's Eve, two nights later, Krake sat alone in the Hilliards' kitchen throwing playing cards into a hat. The kids were in bed. Jocelyn and Matt had gone to a party at a director's house in the Valley. Krake kept missing. Every time the spotted rectangles skidded across the linoleum, she swore. "God damn, son-of-a-bitch, mother-fucker!"

What is it with me? Here I am, an honest-to-God STARLET for Christ's sake, and no date on New Year's Eve. Just like the night of her senior prom when she and Marilee smoked cigarettes and drank olive Cokes at the Hogshead in Belton. Dateless! I'm not even an object tonight, more like a doll on a shelf, not real, only to be looked at and envied. If only people knew. Their jealousy would be laughable.

She recalled when Ben had sent her on a "cattle call" for six exotic dancers for an Arabian nights film at MGM. Her only instructions were to bring a bathing suit. She took her one-piece white number, and arriving late on the soundstage, saw an endless line of young women in swimwear and high heels snaking across the cement floor of the warehouse. Quickly discarding her clothes and donning the suit, she was placed in line according to height. Two men, assistant directors she assumed, went up and down the row saying, "You, you, you, you." Those not picked left. Finally, it was down to Krake and nine others. They were instructed to dance individually on cue. One by one, they moved forward and waltzed around. At least, that's what Krake did. She was so overcome by self-consciousness she could hardly move, much less dance. If she had had a couple of martinis, she would have most likely stripped, but sober, it was impossible to relax. Humiliated and feeling inadequate, she was grateful to get out of there.

No Arab dancer, no date on New Year's Eve. She continued to toss cards and swear.

The day after New Year's, the phone rang. It was Monica Howser. She said, "Congratulations, dear, they picked up your contract. It wasn't the scene they liked so much as the interview. Come to my office on Thursday, say about eleven. We'll sign the papers and talk about getting you an agent."

"Monica, I'm so thrilled! What about Bradley?"

"They picked him up too and one of the girls from New York, the brunette. They didn't like the little blond, for some reason."

"Thank you for all your help. I can never repay your kindness."

"Don't be silly, dear, you deserve it. See you on Wednesday. By the way, what do you shout when you play Blockhead?"

Krake laughingly told her then put down the receiver. She couldn't believe it.

"Jocelyn, I got it! I got the seven-year contract!" Krake shouted.

"Congratulations, darling. I'm very happy for you. Matt will be so proud." Jocelyn hugged her.

Krake, suddenly self-conscious, said, "Well, it's about time. I've been here two and a half years!"

Jocelyn stepped back in amazement. "Two and a half years! Why Krake, most people are here five or ten years and never get a job and you have a seven-year contract."

Monica suggested Krake use Creative Talents Associates as her agents. One of the two men who ran the agency was related to Lew Wasserman, the president of Universal Studios and Revue Studios. Nepotism prevailed in Hollywood.

"Why do I need an agent?" she asked. "I got this contract without one."

Monica stared at her sternly, "They handle the business end of things for you, negotiate salary, see that you have all the proper facilities during the making of a film. Since you'll be working mainly here, I think being a client of the president's son-in-law would be helpful. This is just my advice. If you want to sign with someone else, that's up to you. But you must get an agent."

Krake signed with Creative Talents Associates, who never sent her on an interview. The main thing they did was go around town bragging how they had gotten her the contract.

The first year she was to be paid only when she worked. She still had to be cast. After that she would be paid weekly, the amount increasing every year. This left her struggling to make ends meet. She mentioned her finances to Monica saying maybe she ought to get a part-time job. Monica discouraged this telling her she needed to be available for interviews whenever one came up.

On the next visit to her office, Howser handed her a check for $300, an advance on her salary.

"You'll need this to tide you over. Don't thank me, you're going to earn it."

Krake could hardly believe this woman. She was constantly finding ways to help her. She hoped she could repay her someday.

16

Krake's career had reached a low pinnacle. Being under contract sounded better than it was. Monica sent her on interviews for second leads in current TV series, but lack of film experience was a drawback. Everyone was fearful of using her because she hadn't been proven. If only someone would take a chance. She longed for a part, yet dreaded that if cast she would be found lacking.

After the first few interviews at Revue, in Universal City, a long way from the Hilliards', Krake decided she either had to learn to drive or move closer to the studio. Since the automobile accident that had killed Burg she had been afraid to try.

With help, she found a small bungalow on a quiet, residential street six blocks from Universal. $75 a month, unfurnished. Hardwood floors, clean white walls and a small bay window at one end of the living room which looked out on a courtyard planted with pansies and daffodils just beginning to bloom.

Jocelyn gave Krake a big box of mismatched dishes, pots, pans and silverware. Matt took her to Akrons' on Sunset to buy a bed. At a second-hand store, she bought two chairs, a table and an old lamp to put in the bay window. She planned to refinish the furniture which had chipped paint and looked shabby. Jocelyn gave her an old, blue madras bedspread and a blue flowered tablecloth to hide the ugliness of the used table. She was busy preparing to build her nest and would move in on Saturday.

Thursday afternoon the telephone rang. Krake answered it on the extension in the garage. A vaguely familiar voice asked to speak to her.

I know that voice, whose is it?

"This is Damien. How are you?"

It's him, it's him! "Fine, how are you?"

"I'm better now. Kennedy's assassination really upset me. I've been depressed ever since it happened."

"Yes, that was terrible. I guess everybody was disturbed by it. I know we were here."

"I just got back from visiting my family in Pennsylvania. That always helps, especially seeing my mother. Did you go anywhere for the holidays?"

"No, just stayed here and got a seven-year contract with Revue Studios."

"Congratulations! Umm, are you working now?"

"No, just going on interviews," Krake replied.

"Are you doing anything tomorrow night?"

Damn, she had a date with Sam, the boy-student from *Chandler*. She had been having a "fling" with him for the past month. "No," she said.

"Would you like to see the new Rock Hudson picture, *Man's Favorite Sport*?"

"I'd love to."

"Good, I'll pick you up around eight-thirty."

"You remember where I live?"

"Yes."

"OK, see you then." She placed the receiver back on the phone and hugged herself jubilantly. He's finally asked me out. I can't believe it. Her heart sank. What about Sam? Oh, she'd make up something. I'll tell him I'm sick, that's it. What to wear? What to wear? Nothing was right, but she finally settled on a rust sweater with a rust and olive-green plaid skirt. It set off her hair.

The next day time seemed to stop. She and Becky took a walk after breakfast, pushing Andrew ahead of them in the stroller. They picked an early daffodil which he managed to tear apart before they got home. She spent time cleaning the vintage silverware Jocelyn had given her and ended up reading her outdated copies of Bazaar and wondering if it was true that she looked like Suzy Parker.

At five Sam called, suggesting they go to the Hamlet for lobster bisque.

"Gee, Sam, I'm really sorry, but I'm not feeling well. I woke up this morning with a bad headache and now I'm getting chills. I think I've got the flu."

"I'll get something at the drugstore and bring it right over."

"No! I'm in bed. Jocelyn gave me some antihistamines and they're making me sleepy. Give me a call in the morning."

"All right. Get some sleep and feel better."

"I will. Thanks, Sam." She felt guilty, but not enough to keep her from going out with Damien. He was a teen idol, handsome, sexy and she was starstruck. She couldn't take the chance that he might never call again.

The whole family was eating dinner when a car pulled up in the driveway and soon after, Sam came in. He thrust a small paper bag at her. "Here, I got some cough drops and Anacin just in case. How are you? I thought you were going to stay in bed?"

"I did sleep a little, but I knew I'd better eat something." Her face felt warm.

Jocelyn looked puzzled. "I didn't know you weren't feeling well," she said. "Are you still going to the movies?"

Krake felt a hot flush rise from her toes and envelop her entire body.

Sam's voice rose, "The movies? You're going to the movies? With who?"

"Er," gulp. "I'm ..." she stuttered and stammered.

"You broke a date with me, didn't you? Why? Who are you going with? At least tell me that."

Quietly she replied, "Damien."

"Damien! That dumb teen idol?"

She nodded.

"I see, I'm not a big enough star for you, huh?"

Matt, who along with everyone else had been unwilling spectators to this confrontation, said, "Krake, why don't you and Sam discuss this in the living room?"

"I've got nothing more to say!" Sam turned and walked out of the house. They heard the car start and he drove away, grinding the gears.

"Krake, whatever possessed you to do this?" Jocelyn shook her head.

"Jocelyn, I've had a crush on Damien ever since we did that photo layout together in November. When he called and asked me out, I just said yes."

"You have to be more considerate, darling. You obviously hurt Sam. If Damien really wants to date you, he would have called again. You've got to believe in yourself."

Krake was silent, excused herself and went out to the garage. She lay on the bed and cried. She hadn't meant to hurt Sam, she liked him. She just couldn't take the chance Damien wouldn't call back. Hating herself, she couldn't quell the excitement of seeing him.

Damien arrived promptly at eight-thirty and she was back in XKE Heaven.

The movie was mediocre. Damien didn't try to hold her hand although she left it lying open on her lap. A good downpour greeted them as they exited the show and he left to bring the car around so she wouldn't get wet. A lot of men were doing the same thing as the women waited under the marquee for their chariots. At last the sleek, blue vehicle pulled up. She ran to it, opened the door and backed in, the only way to enter such a low-slung car while wearing a skirt. Swinging her legs around, she closed the door and set her purse on the floorboard. A smiling, very pretty woman tapped on the window. Who is that? Probably an autograph hound. She rolled the window down a crack and heard her say, "You're in the wrong car." She looked at the driver. It wasn't Damien! Wait, he looked familiar. It was Gary Lockwood. Later she realized the woman was Stefani Powers. She was very embarrassed and excused herself saying her date was driving a car exactly like this. The woman laughed and Krake had to laugh with her. She got out and looked around for Damien. She saw his face smiling through the rain streaking the windshield of the car behind.

"What were you doing?" he asked as she got in.

"I got in the wrong car. I thought it was you." First the mix-up in the restaurant and now this. He must think I'm a total idiot. He'll never ask me out again.

He kept laughing over her mistake as they drove home. He didn't ask me out for coffee. He doesn't want to be with me. I don't blame him. He walked her to the door, said he had had a good time and left. No kiss, no next date. Here she had ruined her friendship with Sam and for what?

She didn't sleep well that night, tossing and turning, going over the whole evening, beating herself up with her mistakes. Somewhere around three a.m. she crept into the house, opened the china cabinet in the dining room and stole some of Matt's scotch, just like Daddy's at home. She filled a water glass and back in bed drank it all. She began to relax and not feel so bad and eventually fell asleep.

Saturday morning came too early. It was her official moving day. Matt borrowed a small truck, the Hilliards accompanied her en masse and everything was unloaded by noon.

Sadly she watched her family drive away and began to put the place together. The madras bedspread and the flowered tablecloth made it look cheery. Only the straight chairs, bereft of paint seemed needy. By late afternoon, everything was put away and she sat in the living room.

The silence was deafening. No radio, no TV, no stereo. HELP! I'll get out and take a walk, explore the neighborhood. By the time she walked the four blocks to Lankersheim Boulevard, it was almost dark. She stopped at a small grocery store. They didn't have much, but she bought a chicken breast and a bottle of white wine, less calories you know. With these purchases and the staples she had brought, she prepared an elegant, lonely meal. I miss the sounds of the Hilliard household. Andrew's cries and gurgles, Becky's running feet, Jocelyn's laugh and Matt's voice. She felt cut off. She knew almost no one in the Valley, only Monica at the studio. All her friends were over the hill (logistically) in Hollywood.

She drank the entire bottle of wine and went to bed. Sunday she slept late, then walked miles down Lankersheim looking in the closed shop windows. Stopped and got two bottles of white wine on the way home. Two, just to be safe. To make sure I don't finish one and still want more. She knew that agony well.

Monday morning, groggy from the effects of the wine she let the telephone man in and he installed a connection to the outside world. She was finishing her makeup when there was a knock on the door. It was Sam.

"Krake, let's just forget the other night," he said. "I was tired and got too upset. Can I come in?"

She opened the door and he entered her silent domain.

"It's so quiet here," Sam said.

"Too quiet," she agreed. "I miss the noise at the Hilliards. I guess I'm going through, as Tennessee Williams would say, 'a little period of adjustment.' I'll get used to it. Come in the bathroom while I put on some rouge."

"You don't need that." He took the oval compact out of her hand. "I'll put some roses in your cheeks." He put his arms around her and gave her a big kiss. He was a good kisser. Fragments of desire began to stir. She pushed them and him aside and went back to her magic palette. She was stroking the fluffy brush with the peach-colored rouge onto her cheeks when he came up from behind and began to kiss her neck. She could feel his stiffness pressing into her ass. His hands slid down her body, opened her robe and began to touch her clitoris. He lifted the robe and entered her from behind. Passion stifled protests.

When they were finished, he kissed her neck and shoulders. "Krake, I'm crazy about you. You're all I think about, dream about, want."

She kissed him, murmuring how much she cared for him too. If only she could forget Damien. I'll probably never see him again.

One afternoon, that first week in the Valley, as she was on her way home from an interview, practicing walking with her hips thrust under and through, pelvis forward, the way Jocelyn had shown her, a red sports car pulled up alongside her. A young Asian man looked up and said, "Hello, could I ask you a question?"

It was bright daylight close to a busy street, so she stopped. The car stopped too. "What?" Krake asked.

"Do you do any modeling?"

"I have modeled, but I'm an actress. I'm on my way back from an interview at Universal."

"I'm Roy Ling, a commercial photographer. I do the Cooking With Gas billboards along the freeway. Have you seen them?"

"Yes."

"I'm always looking for models to use. You look perfect. Here's my card, give me a call and we'll set up a time to do some test shots."

"OK, thanks." She took the card and put it in her purse.

"Be sure and call," he said as he drove away.

She walked on air to her apartment. Whenever anyone expressed approval of her she felt great, at least for the next five minutes. Changing out of her interview clothes into jeans, she began work refinishing a little rocking chair. Self-doubt crept in. What if the test shots are ugly? What if he doesn't want to use me? I'll probably photograph badly and be rejected. How will I get to his studio? I hate to ask anyone to take me. Can I expect Matt to drive way out here and then over to Encino? He'd have to wait. No, I just can't. The bus, what about the bus? I'd probably have to take two or three and I might get lost. And what's the point anyway? I won't be what they want. The mind fuck continued and by the end of the afternoon she went to the grocery store, got two bottles of wine and drank herself into oblivion. She came to the next day and couldn't find his card, anywhere. Had she flushed it, or taken it outside and buried it, what? She only felt relief that she had been saved from possible rejection.

While she was in bed nursing her hangover, Damien called. He wanted her to go to Palm Springs next week, for three or four days. She said yes, and immediately called Jocelyn.

"Jocelyn, Damien just called and invited me to Palm Springs next week."

"Darling, that sounds great. How are you doing, any interviews?"

"A couple, but I haven't been cast yet. Monica sent me to Columbia. I read with Arthur Penn. He's directing a new movie, *Mickey One*, starring Warren Beatty. He called me back for a second reading, but I haven't heard anything. I guess he's decided to use someone else. Probably just as well. Knowing me I'd fall madly in love with Warren and have my heart broken."

Jocelyn laughed. "You know what? I'm going to send Matt out there to get you. We miss you."

She spent the night and most of the next day at the Hilliards. Jocelyn had learned a new dance step which was becoming popular called the "twist." It didn't take long to master and when Lasalle came by that evening they "twisted" late into the night.

Home again the next evening, the loneliness was dissipated somewhat by her upcoming trip. The main item on the agenda was what clothes to take. Three or four days, this was monumental. A bathing suit. For years she had refused to wear a bikini because of the appendix scar crossing her abdomen. Recently she mentioned this to her gynecologist during a routine checkup and he said, "Wear one, it makes you look worldly." So a bikini. What shoes, what jewelry? Should I bring something dressy? Finally she decided on three cotton dresses, one rather fancy, and several pairs of shorts, tops and slacks.

The Monday morning she was to leave she was on the phone talking to Matt about developing a characterization for a part she was scheduled to read for the following week. Suddenly the operator's voice interrupted, "I have an emergency call from Damien." Krake's heart sank. He was canceling.

She replaced the receiver and the phone rang immediately.

"Hi, I had to let you know I'll be picking you up at one-thirty instead of noon. I've got to meet with my business manager before we leave."

She assured him this would be fine and hung up, giddy with her own importance. A movie star broke in on my phone conversation, I'm a part of this glamorous and exciting world at last.

Her suitcase just fit in the small trunk of the XKE. The day was cloudy and the top was up. Damien drove fast. As soon as they swung off the freeway and onto the road leading into Palm Springs, the magic began. Mt. San Jacinto rose so high part of the sky was blotted out. Only a thin sliver of pale blue crested the dark peaks. The temperature had risen twenty degrees at least. Los Angeles had been mild, but here it was hot. In February, how exotic!

A fantasy setting, the town looked like a tropical version of Carmel. No quaintness here, instead, pastel picturesque. Their hotel was a pale pink adobe building with bungalows. Theirs had a sitting room facing the kidney-shaped pool. Krake quickly opened the drapes to let in the afternoon sun. They left their suitcases in the bedroom and went to a pharmacy so he could pick up some things. These turned out to be sunglasses, suntan oil, and two bottles of Dom Perignon. Some corner drugstore. Returning to the room, Damien asked if she wanted to go swimming.

"No, I'll wait until tomorrow," she said. The truth was she didn't want to redo her hair and makeup.

They decided to go out to eat. Damien rose and extended a hand to help her up. His fingers closed around hers, he pulled her to her feet, close to him. Her heart was beating wildly.

"You know I can sleep out here on the sofa or get you another suite, if you like." He spoke softly in her ear.

"Why?"

"If you'd rather not sleep in the same …"

"Let's see how it goes." His shyness was charming. This whole attitude of concern for her welfare had such an appeal. Fame hadn't made him arrogant or self-serving.

In the restaurant, people kept staring. Finally a young woman with a little boy approached.

"Are you Damien?" she asked.

He nodded.

"I thought so. My name is Darlene Hoyt. This is my son, Barry. Could we have your autograph?"

He graciously signed the piece of paper, smiled and patted Barry on the head. They went back to their table, obviously enchanted.

Krake was thrilled. She felt so important being with a celebrity. Almost like it was happening to her. The Italian wine they had with dinner didn't raise her endorphins like the adoration of Damien's fans.

Dinner over, they cruised Palm Canyon Drive so she could get a glimpse of paradise after dark. Sitting in the open car, head resting on smooth leather, Krake felt like she was in a dream. The street lights hidden in the fronds of the palm trees lining the broad streets shone down on the fashionably dressed, tanned, upper middle-class populace. I'm riding in an actual Jaguar convertible, with an actual teen age idol! Me, me, Krake Forrester, from Podunk, U.S.A.. I'll remember this all my life. She intimidated herself into silence during the drive.

As soon as they got back to the room Damien opened the champagne. The pool lights cast rippled reflections across the windows. He closed the drapes and turned on the radio. Soft, romantic music filled the night and he drew her close. They set their champagne flutes down and kissed. Heady with the fantasy of the situation, the kiss was glorious for Krake. They were soon in bed. Damien was so gentle, not much foreplay, but he had put a quarter in the vibrating bed. Besides, the last few hours had been arousal enough.

The next day, they lounged by the pool, listening to music on a portable radio. Over dinner Damien had revealed that he had turned twenty-one the week before. No one gave him a party or even a present. He had treated himself to a new stereo system and the portable radio.

This famous man has no friends, not like my friends, Krake concluded. No birthday party, how sad. She found herself pitying this teen idol.

Just before noon he went inside to make some calls. She baked in the sun as the West Coast's answer to Walter Winchell, Jimmy Fidler, came on the radio with his five minutes of Hollywood gossip. "Damien, the heart throb of millions is currently dating Revue Studios contractee, Krake Forrester. Looks like love." She didn't hear the rest, only wanted to shout to anyone within earshot, "Hey, that's me! I'm Krake Forrester!" The pool area happened to be deserted, fortunately.

After another Italian dinner, they saw *Charade*, with Audrey Hepburn and Cary Grant. A short subject preceded the main feature and held their attention because of a haunting background melody called, "Stranger on the Shore." It became their song. After the movie they had another night of passion accompanied by the second bottle of Dom Perignon. This time Damien vibrated the bed himself.

The next morning, Damien wanted to do a little shopping. He was leaving for Hawaii shortly to do a surfing feature and needed some shirts and shorts. While Damien was looking at shirts, he suggested she try on bikinis. She had told him the one she was wearing was borrowed and he wanted to buy her one. She tried on several, all of which he said he liked. Krake quietly asked the saleslady if she thought he liked one particular suit over another and the woman replied, "I think he'd like you in anything." Smiling, Krake chose the bright yellow bikini and began to look at dresses. Noticing, Damien told her to get one if she found anything she liked. They left the store loaded down with packages. She could have bought several items, but restrained herself and chose one elegant, black-and-white checked sheath. It looked stunning.

Back at the hotel, she tried on the new bikini. As she was descending the steps into the shallow end of the pool, an older man said to Damien, "If I had someone like that in my pool, I'd never set foot on dry land." She blushed as Damien nodded his head in agreement. They floated and dived and kissed in one corner until the phone in their room rang and Damien went dripping to answer it. He talked for quite awhile then rejoined her outside.

"I have to go back to LA tonight," he said. "The film in Hawaii has been moved up. It starts in two days. I'm sorry, I wanted to stay at least another day."

Disappointed, she went inside to pack. When the *Ed Sullivan Show* came on, she had showered and was doing her makeup. It must be Sunday. I've lost track of time. Damien sat at the foot of the bed, watching. He knew and liked Sullivan, and had appeared on his show a couple of times. He shouted for Krake to come in and see a new musical group from England. He had heard they were really good.

A group of four young men began to sing, "I love you, yeah, yeah, yeah." They were good. She liked the harmony and the beat.

"Who are they?" Krake asked.

"The Beatles. They're going to be big," Damien predicted.

"Maybe so," she said, more concerned with putting on her new dress than with any singing group.

They went to Don the Beachcomber's for dinner. The dark waiting room was full as they pushed their way to the reservation desk. The maître d' took one look, picked up two menus and said, "Damien! Right this way." He led them to an empty booth in the main dining room. Wow! He seated us like that, no waiting, no nothing. She had never been with anyone who was catered to like this.

The meal was delicious and she was sad they were leaving. The car was already loaded so they headed straight back after dinner. He asked if she would mind spending the night at his place in Beverly Hills. Mind? Hardly.

The building was small, only three stories and a penthouse where Damien lived. The elevator door opened onto a hallway leading to his front door. Inside was a large living room with a grand piano in one corner, a small, well-equipped kitchen, one bedroom with a dressing alcove and a tiny bathroom. A balcony ran along two sides with sliding glass doors. In the darkness, discrete lights dotted the hills of Beverly.

Damien made a call to his agent while Krake slipped off the new dress and slid under the covers of a king-size bed. Damien had turned on the television as soon as they arrived and the eleven o'clock news reprised the Beatles appearance on the Sullivan show, calling this a revolution in rock 'n roll.

"I must call Monica in the morning," she said sleepily as Damien took her in his arms. His kisses soon aroused her drowsy body and the lovemaking was sweet. She fell asleep snuggled next to him. The ringing of the telephone woke them. The clock on top of the TV read seven-thirty.

After breakfast, Krake made her phone call to Monica. A loud, angry voice said, "Where have you been? I've been calling all over for the last two days. Where were you?"

Meekly, Krake answered, "I was in Palm Springs."

Monica's voice was stern. "Never, never go away like that without leaving word where I can reach you. How soon can you get to my office?"

"Just a minute, let me see when I can get a ride." She put her hand over the receiver and asked Damien how soon he could drive her to the Universal lot. He said whenever she was ready. She spoke to Monica, "In an hour."

"I want you to read for a part on an Alfred Hitchcock that's shooting next week. Get here as soon as you can."

"Will do." She hurriedly made up her face and gathered her things, giving Damien her apartment key so he could drop off her suitcase and his old stereo. When she had mentioned she didn't have one, he was quick to offer his, along with some albums she liked.

The XKE pulled up in front of the studio gates. As he kissed her goodbye, a small blond jumped out of a convertible that screeched to a halt in front of them. Krake recognized Sandra Dee and the car's driver, her husband, Bobby Darin. I am becoming a part of things, she concluded with excitement.

That feeling lasted until the reading, which was a disaster. The part she read for was a hillbilly type, so she took off her sneakers and read barefoot. Apparently her feet and shoes were rather gamy. While she was reading, the director and producer turned away, put their hands up and covered their noses.

Involved in the reading, she didn't register their responses until she got home and taking off the offending shoes, got a whiff herself. Awful! She was so embarrassed. Monica called later and said they had decided to use someone else. She knew it wasn't her reading that stank!

17

The three weeks Damien was in Hawaii dragged by. Krake wrote to him every other day. He called each weekend and the conversations went on for at least an hour. She called Sam and asked him to stop by, she needed to talk to him. It was difficult, but she told him she was in love with Damien. He was hurt, said he loved her. Surprised, she told him it wasn't love for her, but for the life at the Hilliards he felt the emotion for. He wasn't convinced, but left. Relief was her primary emotion.

Finally it was the day of Damien's return. She had bought a new, vivid blue sleeveless dress and made him dinner at his apartment. He arrived home with the entourage of people who usually accompanied him: his business manager, agent, valet and several flunkies whose jobs were never clear. After brief introductions, he made everyone drinks while Krake busied herself in the kitchen.

She thought they would never leave, but after nearly two hours, Damien showed the last of them out. Soon Krake and Damien were lying in a tangle of bedclothes and people clothes.

"I missed you," he murmured.

"Me too."

"I kept all your letters. You don't throw away letters like that." The admission surprised her. She was only beginning to realize how lonely this man was. How hungry for genuine love and affection. Despite all his fame, he was an innocent creature, sinking in the quagmire of Hollywood. Krake was like a breath of fresh air in his life. Her sweetness and honesty constantly amazed him. He was afraid to admit how much he cared. He had had no chance to be young and in love. His childhood and adolescence were torn away from him when he was thrown into the limelight at the age of fifteen.

Krake was five years older, but with her emotional immaturity and his veneer of adulthood, they were equal. She helped him unpack, pausing only to exchange caresses or a kiss as they passed.

They lingered a long time over dinner. He was impressed by the meal of chicken Kiev and pureed carrots. He talked about his trip home the previous Christmas. He had just purchased a brand new house for his parents. In a suburb of Detroit, it stood on ten acres with a creek and woods covering the back eight. While there, he went hunting every day. One afternoon, when the winter sun was casting purple shadows on the snow, he sat down on a log and reveled in the stillness and beauty of the setting. As he was gazing around a magnificent buck came into the clearing. He didn't see Damien right away and nibbled on a few sprigs of dried grass poking through the icy covering. When he saw him, he stopped.

"He stared at me with those brown eyes for about thirty seconds, turned and walked back into the forest. For the longest time I stayed still, but he didn't come back. I'll never forget that. You know Krake, I hate it here. Beverly Hills, the rat race, someday I'm going to live in Michigan. That's where I feel like myself." He poured another glass of wine.

Damien was different from the person Krake thought he would be. The image of that winter panorama struck a chord in her. It brought back memories of walking in a flurry of snowflakes, snow crunching under foot while Boots bounded through high white banks at her side. I think we may belong together she thought as she finished the last of the chocolate mousse.

She brought candles into the bedroom which she lit and they lay in bed together. "Tell me you love me," she said. Two bottles of wine had loosened her tongue.

He looked at her in silence.

"Tell me you love me, even if you don't. I want to hear you say it." Silence. "I love you," she said. Silence. "Nod your head then."

He nodded slightly. She had to be satisfied with that.

The next day they spent lazily watching TV in the bedroom with the drapes drawn. Krake opened them once and he closed them right away. They talked and he told her why he had quit singing the year before.

"I couldn't take it anymore. No one said I was good. I knew that I wasn't and refused to do it anymore." He lit a cigarette and offered her one.

"How did it all start?"

"I was working as a janitor's assistant, making six dollars a week, when Herb Marioni, the promoter, saw me and decided he could make me a star. I was scared. The first time I walked out on a stage and those girls started screaming, I couldn't believe it. Screaming for me! Me, a janitor's assistant! When I tried to get from the limousine to the theater, girls would tear my clothes, grab me and say things you wouldn't believe. I didn't know fans behaved like that. I was only fifteen and a half. After four years, it got so I couldn't walk out on that stage one more time. Now that I've given up singing I want to act. I've done movies and TV and I enjoy it. I'm studying acting and maybe I'll be good someday."

Krake listened with compassion. The demanding, highly critical, amoral, unscrupulous world of fame and fortune was his and he was in therapy three times a week to try and deal with it.

Damien said he didn't have time to run back and forth to the Valley. Would she be willing to live in the penthouse? She agreed, but kept her own apartment, although she only went there to pick up mail. Damien introduced her to the local grocer and told her she could charge on his account. They established a routine. He took her to Universal City when she had interviews and the remainder of the time she spent at the penthouse. After planning the evening's menu, she would go window-shopping on Rodeo Drive, stop at the grocery store to purchase the makings for dinner and perhaps steal a rose from someone's yard on the way back.

Damien admonished, "Beverly Hills cops are really strict about things like that. They may even stop and question you if they see you walking in a residential area. No one walks here."

She had always walked and continued to.

Washing the dinner dishes, she would gaze out the window and watch him shoot pigeons out of the trees with his 22-caliber rifle. Recalling the incident with the deer in Michigan, Krake guessed Damien was trying to bring the woods to Beverly Hills. What a bizarre domestic scene. Not how I thought life would be at all. Three children, a bungalow with a picket fence and my husband reading the evening newspaper after a hard day at the office.

On some mornings, waking up at six, she went to the kitchen and drank brandy. This was highly dangerous since her capacity for liquor was so low she would be slightly drunk by the time he woke up. But her anxiety about the relationship drove her to it. She was worried about blowing it. The unreasonable fear of losing another man she loved was overpowering. Only alcohol kept her from screaming it to everyone. She tried to limit her drinking to the evenings when Damien would drink too, but sometimes she couldn't help it. She felt like everything was in the palm of her hand and she couldn't make a fist.

Krake tried to appear normal, cheerful and happy, but inside she was falling apart. The constant anxiety of losing him and the contract drained her. The descent was rapid and she was unable to stop it or ask for help. To an outsider it would have seemed ludicrous perhaps, but she had been drawing upon her meager inner reserves for years, long after they were depleted.

Monica informed Krake that she was going to represent the studio at a golf tournament in Las Vegas in two weeks, and should come to Monica's office and decide what clothes she could borrow from wardrobe. Krake hardly slept, indulging in fantasies of being a studio representative. The next morning Monica informed her there had been a change, she didn't have enough screen credits and the studio was sending someone else. Another disappointment and another drunk.

A month of similarly neurotic behavior and Damien announced she would have to move back to the Valley. The thought of the isolation and loneliness brought tears. He comforted her by saying they would find her an apartment on this side of the mountains and could see each other nearly as often.

"You need to find a job too," he said.

"I know, but what?" Fear clutched her.

"Go to Flair, the big modeling agency. I bet they'd find you something."

Bradley's agency? Why not?

A cursory glance in the Sunday morning newspapers unearthed a perfect studio apartment on Doheny Drive. It once was the music room in a large mansion with a private entrance, knotty-pine paneling, a hot plate and a minuscule bathroom.

Damien paid the first month's rent.

They moved her out of her bungalow apartment. She had lived there six months. Krake gave away the furniture and returned what she had borrowed from Jocelyn.

After settling into the music room, she called Flair and made an appointment. The agency took one look and sent her on an interview for a hostess position in a small restaurant on Wilshire Boulevard. She was hired immediately.

Being a nervous wreck over what to wear and whether she would look all right robbed her of any sleep the evening before she started. Still spending nights with Damien, she took the bus down Wilshire to begin work. Suddenly she couldn't talk. In a daze, feeling other-worldly, she led customers to a table, gave them menus, then retreated to the bathroom to cry. At the end of the third day, the manager called her into his office and told her it wasn't working out. It was no surprise.

She managed to get on a bus headed to Damien's. Looking at her reflection in the window, she began to weep. He was proud of me and now what? What's wrong with me? I can't do anything. I hate myself, I'm such a failure.

In the midst of this weeping and self-flagellation, she became aware of an intense pain in her lower back. She had suffered a kidney stone a few months before and this felt like it could be another one. She stayed on the bus and got off at her doctor's office.

With a temperature of 103, she was admitted to the Cedar's Clinic immediately and assigned to a small private room.

Shortly, Damien appeared and she quietly told him she had been fired.

"Never mind that," he said. "We've got to find out what's wrong with you and get you well." He took her hand. Take care of me, you idiot, she thought.

A couple of floor nurses peeked at Damien, giggled and disappeared. He left soon afterwards because she was getting sleepy from the sedative they had given her.

The diagnosis was acute kidney infection. Damien sent a lovely bouquet of white daisies and yellow roses and came faithfully each evening to spend an hour or so talking and holding her hand. Krake was very content. After the first several hours, she had had no pain and was receiving excellent care. For a short time, she didn't have to face the real world and try to make her way in it.

She stayed for ten days, at the end of which Damien offered to have her spend the first few days recuperating with him. He picked her up at the hospital's side entrance in a new, black Cadillac convertible.

"What happened to the blue hornet?" she asked as she slid into the front seat.

"I can't afford the rental," he said quietly.

"What?"

"Insurance on a sports car is too high. My new business manager told me a couple of days ago I had to make some changes in my lifestyle."

She looked puzzled. "I thought you'd made a lot of money when you were singing, all the concerts, tours, records, movies ..." her voice trailed off.

"You know Herb Marconi, the one who 'discovered' me? I just found out that he swindled me out of a lot of my earnings when I first started. I was unfamiliar with any of the financial end; I let him take care of it all. He really did. He must have siphoned off big bucks during the years he was working for me. I had no idea until a few months ago when I hired an accountant to do my taxes. Large sums of money were missing. Marconi denied it, but I know he's guilty. Harvey suggested I hire Joel Levy and he seems to be doing a good job. But he's been putting limits on my spending. My family's used to getting anything they want. I've explained the situation, but they don't seem to understand. A stack of new bills came in yesterday. I've got to call and try and make it clear. Since his retirement, my Dad buys champagne by the case. Levy warned me this has to stop. What am I going to say to my Dad? I don't want to hurt his feelings."

"Explain what's going on and I'm sure he'll be agreeable," she offered.

"I've tried before. He either doesn't believe me or doesn't realize the seriousness of the predicament."

"Why doesn't Levy call him?"

His father had suffered a heart attack two years before and everyone handled him with kid gloves. Damien seemed closer to his mother. She was always calling and they had long talks Krake envied. Her estrangement from her family bothered her a great deal. Her father never called her and rarely wrote. Her parents had not been impressed with her seven-year contract and only seemed ashamed of her, that she wasn't working steadily and making money. She felt rootless without that core of support.

Damien's concern for his finances was a surprise. He wasn't wildly extravagant, but never looked at price tags the way she did. To her, that was close to wild extravagance. With every purchase Krake made or thought of making, she heard Lorraine's voice, "You can't have that. We just don't have the money. Do you think we're made of money?"

The fact that Damien had taken her into his confidence made her feel much closer to him. And worry about money was a subject she could readily relate to.

He lit a cigarette as they headed down Wilshire towards Ah Fong's, one of their favorite restaurants, and began to talk about a man named Martin Luther King who had been interviewed on TV that morning. Damien was impressed with his views on equality and integration and said that he believed in twenty years or less a black man would sit in the White House.

"Sure, after he's cleaned the floors," Krake retorted "I lived in Texas for seven years and I know what racism is." Her voice rose as the injustices she had witnessed came to the surface. "I've heard high school boys discussing whether to go 'gator giggin' or 'nigger knockin.' I've seen Negroes forced to drink from Negro-only fountains, sit apart from white folks and in the rear of public vehicles."

"That used to exist, but not anymore. The Supreme Court ruling made that illegal."

"So it's hidden, but it's the same. All you have to do is spend some time in the South. They'd as soon lynch a Negro as look at him."

"Krake, you're exaggerating."

She began to get angry. "What do you know about it? Have you seen the poverty Negroes live in or the injustices the Negroes suffer in the legal system or the blatant double standard imposed?"

"Look at Sydney Poitier, Sammy Davis Jr., Lena Horne and all the others out here. Poitier just won an Academy Award for *Lilies of the Field*." He angrily stubbed out his cigarette.

"I know, but the movie industry society is different. In the arts, people are more tolerant of others."

"I guess that's what makes me think we'll have a Negro president in twenty years."

"You have to have the votes of the entire country to elect a president. The South alone would unanimously vote NO. Maybe someday there will be a Negro president, but I doubt if it'll happen in our lifetime."

Damien looked straight ahead as he parked the car in front of Ah Fong's. She got out when he opened the door. Halfway up the narrow walk to the entrance, he stopped abruptly. "I can't take any more of this, I'm taking you to your apartment." He went back to the car. She followed slowly, not understanding.

"What did I do?" she pleaded, puzzled.

"It's too bad you don't think as much of yourself as you do of Negroes."

"What do you mean? I don't understand. Why are you taking me home?"

"It's over, I can't take it anymore," he said firmly.

"Can't take what anymore?" she asked, her heart in her mouth.

He didn't answer and the rest of the short ride to her little place on Doheny Drive was made in complete silence. She got out and he helped carry in the few belongings she had had at Cedars.

"Goodbye," he mumbled, got in the car and left.

She sat on the bed in shock. She couldn't bear to think about it being over. A drink, I need a drink. There isn't a drop of anything in the house and I don't have any money either. What'll I do? She thought for a moment. I'll walk to the grocery store where I can charge on Damien's account. She recalled Dr. Wasserman telling her that cranberry juice was good for the kidneys, so she bought a quart of it and a fifth of vodka. She emptied both bottles over the next few hours.

In the early morning while regaining consciousness, she had a vision, or as some would say, a hallucination. Nestled in the green-gold hills of California was a group of two-story, white stucco, Spanish style buildings with red-tile roofs. The windows were covered with black wrought-iron scrollwork. Like a scene on a postcard, it came with a startling clarity, but it wasn't a place she had ever seen before.

The cold, gray morning light crept in. Her hangover was horrendous. It almost blotted out her grief over the loss of Damien, but not quite. Three aspirin helped only a little. What was she going to do? From this fall, she couldn't get up. She couldn't do it anymore. Not any of it. No more interviews, no more rejections, no more scrimping to pay the rent, no more dates, no more being dumped. The ache of disbelief in herself outweighed all other emotions.

Desperately she dialed Belton. It was Saturday and miraculously her father answered. She couldn't have handled Lorraine.

"Hello, who is this? Krake, is that you? I can barely hear you." Her father's voice was clear. He sounded so close. She wished he could reach out and hold her.

"Daddy, I want to come home." Despair was evident in her voice.

"You mean you want to come home for a visit?"

"No, Daddy, to live. I can't take LA anymore."

"Krake, you know there's always a place for you, but there's nothing here you'd want."

With a sinking heart, she knew he was right.

"What's happened? We thought you were doing fine. You sounded so good at Christmas."

The call to which he was referring had taken place right after the New Year, the day she learned about the seven-year contract. Her mother's response when she had told her was, "That's nice. It's been so cold here I think the azaleas in the front may have frozen." She repeated the news to Daddy when he came on the line. "Yes, dear. Your name was on the front page of Variety, my, my." No excitement, no questions, no support. Never any support.

In the five years since she had left home, her father had gradually assumed a different attitude towards her. His belief in her had diminished and his former pride in her achievements was replaced by disappointment that she hadn't accomplished more. He didn't realize how slim the chances of being given a seven-year contract were and his casual response told Krake it should have been easy.

She clutched the bedspread in her hand and said, "Daddy, I don't know what to do. Help me!"

"I love you, honey, but I don't think you'd be happy at home."

"I know, Daddy, I just needed to hear your voice. I'll be okay."

"I know you will. I love you, sweetheart."

"I love you, too." She put down the phone and lay

unmoving. She had always counted on him to stand by her and believe in her. It felt like he had cut the cord. She knew he loved her, but he couldn't handle her being at home again. The relationship between her and her mother was so volatile she guessed she couldn't blame him for not wanting to be a referee again. Her needs were beyond him.

Later, Damien called, "How are you?"

"Hung over."

"I bet. What were you drinking anyway?"

"It doesn't matter, whatever it was it worked," she groaned.

"That was some phone call at two this morning."

What was he talking about? She had absolutely no recollection of making any call. "Yes," she said vaguely, wishing she had enough nerve to ask him what she had said.

"Call me if you need anything," he invited before hanging up .

She phoned Matt directly after Damien's call. As soon as he could get away, he came for her. They sat talking in her old room in the garage. She told him she couldn't go on. He suggested she see a therapist. He had been in Freudian analysis during his teen years and said it helped. Since she had no income, he proposed she go somewhere the therapy would be free.

"Where would that be?" she asked.

"A state institution. Camarillo State Hospital is just up the coast."

A state hospital! Visions of Olivia de Haviland in *The Snake Pit* flashed through her mind.

"Honey, you have no money," Matt said. "If it's not suitable, you won't commit yourself. It'll be on a voluntary basis, so you can leave whenever you want."

In acute pain, clutching at anything, she agreed.

"Matt, can I stay here tonight?" She began to cry. Matt held her while she sobbed and sobbed. The pain was excruciating. She felt like she had fallen into a cleverly concealed pit. It was black and bottomless and there was no way out.

Jocelyn brought her dinner on a tray in the garage and she cried herself to sleep.

The next morning the old Peugot hummed along with only an occasional sputter. In less than two hours, they left the main highway and took a narrow, winding road over the hills to a group of white stucco, Spanish-style buildings nestled below. It was the place in her hallucination! What coming attractions were in store?

Matt drove up the lovely, curving drive and parked in a visitor's spot not far from the entrance. They ascended stone steps and went through the arched door. A woman in a severe, navy-blue dress sat behind the desk. "What patient did you come to see? We don't usually have visitors on Monday."

Matt spoke, "We're not visitors. We'd like to see the administrator, a Mr. Douglas, I believe." He had called earlier to arrange an interview. An interview for the loony bin! Would she measure up or what? She was terrified that Mr. Douglas would take one look, tell her to take two aspirin and don't call him in the morning. Her impression of her surroundings was limited after that. She felt deprived of all of her senses. The only thing left was the pain. Mr. Douglas's curly mustache vibrated as he asked them to be seated and inquired how she felt.

She had trouble talking. Pain clutched at her vocal cords. She tried to tell him and he must have understood.

Douglas came out from behind the desk and stood looking down at her. "I think we can help. We'll put you on a ward right away and have our psychiatrist stop by and do an evaluation this afternoon."

"Today? Now? I can't. I have to close up my apartment, store my things and attend to some business affairs first," she said.

Douglas shook his head skeptically. "You won't be back."

"Yes, I will. I'll be back on Friday," she promised convincingly.

"We'll see. I don't think so."

He was willing to have her commit herself. The only contingency was that she stay seventy-two hours. After that, she was free to leave at any time.

Relieved some solution was forming, she and Matt took the beach road on the way back and pulled over in a deserted spot.

They got out and picnicked on sandwiches Jocelyn had packed for them. Matt said, "Look at this time at the hospital as an opportunity to discover who you are and what you want. You seem sort of rootless, drifting."

"I just want to curl up under the covers and suck my thumb. I don't know what to do," said Krake.

"Forget about what to do and just let yourself be. When you're stronger, you'll know."

"I will?" she asked.

"Trust me," he said.

She kept hoping for a miracle, a prince, a daddy, any kind of rescuer. No one arrived. All she had wanted to hear since leaving home is "Krake, will you marry me? Krake, I'll take care of you."

When Krake told Monica she was committing herself to Camarillo, she was very understanding. "Don't worry, it'll work out. I'll tell everyone you're in Texas visiting a sick relative. Call me when you're back."

Damien helped her move her wardrobe over to the Hilliards'. In the midst of the shift, he said he would like to drive her to Camarillo. So she spent her last night in Los Angeles with him. He made love to her so sweetly, like she was a delicate Dresden figurine. She didn't feel she would break, only that she had disappeared. Afterwards, lying side by side, toes touching, he said, "You should get out of this town, you don't belong here."

"You don't either," she said.

"I'm in too deep, I can't."

She slept well and the next morning the Cadillac headed north. They had almost no conversation. "Stranger on the Shore" came on the radio. He reached over and touched her hand. Only four months ago, they had decided it was their song. Now her life had crashed down around her and she was lost in the rubble.

Too soon the Caddy swung up the curving drive. He pulled over and shut off the engine.

"Krake, I feel like this is my fault. I'm sorry. What can I do?"

Aside from marrying me, nothing. Aloud she said, "It's not your fault. It's so many things. I can't explain." She couldn't, because she didn't know herself how it had all gone wrong.

He took her small suitcase from the trunk. She was allowed to bring three dresses. That would cut out a lot of stress right there. They went inside. With a swift kiss on the cheek and a "take care of yourself," he left her at the desk. She watched him run to his car, seemingly anxious to get out of such a depressing place. Gone. She turned, sat down on a wooden bench in the foyer and waited to be taken to her ward.

18

She waited and waited. Low, guttural moans followed by cries and occasionally a sharp scream seemed to be coming from a room off to the right. She listened until her curiosity got the better of her. Halfway down a long corridor, she looked in a doorway. The scene that met her eyes filled her with horror. Right in front of her were large, wooden cribs. Behind the bars were human forms distorted by disease, cries came from misshapen mouths. The stench of feces and vomit filled the air. Behind the cribs were a group of wheelchairs and beds, the occupants of some writhing around while others lay unmoving. No one noticed her. If this is what it's going to be like on 4C, I'm leaving. Fuck the seventy-two hour rule! This made *The Snake Pit* look like *Father Knows Best*. She whirled around as a hand touched her shoulder.

"Miss Forrester, you shouldn't be here." A gray-haired nurse, with Mrs. Chalmers printed on her name tag, stood beside her. "You were supposed to wait on that bench down the hall."

"I heard all this noise in here so …," she gestured towards the scene.

"This is the ward for the physically as well as mentally handicapped. These people can't walk or dress themselves. They have to be cared for in every way." The woman took her arm. "Come and have some lunch, then we'll go up to 4C."

She was guided down the hallway and into a brightly lit dining room where food was being served, cafeteria style. This was the employees' dining room. The patients had already eaten in their dining room and lunch was over. Krake selected some unappetizing-looking meatloaf, molded lime salad and a piece of white bread. She sat at a table alone and tried to eat. She couldn't swallow. Pictures of the handicapped ward kept returning, turning her stomach.

Finally, Chalmers came back and took her up three flights of stairs to a set of big double doors leading to Ward 4C. She opened them with one of the keys in a large bunch dangling from her belt.

The room was large and airy with windows along the far wall. The entire place was ringed with straight-backed wooden chairs. Half of them were occupied by women ranging in age from around twenty to perhaps past seventy. Small tables and chairs, couches and armchairs were scattered in the middle of the open space. Groups of women played cards or board games. At most of the tables, people sat alone staring off into space. A few crocheted and one woman was writing on a yellow tablet.

Everyone stopped what they were doing to look at Krake. She followed Chalmers across the expanse and into a long, narrow room with a row of beds lining each wall.

"Yours is number sixteen. I'll take your suitcase. You'll have to wear a uniform until you earn a red card." Chalmers opened a closet lined with sheets and pillowcases and folded uniforms. Krake chose a red-and-white pinstriped dress and a navy-blue one for her change of clothes.

She changed quickly and went into the Day Room. No one paid any attention so she wandered around looking at the various women. Few even glanced up. She finally found a good-size drawing pad and some pastel pencils on a large library table in a corner, sat down and began to aimlessly color on a blank sheet. She drew mountains and flowers and stick figures. Gradually relaxing, she became absorbed in her endeavors. Two women sat down at the table.

"Are you a nurse?" one of them inquired.

"No, I'm a patient like you."

"No, you're not. I bet you've been sent here to spy on us," the other accused.

"No, really, I'm just a patient. This is my first day here. I'm Krake."

Silence. They moved away.

The afternoon dragged on. At last the buzzer announced it was time for dinner. Mrs. Lictner, the head nurse, and two attendants herded everyone out through heavy double doors and down the two flights of stairs to the patients' dining room, located in a different building. A disagreeable odor stopped her at the entrance. She never found out what it was. Maybe decayed garbage, who knows? The smell was there at every meal.

The food wasn't bad, for institutional fare. The hospital grew most of the vegetables and grains in the large farm behind the buildings. The male hospital population worked there to earn grounds privileges. They also tended herds of cattle and sheep which provided the milk and some of the meat. But odor is so closely connected with taste, it was some time before Krake could separate the two and enjoy the meals. The dining hall sat several hundred and the rows of long tables and benches seemed endless. Everyone served themselves, again cafeteria style.

The first dinner over, she went back to the ward. A thin, faded elderly woman she had noticed earlier sitting alone on a couch stopped and asked if she would write a letter to her mother. Rose said she had been a patient here so long she had forgotten how to write. Asking around, Krake obtained some stationery and a pen. Rose rambled on, repeated herself and constantly lost her train of thought, but at last the letter was finished. When Krake told one of the other women what she had done, the woman laughed and replied, "Rose gets every new patient to write letters for her. Her mother's been dead, for years."

This really was the nuthouse!

It was hard for Krake to remember that the seemingly normal people she was living with, weren't. She was conned frequently during the first few days and was issued a warning to keep her purse with her at all times. Kleptomaniacs, you know. Not just a word in a beginning psychology text, but a reality.

One more communal room awaited her discovery. The bathroom. A long row of sinks and mirrors on one side of the tiled space was complimented by an equally long row of toilet stalls sans doors facing them. Every night Ward 4C lined up to use the facilities before bedtime at nine-thirty. There were a dozen showers beyond the sinks and shifts of twelve showered together. Krake felt awkward brushing her teeth with one hand while holding her purse with the other.

The ward lined up at lights out to receive a small paper cup with medication for their particular illness and sedatives to help them sleep along with another paper cup of water. They had to swallow their pills in front of the head nurse who noted their consumption on a large pad. Krake fell asleep easily.

The next morning after breakfast, Krake was assigned to the laundry. Giant machines were washing and drying linens for the entire hospital. The noise was deafening. Her job was emptying the huge dryers and folding uniforms, sheets and pillowcases. Conversation was impossible over the din of the machinery so she was left with her thoughts. Two persisted; I look like Ida Lupino in a prison movie and wouldn't my mother just die if she could see me now?

That night was movie night. Of all movies to be playing, it was *Alaskan Adventure*, starring John Wayne and Damien!

As 4C marched in a double line to the auditorium where the movies were shown, she said softly to Mary walking beside her, "I used to date Damien. In fact, he brought me up here two days ago."

Mary looked at her from under bushy brows and said, "Sure, honey."

It was the first time she had seen Damien on the big screen in living color and she missed him even more. A few months before, they had watched a *Twilight Zone* episode in which he played a deranged killer. He was good. His performance in this wasn't as polished, but his natural charm and genuineness came through.

Back on 4C after the screening, in the line waiting for an empty sink, she sensed someone behind her and started to turn when two strong hands grabbed her shoulder and shoved, hard. It was Maudie, the catatonic. Krake's head hit the tile floor and she lost consciousness for a moment. The contents of her purse scattered everywhere. Maudie fled. After that, when Maudie stood next to her in the lunch line, tremors of terror coursed through Krake's body, but Maudie never touched her again. She never found out what had provoked Maudie's violence.

The afternoon of her third day, Krake met with a psychiatrist. Dr. Helen Powell was an efficient, middle-age woman who never had enough time for anyone. Krake saw her on only one other occasion during her two-month stay. The problems of understaffing were monstrous.

"Briefly tell me about yourself," said Dr. Powell.

"I'm under contract to a movie studio. I've been a professional actress for five years." Krake stated this information matter of factly, but hoped to impress.

Dr. Powell didn't appear to be. "In that case, I don't want you to be involved in the closed circuit TV station here. In order to have grounds privileges, you have to work. You started in the laundry. You'll be assigned that duty for the next two weeks, then you'll be issued your red card, which allows you to leave the ward during the day. The hospital will write your family to tell them you are here. If they agree to send 25 dollars, you can buy snacks at the canteen. You'll eat all meals with your ward and participate in any activities provided. We show movies once a week, have dances and play bingo.

As far as your treatment's concerned, I'm assigning you to group therapy once a week on Tuesday afternoons. There's also ward group therapy every Wednesday morning at ten. This hospital has a Patient Government Association which meets weekly to decide on policy issues and arrange the outside entertainment programs for the patients. Next week, a traveling circus will be here performing on the grounds. Would you be interested in attending a PGA meeting?"

"I guess so." Why not?

"Good, I'll schedule you. The meeting is on Thursday afternoon at one, on Ward 2A. When you have your red card, you won't need my permission. If you ever have any questions concerning the hospital, let me know. I'm sorry I can't give you more individual attention, but I don't have the time. With a patient population of 1500 and a staff of three psychiatrists and five psychologists, you can see why."

She rose, indicating the interview was over. An attendant escorted Krake back to 4C.

The next afternoon she was taken to the PGA meeting. She felt right at home. It was like her Alexandria Mills school days as she listened to various patients read minutes, propose ideas and make motions. Several people came up to her and began to talk. The next thing she knew she had agreed to be nominated for vice-president. She was feeling more at home. Her job in the laundry, the scheduled mealtimes and the regimentation of activities gave her the security acting hadn't. At least, not in Hollywood.

On Saturday she sat with a group from 4C to watch the traveling circus. Carla, who had appeared on the ward yesterday, sat to her left. This was Carla's third time in Camarillo. A kindergarten teacher, she had that all-American, blond, blue-eyed, girl-you-wished-lived-next-door look. She and Krake, sensing kindred souls, were soon sharing confidences.

Carla and her high school sweetheart had broken up before she discovered she was pregnant. When she told her parents, they sent her away to her aunt in Seattle until she had the baby, which was given up for adoption. Carla moved back to her parents in Oxnard and when her drinking became a problem, they brought her here. Camarillo was close by and she seemed to improve. Within a few months on the outside, however, she began drinking again and exhibited "irrational" behavior, such as wrecking the family car and picking up men in bars. Back she came. Again, she returned to Oxnard, but the pattern repeated and here she was for the third time. Krake could identify with the drinking and irrational behavior, but since she had never dealt with her own problem with the booze, she was unable to help.

Vigorous applause brought her back to the circus performance and she noted the wonder on the children's faces. Their joy at seeing a clown in an orange, fuzzy hat with big, yellow shoes or watching the aerial trapeze artists perform above their heads was catching and Krake found herself oooing and aahing too. She wished she could help these little ones.

When the two weeks in the laundry ended, she was assigned work in the employees' dining room. She earned her red card and could now get soft drinks and snacks from the canteen. Daddy had sent the money, but no letter to her. Dining room work meant rising at six a.m. She worked the breakfast and dinner shift, setting tables, taking orders and delivering them. Sometimes at night, she helped stack the dishes to be put in the industrial-size dishwashers. She saw more of the hospital staff waiting on them than in any therapy session.

The hour-long group-therapy meetings with ten patients and a psychiatric social worker weren't very helpful, but they started her thinking. Everyone had to introduce themselves and tell why they were there. Krake didn't know. She just could no longer function. But she began to ask herself, what do I want?

Through PGA, of which she was vice-president, she became friends with a tall, big-boned German woman named Hannah from Ward 3D. Both were concerned with the inert women sitting in the dayroom chairs. They decided to conduct a survey entitled, "What Would Make You Get Out Of Your Chair?" They were given permission to poll the women's open wards, and the answer was overwhelmingly, work!

Krake agreed. In Camarillo she had a purpose, a reason to get up in the morning. There was someone else to think about besides herself and her so-called career.

One morning hurrying to the employees' dining room for the breakfast shift, she became aware of feelings of happiness and vitality. That evening after dinner she got permission to go down to the pay phone on the first floor and called Damien. He had urged her to do so whenever she wanted. It had been three weeks since they had seen each other and she was feeling stronger. They talked for quite awhile and he seemed glad she called. Just before hanging up, he asked if she would like to come to Los Angeles for the weekend. It was hospital policy to let volunteer patients have weekend visits away after two weeks.

"OK," she replied eagerly.

"Good. Harvey and I'll be up Friday afternoon. We'll have dinner with Harvey and Theresa if you like."

She hung up and her feet hardly touched the concrete steps leading back to the ward. All week she hugged happiness to her. Friday afternoon finally rolled around and the charge nurse told her a guest was waiting in the lobby. Carrying her small bag with two of the allotted three dresses inside, she caught sight of Damien. His face lit up when he saw her. She hesitated a moment, then ran to him. After embracing her, he took her bag and they went to the car parked near the entrance, with Harvey smoking in the front seat. Damien started the engine while Harvey gave her a big kiss. Their obvious warmth and caring felt good and she chatted exuberantly on the drive into Beverly Hills. They seemed to share her concern for the children left in the institution, but could come up with no solutions as to how to provide extended care or what to do about the understaffing.

They met Theresa at her office and drove in two cars to an Italian restaurant in Santa Monica. After dinner, Damien and Krake returned to Beverly Hills. She was exhausted by all the excitement.

As soon as they entered the apartment, his arms closed around her. His kisses felt so good. He sort of slow-danced her over to the bed where he laid her gently on the counterpane. She felt so vulnerable, like an open wound. She felt stripped bare, her soul naked. But he was very gentle until he thrust inside and then the movements were powerful. They both reached an orgasm quickly. Three weeks of abstinence was some aphrodisiac.

They spent the next two days relaxing in the penthouse. Damien watched TV while Krake lay in the sun. Damien preferred to remain inside the heavily-draped bedroom. Krake liked the feeling of the sun on her skin, tension seemed to vanish in its comforting rays. They dined on the balcony and made sweet, gentle love with the ever-present TV blaring. Krake felt they were closer than ever before and was sure Damien loved her.

On Sunday afternoon, they drove the all-too-short ride back to the loony bin. Sadness touched her as they pulled up to the stucco facade of the main building. She was happy too, though, because she felt he still cared. And she had some place to go. A mental hospital ward. Her home.

Lying in bed that night, she realized that while the weekend was lovely, she couldn't wait to get back on 4C. That frightened her. She didn't want to live here forever. Maybe she and Damien would be together again.

Dr. Powell rescinded her rule about Krake not participating in the hospital's TV station. The PGA was sponsoring a thirty minute segment featuring hospital news and interviews and wanted Krake to be the hostess. The association petitioned Dr. Powell who gave in to their wishes. Krake was excited, her head bursting with plans, and stopped by 3D to find Hannah to discuss some programming. She was told that Hannah had gone up on the hill the previous afternoon and tried to hang herself. When she left the infirmary, she was transferred to a locked ward.

Shock waves hit Krake. Not smiling, intelligent, vital Hannah! She had just seen her the day before she left with Damien. Hannah never discussed her problems, so Krake had no idea why this happened. It was a reminder that this was an insane asylum. She always forgot.

On Thursday she called Damien, hoping they could repeat last weekend, but he seemed preoccupied and told her he was leaving on a Dick Clark Tour the following week and wouldn't be in LA for awhile. He had to rehearse on the weekend, so they couldn't see each other. She felt hurt when she hung up. Why hadn't he mentioned it before? She softly cried herself to sleep, not understanding his mood swings or much else.

On Sunday, Harvey and Theresa visited. They listened to her describe all her activities. She talked for nearly a half hour, non-stop.

Harvey said with a smile, "I bet when you get out of here, you learn to drive, buy yourself a little Volkswagen and come up here on the weekends to work with the children." They all laughed.

That night in bed his words kept echoing in her mind. I'm happy here, strange as that may seem. I'm miserable as an actress. What if? Maybe? Could I? Why not? A faint glimmer of light was becoming visible at the end of the tunnel.

After the breakfast shift the next day, she sat on a stool in the empty dining hall and contemplated changing her career. Give up my dreams of stardom, glamour, fame and the adoration of millions? Anonymous love didn't match the shining eyes of a retarded child in a wheelchair, watching a raggedy clown turn somersaults. Helping these patients made her feel she had something to contribute. Planning trips to the beach, hosting a TV talk show where issues directly affecting patients could be discussed, offering a shoulder to cry on or just simply listening filled her with self-respect. She hadn't realized it had disappeared. Ever since she had left Alexandria Mills, she had been surrounded by materialism, the open display of wealth and being treated like an object. Her looks seemed her main asset and she had difficulty relating to them. The shallowness of the lifestyle wasn't fulfilling.

During this short stay at Camarillo, she became aware of her lack of identity. When she put makeup on, the eyes she smudged with shadow, the cheeks she brushed with rouge and the lips she painted, could have belonged to anyone. She didn't recognize them as her own. Whenever she saw herself reflected in a mirror, tiny shock waves ran through her. Is that me? Gee, I'm pretty. But who am I? Why do I feel empty and scared in the real world and full of hope and purpose here? I can't spend my life in the nuthouse. I must return to the world. I don't want to. I have no money, no place to live and I can't go on one more interview for an acting job. My rejection quota has been filled.

When she had decided to pursue an acting career as an alternative to marriage or teaching, the former because of lack of offers, the latter due to a lack of desire, it never occurred to her that her choice might prove unsuitable much less unbearable.

Now, though she had gotten her foot in the door, she honestly didn't think she could function in that world. She thought getting a contract would make things easier, but the same conditions prevailed. She knew that if she could wait it out she might become a star. But she now realized she didn't want it. She wasn't emotionally capable of living that life. Of sacrificing all for her looks, of being dependent on others for validity, jobs, acceptance, all of which could be taken away in an instant.

The shame, guilt and sense of failure was overwhelming and she went back to bed, curled up and escaped into *The Group*, a book Theresa had left.

The following day she called Matt. He came and brought her home for the weekend. Abner, learning from the hospital that she was at the Hilliards, called and asked if she would go out with a producer friend of his, Stanley Russo.

"Abner, I can't go on a date. I'm on a weekend leave from Loonyville, you know that," she replied, shocked.

"Honey," he said, ignoring the remark, "I had coffee yesterday with Russo, he's Brando's producer, and he was going on and on about how self-centered, boring and egotistical actresses are. I said I knew one that wasn't and he wants to meet you."

"Did you tell him my address?"

"No, you can do that. He'd like to take you to a small dinner party Saturday night. Can he call you?"

"Tomorrow night? You want me to go on a blind date tomorrow night?" She panicked.

"Krake, he's very nice or I'd never ask you. You might enjoy yourself."

"Abner, I don't know if I can. I'd rather not date yet."

"It'll be all right, I promise."

So instead of spending a safe, family-oriented Saturday night with the Hilliards, she found herself nervously answering the door at seven. And soon after, sitting once again in a

Rolls Royce, she laughed to herself. The first time I'm in one, I'm on the way to an AA meeting and the next, I'm out for the weekend from the insane asylum!

Conversation centered on his latest, as yet unnamed film with Brando and Sophia Loren. That topic exhausted, there was a lull and he asked what she was doing. "I'm just home for the weekend from Camarillo."

He never missed a beat. "How do you like it?"

"I hate to say this, but I can't wait to return. I know I can't spend the rest of my life there, but I have no place else to go."

"I thought you lived with the Hilliard's."

"I did until I was put under contract with Revue Studios in January." Was it only seven months ago?

They drove in silence for awhile. She, for the first time, didn't give a flying fuck what a man thought.

"I have a friend, a psychiatrist in Beverly Hills, who runs the California Day Treatment Center on Santa Monica Boulevard in Hollywood. You might be interested in something like that." He glanced over at her.

"What's a day treatment center?" She began to get nervous.

"As I understand it, a patient attends the programs offered there during the day, but lives elsewhere. You would have to find a place to stay."

"Matt and Jocelyn might let me stay there, but I'd have to pay room and board," she said hopelessly.

"Maybe something could be worked out," he said as he turned the car up a curving drive in front of a large, brick two-story house in Brentwood.

During the evening, Krake retreated into silence while pretending to be extremely interested in everything. She hadn't a clue as to what was going on. She felt no connection with any of it, just wanted to get into bed in the garage or better yet, on 4C.

After the meal, one of the guests played the Steinway in the corner while the others sat on couches and easy chairs sipping brandy or espresso. The bitter coffee burned her throat. It was strong, with a lemon slice floating on top. She liked sugar and cream, a no-no with espresso. She drank it, but refused a second cup. Stanley inquired if she was ready to leave. He had an early call at the studio and felt it was time to go.

He deposited her at the Hilliards' promising to have his friend, Dr. Rothschild, call in the morning. The coffee kept her awake a long time. She finally fell into a light sleep, dreaming of falling into pits with strange yellow demons dancing over her and then drifting at sea without an oar.

At breakfast, she told Matt and Jocelyn of the possibility of the California Day Treatment Center as a means for her continued care. They said she could move back, but would need some money for room and board. A reasonable amount of seventy dollars was named.

Dr. Rothschild telephoned before noon and said he would like to interview her in the morning.

"I can't. I'm on weekend leave and have to be back in the hospital by six this evening."

"What if I called and got permission for you to spend another day?"

"That would be OK, I guess." Her voice was weak.

"I'll call you back as soon as I make the arrangements. Don't worry, it'll be all right," he said calmly.

Thirty minutes later, he had okayed it with Douglas and asked her to stop by his Beverly Hills office in the morning.

When she walked into his suite, she sank into thick beige carpeting. The furniture was antique. Impressionist paintings hung on the ivory-colored walls. A heavily carved wooden door opened and out walked a short, trim gentleman with receding gray hair. His deep blue eyes twinkled as he grasped her limp hand.

"I'm Theodore Rothschild and you must be Krake. Come in and sit down."

She followed him into a large wood-paneled office with an ornately carved desk in one corner and a dark saddle-brown leather sofa and several chairs arranged conveniently. He sat her down in one and took the chair opposite.

"Talk to me, Krake. Stanley tells me you're in Camarillo State Hospital and want to stay there."

"Yes, I do. I have no money and I don't know where else to go. Besides, I like it." She explained her career problems and ended by hesitantly offering that she wanted to change professions and work in the field of psychology.

He smiled and said he thought he could help. "I don't have any openings at the treatment center, but I'll make room. Let me explain what it will be like. The day starts at nine and ends at four in the afternoon. We have private therapy sessions, group therapy, career counseling, craft projects and more than enough activities to keep you occupied."

"It sounds interesting," she said.

"It is. Do you have a place to stay?"

"My married friends said I could stay with them, but I'll have to pay rent."

"Don't worry about that, we'll make arrangements."

"When will I leave Camarillo?"

"When it's convenient, but I'd like you to begin at the center on August first."

It was the second week of July.

On the drive back, she told Matt she didn't want to go to Rothschild's center, but knew she had to. Camarillo had become her haven. Even at the low of her life, she knew it was far from the best solution. Let's grow old and gray in the loony bin, hooray!

She walked the grounds the following day savoring the clean air and the pastoral setting. The green hills of May had given way to the golden hills of July, the sky was a clear blue and dark green oaks dotted the slopes. The sight filled her with a serenity she didn't find in the city.

Good-byes were said during her Thursday morning TV show and at group therapy sessions. She knew she would never see these people again and would miss them. Despite their psychological impairments, they were more real than most of her Hollywood associates. Matt came on Saturday morning and as they drove away, she took a last look at the idyllic setting.

She told Matt and Jocelyn of her planned career change.

"Are you sure about this?" Jocelyn asked, pulling her chair closer to Krake's.

"I don't know. I only know I'm miserable being an actress and I was happy helping the patients at Camarillo." She shrugged her shoulders helplessly. "You probably think I'm totally crazy to give up the contract."

"Darling, if you're that unhappy, there's really no question, is there?" Jocelyn squeezed her hand.

"I feel I'm a failure." Tears welled in her eyes.

"You're a failure if you fail to do what's best for you. Only you know what that is, or in this case, isn't," Matt said. "It seems your emotional makeup isn't capable of handling the erratic nature of this business. You're no different than many. Some have committed suicide or turned to booze and drugs, but you're facing things head-on and you're making a choice. We don't think less of you. In fact, you're behaving pretty courageously, for a starlet!" He winked.

She laughed, "From starlet to psychologist, hmmm."

At Matt's suggestion, she talked to UCLA's graduate school in psychology. The counselor informed her that because she already had a bachelor's degree, she would have to get her required psychology credits at night school which would be a long haul. Krake needed a faster solution. Her shaky self couldn't handle too much stress.

Krake met with Monica Howser and explained her decision. Monica seemed to understand and wished her the best. Krake thought she was letting Monica down, but she left her office, feeling as though a weight had been lifted from her.

19

"You can all go to hell," a pimply-faced teenager shouted at the group of five patients sitting in a room at the Day Treatment Center. No one spoke.

"Henry, do you really want us to do that?" Dr. Rothschild asked.

"Yes, I'm tired of psychoanalysis. I'm tired of you. I'm getting out of here." He left, slamming the door.

"He'll be back," the woman sitting across from Krake said. "He does this all the time. Anything for attention. Why are you here?"

Dr. Rothschild had introduced Krake as a new member at the beginning of the group session.

Krake looked at Rothschild for guidance before she spoke.

"I think we'll have you start us off this morning, Irma." He directed his gaze at the woman. "Why don't you tell us why you're here?"

"I don't want to be here, I never want to leave my house. I used to work at a dry cleaners, but I kept mixing up the clothes. Aw, I don't feel like telling her about it." She pointed at Krake.

"We must make our new member feel a part of things by sharing. Try and finish the story, Irma."

Irma picked at the sleeve of her dress. "I once gave a man a sequined dress instead of his business suit. He never looked in the garment bag until he got to his hotel and started to dress for a meeting. I got fired." She started to cry.

An elderly man sitting next to her said, "I'm here because my son won't let me stay at his house unless I do this. I keep setting fire to things."

Krake sat and listened. Rothschild had said she didn't have to participate unless she felt comfortable and she didn't.

At the end of the hour, she and Rothschild remained in the room. "How are you feeling?" he said.

"Like I'm here, but I'm not," she said.

"Explain."

"I don't know if I can. It's strange being on the outside again. I didn't know I'd feel so alien."

"Alien to what?" Rothschild asked.

"To life. I mean, routine functioning, like riding the bus down here, meeting new people, almost everything."

"When have you felt a part of things?"

Krake thought a moment. "Growing up, I guess. In Alexandria Mills, I knew almost everybody. Went to the same church, school, movie theater and lived in the same house until we moved to Texas. She told him a little about the move to Belton and at the end of her session, Dr. Rothschild mentioned that the Rusk Research Foundation for Mental Health needed a secretary-assistant, and asked if she was interested.

"I can't type," she replied.

"We'll send you to typing school if this kind of position appeals to you."

"What would I do?" she asked.

"The foundation is involved in researching various aspects of clinical psychology. I'm conducting extensive studies there on psycho-pharmacology."

She looked blank.

"That's the use of drugs in psychiatric treatment."

Krake felt a glimmer of interest.

"You'll need some background in medicine, knowledge of terminology, etc. I'm looking for a school that teaches the rudiments. I hope to find something by the end of the week. I'll let you know."

In the afternoon, she tried unsuccessfully to stir up some curiosity in observing a class on stenciling. At four, she rode the bus home, ate, and took two Valium which Rothschild had prescribed to help her sleep. Her lower back ached.

The pain persisted so the next afternoon she went to her doctor's office for an exam, hoping it wasn't another kidney stone. After a rudimentary exam and a urinalysis, he told her she was pregnant.

Shocked and overwhelmed, she began to cry. She knew it had probably happened the last time she and Damien had made love. She contacted him on tour in Idaho and he assured her he would take care of everything. Shyly, she said, "You wouldn't want to get married, would you?"

He laughed. "No, not really, it just wouldn't work."

After she hung up, she lay on the bed sobbing. Pregnant! She had hoped to be happily married when this happened.

Jocelyn drove her to the doctor in Watts Damien had contacted. Abortions were illegal. This was what is known as a back-alley abortion. Lying on the table, feet in the stirrups, she began to cry. The doctor stopped his probing and came around the side of the examining table. "I don't have to do this, you know. I'll stop now if you want me to." She shook her head and he continued.

Jocelyn waited in an alley over an hour until Krake felt strong enough to walk to the car. Jocelyn grabbed Krake's hand, "I hope it wasn't too painful, darling."

"No, I didn't feel anything, but I almost fainted when I got up to leave. He made me lie down again. I'm sorry you had to wait so long."

"I know these things can take time, I'm just happy there weren't any complications." They drove, without speaking, back to the house. Matt hugged her and helped her to her room.

Krake felt sad, but not guilty. The thought of bringing a child into a world when she could barely care for herself was unthinkable.

The next morning, Damien called to see how she was feeling. "Was it a boy or a girl?"

Horrified, she said, "I didn't ask."

"I'm glad you're OK," he said and hung up.

Two days later, she was back at the Center, saying she had had the flu. Dr. Rothschild arranged for Krake to attend a school for medical and dental assistants, as well as typing classes. Her tuition, along with room and board, would be paid for under one of his research grants. In return she would become his assistant when she completed her studies.

Medicine became her passion. The language, the diseases, the mysteries of bodily functions, the various treatments, the metric system, taking and developing x-rays, performing simple lab tests, drawing blood, giving injections, she was mesmerized by it all. Full of enthusiasm she wanted to help everyone. When she saw an accident or witnessed an injury, she longed to be able to help.

The first day she wore her nurse's uniform on the bus people looked at her with respect. I'm someone! I have an identity, I'm a Medical Assistant!

Mrs. Hayward, her teacher, became her idol. A former R.N., she had founded the school in 1960 specifically to train young women in the various procedures and requirements needed in a physician's or dentist's office. The initial three months of the course were devoted to the theoretical aspects of medicine. The final months concentrated solely on the practical side; such as taking and developing x-rays, doing EKGs and performing routine lab tests like a urinalysis and a CBC, which required drawing blood. Two days a week, she attended a typing class. Never had she been required to work so hard. Devouring it, she was energized and totally immersed. Well, not completely.

Shortly after starting school, she met Gale Maxwell, a sexy student of Matt's. One night when she came in from studying to fix a cup of cocoa, Matt introduced them and Krake offered him cocoa. When it was ready, she took her cup and headed for the door, saying, "Sorry I can't stay, I've got to study for a test tomorrow," wondering what was in his jeans.

As soon as she got home from school the next day, the phone rang and Gale invited her for a ride to the beach. She hesitated because she had another test to study for, but his seductive voice persuaded her.

They sat on his coat and watched the sunset, after which he drew her near and gently kissed her forehead, both cheeks and her mouth, first lightly, then with .more purpose.

She pulled away. "No, I just want to be friends."

"OK." He took her hand and led them back to the car.

He dropped her off at home and said he would call. She went to the garage and tried to study, but kept remembering the kiss and wanted more.

It was easier to memorize the causative organisms of disease the next morning, but she began to wait for his call. It never occurred to her to call him. She was being coy. It came a week later and he drove over to show her his new car, a green Triumph.

They drove out to the beach. The cliffs were dark, but in the pale light of the new moon they made their way to the edge of the precipice and stood there arm in arm. Relaxing against him, she turned her face up and he kissed her, with a sweetness that won her heart. His arms tightened and the kisses became passionate. She pulled away and started to run back to the car. He caught her from behind. With his body pressed into her back, he said strongly in her ear, "I don't want to hurt you. Matt told me about Camarillo. I know you're fragile, I don't care. We'll wait as long as it takes. Krake, you can trust me."

She burst into tears. "I don't know why I'm crying, I can't help it," she sobbed. Inside she felt pain and terror.

He turned her around and held her, murmuring, "It's all right, it's all right." When she stopped crying, he handed her a handkerchief. "I'll take you home now."

On the way into town, she dried her eyes and took the cigarette he offered. She usually smoked only when drinking, but she needed one now, the closest thing to Mommy. Her thoughts were confused. She didn't want any involvement, but that seemed hard to achieve. She was lonely. He dropped her off and told her he would call.

"Thanks for everything," she said. He was sweet. His rugged good looks and 6'1" muscled body appealed to her also. The blue eyes had a coldness she didn't like, but his concern and patience canceled that out.

He came for dinner at the Hilliards and afterwards, walked her out to her study chamber.

"Better not come in," she protested. "I have a feeling we'd have a hard time parting."

"Just for a minute." He opened the door, she followed, switching on the light. He switched it off and kissed her. It felt so good to be in a man's arms, the object of desire and passion. Not wanting to, she insisted he leave. She wasn't ready to make love. Before going, he asked if she wanted to go dancing on Friday night.

Gale was a superb dancer. He later told her that when he hopped a freight in Iowa and left the family farm at seventeen, he earned money dancing in the streets of New Orleans. They whirled and dipped to a Mariachi band and drank too many margaritas. By the time they arrived at the Hilliards, she could hardly stand. Gale carried her to the garage and carefully laid her on the bed, lying down beside her, ignoring the feeble protests.

Kissing her, he unzipped her dress and unhooked the black lace bra. She didn't remember much after that, just his mouth covering her breasts with kisses and then his tongue on her clitoris. She never heard him leave.

Naked on top of the sheets, with a blanket thrown across her, she woke to shame, guilt and remorse at being so easy, accompanied by a splitting headache and queasy stomach. She stayed in bed until early afternoon when Gale called to express regrets.

"You'd had too much to drink, but I couldn't help myself, you're so sexy. I hope you'll forgive me, it wasn't fair." His voice was high-pitched, full of anxiety.

"I didn't exactly fight you off, you know." She didn't want him to suspect that she only remembered fragments.

"I should have controlled myself. I'm sorry. Forgive me?" He sounded sincere. How could she not? "Can I see you today?"

"I'm not feeling that well and I have to study for Monday's exam." She wanted to stay in bed. "Give me a ring tomorrow, OK?"

Relieved at not having to face him, she fixed some chicken noodle soup, ate it with saltines and began to think she might recover. She had had to stop her therapy sessions once she started school but now wished she could talk to Dr. Rothschild. The homework required every spare second. She didn't think she wanted an intense relationship with a man right now. She didn't have the stamina for both.

On one of their outings, Gale told her about his Navy experiences during the Korean war. Trained as a frogman, he worked on a demolition crew off a submarine in the South Pacific. During a mission, a bomb exploded underwater killing his best friend and injuring him severely. His right lung collapsed and he was in a decompression chamber for days, then in a Navy hospital in San Diego for months. He still received treatments to restore full-lung capacity. Tears filled his eyes as he related seeing his friend die in front of him.

Krake was moved. He appeared tough and invincible, but had an emotional depth that touched her heart.

She pulled back, "Let's take it slow."

"I don't know if I can. Krake, I love you. I've loved you from the first time I saw you."

"Gale, I care a lot, but I need to go slow. I'm in a school that takes ninety-nine per cent of my time and I'm scared."

"Of what?"

"Of myself, of you, of love, of being hurt, everything."

"I'll never hurt you, I promise."

He looked so sincere, she kissed him. "I've got to finish studying for tomorrow and it's late. Call me in a couple of days."

"I'll do my best to be patient."

"Thanks, 'night." She pushed him out and closed the door, leaning against it. Is this what she wanted? She didn't know.

Her school work was excellent. At the head of the class, she was a star instead of a starlet and loving it. Krake felt like she was finally growing up, but there was no Daddy to praise her.

In January, she began the practical part of her training. Developing x-rays was her favorite. When she lifted the film from the tank, she was in awe to see a ribcage, a white bony arm or hand displayed before her. Magic!

In early February, Mrs. Hayward spoke to her about a job for an internist. Krake, nervous and afraid she wasn't ready, went for an interview and got the job. Only a few hours a day to start, she worked before and after school. Krake worried about maintaining her high marks. That part proved easy, but the job was demanding. The hours she spent working were nerve-racking. Everything was happening so fast, she was scared and not at all confident.

There were two doctors in the practice, Dr. Lehman and Dr. Coleman. Dr. Lehman was easygoing, laughed a lot and was pleasant to be around. Dr. Coleman was high-strung and a perfectionist.

The patient contact was her favorite part. People were so appreciative of the slightest thing. If she brought them a glass of water or helped someone undress or laughed at a joke, they adored it.

Graduation loomed and Mrs. Hayward asked her to give the valedictory address.

"What should I talk about?" she inquired.

"Emphasize a unique aspect of being a medical assistant," the older woman suggested.

When she mentioned it to Dr. Coleman, he said that empathy was the single most important quality anyone working in the medical profession could possess. He loaned her some medical journals containing articles on the subject and she wrote what she considered to be an excellent speech.

Communication with her family had been non-existent for the two months she was in Camarillo. She kept hoping for some letters, but none had arrived. She had written them when she enrolled in school and Daddy corresponded occasionally. Lorraine sometimes added a footnote of chatty gossip. When she told them that she was number one in her class and had been asked to make a speech, her father wrote his congratulations. He expressed a desire to be there if only he had the money. If only ....

On graduation night, flowers arrived for her, a dozen long-stemmed red roses. They must be from Gale, she thought, how sweet. She opened the card. "Dearest Krake, I wish I could be there. Congratulations! Love, Daddy."

Hugging the flowers to her, she ran to her room, sat down on the bed and cried. She missed him so much. More than anything, she wished he could be here.

Gale appeared in the doorway. "Who sent those? I know,

a secret admirer."

"Not so secret. My father." She started weeping again. "I miss him."

Gale sat beside her, one arm circling her shoulders, "I'm here. That's something, isn't it?"

She nodded. But not enough.

At the ceremony, Krake walked to the podium for her speech. Her notes in front of her, she began. "Ladies and Gentleman." Her hands and her voice started to tremble. The years of stage experience vanished. She clasped her hands tightly behind her. She saw Dr. Rothschild sitting way in the back. Gale was with the Hilliards. Andrew didn't recognize her immediately. When he did, his voice rang out, "Hi, Krake, you sure look pretty." The audience broke up and so did she. When her composure returned, her confidence came with it and she finished with poise and conviction.

On the way home, she asked Gale if the speech was all right and if she appeared nervous.

"Yes, at first, but as soon as Andrew spoke and everybody laughed, you were great. I'm proud of you."

"Thanks." She was tired, so he took her home promising they would go dancing the next night.

She lay in bed after he left, the scent of the roses filled her room. She fell asleep with one in her hand.

20

Before the month of internship with Coleman was over, she had decided not to work as Rothschild's assistant. The job would be dealing in the abstract which meant no patient contact. That was the most healing part of the experience. Helping people directly, receiving their appreciation and validation was essential for her recovery.

Awkwardly, she told him. She expressed regret at not being able to fulfill their initial agreement, but he seemed happy that she had found a profession she liked and agreed her being fully restored to health was more important. She thanked him, grateful for his understanding.

This was the final month of the grant so there would be no further subsidizing. Starting salary at Dr. Coleman's was fifty cents above minimum wage. That seemed adequate for the present, besides she couldn't risk rejection looking for another job. Mrs. Hayward was appalled when she learned Krake's salary. "You're making how much an hour? Krake, you should be earning a lot more." A bird in the hand and fear kept her there.

She did change residences. The Hilliards were her family, but she had to bus it forty-five minutes each way to work. Finishing sometimes at seven or seven-thirty, arriving home at eight-thirty, eating dinner and falling in bed at nine-fifteen was too limiting. There was no time to have a life. She moved to a large studio apartment just off Wilshire Boulevard, a half-hour walk from work.

Gale liked to spend time at her new place. She couldn't understand why. He and his roommate shared a quaint apartment in the hills above Sunset Boulevard. The building cantilevered out over the side of a hill and to reach the apartment you had to walk down twenty-seven steps curving through the foliage and flowers.

Although Gale's apartment had a fairy-tale quality, it was a typical bachelor pad. Dirty clothes were piled high in the bedroom and used dishes filled the sink. Inch-thick dust covered every surface. When she saw all this, it was clear why he liked to spend so much time at her place.

Soon after she had started full-time at Dr. Coleman's, she had a patient to whom she administered ultrasonic therapy for an arthritic shoulder. His name was Walter Enthro. With his profession of psychiatric social worker, he shared her love of medicine and people. During one of their sessions, she revealed that she had been a patient at Camarillo State Hospital. She described her stay and subsequent enrollment in the California Day Treatment Center.

When he heard that she was no longer in therapy, he told her that he conducted both private and group therapy sessions, fees on a sliding scale.

She thought about it for a few days and then decided to pursue it. She knew there was a tremendous amount of emotional turmoil churning inside of her. The group therapy at Camarillo and the day treatment center had merely scraped the surface.

At his suggestion, they had a few private sessions first. During one of these he called her, "skin hungry."

"What's that?" she asked.

"You're starved for love and affection. You're so needy and vulnerable, it's difficult for you to connect fully with another person. Love relationships require you to give more than you receive. That takes a lot of self-love. You need to learn to love Krake more."

Among other topics, they discussed her childhood; mainly her close relationship with her father and her inability to relate to Lorraine.

"What's the severest trauma you've experienced?" he asked as he filled the bowl of his old pipe.

With no hesitation she replied, "The death of my fiancé while I was attending college." She related the story of the accident and felt the old familiar pain. "It's been eight years and it still hurts."

After brushing a lock of his salt and pepper hair from his face Walter said gently, "It may always. Have you shared this with many people?"

"No, it's on my mind constantly. When I first meet someone, I have this urge to tell them about it, but I'm afraid they'll think I'm full of self-pity."

He tried to draw her out about Burg by asking her what he was like and what things they did together, but she couldn't open up. Walter inspired trust, but the block remained. Drunk, the restraints were released, sober it was impossible. This proved to be the last of the private sessions and on the following Tuesday she began meeting with a group.

This assemblage consisted of ten men and women near her age. They were a curious mix. The youngest, Meg, was twenty-five, unmarried and embroiled in a year-long affair with a Catholic priest. Quiet Don was a slightly overweight, Jewish accountant whose low self-esteem was palpable. Irwin, a married man with two young children, usually sat opposite her, so he could look up her dress, he informed her later.

Krake looked forward to the weekly meeting. The group began at seven, broke up at nine-thirty and continued on at a nearby coffee shop. Often, Krake didn't arrive home until after midnight. Then she was so stimulated, she frequently lay awake until two or three. Wednesdays weren't her best days at work.

Krake and Gale spent weekends at the beach. One Sunday afternoon she walked to the farthest edge of the cove and sat on a rock watching dim figures of ships on the horizon wondering where they were bound. A hand on her shoulder startled her. Looking around, she met Gale's gaze. "You scared me, I didn't hear you."

"Move over, I want to be near you." He sat down. Silently, they observed the sea's travelers.

"I'm getting cold," she said after a while, "want to head back?"

As they were walking in the wet sand, foam lapping at their toes, he asked casually, "Krake, will you marry me?"

"What?"

"I know you heard me, but I'll say it again. Will you be my wife?" He looked straight ahead.

She stopped. "Gale, look at me." He did. "Are you serious?"

"Oh, no, I always ask people to marry me as a joke." He grabbed her around the waist, lifting her off the sand, his mouth on hers.

Finally, she drew back, catching her breath. "I'm surprised. I didn't think you wanted to get married. You spend so much time at the college it seems like you're interested in directing and nothing else."

"Krake, I love you. You're right, I want to direct, but I want you with me. What do you say?"

She didn't answer. Damien's face flashed in front of her. She had never stopped loving him, but hadn't heard a word in eight months. The last time she had called, a recording announced that the number was no longer in service. Anyway, she lived in a different world now. Her job, friends and life were all new. Most of the people she had known while acting had vanished. It was almost like it had never happened.

"Krake, answer me." His voice was insistent.

"I'm sorry, I was thinking."

"About what? What's there to think about? Either you want to or you don't." He was getting angry.

"Gale, you don't understand. I need time. Where would we live? I'm working, but I don't earn very much. What about you? You'd have to find something when you finish the course at Bainbridge."

"Don't you care that I love you and want to marry you?"

She flung her arms around his neck. "Of course I do. I'm thrilled and I guess, scared. I've wanted to get married for a long time, now it's here and I'm afraid. Isn't that typical?" She laughed.

"Honey, there's nothing to be frightened of. Sure, I'm gonna get a job when I graduate. I've put my name on the NBC hiring list as a page. It doesn't pay much, but I'd meet a lot of important people and be working in the heart of the industry. I'm pretty sure they'll call when there's an opening."

She took a deep breath, "'Yes I said, Yes I will, Yes!' Know what that's from?"

He shook his head. "I don't care, you just said yes!" With that he picked her up and carried her back to the blanket where their friends lay in the sun.

Holding her aloft like a trophy, Gale said, "She's mine! She said she'll marry me."

"Put me down, I feel like a winner's cup at a bowling tournament," Krake protested.

Later, lying in bed, Krake wondered if this was right for her. Do I really love him?...I don't know. How stable is he? He's consumed by his film projects and I don't see him for days. That was fine while I was in school, but I'd like someone to be there when I get home from work. He's moody and unpredictable. On the other hand, I am twenty-eight. That's old. Old enough to be called a spinster not that long ago. I'll never see Damien again, Burg's dead, Will's with his wife, why not? What the hell! I wonder if Walter will approve?

She called her parents to tell them and her father asked what she wanted as a wedding gift.

"You!" she answered. "I want you to come out and give me away."

"I don't know if I can. We'll see."

"Please, Daddy, it would mean so much," she pleaded.

"We'll see, Princess."

It was early June and they chose late October for the wedding, when the air would be crisp, the sky hopefully free of smog. When he learned the date, Hank wrote that he couldn't come because Lorraine had to have a hysterectomy. He wouldn't have much money after the medical expenses. The reason for the surgery, some growths on her uterus, didn't alarm Krake. Not only was Lorraine a chronic complainer about her health, but Krake knew that most doctors would jump at the chance to remove a woman's uterus. It was the operation of the 60s. Her mother had been trying to get cancer since the disease came on the scene. Nothing Krake could do would convince Lorraine that perhaps the operation wasn't necessary. Krake felt that her mother would go to any lengths to keep Hank away from her wedding. The contest was still on.

Acute disappointment! I don't have anyone to give me away. Daddy and I can't play *Father of the Bride*. Who to ask? There was no one but Daddy to enact this role.

Then Walter came to mind. Because of him and with the aid of the group, she was beginning to discover herself. She was so accustomed to pleasing others she didn't know how she felt or even what. A major break came when she discovered she didn't enjoy watching football games. Since childhood, she had sat next to Daddy and various boyfriends, cheering. She never knew which team had the ball, never was able to decipher what action was taking place on the field, or if she should shout Hooray or Boo! Along with this self-discovery, she was starting to understand that she and Lorraine had always been in competition for her father's affections.

Upset by Hank's letter, she spoke with Walter after the Wednesday night session. "I don't understand why he can't come out. I told him it would only cost plane fare. He could stay with me. We're not having a conventional wedding with a rehearsal dinner or any of that."

"Why don't you write or call and tell him how you feel?"

"It won't do any good. He already knows. One reason I told you is because I wanted to ask if you'd be willing to be the one to give me away."

Smiling, he hugged her. "It would be a pleasure."

She did write Daddy and asked if he could help with the wedding expenses; dress, food or flowers? He wrote that he couldn't, no money. Angry and hurt, she vowed never to speak to him again. I don't need you, I'll do it on my own.

In a bridal shop, she found an ivory linen bridesmaid's dress that she considered perfect for a bride, simple and classic. Jocelyn, her matron of honor, volunteered to make the veil. It was ivory tulle cascading from white silk lilies of the valley fastened in her hair. They made the invitations out of a oatmeal textured paper with a yellow circle glued in the center. Underneath was the quote from Molly Bloom's final speech in Ulysses: "Yes I said, Yes I will, Yes!"

Krake and Gale found a new apartment. She wished she had more money to spend on furniture, but Gale had a double bed and dresser and she had her wardrobe.

Her salary barely covered her expenses. She had been putting out feelers for jobs, but so far nothing sounded good. Gale had his Navy medical disability checks which kept him afloat.

In August, her therapy group went to a marathon weekend at San Felipe College, situated in a rural area above La Canada. Gale wasn't too pleased when he learned she was going. He felt threatened by her group anyway, was paranoid, thinking she was saying derogatory things about him. She told him if he didn't get off it, she would.

Thirty people attended, quite different from her intimate circle in Hollywood. Everyone but two of Krake's group was there.

She shared a room in a dormitory with a quiet woman named Rita who seemed sad. She said she had been in private therapy with Walter for the last two years and preferred his gentle approach to her first therapist, a Reichian.

Saturday morning they met in small groups to discuss any pressing personal problems and that afternoon participated in various exercises. One involved falling backwards with your eyes closed, trusting the others would catch you. Another required a person to lie on the ground while other members touched and held you. This was Krake's favorite. Her skin didn't go away hungry.

Sunday dawned bright and clear. Sweet flower fragrances filled the air. The entire membership gathered on the lawn, seated in folding chairs arranged in a large circle. Walter began by asking a general question, "What do you fear most in a relationship?" Several people responded, offering comments ranging from having someone see them naked to having to make conversation over breakfast. Then soft-spoken Rita admitted she was afraid of intimacy. Silence.

Walter broke it. "Krake, tell us what happened to you."

She looked at him blankly, "What?"

"You know."

Then it hit her, "You mean Burg?" Still unsure.

He nodded yes.

Self-consciously, she began, "It was my junior year in college ..." She had meant to hit only the highlights, but it was like a dam bursting. Halfway through, she was in tears. Talking despite the pain, she sobbed, taking in huge gulps of air. Near the end, Louise, an older woman came across the grass and held her. She had lost her husband in World War II.

The remainder of the encounter group was hazy. Krake was very drained, but she felt a thousand pounds lighter. The knot of pain lodged in her solar plexus was gone. She felt at peace. She was thankful for Walter, that he forced her to communicate her feelings sober. Krake didn't know if the ache in her heart would come back, but right now it was gone.

When she saw Gale two days later, she felt love for him. Not a wanting to want to, but a strong sense of caring. She explained Sunday's release and he said he had felt her holding back, not giving completely. They made love that night and she seemed connected to him spiritually as well as physically.

Plans for the wedding progressed. They were going to be married at the Little Brown Church on Coldwater Canyon. Although located on a busy thoroughfare, the chapel was small and quaint. The Little Brown Church was painted white, the interior paneled in knotty pine with dark mahogany pews, paned windows and deep maroon carpeting. Simple and charming, it had a distinct country air.

Krake moved to the new apartment on October first. With a salvaged sofa-bed and a small wooden table and chairs in the dining room, she and her clothes rattled around. Gale wasn't moving in until after the wedding.

Gale's long-awaited interview at NBC materialized and he was hired. Fortunately, his studies at Bainbridge had ended the previous week. He began working nights and she saw little of him.

Gradually the apartment was acquiring more furniture. Gale brought his bed over along with a cable spool table. His mother sent a Tiffany style lamp, circa 1930, as a wedding gift, which was promptly used to cover the hole in the center of the cable spool. Gale's desk occupied the glassed-in space beyond the living room.

The wedding day approached. Krake prepared most of the food for the reception, with salads and appetizers contributed by friends. Jocelyn made an Irish wedding cake frosted with marzipan.

The day before the ceremony, Krake and Gale cut chrysanthemums at his apartment. His landlady had kindly offered her prizes. They decorated the church the morning of their wedding, with the yellow and amber flowers and gold velvet ribbon festooning from pew to pew.

Just as Krake was preparing to take a bath, there was a knock on the door. It was a telegram from Texas. "Thinking of you on this special day. Wishing you the best. Daddy."

She checked where it had been sent from; his office, so Lorraine wouldn't know. Crying, she nicked her shin with the razor. Damn, why, Daddy, why couldn't you be here? My whole family should be participating, helping, supporting, loving me. Why aren't they?

As she was slipping the white dress over her head, Pam arrived to drive her to the church. Carrying the veil and extra makeup in a bag, they hurried out to the car. It wouldn't start. They looked at each other, stricken.

"We'll have to call Dave. He's right down the hill," said Pam.

Inside they went, telephoned and in ten minutes he arrived in his dusty 1957 Porche. Jamming her belongings down by her feet, off they sped to the Valley.

She ran up the walk of the church and entered the Bridal Bower. Jocelyn and the Reverend Holyford were waiting. Holyford was a misnomer. It should have been Lustford. Granted Jocelyn's dress was low-cut, as was hers, but this man never glanced above the neck. He wouldn't have seen them thumb their noses at him if they had had enough presence of mind to do so. He questioned Jocelyn as to her faith, her marital status, birthplace, anything to be able to stare directly at her tits. Finally, Walter knocked on the door and announced that it was time to start. He gave Krake a big hug.

Veil in place, carrying a single yellow rose, she felt beautiful. They had had no rehearsal, but she knew what to do. She had been preparing for this all her life. Sixteen ivory candles were lit and the organ music swelled with "Here Comes The Bride." The congregation stood smiling as they walked slowly down the aisle. Walter left her at Gale's side and they knelt before Holyford. Jesus! The man never stopped looking down her dress as he guided them in exchanging vows. Krake cried through the whole ceremony, could barely get out the proper responses. It was when she knelt at the altar that she suddenly knew this was wrong, very wrong, but it was too late to stop it. Then it was over. They stood up, kissed and marched out of the sanctuary to the Bridal Bower to sign the license. Afterwards they drove off in the Triumph, brushing the rice out of their clothes and hair. Gale stopped a few blocks away and untied the shoes and cans dragging behind.

The reception was fun. No one seemed aware that she had sobbed through most of the service. Gale never mentioned it. She passed it off to herself as nerves. During the entire day, she had felt she was observing the event and wasn't a part of it. The food was delicious, but the marzipan frosting was uncuttable. Jocelyn lifted it off whole and served the fruitcake underneath.

Gale had rented a cottage in Laguna Beach for the weekend. They walked the beach, ate in Laguna's finest and gradually Krake felt herself re-enter her body.

A few weeks into wedded bliss, she found that work was taking its toll. There was no time to enjoy the new apartment or married life.

Through the school, she found a job in a surgeon's office, taking x-rays and EKGs, drawing blood and performing minor lab tests as well as assisting in office surgery. The surgeon was also the Yellow Cab company's doctor.

When she told Coleman she was quitting, he offered her his other assistant's job and $400 a month, to match what the new job was paying. She mumbled she would think about it. Later, talking with Gale, she was indignant. "Edith's been with Coleman for ten years! She works harder than any of us. I've left that office at seven-thirty at night and she was still developing x-rays or doing lab work. He couldn't pay me enough to take that job. As if I would betray her! Don't medical ethics apply to doctors' treatment of their employees?"

However, she gave Dr. Coleman the age-old excuse, "I have to decline, Doctor, Gale says he wants me home more."

Her new work schedule was agreeable. She started work at nine. Dr. Kiley arrived at nine-thirty to finish the cab drivers' exams which she had begun. She had her own office; a small room with three gray-metal file cabinets, storage boxes full of drug samples and a large color photo of President and Mrs. Kennedy on the wall by the door. Several months after she began, Kiley revealed that one reason he had hired her was because she looked like Jackie.

Gwendolyn Thatcher ran the front office. A former R.N. in England, she had never taken the U.S. exam, so couldn't work as a nurse in this country. Krake was forever grateful for her extensive medical knowledge. It bailed them out of many a predicament.

She took patients' histories before Kiley saw them. With the cab company's industrial accident cases, she took the history and x- rays immediately. She learned his standard treatments and on the days he didn't make it in due to lengthy surgeries, even prescribed. The work day ended at five, except for Wednesdays when they left at four. This job was what she had dreamed about while attending school.

It wasn't uncommon for her to see certain patients weekly while Dr. Kiley met with them once a month. She welcomed the responsibility and she felt she had found her niche. Looking forward to the time spent on Third Street, she gave it everything she had.

At Christmas, Kiley decided to close the office for three days. Gale wanted to go to Tijuana. Krake eagerly agreed, visions of colorful fiestas and breaking piñatas filling her mind. The reality was far different. They soon learned that the Mexican's are family oriented and spend holidays at home.

On Christmas Eve afternoon, they arrived at their hotel in the heart of Tijuana. The hotel was deserted and the streets empty, so in search of adventure they drove to Ensenada. The shrimp and margaritas in the seaside restaurant were excellent. Slightly drunk, they went to a dive called Hussong's. They drank tequila and danced to a Mariachi band in the dirty, smoke-filled room. They had no idea how they got back to their hotel.

Christmas morning, Krake awoke with a monumental hangover. Breakfast in the hotel's empty dining room wasn't too bad. She couldn't have handled much noise.

"People are home opening presents, they'll be celebrating in town later," Gale said confidently. After wandering the empty streets, past closed shops, they had an early dinner, went to bed and drove back to LA the next morning. Krake wondered if she was doomed to having unhappy Christmases. New Year's Eve was better, but the expectations connected with these holidays was always greater than the reality. She was glad they were over.

She continued to be grateful for the one area that never let her down, her job. The only drawback was transportation. The three buses home could take up to an hour and forty-five minutes. Moaning and groaning, she continued to ride the frustratingly inadequate public transportation system rather than learn to drive. She just wasn't ready.

In March, a letter arrived from Daddy. Inside a wedding card was a check for three hundred dollars. The note read, "Sorry this is so late in arriving. Your mother and I wish you the best. Love, Daddy." Krake put her head down on the table and cried. He does love me, kept running through her mind. Still sniffling, she ran to the phone in the bedroom and dialed Texas.

Hank answered.

"Daddy, I just got your card and the wonderful gift. Thank you, thank you." She started to cry.

"Didn't you think I'd send anything? I said I would."

"Daddy, I've missed you. I wanted to write but I thought you didn't care. I really did."

"Of course I care. Don't you know you're my favorite daughter? Now, tell me about the wedding and Gale."

She did and promised to send him the only four wedding photos that came out. No one's camera had been working. Happy, she hung up with the parting words, "I love you, Daddy, come out and visit us soon."

"I will, Princess, I promise."

She sent the photos and a long newsy letter telling of her job at Dr. Kiley's and the apartment and married life, which with them both working different hours was rather lonely. He wrote back complimenting her on how beautiful she looked in her wedding dress and how much he regretted not being there. It was so good to be reconciled. The pain of estrangement vanished.

Two and a half weeks later on the first Wednesday in April she commented to Gwen over lunch, "I've been writing the date 4/5/67 in the charts all morning. That's unusual, there won't be another date like this again until 1978." They laughed, finished eating and returned to the office.

That night the phone rang and her brother's voice said, "Hi, Krake, this is Hank Jr., I have some bad news. Your father passed away at noon today." That phrase, "your father," rang in her ears. Why didn't he say "Daddy" or "Dad?"

With the phone pressed to her ear, she said "No!" and kept repeating "No!" as she backed over to the bed and sat down, crying and gasping for breath. Then her mother came on the line and they made arrangements for her flight home. Ironically, the wedding gift turned out to pay for her flight home to attend his funeral.

In southeast Texas, people are buried within two days because of the heat. By the time Krake arrived the following evening, the funeral arrangements were all made. Hank Jr. took care of everything.

The death had been so sudden. So violent. So final. A cerebral hemorrhage at noon. His secretary said he had had a severe headache all morning and at lunchtime went to visit the nurse downstairs to get something for it. He collapsed in her office and died in the ambulance on the way to the hospital.

Now they were in the stifling heat of an April afternoon in Texas, following the body of her father to its grave. Sweat rolled down her sides and made the black and white polka-dot dress stick to her flesh. The dust of the rutted, two-lane road swirled around the tires of the hearse ahead. Is it normal, she thought, to feel so alone, so isolated in grief, so damn unreal? I could be watching a movie of a funeral.

It's over. My father is dead. Dead for always. Never, never to have another wet kiss, or see the nicotine-stained fingers holding a Camel or touch the snow-white hair or have him wiggle his ears or blow smoke rings.

Daddy had been her link to the family and now he was gone. Krake felt better when after the service at the graveside, as she was stumbling along in her black patent heels, Hank Jr. came up beside her, put his arm around her shoulders, pulling her close, and together they walked back to the black limousine. The gesture was moving and gave her the strength she needed.

As she settled back in the soft upholstery of the limousine, her thoughts were scattered. Maybe she and Hank Jr. could be friends. Daddy was gone. She had spent years trying to find someone like him, but why? Hadn't he abandoned her long before his death? Yes, they had reconciled and she was thankful for that, but his sporadic attempts to connect with her were far from adequate. However, she had managed to hold onto the myth of the perfect father anyway.

21

Miraculously, after the funeral the pain of loss vanished. Krake knew Daddy was at peace. She decided to stay with Lorraine until she felt her mother could be alone. Hankie, the friendliest since she had known him, had to return to Houston the day after the funeral. Both he and Mae's jobs awaited. It was a strange feeling to be friendly with him. While growing up they had only communicated in anger and since she had left home, there had been no communication.

One afternoon, Lorraine came into the dining room where Krake had just finished the thank-you notes for flowers and condolence gifts. Lorraine, almost prostrate with grief, clung to Krake in a way she never had before. She seemed to need her so much, Krake didn't see how she could return to LA. Krake's experience with Burg's death heightened her awareness of the kind of pain her mother was in and she wished she could do something to alleviate it. It seemed that their roles were reversed and she was the older maternal figure, while Lorraine had become a child. It was a nice feeling that her mother needed her instead of being ashamed of who she was.

Lorraine's voice was dull. "I think I dozed off for a little while."

"Good. Is your headache gone?"

"Almost. Thanks for writing those notes, I just can't seem to get my thoughts together."

"Mom, I'm so glad Daddy sent the wedding card and check before he died. If we had been out of touch, I don't think I could have stood it."

Her mother looked at her with swollen, red-rimmed eyes. "He told me he was sending you a gift he'd promised and I said not to, that you didn't care about us, but he went ahead anyway. I'm thankful now that he did."

"Why did you think I didn't care?"

"You moved away and never came home. I kept reminding him you didn't love us."

A hot poker of pain jabbed her gut. "That's not true! It's you who doesn't love me. Hankie said that when I was in Camarillo he was told not to mention my name outside the house. Do you know how that makes me feel?" Her voice rose. Normally the emotions would have accelerated into a bitter quarrel, but since the interment a sense of peace had enveloped her. The invisible bands of dependent love attaching her to her father were loosed and in their place fibers of strength and maturity held her together.

"We felt it was a private matter that you were in a state hospital," Lorraine answered. "No one in our family has gone insane. It just doesn't happen."

"I wasn't insane. I needed somewhere to go to sort things out. Why didn't you write to me? I wanted to hear from you." Her calmness created a space for communication.

"We didn't know we could."

"Why not? Even prisoners get mail."

Lorraine ignored the jibe and continued, "Money, that's all we've been good for. When we couldn't send any, you wanted nothing to do with us. I've always known that!" She was starting to sound like her old self.

"Mom, that's not true. In high school I wanted the things my friends had, like everyone that age. After I left home, I needed your emotional support more than money. You have always reduced love to dollars and cents. I don't think that way. I wanted Daddy to give me away at my wedding. It was always my dream. I wanted you and Hankie there too, but I knew that was out of the question financially."

"We talked about it. Your father was seriously considering going, but I told him he'd have to pay for the rehearsal dinner and the reception. The bride's family pays for everything." Lorraine rose and went into the kitchen for a glass of water.

Krake followed. "I wrote that it wasn't going to be conventional. He could have stayed with me. I catered the reception, there was no rehearsal dinner. Oh, Mom, why didn't you encourage him to come?"

The hazel eyes met hers and glanced away. Shrugging her shoulders, Lorraine put the glass down on the edge of the sink, turned and stared out the window. The sunlight streaking the pines in the backyard lit the silence. Softly came the reply, "I don't know."

Suddenly the broad back that had always been so strong, shrunk. Krake, responding to it's vulnerability, crossed the space between them, put her arms around the sturdy figure and laid her head between the protruding shoulder blades. "Mom, I love you."

A sigh escaped, "I love you too, dear."

They left it at that. Some things would never be resolved.

When Krake stepped off the plane at the LA airport, Gale was waiting. He took two steps and they embraced, kissing hungrily. She was glad to see him, but a brown haze of smog made her eyes burn.

The apartment was a disaster! Bed unmade, dirty dishes filled the sink, trash in every room, clothes dropped on the floor. She wanted to run back to the air-conditioned order of her mother's house. Gale's total self-absorption was amazing. He acted as if nothing was amiss, that she had been on vacation and would be happy to cook and clean for him again.

As soon as he put the suitcases on the littered bedroom floor, he turned and grabbed her, kissing, caressing and saying as he unbuttoned the olive-green dress, "You've got to shorten your skirts, everyone's wearing minis. You looked so old and dowdy when you got off the plane." Not too repulsive to fuck, however. Which he did, then announced she shouldn't wait up because he was working the Carson show.

After he left, as she lay amid the clutter on the bed, her father's voice spoke in the deepening twilight, "Princess, are you happy?"

"No," she replied, putting on jeans and an old shirt.

Silently she set about unpacking and cleaning up, missing her mother, for the first time in a long time, and the old college friends she had seen in Belton. Something happened at Daddy's funeral. Her perception of things had changed. Just how she wasn't sure. Except that she felt relief that she no longer had to please her father or compete for his love. There was a lightness between her and Lorraine that had never existed before.

Back at work, the world resumed its familiar shape. Missing a bus the first week of her return, she was sitting on the bench cursing the LA mass transit system when a red 1963 Corvair pulled up. A blond, mustachioed, goateed version of Errol Flynn rolled down the window on the passenger side, "Hi, need a ride?"

She hesitated. "Where are you headed?"

"Downtown."

She rose. "I missed my bus to Seventh Street, the one that stops near Bullocks. If you're going near there, I might be able to catch my second bus."

"Sure, hop in. Just put that stuff in the back seat."

She moved some large drawing pads and got in. "Whew, thanks. I don't know when I'd have gotten home. The next bus isn't for forty minutes. I have two more after that. It takes forever!"

"Is your car in the shop?"

"I don't have a car."

"No car? In LA? That's like painting the Mona Lisa without a brush. You've got to have wheels here." He offered her a cigarette.

She took it, leaning towards his proffered lighter flame. Inhaling, she said, "I don't drive."

"Against your religion?"

She smiled. "I don't know how."

"My God, woman, you've got to learn. If I had time, I'd teach you right now, but I have a figure drawing class at six." In front of Bullocks, he pulled into a NO PARKING zone. "You know, I'd really like to teach you to drive. I see by the ring you're married. Would your husband object?"

"I don't know. Let me think about it."

"My name's Peter Gibson, by the way. What's yours?"

"Krake Maxwell."

"What?"

"Krake, like rake, a family name."

"I like it. If you decide to learn, you can reach me at the Chenley Art Institute. They'll know where I am. Here comes a cop, I've got to move."

Her bus arrived seconds later. During the ride she thought about the chance encounter. He was dashing! And so friendly! Learn to drive? She knew she had to. Without it, she was like a prisoner. Her territory extended from the apartment to work. She never went anywhere else unless it was with Gale or Pam. Since starting to break the dependency ties with Daddy after his death, freedom was more important to her, but she was far from free. She longed to be mobile, to go to a movie or an art exhibit or out to the beach or to a GIGANTIC CLEARANCE SALE! By herself.

She felt certain Gale wouldn't approve of her learning with Peter. He had tried to teach her the second month they knew each other, but shifting plus trying to steer and avoid road hazards (LA traffic) plus Gale's constant criticism rendered it hopeless. Her old depth-perception problem left her not knowing exactly where in the road she was. This was terrifying, but she felt it was her own inadequacy that prevented her overcoming it.

On second thoughts, maybe it would be OK with Gale. She'd ask. She wouldn't see him long enough to broach a subject like this until Saturday night. That and Sunday was the only time they had together. Both worked Monday through Friday; she nine to five, he, five to midnight or later. Usually he decided after she was dressed and ready to leave in the morning that his cock needed attention. Ingrained as wifely duties were in her, she reluctantly complied, looking at her watch as he satisfied himself. Still, she found it flattering, if inconsiderate.

That Saturday night over a candlelight dinner of rare steaks and cabernet in a restaurant in Glendale, she related her unexpected ride to the bus the other evening. Gale froze, his smile faded, the blue eyes iced over. "You got in a car with a total stranger? Are you nuts? You could have been raped and killed."

"I never thought of that. I just wanted to make my downtown bus connection. Otherwise I wouldn't have gotten home until midnight."

"You would've gotten home, though. I can't believe you're so stupid! You disgust me. You act like a tramp! What's the matter with you, huh? Answer me." His voice was hissing and people at nearby tables stared.

"I'm sorry, I wasn't thinking, I'll never do it again." She pushed down her anger at his false accusations, not wanting to cause a fight.

"You're damn right, you'll never do it again. Not my wife. Don't speak to me for the rest of the meal. Wait until I get you home."

They ate in silence, she rather fearfully. The wine was finished and she wished she had another bottle. He paid the check and held her elbow as they walked to the car. The silence on the way home was broken only by her feeble attempts at conversation. Gale never spoke. Once inside, he took her by the shoulders and shook, forcefully.

Her anger rose, "Let go of me, you bastard! I didn't do anything wrong, don't touch me again."

He slapped her hard. Again and again. She began to cry. He left, slamming the door. Stumbling into the kitchen, she grabbed an open bottle of Red Mountain Burgundy and poured a tumbler full, drained it and poured a refill. Calmer, she walked into the bathroom and looked in the mirror. Her right eye was red and swelling. She put down the glass and soaked a washcloth in cold water. Undressing, she lay on the bed, eye covered and drank almost the whole half-gallon of cheap wine. Her thoughts were jumbled. She must be an awful person to be treated this way. Did he sense she found Peter attractive? What would have happened if she had asked him about driving lessons? Miserable, she fell asleep. Gale got home at dawn.

When her eyes opened, the sun was high, her head ached and the empty glass lay on the floor. He was still asleep. Quietly she slipped from underneath the comforter and tiptoed into the bathroom. A glance in the mirror revealed a Technicolor face, blue and purple blotches circled her right eye and cheek. God! I have to go to work tomorrow. What will I do? My husband hit me, how shameful! No one must know.

She was sipping her second cup of coffee when Gale came into the kitchen and silently poured himself a cup.

Sitting down at the table, he asked casually, "How are you feeling?"

“ ”My face hurts."

"I'm sorry about that. I just saw red thinking about you and another man. Putting yourself in danger like that. Krake, you must be more careful." His hand covered hers.

Remembering the blows, she flinched at the touch. "I will. Please don't hit me again. It's awful. I have to work tomorrow. Look at my eye."

"I won't, I promise."

The remainder of the Sunday, Gale spent lazily reading the paper and Krake did some house-cleaning and a washing. Gale sent out for a pizza and they watched TV until she pleaded fatigue and went to bed. He soon followed and made overtures for sex. She didn't want his touch. Sensing her unwillingness, he rolled over and started snoring almost immediately. She slept fitfully, tossing and turning until the wee hours. I'm trapped with a man I don't love. Help! She didn't know why, but a single thought persisted, I must learn to drive. It was scary to contemplate what Gale might do if he found out, but she had to do it.

On Monday morning, forty-five minutes and layers of clown white later, the bruises were hidden. Her years in the theater proved useful in camouflaging. No one at work seemed to notice, at least nothing was said.

She decide to wait until the marks were gone before contacting Peter. A week later, when only faint smudges remained, she called Chenley and asked for his number.

"We're not allowed to give out students numbers," the voice on the line informed her.

"Mr. Gibson said I could reach him here. Could I leave my number? Would he get it?"

She gave her name and work number. Hanging up, excitement raced through her. I'm scared, but I have to do this. She motioned in the first cab-company applicant and began his eye exam. Every time the phone rang, she hoped it was Peter. No such luck. By the third day, she had concluded he hadn't meant what he said, but right after lunch Gwen's voice came over the intercom in her office. "Krake, call for you on line one."

Eagerly she picked up the receiver. "Hello."

"Hi, It's Peter. I just got your message. I've been up north checking out the California College of Arts and Crafts in Oakland. What's happening?"

"Peter, if you meant what you said, I'd like to learn to drive."

"Hey, good for you. When shall we start?"

"The office closes at four today. How about this afternoon?"

He said that was fine and she gave him directions.

"Your husband said it was OK?" he asked just before hanging up.

"Not exactly. I'll explain when I see you."

"Whatever you say. Later."

As soon as she replaced the receiver, a chill ran over her. What if Gale finds out?

With two EKGs and a set of cervical spine x-rays to complete, four o'clock arrived at three.

Gwen entered her office, smiling slyly, "There's a handsome blond in the waiting room asking for you."

"Thanks, he's a friend of Gale's who's going to teach me to drive. Don't tell anyone, especially Gale, it's a surprise."

Gwen winked. "My lips are sealed."

He is good-looking, she thought, as she entered the waiting room.

In the small parking lot behind the building, she slid behind the wheel. Terror gripped her. White-faced, she turned to him, "What do I do?"

"Change the gear to DRIVE, take off the emergency brake and push on the gas pedal, the one on the right." She did as instructed and the car leapt forward. "Gently, easy on the gas, lighten up on the pedal." The car slowed. "Now drive around the parking lot."

Bumping, starting, stopping, jerking, they spent an hour circling the small cement area. Finally, things began to go smoother and she relaxed slightly.

"Now, move out of here and drive around the block."

Her eyes widened, "Do you think I can?"

"Yes."

Cautiously, she waited until there was a large opening in the evening traffic and made a wide turn into the world of rush hour. Misjudging the first corner, she bumped over a curb. Frightened, her foot left the accelerator and the auto stalled. Immediately, the car behind began honking and others joined in. Panicked she wanted to get out and run.

Peter's voice was calm and steady. "Turn on the ignition and give it some gas, slowly."

The car lurched ahead and with sweat pouring down her sides, she slowly drove around the block. She forgot about the turn signal, incurring loud honks as she swung into the safety of the parking lot. Gratefully switching off the ignition after putting the gear in PARK, she sank back in the seat.

"Peter, I was awful, I'll never learn, I'm sorry."

"For what? We're still here, aren't we? Tomorrow we'll do it again."

"Tomorrow?"

"If you're free, that is. Better to practice as often as you're able. It is OK with your husband, isn't it?"

She looked away. "To be honest I haven't told him."

"Why not?"

"I want it to be a surprise. He's been after me to learn."

"Why doesn't he teach you?"

"Umm, well, he's too impatient, too critical. I can't even start his Triumph."

"I assume it's a standard shift." She nodded. "That's too complicated to begin with. This automatic lets you concentrate on steering and handling traffic. I don't know why it stalled, it doesn't usually. Later on you can learn the gear box. What time tomorrow?"

"I'm through at five every day but Wednesday."

"I'll be here." He glanced at his watch. "My night class

has been changed to seven, would you like a ride home?"

Gale was working from five to midnight so she accepted the offer. He left her in front of the stone steps promising another adventure the following day and assuring her she was doing fine. His words were of little comfort, she knew her driving was terrible. But it was a beginning. I can't give up, I've got to conquer this.

The next evening she successfully negotiated the block five times and was elated at her progress.

So was Peter. "See, you can do it, you just have to be patient. I'm going north again for the weekend, but we'll continue next Wednesday."

Relieved at a few days reprieve, she thanked him and walked to the bus stop. Projects at school were pressing and he didn't have time to take her home. The bus ride was more tedious than ever and she looked forward to the day she could drive the distance herself.

Meanwhile, Tuesday night therapy sessions continued. She revealed her secret tutor, provoking mixed reactions. All endorsed her learning to drive, but Irwin voiced loudly that she ought to tell Gale.

"He wouldn't like it, I know that," she said firmly.

"How do you know? If he finds out, he'll like it even less," Irwin stated.

She had to admit that was true, but hoped to keep it a secret.

"Why don't you think he'd like it?" Walter asked.

Looking in his concerned eyes, she couldn't avoid the truth. "When I told him Peter gave me a ride downtown, he got very angry and hit me."

"What happened?" Walter's brow was creased.

The attention focused on her as she related the incident. The comments ranged from "Leave him" to "Get him into therapy."

"I can't leave him. We've been married less than a year. He would never consider therapy, he hates me coming here.

He's never hit me before and promises he'll never do it again."

"That's what they all say," advised Marion. "once they start, they never stop. At least that's what my husband was like." Marion was a new group member who had shared little in the month she had been participating. She now spoke at length of being married to a man who beat her if she hadn't dusted. He was a member of the military and conducted a white-glove test whenever he had been away. If the glove was the least bit smudged, he hit her. She stayed for seven years, but when he began to strike their five-year-old son, she left. Her mother provided refuge until she was able to secure a position as a legal secretary and live on her own with her child. The divorce was difficult. He denied all aberrant behavior. She opted for freedom in lieu of alimony and received monthly child-support checks. She wrote her phone number on a piece of paper and handed it to Krake. "If you ever need a place to stay, call me." Krake put the number in her wallet. She would never have to use it.

The weekend passed without incident. Gale was working double shifts and they hardly saw each other. On Wednesday, the lesson went well. She ventured several blocks further from the office and practiced parallel parking, the use of hand signals and changing lanes. A week later, traveling down a crowded street, Peter instructed her to turn right. Suddenly they found themselves going up an on-ramp of the Hollywood Freeway.

"I didn't mean to turn here. I wanted you to take the access road." He sat up straight. "Just stay in the right-hand lane and get off at the next exit."

The din of rubber on cement, the roar of engines, the screeching of brakes and horns honking was deafening; something of which as a passenger she had been unaware. "Peter, I can't, I'm too scared." It was rush hour on one of the heaviest traveled freeways in Los Angeles.

He leaned over and took the wheel. "Just give it gas and we'll get out of here." He steered them down the next off-ramp and pulled over to the curb. "Shut off the engine."

"I can't believe the noise. I couldn't think." She took the cigarette he handed her.

"You're not ready for that yet, but you will be. You startled me heading up that on-ramp." He laughed.

She vowed never to drive on the freeways.

When she got home, Gale was unexpectedly waiting. "Where have you been? You've never gotten here this late. I called Kiley's and got the answering service." He grabbed her arm.

She backed away. "I stopped at Bullocks and tried on clothes. I didn't realize the time. What are you doing here?"

Fear rose. Had he discovered her secret?

"They decided to transfer me to daytime for the rest of the week. I'll be home every night till next Monday. You got some new clothes? Mini-skirts, I hope. I'm sick of you looking like an old lady."

"Gale, I've been choosing my own things since I could walk. Mother always said I knew what looked best on me. Daddy said I should be a buyer for a department store."

"You? You look like shit!" He headed for her closet and grabbed a colorful pink and blue gingham banded in orange. She called it her cotton-candy dress, one of her favorites. "Look at this, it belongs in the rag pile." He took it off the hanger and deliberately tore it in two, throwing the garment at her feet. She sprang at him, clawing, yelling, hitting. He fended her off and socked her in the jaw, twice. She crumpled to the floor next to the ripped dress.

When she came to, he was gone. Her whole head ached. She looked at the remnants of the beautiful dress and began to cry. Quieting down, she went directly to the cabinet where two bottles of rot-gut burgundy sat waiting. She drank them both.

When she awoke, still alone, she didn't know if it was the booze or the blows causing the most discomfort. Calling work, she left a message that she had the 'flu and wouldn't be in until tomorrow. All day she tried to figure out what to do. She called Walter who wanted to see her immediately, but she didn't feel well enough to make the journey. He advised her to say nothing to arouse Gale and come in for a private session the following evening. She thought about leaving Gale, but the prospect was overwhelming. Where would she go? It would be another failure. Was she so awful? Did she look like shit?

Gale didn't appear until after dinner. Not a word was said about the previous evening. They barely spoke.

Another forty-five minute makeup job in the morning covered the latest damage and she went to work.

"You're so pale," Gwen commented. "Do you feel well enough to stay?"

"I'm weak, but I'll live," she replied.

After lunch, she called Chenley and left a message for Peter. Late in the day Peter returned her call. She told him they would have to postpone that afternoon's lesson until next week. Gale's schedule had been changed.

"Are you all right?" he asked. "Your voice sounds different."

"Sure, I just had a flu bug, but I'm better now. Have a nice weekend."

"You too, get some rest."

Much to her surprise, Gale picked her up after work and took her out to dinner. Using the excuse of visiting the ladies' room, Krake called Walter from the restaurant, explaining why she couldn't keep their appointment. They arranged a session before the next group meeting.

By the end of the evening, she felt better. They had shared a bottle of Chianti with the veal parmigiana and it seemed reminiscent of their dating days. He was funny and told her she was his dream girl. At home, he wooed and caressed her passionately and she enjoyed the lovemaking for the first time in many weeks.

But Monday morning when he attempted a fuck, she resisted. "I'm all dressed for work. We've only got twenty minutes to get there, just not enough time."

He pouted, slamming around as he got ready to take her to the office. She attempted conversation on the ride there, but he didn't answer and roared away as soon as she got out. Her day was busy and she forgot his moodiness until she got home and walked into the living room to an appalling sight. Every photo, every newspaper clipping, every theater handbill, even the Ford Grant writer's poem to her had been methodically torn in two and then placed carefully together on the blue carpet. At first glance, it seemed it was just an array of memorabilia. Stepping closer, the jagged-edged tears became visible.

No, no, no, not this, all my mementos of my acting career destroyed. Why does he hate me so much? Because I wouldn't have sex this morning? Crying, she fell to her knees, gathered up the pieces and threw them away. The pain of this was greater than the physical blows.

That evening in her private therapy session, she ranted and raved and sobbed out the story. She had been proud of her achievements in the field of acting, the photos and writings were irreplaceable, she felt such rage at Gale, she wanted to kill him.

Walter handed her a box of Kleenex. "What do you want to do?"

She blew her nose, shaking her head. "I don't know."

"Krake, I can't tell you what course to take, but you may be in danger. I'm not sure what's triggering this behavior, but I fear for your safety. Do you know that his hands are registered with the Navy as weapons?"

Krake was aghast.

"Gale told me that during the wedding reception. He was very proud of the fact. He could really hurt you."

"Where would I go? What would I do?"

"You tell me you pay most of the bills. You have a good job, you'd manage."

"We'll see, Walter, we'll see."

He hugged her and they arranged the chairs for the group. When everyone was seated, Walter asked if she would like to share her recent experience. She did. Marion immediately offered her apartment.

Krake thanked her and others in the group who encouraged her to leave, but she just wasn't ready.

On Wednesday afternoon, Peter arrived promptly at four and suggested they drive over to Hancock Park. The wide, tree-lined streets and stately homes provided a quiet, stable background for driving. Her turning and parallel parking were excellent and she experienced a few moments of pleasure behind the wheel.

Peter offered to treat her to a sundae, in celebration.

At Will Wright's, as they devoured giant caramel sundaes with coffee ice cream, he asked if everything was all right. "I sense some worry that wasn't there the last time we met. Has anything happened?" he asked.

She studied the ice cream melting on her spoon.

"You don't have to tell me. It's none of my business."

"Gale and I have been fighting lately."

"Not over me, I hope."

"Only once, when I told him about you giving me a lift downtown. He's so jealous."

"Does he know about the driving lessons?"

"No, he has no idea and never will, I promise you."

"He'd probably kill me," Peter nervously laughed.

"Not you, me. He's knocked me out before."

"He what? Knocked you unconscious?"

She nodded.

"That son-of-a-bitch! Hitting a woman. You don't deserve that."

"No, I don't, but he's always sorry afterwards. He loves me, says I'm his dream girl."

"Sounds more like a nightmare to me. Are you going to stay with him?"

"I don't know, Peter. I'm confused." Her voice broke and he reached across the table to take her hand.

"You're a beautiful woman, don't you know that? You're sweet and funny and kind and might even learn to drive one day. Any guy in his right mind would give whatever to have you."

Looking away, she thanked him softly.

"It's true, God damn it! Is there anything I can do to help?"

"Just be my friend and teach me to drive."

"That I can do. Back to the steering wheel."

He paid the check and she drove to the office in the silvery dusk.

"Need a lift home?"

"Better not. He's due home at midnight, but you never know. See you tomorrow after work."

He hastily scribbled something on a scrap of note paper. "I've been meaning to give you my phone number at the apartment. He gives you any trouble, I'll drive this thing faster than any white horse to your rescue."

The following evening Peter cajoled her onto the freeway, this time with the windows rolled up. "You've got to use the freeways occasionally. Drive to the next off-ramp."

Anxiously she kept the car in a straight line and exited without incident.

"Proud of yourself?"

"You bet!"

He told her to drive downtown. She protested that she couldn't, but he insisted. It wasn't that bad, but negotiating the intricacies of downtown traffic and pedestrians was exhausting. Back at the office, she pulled into the parking lot just as Gale was turning up the street away from them. "My God, that's Gale. He's supposed to be working. I hope he didn't see us!"

"In that dark green Triumph? No, he was eyeing a blond walking up the hill. Her mini-skirt covered her waist, that's about all."

For once she was grateful for the existence of testosterone and quickly exited the car. "I'm going to run to the bus stop. See you next Wednesday."

"Call if you need me." His voice trailed after her.

She figured out her story on the way home. Open the door, deep breath, big smile, "Hi honey! Gwen invited me to supper. Why are you home so early?" She began taking off her uniform, talking all the while. He followed her into the bedroom. "Her apartment's so cute, not my style, but cute. We had a potato-cabbage pie, English, I guess."

"I came by the office, but you'd already gone. I haven't eaten. Want to go out to the Mexican place?"

"I'm kind of full, but sure." Actually she was starving, not having eaten since lunch.

"You're really going through those chips," he commented, drinking a Dos Equis.

"Can't stop once you start," she laughed, stuffing her mouth, salsa dribbling down her chin.

"Clean your face, you're a mess." His tone was imperious.

What had happened to him? she wondered. He used to be fun, teasing her affectionately and laughing a lot. It had all changed. He acted like she was an object for display only, something to wear on his arm.

"Gale, nobody's in here but us. Who cares? Smile, Señor." She held the napkin in front of her face like a veil and rolled her eyes at him.

He grabbed the white paper square and crumpled it. "Don't laugh at me. I work hard, I try to do my best!"

Incredulously, she said, "I'm not laughing at you. Gale, what's wrong? You don't have fun anymore, at least not with me. Aren't you feeling well? What is it?"

"Nothing's wrong. You don't take me seriously."

"I take you very seriously. But sometimes I like to play, don't you? Life's hard enough, there's a need for silliness."

No answer. The meal was finished in silence.

He worked double shift again all weekend. On Saturday night, she drank a whole jug of burgundy. Gale told her the next day that he found her lying outside on the patio clad in nothing but a bra and panties, a half-empty glass by her side. He tried to wake her, but couldn't, so carried her inside to bed.

The hangover was as treacherous as ever. She threw up and spent the day in bed. At four, the phone rang. It was Lorraine.

"Hello, dear, it's Mom."

"Mom, hi! Is everything OK?" Lorraine never made long-distance calls. Something must have happened.

"Everything's fine. Well, you know. I mean I'm all right. I appreciate your letters, but I haven't felt like writing. I think I'm going to take a trip back to Hillsburg and Alexandria Mills. I want to see our old friends."

"That's a wonderful idea. I wish I could go."

"That's what I was wondering. Could you get time off from work and come with me?"

"I don't think so, Mom. Dr. Kiley docked me three days pay when I was home for Daddy's funeral. I can't afford to miss any more right now. I'd love to go though. How are you getting along? Did you figure out the bills?"

"I almost lost the house."

"What happened?"

"I was under the impression they sent a bill regularly. After three months, I called the bank. They were on the verge of starting foreclosure proceedings. I had the payment vouchers here and was supposed to send the money in monthly. Dad did all that. I should have paid more attention. I hunted and hunted for that darn bank book and finally found it in the desk. I feel so foolish not to have known."

"You shouldn't, Mom. How could you've known that? A lot of widows have the same problems. Do you know when I left home, I didn't even know how to ride the bus? I sure learned."

Lorraine asked about her driving lessons which Krake had mentioned in a letter.

"They're coming along. Gale doesn't know. It's going to be a surprise."

"Just think, you'll be married a whole year next month and I haven't even met my son-in-law."

"Why don't you visit us for Christmas?"

"I'd like to. I'll talk to Hank Jr. and Mae and see what their plans are. How are you and Gale?"

Krake swallowed, "We're fine. Adjusting. I think when I get my driver's license and a car things will be better. He's gone a lot of the time and I'm stuck here."

"As long as you're happy. Well, I'll say goodbye."

"Bye, Mom, I love you."

"Bye, dear, I love you, too."

As she hung up, Krake realized this was the first time Lorraine had called her. It was a good feeling knowing her mother wanted her company on a trip. Daddy's death really seemed to have united them.

After Wednesday's lesson, Peter said she was ready to take the driver's test.

She was in seventh heaven when she passed and ran to find Peter who was in the waiting room. Pulling him to his feet, she hugged him, jumping up and down. "I did it. You did it! Anyway I passed!" He kissed her on the lips. It felt good, but she ended it quickly, she didn't want any complications just now.

All weekend she wanted to tell Gale, but refrained, too dangerous. She had to figure out the best place and time for this revelation.

With Peter's help, she found a 1961 Corvair in good condition and talked the owner into letting her pay it off on time. He also let her keep the car in his garage until she could pick it up. Now she had two things she had to tell Gale.

22

"Out of reindeer? We drove down from Santa Barbara for some. I'm very disappointed." The pudgy, strawberry blonde's gold bangles clinked as she took a long drink from her lipstick rimmed martini glass. "What would you recommend?"

"Do you like whale, Madam?" the waiter inquired.

"Is it tough?" the blonde's companion asked.

"No sir, they don't swim much," was the sardonic reply.

Gale had chosen The Blue Boar on La Cienega Boulevard for their anniversary dinner. They had chateaubriand and eavesdropped on their neighbors' conversations. After key lime mousse, coffee and Calvados, they drove out to the spot on the coast where they had gone that first evening together a year and a half ago. She recalled Gale's tenderness and understanding at her reluctance to become involved. Tonight the gentleness was a part of him again. He spread his jacket on the ground and kissed her so sweetly as he sat beside her.

"Happy anniversary," she said, snuggling closer.

"May we have a lifetime together." Gale placed a small velvet box in her lap. "This is for you," he said.

"Gale, we agreed, no presents, money's too tight. I feel awful, I don't have anything to give you."

"I'll think of something," he said, laughing. "Open it."

"I can't see very well," she said, opening the lid. A small, exquisitely carved cameo pin gleamed in the pale light.

"Gale, it's lovely, thank you." She kissed him. The memory of the violence of recent months faded. Things will be all right. Everything will work out. Under a canopy of stars, they made love by the faint light of the new moon.

The next morning, Gale woke her by licking her toes and they made love again. Afterwards, they lay on the carpet in the living room sipping cinnamon coffee and listening to a new Beatles album he had brought home, "Sergeant Pepper's Lonely Hearts Club Band." She felt like Lucy, except the kaleidoscope wasn't in her eyes, but in her brain. Pictures of Peter and Gale tossed around there all afternoon. She had to tell him about the car and that she now had a driver's license. How? When? Not today.

Early the following week, Peter called to see if she was using her vehicle.

"Not yet. I have to decide the right time to approach him."

"Do you enjoy not being able to tell him something like this? We're friends, not lovers. You should feel free to let him know of your accomplishments."

"Peter, he's never hit you. It'd be great if I could be completely honest, but I know better. He's crazy and jealous where I'm concerned. It's because he loves me."

"Spare me that kind of love."

"We had a lovely time on our anniversary. Maybe things will be different from now on."

"For your sake, I hope so, but don't count on it."

The next day over coffee, she asked Gwen if she would help her out of a predicament.

"If I can," the Englishwoman replied.

"You know I got my driver's license a few weeks ago," she began.

Gwen interrupted, "Yes, and I'm proud of you. Was Gale pleased?"

"That's the problem, he doesn't know."

"You mean you and his friend spent all that time together so that you could pass the test and he doesn't know?" She put her cup down.

"Gwen, Peter's my friend, not Gale's. If he knew who taught me to drive, he'd be furious."

Gwen looked puzzled. "Why?"

"Because he's extremely jealous."

"Has he hit you? Is that why you wear so much makeup sometimes? I thought so." This conclusion was drawn before Krake had a chance to answer.

"He's promised not to do it again." Gwen shook her head. "Could I say you taught me after work?"

"Me? I just got my license a few months ago and I still can't get used to driving on the wrong side of the road."

"He doesn't have to know that. Would you, please?"

"I guess so. If it'll help you out." She looked at her watch. "Nine o'clock, better let the hordes in."

After group therapy the following evening, she waylaid Marion in the hall. Marion agreed to say she had heard about the Corvair through a friend. The car was too small for her and her son Justin, so she'd mentioned it to Krake one evening in group. They had gone together to see it and the rest was history. If only Gale bought the story.

Krake picked up the car and bought champagne and groceries for a sumptuous meal.

Gale's first words as he came through the door were, "You look beautiful, is that a new dress?"

She twirled in the pale blue, imitation leather, micro-mini jumper and knee-high white boots. The cameo was fastened to the old-fashioned, lacy blouse she wore under the jumper. She urged Gale to shower and change because this was going to be a night to remember.

Willingly complying, he soon emerged, looking handsome in a beige Nehru jacket and navy slacks. They began the meal with stuffed mushrooms and the first of two bottles of cabernet. The steaks were rare, potatoes fluffy and the salad crisp. During desert, with the candles flickering, she cleared her throat. "Gale, I have a surprise."

Drowsily, he said, "Yeah?"

"Guess what?" she prompted nervously, stomach churning.

"What?"

"Promise you won't get mad."

"Yeah."

"Gwen, you know, at the office …"

"I know, get on with it."

"Well …"

"Well what?"

"She's been teaching me to drive."

"She's been teaching you to …. Ha! That's a laugh."

"Why?"

"I've seen her weaving around near Third Street. Lucky she hasn't hit someone."

"Maybe she's a better teacher. Anyhow, we've been practicing after work and I took the test and passed it! I've got a driver's license!"

The two bottles of wine had dulled his reflexes. He slowly reached across the table and clasped her wrist tightly. Her heart stopped. "Congratulations, honey, that's great!"

Relief spread warm fingers through her. Round Two. "There's more." She was on a roll.

"More? I suppose you bought a car?" He laughed heartily.

"I did."

"You what? You bought a car? Not a new one, I hope. How can we afford it? The Triumph needs a tune-up. Where is it?" He pushed his chair back and stood up, looming over her. She led the way outside to where the Corvair was parked up the hill in a curve, hidden from the apartment.

"Looks all right. You should have the wheels pointed into the curb in case your brakes fail. It's steep around here."

"Want to take her for a test drive?"

They got in, Gale driving. "How much did you pay for this heap? Not a lot, I hope."

"$450. I gave the owner some money down and he's letting me pay it off on time."

"Who's this guy? Some stud patient of yours?"

"No, he's real old. So old he can't drive anymore. Marion from group took me to see him. The car was too small for her, but it's perfect for me. What do you think?"

"I only hope you didn't get taken." He parked the vehicle behind the Triumph. "I didn't think you had it in you. Now I can sleep in every morning. No more early trips to Kiley's."

Couldn't he be more positive? Rain was definitely falling on her parade. On second thought, her main concern was that he believe her stories. He seemed to. Hooray!

Driving to work took all of fifteen minutes. She followed carefully the route Gale took and easily found her way. The first Saturday she had transportation, she drove slowly down Beverly Boulevard to La Cienega. The night of their anniversary dinner, they had taken a stroll along the boulevard. She had been drawn to a shop with bold, striking clothes in the window. She had promised herself she would return in her new car and here she was. She bought two dresses. There went her paycheck, but she didn't care. The feeling of freedom mixed with power was heady.

Back in the apartment she tried them on again. Which one to wear tonight? The black and white flowered print mini with the dropped waist? Yes, it was cute and sexy.

Gale got home late, said he had been rehearsing a scene. A friend from NBC had talked him into joining an acting class, promising that it would be an aid in directing. Krake heartily agreed, remembering her frustration at the lack of communication between herself and the directors in Hollywood.

Showered and changed, he looked up from fastening a

cuff link as she walked into the bedroom decked out in her new finery. She stood waiting. "Well?" she asked. Silence.

"You look grotesque!"

She wanted to run but couldn't move.

"That dress is the ugliest I've seen. Is it new?"

"I bought it this afternoon."

"What can I say. You did a lousy job. Change into something else, that is if you want to go out with me. And hurry, the reservations are for eight o'clock." He left the room, went into the kitchen and she heard him pour a glass of wine. Still reeling from the critical blows, she took off the dress and put on the blue jumper. Fastening the cameo she was filled with such hatred she could hardly see the clasp.

"Let's go! Chop, chop!"

"Be right there," she chimed, grabbing her purse and heading for the door. I hate him! I hate him! I hate him!

The new restaurant on the strip was pretentious. Gale loved it. The portions were small, the lamb overdone and the haricots verts, inedible. He praised the food, flattered the waiter and virtually ignored her. She drank. As much as she could. Insisted on a double Calvados afterwards. Then wanted to go dancing.

The Whiskey was jammed so they found a small bar on Santa Monica with a trio. She had brandy and soda—five of them. Finally the place closed and they went home. Gale had to carry her in. Gale woke her sometime during the day to say he had another rehearsal and would be back late.

Rousing herself to take an Alka Seltzer, she fell back on the bed in misery. Lying there, she tried to remember how the evening ended. No use. Getting up, she opened the door to her closet. Her bloodshot eyes filled with tears when she looked at the new dress. As she held it in front of her before the full-length mirror, his word echoed in her head, "Grotesque!" Am I nuts or is he?

Monday morning, she called Peter and met him after work.

"I was surprised to hear from you."

"Peter, I don't know what to do."

"Have you told him about the car?"

"Yes, a couple of weeks ago and I guess he likes it."

"Guess he likes the car? What's not to like?"

"I don't know. He acted strangely about it, made fun of it."

"Jealousy. He's jealous because you have your own car. You're mobile and can leave him if you want to. Has he hit you again?"

"Not with his fists. But Saturday night his comment that my new dress was grotesque was devastating." As soon as she spoke, it hit her. She wanted Peter's approval. Am I never going to break this dependency that Daddy had begun? The realization blotted out Peter's response. She looked at her watch. "Peter, I've got to run. Thanks for listening."

On the way out, Peter said, "Krake, I've got some news, too. I have decided to transfer to CCAC in Oakland at the end of the semester. You can always reach me at school. I'll give you the number there as soon as I know it. Don't be shy about calling. I think you should do the communicating. After all, you may decide you never want to see me again."

She shook her head and wished him a happy Thanksgiving. Driving home, she made herself a promise to change this pattern with men, although she wasn't sure how to go about it.

The holidays approached. Lorraine was coming and so were Gale's parents. They rented a single bed to put in the study for Lorraine. Gale's parents would have their bed and Krake and Gale would sleep in the living room on the sofa bed. Krake spent the week before their arrival cooking meals and freezing them. She would be working through the twenty-third.

On the 20th, Krake drove to the airport to pick up Lorraine. The flight landed, passengers poured out. No Lorraine. She waited and waited, looking everywhere in vain. A pale-skinned blonde, wearing the Continental Airlines uniform, approached her. "Are you Krake Maxwell?" Krake nodded.

"Your mother is waiting near the baggage carousel." The woman led the way.

Her mother was sitting on Krake's old blue Samsonite luggage. Seemingly calm, she smiled, rose and embraced Krake. "I knew you'd find me, dear. I was prepared to wait all night. Thank you, Darlene. Tell your mother I always take Pepto Bismol during those times." The blond from Continental gave Lorraine a hug and wished her a Merry Christmas.

"Do you know that poor girl has to work another Christmas? It's her third in a row. Seems unfair, doesn't it? And her mother so ill with diverticulitis. I have her phone number. I promised I'd call during my stay."

Krake marveled at Lorraine's ability to learn strangers' most intimate secrets within five minutes of meeting them.

In the car, driving across town, Lorraine complimented Krake's driving, which made Krake feel very good.

"I'm taking the long way," said Krake. "I won't drive those freeways, everyone's going so fast."

"I don't like to go fast."

"What?" Remember that speeding ticket you got right after we moved to Belton?"

"I had the air-conditioner running, the windows rolled up and didn't realize how fast I was going."

"That was a bit of irony, considering how much you nagged Daddy if he went over forty."

"I was awful, wasn't I?"

"Yes, I don't know how he stood it. Sometimes I wanted to scream."

"Sometimes you did. But he didn't, I wonder why."

"Think it was because he loved you?" Krake's eyes filled with tears.

Lorraine's were also brimming. She fished around in her purse, found a Kleenex and blew her nose. "Want a Chiclet?"

Hey, my Mom's here, Chiclets and all.

Lorraine thought the apartment was charming and that Krake had done an excellent job of decorating it and the tree. Her mother used a decorator, but had excellent taste and an appreciation for original things.

They had wine with dinner and Krake kept on sipping while she did the dishes.

"I wish you wouldn't drink so much," said Lorraine. "It always worried Dad and me."

"Daddy drank a lot, what's wrong with it?" Krake's voice was hostile.

"Don't get upset. Dad got so he'd have two martinis before dinner, that's all."

"I never knew Daddy to quit at only two, unless he was out of booze." Krake slammed the dishes around in the water.

"You're right. We used to go to parties in Hillsburg and he always drank too much, first staggering, then falling down and passing out. Some of his friends liked to see that and they'd egg him on. It made me so mad. We'd talk and he'd say he'd never do it again. At the next party, it would be the same. Dad just had to smell the cork and he was off."

"I'm just like him, I suppose?"

"Yes, you are. You get so mean and won't stop. Don't you have to go to work in the morning?"

"Yes."

"Then let's go to bed. We'll talk more tomorrow. I've been up since four this morning, I was so worried about the trip and I couldn't sleep."

"Mom, I'm glad you're here."

"So am I. Good night, dear."

"Night." Krake poured another glass of Red Mountain Burgundy and sat on the foot of the bed.

"Don't let the bed bugs bite," drifted in from the study. Her mother's familiar saying was comforting. She had never fallen asleep in the same house with her and not heard it. Somehow it transcended the years and separateness, binding them together in love. Krake had overlooked these moments, they had gotten lost in the bitterness and resentment when she was younger.

Hung over the next morning, she got dressed for work, barely introducing Gale and Lorraine. At noon she called the apartment. No answer. Where were they? Gale didn't have to leave until three-thirty. He must have taken her mother somewhere.

When she returned that evening, there was a note stuck in the dish drainer. "Krake, Gale's taking me on a tour of NBC. Go ahead and eat, he says we're going somewhere exciting for dinner. Love, Mom."

Her feelings ranged from resentment at not being able to go with them to relief at having a few hours to herself. Washing her hair and painting "Fire and Ice" toenails took over an hour. She ate a salad, lay down for a little while and fell asleep. Lorraine tiptoeing around in the bathroom woke her. "Mom, is that you?"

Lorraine sat on the edge of the bed and told her about watching a Jack Benny Special being taped at NBC. Then Gale had taken her to a bar for dinner. She fell asleep, happy that her mother and Gale had gotten along so well.

The next morning she left her husband and her mother drinking orange juice. Gale and Lorraine were going out to the airport to meet Gale's parents who were arriving that afternoon.

23

The Maxwells had rented a Plymouth sedan. It was parked behind the Triumph when Krake got home from work. They're here. Hope they like me. Hope I like them. She went in through the back door and hearing voices, stopped in the hallway to listen.

"Harley," a woman's voice said.

"What, Mom?" My God! His name's Harley. Mrs. Harley Maxwell? No, thank you.

"Those red bows on the tree, couldn't you and Krake afford regular ornaments? Your father and I would have sent the money to buy some."

"We like these better." Gale's voice was subdued.

"The tree is unusual, but beautiful, don't you think, Floyd?" Lorraine spoke firmly.

Thanks, Mom. Well, here goes. She walked into the fray.

Lorraine greeted her, "Krake, we're admiring the tree, it's so unique."

A short, pudgy woman with brown bangs helmeting her brow said, "It's different all right. I'm Gale's mother, Ethel. This here's Floyd." A tall, rangy man smiled, eyes twinkling. "Krake, welcome to our family. You're so pretty. Those wedding pictures didn't do you justice." He gave her a big hug.

"I'm going to change," said Krake. "Gale, why don't you make some drinks for everyone?"

Ethel spoke sharply, "I don't drink, young lady."

A silence descended.

Gale broke it, "I know you'd like a beer, Dad. Lorraine, why don't I make us one of those martinis you liked so much last night?"

"I'll wait awhile, thanks. Ethel, tell me more about Iowa. That church social every Christmas Eve sounds so nice."

In the bedroom, changing into purple corduroy jeans and matching turtleneck, Krake blessed her mother for her abilities as a conversationalist.

In the kitchen, Lorraine was telling Ethel, "Krake loves to cook. She prepares the most exotic dishes. I've always had ordinary food like meatloaf or roast beef." Lorraine poured two glasses of 7-Up and handed Ethel one.

They talked about Christmas dinner, then Ethel asked, "What church service shall we attend on Sunday?"

Krake looked startled.

"We're Baptists. Our minister at home is so full of enthusiasm. It always gets me going," said Ethel.

"How so?" Lorraine asked.

"I want to go to Africa and convert all those black heathens. Our Reverend Blakeley worked as a missionary for several years before deciding to attend the seminary. If it weren't for my family, I would be over there. But how would Floyd get along without me?"

Krake saw Gale and her father-in-law exchange winks over their beer. Did I marry into a bunch of holy rollers?

"I saw that wink, Harley. You and your father never take me seriously. Just you wait. I'll up and become a missionary one of these days, then you'll be sorry."

"I didn't know your name was Harley" Krake said.

"Mom always calls me that. My name's Harley Gale. For obvious reasons, I dropped the Harley."

"That was my father's name. You should be proud of it." Ethel's face was pink.

Dinner went well and the next morning, Ethel made breakfast for everyone. Sitting in the living room with the smell of bacon wafting from the kitchen, Krake felt joy welling up inside. Their families liked each other. They were going to have a wonderful Christmas.

But the next night after a long day of sightseeing, Lorraine rushed into the bathroom where Krake was redoing her eyeliner and mascara. They were all going to the movies.

"Oh dear, I've done something, said something to offend Ethel. She won't speak to me!" Lorraine's face conveyed puzzlement and concern.

Looking in the mirror, Krake asked what had happened.

"I don't know. We were doing the dishes, I was drying and mentioned something about how she and I would have to brush up on our cooking skills to come up to yours. She threw the dishcloth into the sink and went into the bedroom and shut the door. I finished washing and drying, hoping she'd come out. I didn't mean she wasn't a good cook. She'd just finished complimenting you on the tarragon chicken. What can I do?"

"I don't know. Talk to her. Knock on the door and go in."

Her mother left, she heard a faint knock and the door opened. Her mother's voice was muffled, she spoke a few sentences, the door closed. Lorraine reappeared. Krake looked at her questioningly.

"She won't speak to me. I apologized, told her I wasn't criticizing her."

"What'd she do?" Krake put the blue liner back in her cosmetics bag.

"Stared past me and when I finished, shut the door. I feel terrible. Will Gale be mad at me?"

"No, you didn't do anything wrong. If she's going to act like this, we'll leave her alone."

Gale, informed of the incident, knocked on the bedroom door. "Dad, can I speak with you?" Floyd appeared and the conversation was brief.

"They're going to the movies in their car. We'll have to take yours, Krake." He drove. His only comment was, "She's always been like this, real temperamental."

Christmas morning, the Maxwells were still barricaded in the bedroom. Floyd told Gale they were going to church. Gale, Krake and her mother went out to brunch. The abrupt turn of events was troubling to Krake. This conduct felt familiar; like mother, like son.

After brunch, Krake and her mother went to the ladies' room. Krake assured Lorraine that whatever happened with Gale's parents would be for the best. Both Krake and Lorraine wished Hank was there to smooth things over. Krake felt such anger at these strangers making her mother feel bad, so she tried to be very cheerful.

When they returned to the apartment, Krake tripped over the pile of packages sitting on the floor just inside the door. The Maxwells had left the gifts Krake and Gale had given them. Krake could only assume they were on a flight back to Iowa. Krake's anger subsided because she had to reassure Lorraine that she had not caused this irresponsible behavior.

Gale made Tom and Jerry's and the opening of the presents turned out to be fun.

"Mom, thanks for the slip and panties." Lorraine had picked out sexy leopard-skin ones. Gale's gift was a dowdy cloth coat. She hid her disappointment from all but Lorraine, who mentioned it later. How dare he criticize my taste in clothes, Krake thought.

Gale mixed more drinks while her mother told them stories about her youth. "I remember once when your father and my cousins Herbie and Caroline drove to Toronto during prohibition. We found a bar where we could drink and dance. Herbie was the best dancer, he and I did the Swing all night. About two in the morning we started back to Hillsburg. Since I was the only one nearly sober I had to drive. Snow covered the windshield and I had to stick my head out the window to see anything. Everyone else was passed out. I kept on plowing through until we came to a bridge. It was the strangest thing, I had an urge to drive right off. Of course I didn't. It's always bothered me that I had that impulse." Krake remembered hearing this story before, but now she felt a bond between her mothers' impulse and some crazy ones she had had.

Just as it was getting dark, Krake and Lorraine decided to leave Gale to his football game and went for a walk in the chilly December air. The streets were deserted, faint strains of Christmas music drifted out from houses as they passed.

"How are you, Mom?"

"I'm all right, I guess. Your father loved Christmas, especially when you were little. You gave him the magic he needed. I never could."

She turned and looked at her mother. "What do you mean, magic?" They stopped before the stone steps leading to the apartment.

"The wonder, the belief that anything was possible. You have a joy in you that sparked his. Together you were enchanted."

Tears rolled down her cheeks. "Why did you keep us apart, Mom?"

"He said you had to learn to be on your own. When you left he began to turn to me. I'm not affectionate like you. It was difficult to let him know how much I cared."

"He knew you loved him. You left Alexandria Mills and moved to Texas when he got a new job."

"But I never said I loved him. I shouldn't have made him eat all the leftovers and I should have made him exercise more." Lorraine touched Krake's arm. "Do you think he was having an affair with his secretary?"

Krake was surprised at this remark. "Mom, why do you ask? Of course not."

"There was a woman at the funeral who cried a lot. That was his secretary."

Krake hugged her mother. "She just liked Daddy. He would never do that." But she wondered if he had.

At work the next day, she tried to explain to Gwen the Maxwell's unexpected departure, but didn't comprehend it herself. "My mother and I are having a great time though. I never realized how much fun she is. I mean, we've shared good experiences, but then something always happened to change it. She'd become overly critical and angry, at what I never knew. Things seem easier since my father's gone. I'm glad we have another week together."

"Were you competing for him?" Gwen asked.

"I suppose so, but I never realized it. I didn't want to be his wife, only his daughter. Mom may have thought differently. She likes Gale, who's been behaving perfectly. He's been sane. I sure could get used to that."

The school called and Mrs. Hayward offered her a teaching position at night. She felt a surge of hope at this new development, coupled with insecurity at having to teach, a double-edged sword, as usual. Would she be good, would the students like her?

That night, while dinner was in the oven, Lorraine and Krake tried to open a bottle of cold duck to celebrate her teaching job. Together they probed, twisted and prodded until with a WHOOSH! the white plastic cork flew across the kitchen sending a ruby-red wine glass on the sink crashing to the floor.

"Gale'll be furious," said Krake in dismay. "That was a wedding present from Pam and Dave. I'll call and find out where they got them and replace it."

"Don't be silly. He'll never give it a second thought. It was an accident, you didn't do it on purpose. Tell him I dropped it putting it in the sink to wash," Lorraine volunteered.

"Maybe he won't be upset if he thinks you broke it," said Krake, gathering up the ruby remains and burying them in the trash.

Lorraine looked at her closely. "Are you afraid of him?"

"Of course not. He gets angry easily, but recovers fast."

"Sounds like Hank. After a couple of drinks, Dad could get so angry. He'd swear and yell. It was awful."

"I remember, but he never hollered at me. I never thought how you must have felt." Is that why I'm attracted to Gale? I thought he and Daddy were so different, but maybe not. She poured two tumblers full of sparkling wine, handing one to her mother. They clinked glasses.

"To us, Mom."

"To us, dear."

They drank the entire bottle. It went flat if you didn't. Gale wasn't particularly fond of it anyway. She left some stew warming in the oven for him and went to bed. Lying there, the urge for another drink was so great she sneaked out to the kitchen and helped herself to the rest of the Red Mountain, passing out under the covers before Gale got home.

On the way to pick up some groceries one afternoon, Krake made a joke about being in Camarillo.

"How can you joke about something so serious? You went crazy," her mother whispered.

"Mom, I'm not now nor ever have been crazy. I had a nervous breakdown, quote, unquote. Camarillo was a place for me to try and figure myself out."

"You always made good grades. Couldn't you have found the answer someplace other than a mental hospital? Nobody in our family has ever been in one."

"What about Grandma Krake? I thought she died in an asylum?"

Startled, Lorraine looked away. "I don't know what was wrong with her, I never asked. All Mother said was that Gramma had to go away to the home."

"Mom, do I embarrass you?"

"You always do the most outlandish things."

Her mother was gazing out the side window. "Oh, Krake look, there's a man dressed in a Santa Claus suit, or half of it. He doesn't have any trousers on! Don't look! He's waving his you-know-what at us." She covered her face. "Is he still there?"

"I can't see, I've got to drive. Want me to pull over?"

"No, get out of here as fast as you can. Now he's turned around and he's waving his fanny. Hollywood! What a place! I'm glad my flight leaves in a few days. How do you stand it?"

"Mom, I thought you were having a good time."

"I am, dear, but it's all so different. Full of weirdos."

"I have to admit a flashing Santa's a first for me."

On New Year's Eve, Pam and Dave came over and they all watched a movie. Gale turned on the radio in the living room and asked his mother-in-law to dance.

Krake was happy to see her mother dance beautifully. "Dad didn't like to dance, but I've always loved to," she said when Gale told her she was a regular Ginger Rogers.

Another tune began, Gale pulled Krake to her feet and swept her away across the room. It was a magic moment and Krake felt a real sense of family again.

From the TV in the bedroom, horns sounded, reminding them of the expected ritual. Gale kissed her long and hard, "Happy New Year."

"Happy New Year," she replied, turning to see Pam and Dave locked in an embrace. Her mother looked alone and forlorn on the couch. She and Gale ran over, lifted her to her feet and enveloped her in a hug.

"Champagne, where's the champagne?" Pam asked.

Krake left to retrieve the bubbly and guiltily returned with four ordinary wine glasses and the remaining ruby one.

"I accidentally broke the other opening a bottle of cold duck," she explained, handing Gale the unopened bottle.

"You what?" he asked loudly.

"I broke it," Lorraine said quickly. "I set it too near the edge of the counter. When that cork flew off, it scared me. I jumped and knocked it off. I've given Krake the money to replace it."

Gale didn't seem to be upset. Thanks, Mom.

"Did your mother really break that glass?" Gale asked sliding under the covers.

"Really," she replied, her fingers crossed as he caressed her breasts. Making love after a few days abstinence heightened desire. She responded immediately to the foreplay and the inevitable coupling was satisfying. After orgasm, he fell asleep on top of her. Gently she rolled him onto his back, then lay wide awake at his side.

Insomnia persisted. She stole into the kitchen, found the trusty Red Mountain and poured a glass. And another. And another. Lorraine found her the next morning, slumped in a kitchen chair, snoring, a half empty glass on the floor.

She shook her. "Krake, wake up. What are you doing here?"

"Is it time for school?" Krake asked groggily.

"What?"

Krake was awake now. "I thought I was back in Belton and you were waking me up to go to high school. Did I sleep here all night?"

"Apparently. Did you and Gale have an argument?"

"No, I couldn't sleep. A glass of wine sends me off lots of times."

"One? I'd say several."

"Mom, I've got a beastly headache. Would you get me some aspirin? They're in the medicine cabinet, top shelf."

Over breakfast, Lorraine said, "Krake, I'm worried about you."

"Why? Because I drink a glass of wine to help me sleep?"

"How often do you wake up in a kitchen chair?"

"Hardly ever. When Gale's working, I take the wine into the bedroom." Krake squirmed uncomfortably.

"I don't think you're aware of how much you drink. Several times during my visit, you've consumed quite a bit. I'm worried because it's so dangerous. Suppose you decided to take a drive somewhere?"

"I'd never go anywhere like that, I know better," she stated firmly.

"Don't be too sure. Have you discussed this with Walter?"

"All he says is that I'm allergic to alcohol. I don't break out in a rash or get a stuffed-up nose when I drink, so how could it be an allergy?"

"Do you remember what you do after a few drinks?"

"Yes. Unless I've drunk an awful lot. I never told you, but I went to an AA meeting while I was working at the Alley Theater. People from the National Board of Alcoholism told me I wasn't an alcoholic, but could become one. I've never lived up to my potential."

"You may be headed that way. Krake, promise me something."

"What?" Krake was wary.

"If you wake up in the kitchen chair again, will you go to an AA meeting?" Lorraine pleaded.

"Sure, Mom, I promise."

Lorraine put her hand on her daughter's wrist. "Please, dear, for me."

"OK, Mom," Krake said.

Before nodding out in a nap later, Krake replayed the morning's conversation. AA meeting, promise me. Shit! I won't do it! I'm not an alcoholic!

The night before Lorraine left, Krake, in her nightgown, went to her mother's temporary bedroom in the study. "Night, Mom. I'm going to miss you. You know I'd rather be at LAX in the morning than giving Yellow Cab Company exams."

"I know, dear. Thanks for a wonderful Christmas. I'll miss you too. Good night."

As Krake was crawling under the covers next to Gale, the familiar voice drifted in, "Night. Don't let the bedbugs bite."

24

The apartment was cold and dark when she walked in after work. And quiet, so quiet. She already missed her mother. The place seemed empty without her.

The month of January began one of the busiest times in her life. Observing classes and working, in addition to preparing her first lecture, left little time for a social life. Peter called and gave her his phone number in Oakland. He was leaving the next day. Gale was involved in directing a scene for his acting class and they hardly saw each other. They made a date for the evening before she started teaching. She was nervous and excited about her debut.

They went to their favorite Mexican restaurant near the lake and drank a pitcher of Margaritas.

Slivers of pain shot through her head. Something cold and hard pressed against the flesh of her cheek. Her eyes burned when she opened them. The gray light of dawn filtered feebly through the window. Where am I? Turning her head, the white porcelain toilet met her gaze. Half clothed, her body began to shiver. Suddenly, uncontrollably, the contents of her stomach heaved itself on the tiled floor. Unable to move, she tried to think. What happened, how did I get here? Slowly, memory returned.

The margaritas were excellent and they ordered another

pitcher after the first. Enjoying the novelty of each other's company, they flirted and got progressively drunk. When the second pitcher was empty, Gale was suddenly anxious to get home. Flattered by his obvious desire, Krake undressed quickly in the bedroom, leaving on the leopard-skin panties and slip Lorraine had given her for Christmas. Arranging herself provocatively on the bed, she wet her lips as he entered.

"You look like a whore in that," he pronounced.

"My mother gave me these," she protested.

"That's where you get your lousy taste in clothes. I should have guessed." Sitting beside her, he pulled the slip straps down and looked at her breasts. "Well, whore, give me what I want." He ripped the slip and panties off, pushed her on the bed face down and pulled her legs apart. "You whores love to get it in the ass. Here goes, baby." He rammed his swollen cock into her unyielding anus. She cried out in pain. A hard slap on the face shut her up. Thrusting and shoving, he finally gained entrance. She writhed in agony. He laughed, pumping in and out. "You know you love it." His orgasm left him limp on top of her. Finally, he rolled off and fell asleep.

When she was sure he was unconscious, she crept into the bathroom and washed herself, afraid to shower for fear he would waken. She then got a glass of Red Mountain from the kitchen, returned to the medicine chest and swallowed four aspirin. Sitting on the bathroom floor, propped up against the toilet she finished the wine and then passed out on the tiles.

Sick, hung over, the thought of going to work was impossible. The travel alarm on the sink showed seven forty-five. With difficulty, she managed to make it into the living room and lay on the couch. At eight-thirty, after drinking Pepto Bismol and consuming more aspirin, she called Kiley's answering service, leaving a message that she had contracted food poisoning and wouldn't be in. She had just placed the receiver on the hook when Gale came in.

"Boy, those margaritas! Am I hung over! Two pitchers, no wonder. I've got a scene rehearsal, do you have time to make me a chili pepper omelet before work?"

"I'm too sick to go to work," Krake said, starting for the kitchen.

"We had a good time, yeah!" He smiled. She continued silently towards the refrigerator. The eggs and pepper-cheese seemed to revitalize him and after a shave and shower he left, kissing her on the brow. "Good luck, tonight."

Tonight! Her first class. She had completely forgotten about it. She ran into the bathroom and looked in the mirror. The ache in her head wasn't all on the inside. A large purple bruise embraced her right eye. Shit! How am I going to teach looking like this? Cold compresses lessened the swelling and pain, but the discoloration remained. She spent the rest of the day in bed trying to memorize her lecture. What had her mother said, "Promise me ..."

Attending an AA meeting any time soon was out of the question. She needed every molecule of energy to recover.

At four, she had tea and toast, then began the arduous task of making up. Again the clown white masked the shame. It was her shame. Shame at getting drunk, shame at being married to a man who sodomized and hit her and never even mentioned it, much less apologized.

Full of insecurity and self-doubt, she set foot in the Med I classroom at six-thirty. Pinning the charts and diagrams illustrating the lecture on the bulletin board, she went to the lounge for a drink of water. Mrs. Hayward came in.

"Hello, Krake. I decided to come down and give you a special introduction. I'd like to hear your first lecture anyway."

Why tonight? Can she see the bruise?

Mrs. Hayward linked arms. "It's nearly time. Let's walk in together."

"Good evening, students," Mrs. Hayward began. "I'm here to join you in welcoming Mrs. Maxwell to the Med I class. Her outstanding performance as a student here as well as a working medical assistant make her an asset to our teaching staff. She has graciously consented to take over for Miss Hawthorne. Let's show her how we feel."

The clapping of hands and attentive countenances inspired Krake to present a superb lecture. Afterwards Mrs. Hayward congratulated her and said she had learned a few things herself.

In bed that night, Krake was so stimulated she couldn't sleep. I need wine. Fortunately, her digestive system rebelled and she had to content herself with some warm milk and a couple of aspirin.

At work the next day, Gwen spotted the makeup.

"Did he hit you again?" she asked when they were alone.

"Shhh Gwen, I don't want Kiley to know." They went in her office and closed the door. "I had too much to drink and Gale got hostile. Called me a whore and was violent. When I cried, he hit me."

"You can't live with a man who treats you like that. Stay with me for awhile," she offered.

"Thanks, but I'll figure something out. I have my group tonight. They'll help."

During that evening's session, after she had related the incident, Don asked, "Are you an alcoholic?"

In group she had mentioned her drinking only briefly, laughing about the blackouts.

He repeated the question. She told him what the AA group in Houston had said.

"Do you think your drinking patterns are normal?" Walter interjected.

"Sometimes."

"Usually?" Silence. "Krake, I'm not accusing you of anything, but alcohol seems to be a part of your arguments and violent incidents with Gale. Am I right?" Walter asked.

She nodded.

He continued. "There's a stigma attached to alcoholism because of the aberrant behavior connected to it, but alcoholism is a disease. AA has the greatest success rate in treating the illness. Would you consider attending a meeting?"

"I'll go with you, if you don't want to be by yourself," said Don.

The group concluded that she should leave Gale and go to AA. Don said he would locate a meeting and call her. As for leaving Gale, the prospect was terrifying.

"There's one on Thursday at eight p.m. at the First Baptist Church on Gower," he said on the phone the next day.

"Thursday? So soon?" she moaned.

"Tell you what, I'll pick you up after work and we'll get a bite to eat first."

"Oh, all right." She was resigned, but the thought of life without a drink was intolerable. The way it tastes with food, how can I possibly enjoy a steak sans cabernet? All my friends drink. I need booze to loosen up and have fun. And what about sex? WHAT ABOUT SEX?

At dinner on Thursday, the waiter asked if they wanted anything to drink.

"Not tonight," Don answered.

"You know, Don, I haven't decided if I'm an alcoholic, I think I'll have a glass of the house red, the entree needs it."

Sipping the dark burgundy, she knew life was impossible without it. They lingered over the meal and arrived a few minutes late at the church. The meeting was underway, the designated door closed. Timidly, she knocked. A flaming redhead opened it and whispered to come in and be seated.

Self-consciously, they sat and listened as various people read passages from the "big book," whatever that was. Presently, the chairman asked if there were any newcomers or visitors. The redhead motioned for Krake and Don to stand.

It was a relief to Krake when the attention shifted from them to a short, heavy-set woman wearing a pair of dirty jeans and a shirt who introduced herself as "Ruth, an alcoholic" and began telling her story. The feelings of inhibition and insecurity she spoke of could have been Krake's. What was most similar was the drinking pattern, the not being able to stop. Ruth's story had some funny moments and laughing at the antics of a drunk was freeing. Maybe I'm not so terrible after all. Maybe I don't have a rare untreatable psychological problem. Maybe I am an alcoholic. Following Ruth's story, the meeting was open for discussion, the topic honesty.

When Ruth asked Krake if she had anything she would like to say, Krake remarked, "I can honestly say for the first time, I think I might be an alcoholic." Everyone clapped. After the meeting, several people approached her, giving her warm hugs and their phone numbers. The redhead filled her purse with pamphlets, saying, "Darling, you're in the right place."

Later in bed, tossing and turning, she went over the entire meeting again and again. I don't want to stop drinking. If I can't handle alcohol, I'm weak and a failure. Everybody drinks. It's glamorous and exciting. Romantic fantasies of champagne glasses and wealth with every comfort at her fingertips; success, happiness, love and booze, they all went together. By morning, she had decided not to go back to the meeting again.

Teaching was exhilarating. Without her realizing it, the constant validation from her students aided her growing feelings of self-worth.

On Saturday, trying once again to create a happy home, she made a special dinner for Gale and dressed carefully in a green caftan with gold dangling earrings and gold braided sandals, her hair upswept in a Grecian knot.

Gale arrived as she was preparing the endive salad. "Wow, who's the beauty queen?" he asked admiringly, crossing the kitchen and catching her up in an embrace. Revulsion rose at his touch. Her mind reasoned he had been drunk two weeks ago and probably didn't remember the brutal incident. Her bruised eye might have reminded him ... come on, let's forget it. He'll never do that again.

He headed for the bathroom, dropping pieces of clothing on the way, jacket, tee-shirt, Levis, shorts.

Slob! When he was in the shower, she picked up the discarded clothing, placing it neatly on a chair in the bedroom. Dabbing some Emeraude behind her ears and knees and, yes, on her crotch, she winked at her reflection in the mirror.

She had bought gin and vermouth earlier to make Daddy's martinis. When Gale walked into the kitchen, she handed him a glass of the concoction.

"To us," she said. Their glasses clinked and the first swallow burned all the way down. Daddy would love this, she thought. The alcohol made her endorphins rocket through the ceiling. If one taste does this, what will several glasses do? They won't be able to stop me. I'll be Queen of all I survey. The smartest, prettiest, the best in all categories.

They went out on the balcony and Gale sat in the hanging chair. She filled his glass, asking, "Can I sit on your lap?"

Gale pulled her down, spilling some of the drink on his shirt. "Damn, clumsy bitch! Get up, sit over there at the desk. No, first get me a towel."

Bringing a cloth from the bathroom, she meekly handed it to him. He swiped at the dribbles on his front.

"Refill my glass," he commanded.

The mood was broken. They sat silently watching the trains coupling and uncoupling. Like us, she thought. Why does he get upset over nothing? "Dinner's almost ready, I'll check on it." She rose, carrying the empty glasses and shaker out to the kitchen.

The meal was exquisite. Chops rare, potatoes light and airy, baby carrots sweet and tender. They finished the wine with the chocolate mousse.

"I'll say this, you sure can cook." He leaned back, wiping his mouth with the napkin. "I'd forgive a hell of a lot for a meal like this. You know, I found some stuff in your wallet last night."

She stiffened. "My wallet? What were you doing looking through my wallet?"

"I was borrowing a couple of dollars and came across a slip of paper. It had some guy's name and address on it in Oakland. I ripped it up. A photo was in there too, I kept that."

"Where is it?" she asked stricken.

"I'll never tell. Who is it anyway?" He brought out the bottomless bottle of Red Mountain, poured them each a glass and sat down, smirking.

She was angry and panicked. "Give me that picture, it's of Burg, the man who was killed ten years ago. I told you about all that."

"That's him? Why do you still have his picture? He's been dead a long time."

"I don't know why I keep it. I like to have it with me."

"Do you still love him?"

"In a way, I guess. I mean he's gone, but my feelings for him aren't. Can you understand that?"

"No, either you love him or me. You have to choose."

"There's no choice to be made. He's dead. You're not in competition with him. I love you."

"No you don't. Not if you carry a dead man's picture and somebody else's address around with you."

"Gale, please give me the photo," she pleaded.

"No."

"Why not?" She felt like she was caught in quicksand with her head barely above the surface.

"You're my wife. Only my picture should be in your wallet and nobody else's address and phone number." He reached across the table suddenly and grabbed her roughly by the shoulder. "Tell me whose it is," he said, slapping her lightly with the back of his hand.

Maybe if I tell him he'll drop it, her alcohol-befuddled brain said. "You remember the art student who gave me a ride to the bus last spring?"

"That bum!"

"He's a patient of Dr. Kiley's and he's leaving to go to art school in northern California. He gave me his address and phone, said in case we were ever in Oakland he'd show us around," she lied.

The next thing she knew she was lying on the floor next to the dining room table with Gale kneeling over her, his closed fist raised. "I told you never to see him again." WHAP! The fist met her jaw and she lost consciousness, and came to lying on the bed alone in the room, but not for long. Suddenly he loomed over her and held a butcher knife to her throat. "Did you sleep with him?"

She shook her head.

"Did you kiss him?"

"No." The cold metal pressing against her windpipe made lying easy.

He threw the knife on the floor and hit her again.

The clock read two a.m. when she groggily tried to lift her head. Pain ricocheted through her skull. She sank back on the coverlet and lay still for another period of time. Finally she managed to stagger into the bathroom. The acrid odor of feces followed. Removing the torn and bloodied caftan, the brown evidence of loosened bowels filled her with horror. Beat the shit out of me, literally! Shame rent her soul. She felt nothing but hatred for him. Tears felt inappropriate. One thing was clear, it was over!

Warm streams of water from the shower began the healing process. She left the robe soaking in the sink, took several aspirin and crawled into bed. I hope I never see him again was her last thought before falling asleep.

The next morning she ached all over. The clock said

seven-thirty, she rolled over and went back to sleep, awakening at nine-fifteen.

She put a call into Walter. "It's Krake. He nearly killed me last night." She related the story, leaving out the embarrassing uncontrollable bodily functions.

"Krake, I've never told you what to do before. I'm telling you now. Get out, today."

"I can hardly move. I'm hung over and beaten, I can't do it today."

"You have to. Marion said that you are welcome at her house. Call her or I will and we'll arrange something."

She knew he was right. She couldn't forget the feel of sharp steel against her throat. "All right, I'll do it."

"Good," he said, relieved. "Let me know where you'll be."

She dialed Marion. No answer. She sank back exhausted. I can barely sit up, much less dress, pack and leave. Dozing, she awoke when Gale entered the bedroom. Fear clutched her. I should have left when I had the chance. He'll probably kill me. She sat up, pulling the covers around her protectively.

Brushing the pile of dirty clothes off the chair, he sat down. "What can I say? I was drunk." He looked woebegone.

Silence.

"I'm sorry, Krake."

"Gale, you almost killed me. You knocked me unconscious three times. Why? Can you tell me why?"

"Don't you know I worship you? I have you on a pedestal and have to keep pulling you off." He began to cry.

Crocodile tears. She felt nothing. A door had slammed shut. "I need time to think things through," she said, praying he would leave.

"You don't want me to stay here?" he asked.

"Not right now."

"I'll see if my buddy Roger will let me bunk with him for awhile. Just till we work this out."

He stood and walked towards the door. "I'll call you," he said as he left. She didn't answer.

Marion didn't get home until late that evening. "We were at a yoga retreat," she said, beginning to enthusiastically tell Krake about it. Krake interrupted her, "I'm leaving Gale, you said …"

"Come right over," Marion almost shouted. "Thank God you've made this decision. Believe me, it's the right one."

"It's too late now. How would tomorrow after work be? I'll pack tonight and see you then."

"Wonderful!" She gave directions to her house.

Krake put a few things in a suitcase, then slept a deep, dreamless sleep.

When she greeted Gwen at the office in the morning, the elaborate makeup did little to mask the battlefield that was her face.

"My God, what happened?" Gwen handed her a cup of coffee.

"It's the same old story, except this time I'm divorcing him. He found Peter's address in my wallet and went crazy when I told him whose it was." She sat down and began to cry.

Gwen's arms came around her. "I'm sorry things didn't work out. Somebody like that needs a keeper not a wife." She handed her some Kleenex.

Dr. Kiley came in. "Hi, girls. My surgery ended sooner than I expected. Thought we'd get started earlier today." Krake turned towards him. He glanced in her direction and did a double-take. "What happened to you? Come over here and let me see." He examined the bruises. "Who did this?"

Silence.

"Gale?"

She nodded.

"That son-of-a-bitch! Gwen get me two cc's of the steroid on the top shelf in the drug cabinet." He injected the solution. "That'll take effect almost immediately. You'll look and feel a whole lot better."

She examined the cab company applicants while wearing dark glasses, explaining she had had an eye examination. By eleven o'clock, the swelling was gone along with the pain and most of the bruising.

Marion's bungalow was in Silverlake, on a quiet street of single-family homes. Huge oaks and maples lined the streets, children played hopscotch on the sidewalks and an atmosphere of peace prevailed.

Marion opened the door before she could ring the bell. "I'm so pleased you're here," she said, picking up the smaller suitcase and bringing it inside. The house was pleasantly decorated with an adolescent boy's sports equipment strewn around. Marion kicked aside a baseball as they entered the spacious guest bedroom.

Krake put the large suitcase down next to a dresser with a carved mirror. "Marion, this is lovely. I can't thank you enough for taking me in."

"If I can play a small part in your liberation from tyranny, I'm grateful." She gave Krake a big hug, telling her dinner was nearly ready and to leave the unpacking until later. Krake followed her out to a small kitchen where the odor of simmering sauerbrauten filled the air. "I'm also making spaetzle. What do you want to drink? A beer?" Then remembering, "I mean, a soda?"

"Milk would be fine, thanks." Just after Krake sat down, Marion's son, Justin, burst in and stopped at the sight of her. He seemed taken with Krake and after dinner asked her to shoot some baskets with him out back.

Standing in the cold February air, Krake wondered what she was doing here. Too confused to come up with answers, she concentrated on getting the ball through the hoop. Her skill wasn't the greatest although occasionally a swish was heard. Justin delighted in demonstrating dribbling and made eleven baskets in a row.

Exhausted by the trauma of the last few days, Krake went to bed early. The flowered sheets and electric blanket were comforting and soon she was in dreamland tossing and turning, running from tidal waves.

She awoke to the thump, thump of a basketball hitting the wall behind her head. Justin was practicing in the early morning light. The sound was comforting and she needed all of that she could get. Marion had breakfast ready and she felt stronger driving to work.

Walter called her aside before group that evening. "Are you all right? You said you'd let me know where you were."

"I forgot, I'm sorry, there's been so much going on."

"Are you staying with Marion?" The blue eyes were full of concern.

"Yes, we drove here together. I didn't realize how lonely I've been."

"You sound better than you did on Sunday," he said.

She didn't want to remember Sunday or the dead feeling she had knowing her marriage was over.

The group supported her decision, but Don probed further. "How about AA? Are you going back?"

Damn him! "I might." He looked at her. "All right, Donald, let's go Thursday night. I'll meet you there."

Aware of her displeasure, he said, "It can't hurt, can it?"

"Who knows?" She left with Marion, glad to put off for two days any further discussion about her supposed alcoholism.

On Thursday, just as she parked in front of the Baptist church at a little past eight o'clock, Don's Toyota pulled up behind her.

"We're on time tonight," she said, giving him a hug.

"Early, in fact." He led the way through the open door. The redhead was laying out pamphlets on a side table. "Hi, Krake and Donald, isn't it?"

"Just Don will be fine."

They were about to take a seat at the far end of the long table when Ray, an extremely thin man with graying hair asked if they would put the baskets of candy on the table. He was busy making coffee and setting out mugs.

"What's the candy for?" Don asked.

"Alcoholics usually have low blood sugar. If someone comes off the booze abruptly, they might experience a seizure or the DT's. The candy helps restore a sugar balance in the body."

As he was speaking, people began drifting in, some looked familiar, some not. Promptly at eight-thirty, Ray, the secretary, banged the gavel and called the meeting to order. The same format and readings were used. Don't they get bored with the repetition? Krake wondered.

That evening, Emily was the speaker. A tall, pale, blond woman in her late fifties, she was an author who had several books in print. Soft-spoken, she revealed a hidden history of drinking for thirty years. Nearly every night for the last ten, she had drunk herself into oblivion. Finally her husband desperately called AA. A member came and took her to a meeting. This very one, in fact.

"I didn't want to go. I didn't want to stop drinking and I continued to at first. But this program ruins your drinking. You people sitting around this table taught me that drinking meant death and sobriety meant life. I chose to live and I haven't regretted it."

Krake was lost in thought when she was called on. "Krake."

Silence. "Krake." Don nudged her.

"Oh, sorry, Emily, I was thinking."

"Who are you?" Emily asked.

Krake looked puzzled.

"Introduce yourself by your first name only, please."

Pause. Can I say it? Clearing her throat, she faintly got

out, "I'm Krake, I'm an alcoholic."

"You think you're an alcoholic?" Emily asked.

"No, I know I am," she answered firmly, suddenly relieved at the admission after all the years of denial.

"The topic's gratitude, any comments?"

She thought for a moment, then spoke. "I'm grateful to be alive. My husband almost killed me last weekend. I was drunk and so was he. It might not have happened if we'd been sober, I don't know. I need to make some changes in my life and this is a big step, dealing with my alcoholism. I've left him and now I need strength and support to get a divorce. Booze doesn't help. I feel invincible when I'm drunk, but incapable when sober. In reality, the opposite is true. I want to learn from you. Tonight I learned that I don't need to be flown to a Viennese psychiatrist for elaborate, lengthy psychoanalysis. I'm am alcoholic. The only treatment is to not drink. I don't know if I can do it, but I'm going to try. Thank you for being here." Unexpectedly, the tears came and she put her head on the table and sobbed. Don comforted her, handing her a Kleenex. Dabbing at her eyes, she noticed several smiling faces looking at her with approval.

After the meeting, Madelyn, the redhead, put a small leather-bound black book in her hand. "This is for you. Start reading it tonight." The gold lettering on the front said, TWENTY FOUR HOURS A DAY.

As soon as she got in her room, Krake sat on the bed and opened the book to the day's date. The words spoke of spirituality, comfort and hope. She sat mesmerized until she had read every day in February. A feeling of peace suffused her. She showered and turning the electric blanket up high, fell into bed.

The familiar thumping of the basketball woke her. Dressed for work, she entered the dining room. Sitting on her plate was a small card which read, "Today is the first day of the rest of your life."

"Justin brought that home yesterday," said Marion, setting a cup of coffee in front of her. "Want some cereal, eggs, what?"

"Half a grapefruit, thanks. I feel like you're my mother."

"Which is what you need right now. I went home to mine when I left the Major. How was last night's meeting? Any revelations?"

"I said I was an alcoholic."

"And ...?"

"Well, nothing."

"No claps of thunder, no bolts of lightning?" Marion set the grapefruit in front of her and laughed. "I'm only teasing. That's wonderful, what a breakthrough. How do you feel about it?"

"Good, relieved. I've been running from the truth for so long, it's nice to stop."

"I bet."

"It's so amazing. They're from all walks of life. Such diversity. Alcoholism isn't prejudiced, it'll take anybody. The stories these people tell. Funny, tragic, they run the gamut. Underneath is a fundamental love so strong it overrides everything. I don't have a higher power like they do. I wish I did. I want that light to shine out of my eyes too." She looked at her watch and jumped up. "Leave the dishes, I'll do them when I get home."

Marion stood at the door waving as Krake disappeared towards Hollywood.

25

It had been six weeks since she had seen Gale. He tried to contact her, but she told Gwen not to put his calls through and not to tell him where she was living. Krake had picked up her clothes with Marion a week after she left, but they didn't see Gale. She stored her belongings in Marion's attic, her out-of-season clothes occupied two trunks in the bedroom.

One night Gale left a single red rose and a copy of Browning's "How Do I Love Thee?" under the Corvair's wiper blade. The minute she saw it she knew who had left it. She only felt disgust. The poem she threw away, but the rose seemed alive and innocent so she took it home.

That evening at dinner, moving aside the bud vase containing the rose, Marion asked, "When are you going to take off that wedding ring?"

"I hadn't thought about it," she lied, unwilling to relinquish her claim to being somebody.

"You're hanging on to him. Let go," Marion advised. "When are you planning to file for divorce? You still want to, I hope."

"Yeah, but it's hard. When I remove this ring and divorce him, I'll have no one. I'll be nothing, floating, shapeless, alone. That scares me."

"Do I look like no one? Go ahead, take off the band of gold and watch me disappear."

Slowly Krake tugged the metal circle over her knuckle and dropped it on the table.

"Well?" Marion screwed up her face and crossed her eyes.

Krake laughed, "OK, OK, so I'm not alone now, but what about when I leave to find my own apartment? It's gonna be loneliville."

Marion asked her if she would like to become a boarder for nominal rent and food. Krake quickly agreed.

"About the divorce, no time like the present," Marion remarked delicately. She had given Krake the name of one of the members of the law firm where she worked. "Chris Weller is the best. I could arrange an interview anytime you like." Shall I speak to her in the morning?"

Reluctantly, Krake answered, "OK, I have to do it sometime, it might as well be now."

At their appointment two days later, Krake felt at ease and trusted Chris Weller immediately. After Krake related all the pertinent details, Chris assured her, "It'll be relatively easy as long as he doesn't contest anything. Since neither one of you has any money to speak of and the property held jointly is minimal, this should be simple."

Krake returned to work full of hope. The weather was warm and she realized that spring was almost here. I hope my winter is over, she thought.

That evening at the AA meeting, she shared the news. "I'd like to celebrate and get drunk," she said without thinking.

Then, appalled at her revelation, "I mean I wish I could have a drink to celebrate, oh, I don't know what I mean."

Madelyn raised her hand and spoke after the mandatory introduction. "I know how you feel. I was standing in my garden yesterday admiring the camellias, when out of the blue I wanted a drink. I've been sober ten years. I thought by now I'd never have that feeling, but it may happen for the rest of my life. I'm only sober one day at a time. At first it was one hour at a time or even less. Don't be upset because you want a drink, that's normal. You're an alcoholic. Don't be afraid of the feeling, use it as a reminder of who you are. Why do we introduce ourselves as alcoholics every time we speak in a meeting? So we won't forget and think we can drink like other people. We can't, not ever."

Harvey added, "Use the energy that your developing spiritual connection gives you to grow, change and live a happy life. If you drank tonight, all the strength you've gained by making a momentous decision would be lost. Celebrate by staying sober. Feel the joy you posses. Booze masquerades as happiness. In reality it destroys everything. Your higher power's miracles are limitless. This success will be followed by many more. God bless you."

The AA meeting was replacing her therapy group in its ability to aid in self-discovery. Here, people weren't afraid to talk about alcohol and its deadly results. Here, it was acceptable to be an alcoholic, there was no stigma. On the outside, caution prevailed. Being able to let down her guard where liquor was concerned opened up whole new areas of exploration. It gave her an objectivity with regard to herself and why she drank. She clung to the clichés. Hearing the words "One day at a time" lightened her load considerably. She did want a drink now and then. The meetings hadn't cured that. It was an incurable disease, wasn't it? On Friday nights, especially, TGIF. Dancing, drinking, sex! SEX?

That Friday, Marion insisted they attend a single's dance the young businesswoman's club she belonged to was giving. Dressed in their finest, they made their way down a long corridor in the Knights of Columbus Hall. No one, not one of the thirty men in the room caused even a flutter or a quickening heartbeat. Krake drank 7-Up, bemoaning the lack of gin, danced when asked, joined in mixers and left early.

Snuggling in bed, she realized it was a relief there had been no princes present. I need space, I'm not ready to give anything to another person now. Who I am is just emerging. Men are demanding, they require attention and I don't have it. That was the reason she hadn't contacted Peter. Also, Gale had instilled fear in her and, although it wasn't likely he would find out, she didn't want to tempt it. Better end the marriage first.

Chris suggested she file a restraining order as a precautionary measure. Krake authorized the firm to do so, along with filing the divorce papers. Both went on record March 21st. It was the first day of spring. A new beginning.

She had avoided telling Lorraine about the situation, but in a letter her mother had inquired after Gale and Krake knew the time had come. Lorraine went on to relate the news that she had enrolled in Belton College and was taking several Special Education courses. Very busy, her grief was taking second place to studying. Krake dialed the Texas number slowly, praying for the right words.

"Hi, Mom."

"Krake, how nice to hear from you. Is everything all right?" Before she had a chance to answer, Lorraine was talking about her last test, the drive to the college at night and the fact that she had been hired part-time at a remedial clinic, teaching emotionally disturbed children.

Krake said, "That's great, Mom. There's something I have to tell you. Gale and I've decided to get a divorce."

"Oh no! Why?"

"It just wasn't working out."

"What do you mean?"

"I hate to tell you, but several times he hit me. A few weeks ago he almost killed me. He always says he's sorry, that he'll never do it again, but I know he will. I can't take it anymore."

"Are you still living in the apartment?"

"No, I've moved in with a friend. My mail's being forwarded here."

"Dear, I'm sorry, it must be hard for you to break up your home."

"Not as bad as being beaten. I tried, but you know what his mother's like, they're both crazy."

"If you want to come here for a visit, please do."

"Thanks Mom, maybe later. I've got a lot to get settled and reorganized, plus I'm teaching my class which I love."

"I'm glad that's going well. I can't believe he hit you. He was so nice at Christmas."

"I know. That was a fluke. Gale's a sick man. I'll give you my new address and phone at Marion's."

"Okay, dear. If you need anything, call."

"I will. I love you, Mom."

"I love you too, Krake."

It was the first time Lorraine had told her she loved her over the phone. Krake felt happy, she had been longing to hear that for a long time.

The day Gale was served with divorce papers was an ordinary one at work. The morning saw two broken bones repaired, a planter wart removed and a routine urinalysis.

Late in the afternoon, Gwen knocked on the darkroom door where Krake was developing some chest x-rays. "Krake, we're on our way out. I'll lock you in. See you in the morning."

After placing the developed films in the wash, she started down the hallway to her office, but was stopped by a loud banging on the side door.

Gale's voice shouted, "Krake, I know you're there. Let me in. I just want to talk to you.

FEAR! PANIC! Where should I hide? What shall I do? I'm alone. He could kill me so easily. Her heart was pounding, her breath came in short puffs. Calm down, calm down, think! She saw the wall phone next to the autoclave in the lab.

Crossing to it, she dialed the operator who put her through to the police.

"Los Angeles Police Department," a man's voice answered.

"I need help. My husband's trying to break in where I work. I'm afraid what he might do. I have a restraining order filed on him. Can you send someone over?" she asked shakily.

"Who and where are you?"

She gave the information and was assured a patrol car would be dispatched right away. "What'll I do if he smashes the door in before they get here?"

"Hide somewhere. The officers will be there soon," he told her.

Krake went back to the x-ray room and hid under the large table in the center. Crouched there, she marveled at the absurdity of the situation. Fear, mixed with a desire to laugh, stayed with her until she heard voices outside briefly, then silence. She waited, barely breathing, until she had heard nothing for several minutes, then crawled out and ran down the hall to Kiley's office. Looking out the window, she saw a patrol car pulling away following the familiar green Triumph as it turned out of the parking lot. They came, he saw, they conquered. Thank you, LAPD.

Hanging the x-rays up to dry, she tidied up, and then let herself out. Locking the side door, she noticed a large crack running the length of one pane of glass on the upper portion. Right through the alarm, better not set it. Nervously, she drove home, glancing in the rear-view mirror constantly for a small green car. None appeared.

She didn't see him again until the court date. He was seated on a bench outside the courtroom with his lawyer when she and Chris entered and sat on a bench a few yards away.

Gale looked at her, smiling. His lawyer approached Chris and they spoke briefly. Weller turned to her. "He wants to reconcile, do you?"

She shook her head.

When Gale heard of her refusal, he glared in her direction his lower lip jutting out in a pout.

The hearing was short. The property was divided equally, there was no question of alimony, because as Gale's lawyer stated, "Mr. Maxwell quit his job due to the stress of the impending divorce."

My heart bleeds, baby. My heart bleeds.

Six months from the filing date, the divorce would be final. Hooray! She thanked Chris. The hearing was at ten a.m., lasted twenty-five minutes and Krake was back at work by eleven. How quickly and routinely these matters were dispensed with. I should be grateful it was so easy. Painless, no. Gale wasn't only a brutal creature. He could be sensitive, gentle and loving. That's what I'll miss, that's what's so hard to give up. If Bluebeard were only a decapitator, why did so many women fall for him? The complexities of human nature were baffling. I know he loves me, but it's not a love I can survive. Her mind started the if only's until her new-found prayer took over. "God grant me the serenity to accept the things I cannot change, change the things I can and the wisdom to know the difference."

Her night class would be ending in two weeks. Mrs. Hayward informed her that the day class beginning in April needed a teacher as well. Krake could soon be teaching full-time.

Mrs. Hayward also told Krake to call her Irene. "I'm not your teacher any more."

"But you're still my boss."

"Let's say we're both career promoters, equally important in guiding women to find rewarding jobs."

After their meeting, Krake stood in front of the white stucco building, marveling at this turn of fate. I'm going to teach full-time in a school I attended only a couple of years ago. She had always planned the hell out of everything with mostly mixed results. Now she realized she had no control at all. She might as well relax and enjoy life. Is that what "let go and let God" meant?

The next morning as she was finishing the last of the applicants, Madelyn called and asked her to chair the Thursday night AA meeting. She declined, due to lack of time. It was overwhelming anticipating the start of two new classes at the end of April. Madelyn said she probably wasn't ready yet. After she hung up, Krake went about routinely writing histories in charts, giving exams, taking and developing x-rays. All the while a voice inside was saying, You've been sober two months, a coveted job's been handed you and you can't chair a meeting? Get off it!

She called Madelyn back and told her she had changed her mind and would be happy to chair.

Thursday afternoon she became fearful of sharing her story with the AA group. What to say? What to leave out?

Anxiously, she parked in front of the church at eight-fifteen. Madelyn arrived at the same time and they walked in together. Krake told Madelyn about the inner voice that had caused her to change her mind.

Madelyn spoke matter-of-factly, "That's your higher power!"

Revelation! "That's my higher power?" Incredulous, she said, "I've been hearing that voice all my life."

"Your higher power—God, I choose to call it—has never abandoned you. He, she or it has always been there. You have to learn to listen."

Supported by this new awareness, unafraid, she began to speak. "Hi, I'm Krake. I'm an alcoholic. My disease began when I was born, I only needed a drink." Relating her story before a group was exciting. The captive audience seemed to enjoy it and the response was gratifying. It seemed that judgment was missing in this room, acceptance and appreciation prevailed. When she finished, she felt closer to the people around the table. They knew her story now.

Gwen and Dr. Kiley gave her a party on her last day. They toasted to her success; champagne for them, 7-Up for Krake. Gwen gave her a tiny gold locket with a picture of the two of them taken last Christmas in front of the office Christmas tree. Tears came to her eyes. This had become her family and she would feel their absence.

Her first day of full-time teaching was marked by the arrival of a bouquet of spring flowers. The card read, "Your knowledge and caring will enhance the Hayward School. Best wishes, Irene." The morning class had an enrollment of twenty-two, the afternoon, eighteen. They were younger than the students in her night class and their eagerness was exhilarating. She was looked up to and admired and she was beginning to feel more confident as a teacher. One day gazing in the mirror, she thought, I like you, K.F. You're OK, in fact you're better than OK.

When group therapy changed its meeting night to Wednesday, she had to drop out because of her teaching. Walter confided he thought AA was more beneficial to her now anyway. She was a trifle insecure at leaving a core link of her recovery system, but her busy workload left little time to worry about it.

On September 21st, exactly six months after filing, the divorce was final. Krake was grateful that Gale hadn't bothered her again. Many women weren't so lucky, she knew.

Krake was grading papers in the teacher's lounge when Chris Weller called to give her the news. Should she call Peter? She got CCAC's number from information, but something stopped her before she dialed. She asked God for guidance and then found herself pulling out her Twenty-four Hour book and turning to September 21. The Thought for the Day was about facing reality and not running away. She had her answer. It was too soon. She had to do a lot of work on herself before she could make that call. Knowing that this was the right decision, Krake returned to grading papers, feeling a strong sense of purpose and a great deal of hope.